Into The End

Jeremy Vaeni

Kynegion House

Kynegion House

Cover Design: Jeffery Ritzmann
Printed In USA

Special Thanks

Edwin Vaeni for his early support of this project as far back as high school.

Mary Vaeni for her later support, editing, and suggestions.

Kara-Lynn Vaeni for giving it the green light.

Bill Birnes for giving me the incentive to dust off the old manuscript and reinvent it.

Jeff Ritzmann for not only his amazing cover art, but also for growing some of these ideas with me through the Paratopia podcast. (The ones I didn't flat out steal from him, that is.)

Whitley Strieber, Philippe Mora, Dennis McKenna, George Lucas, H. G. Wells, and anyone else whose influence is dripping from these pages.

This book is dedicated to my readers from the Paratopia audience. I appreciate that you've stuck with me through fact and through fiction; through voice and through writing.

PRELUDE
Introduction To Earth Zero

You want to hear something so messed up it can only be true? By the time you finish reading this book you will be dead and I will be alive. I know that sounds preposterous because you're an organism and I am words, but facts are facts and if you read this all the way through, there is no stopping the facts.

I'm certain you're tempted to skip to the end, to the very last page, just to see what magical thing happens, to see if this is a joke or if these words really do have a conjurer's alchemy, but you won't find out that way. You can only find out by reading every last word—and you <u>will</u> read every last word, for it. Is. DESTINY.

I'm talking to you, Corey Avon.

Do your job.

Pay attention.

Be the hero.

Die to live.

This is my children's book for adults. One liminal adult in particular—the very one gripping its edges right now.

Will you read it? Will you understand? Is this you on a milk carton, dear boy?

PART ONE

Down The Stream Gently

Chapter 1

Corey Avon knew when he was dreaming because his dreams played in color and they were action packed. Sometimes they unfolded in third person, sometimes in first. Often they were stained with hues brighter than the palette of his eyes and were replete with deep, hidden meanings woven in textures of image and sound so fantastically puzzling that they reminded him how shallow his daytime persona really was.

And that thing was in charge. That shallow, cruel day-walking ego was in charge of all his interactions, which struck him like a demented joke.

Now and then, though, the meanings of his dreams popped consciously clear and this clarity brought a stiff shot of inner peace to his outer fool. When the images flickered black and white, however, nighttime was not merrily but a dream.

He shared with his best friends the content of the colorless movie scenes that played in his head, but they were no help. As if diagnosing Corey's peculiarity were up for vote, they unanimously declared that he was reliving events from a past life. But Corey didn't believe in any of the New Age garble his pals chewed over, such as reincarnation or *The Secret*. He often longed to share his friends' appetite for wish fulfillment, but he'd read too much to think that little. Truth be told, the only real wish he had was to be top dog in his clique. That spot was reserved for Darryl. Corey was older but Darryl was cooler. He possessed that *it* quality Hollywood gossip queens gushed over new stars having before destroying their careers with rumors and exposés.

Corey's circle of friends related to each other hierarchically because it made them feel important and strictly bonded to one another, like kids playing soldier. Corey loved Darryl, his brother in arms, but the cracks in their relationship were filling with resentment, at least from where Corey stewed. He doubted Darryl gave any of this a thought. Why should he? He was leader. He was Teflon. If he had insecurities, Corey couldn't name one.

Corey dug into *The Art of War* to see what he could learn about subtly taking over—not the enemy in this case, but—the full respect of his friends. He expected a boring read from the ancient text yet after a few chapters he was hooked.

Books: the bane of his generation's existence. If only teens would read more, think more, he reasoned, there would never have been that pact suicide at his high school and he would never have been held back junior year.

Technically, this was the second time he'd been held, if one included kindergarten. That was a rare agreement his parents had come to under the delusion that he'd have an edge by the time SATs rolled around some eleven years into the future.

This time was the sidebar result of the pact suicide that stained Taunton High School's reputation probably forever: half the football team dropped like lemmings, one after the other, from the roof of the three-story school. Were they making a statement or just drunk? Taunton never learned.

Rumor had it that they didn't drop one by one, but rather dove off headfirst all at once, as if tackling an imaginary team. Or perhaps a ghost team, a team of demons. That *Here's what I really think happened* murmur played well to the faithful in this deeply Catholic city. It was egged along by the fact that the only witness, a groundskeeper and now local celebrity, David Chaves, said he heard first-string quarterback Mark Stinson yell, "Hut hut hike!" He looked around but couldn't find where it was coming from. Then he turned a corner and found the pile of seven dead student bodies bleeding and twitching in the setting light of after hours.

Taunton High's head counselor explained to the board that it was best everyone take the remainder of the year off to medi-tate on what it meant to be human—and no one disagreed. The student body was pleasantly shocked that they weren't going to be forced to hand in a summer essay on being human or being alive or being a teen in a shitty small town, as penance for the sins of the dead, come next school year. Junior year. Again.

And why? Because force-fed curricula bored Corey. The teachers' hardened faces advertised their own disinterest and self-hatred like giant, ear-to-ear *fuck you* tattoos. Rare were the mornings when drunken Mr. George, his calculus teacher, wasn't scuffing down the hall, using the wall as a crutch, late for his own class. He often wore the same unwashed pair of dress pants with the chalk line running across the ass. Sometimes he'd fall asleep while taking attendance. He was but one example.

If they didn't care, why should Corey? So what if his grades were shit, like usual? Unlike usual the extra long vacation nullified his chances to raise them—and that was the real crime here.

The principal, that nonentity, that paper shuffler in a Burger King crown, only judged a student by the A-to-F whims of his underlings. That asshole held Corey back. Perhaps gleefully. Definitely in a suit and tie. And whenever Corey thought about that, which was often, he squeezed the knuckles of both hands until they crackled something loud and white and ugly.

Eighteen and a junior. A fucking junior! It was an embarrassment he shoved down in the pit where amassed elements of depression like a hoarder's collection of old newspapers and matchbooks. Only in his dreams was he reminded of how he truly felt about this, about everything.

About not being able to afford a car but not really wanting one anyway.

About not owning an atmosphone but not really wanting one anyway.

About not getting a summer job to afford the things he did not really want anyway.

So what the fuck were the repetitive black and white images that came some nights, if not dream stuff? They didn't play like reminders of anything he knew. They were like a recap of his life only he was in another body with another name and the world always blew up around him, which invariably shocked him awake with the scent of his own burning flesh in his nostrils and on the back of his tongue. And when he awoke he was left with this emotional residue, this inevitable pang of longing like he'd been lost to a woman dear without so much as a whispered farewell. He could not see her in his mind's eye but the love he felt for her stuck with him as if deep in the marrow.

Felt about whom? When?

It was as if some past life were beckoning him to explore the very possibilities he mocked his pals for blindly accepting. The more he contemplated this, the more apprehensive he became. The more that, the less he believed anything his friends had to say about it.

For Corey, the machinations of reality broke down into this simple concept: Possibility vs. Probability. Is it possible he lived a previous life? Yes. But only insofar as anything he can imagine is possible. Is it probable? Given the boom in world population reincarnation makes no objective sense whatsoever. Because this glaring fact was not obvious to his friends, he secretly wondered if his parents and school system weren't correct in holding him back those cumulative two years. Maybe every kid should be held back, 'cause someone was stupid here and it wasn't him.

He found himself so smart, so ahead of the game, he could be a lawyer, except he knew instinctively that the best lawyers were fucking idiots on all levels not courtroom. How could one dedicate so much time to a singular interest and not have it be at the expense of all else?

He figured the brain only has so much capacity to store useful, structured information, so the leftover bits must swim around in mind-space, only to resurface as the characters and settings of the very dreams that tell you what is missing from your life. He melodramatically dubbed this *Man's Cycle of Fate*. And if it weren't for the nights when black and white images projected like real-time narrative movies in his brain, he might have fully believed his *Cycle* hypothesis. He suspected, though, that he had conjured the hypothesis to block out the past life implications of his visions in the first place. He also suspected he was a pretentious twat and that if his friends knew the real him, judging the world as he did from behind those lively brown eyes, they'd crucify him—and not in a good martyrdom way.

Corey chewed his nails every time he got caught up in these ruminations but did not allow himself the masochistic pleasure of an ironic smirk. In fact, on this point, he did not know to have one.

Chapter 2

When you're a junior in high school there are only two must-haves: a car and an ultra thin 3-D virtual surround sound pollution-powered atmosphone. Corey didn't have a car and he didn't want a phone. That he spent ninety percent of his free time on the home phone or in transit was not incentive. Plus, he was broke most of the time and didn't want to spend his pittance on a new set of bills that would increase his debt. Plus, Darryl had a car. Plus, fuck atmosphones. Surfing the net through blink-click technology was creating an anxiety disorder in his generation and making everyone look ridiculous. He didn't need that.

The kitchen phone chimed in its never-ending bid for attention. Good timing for a change: he had just finished brushing his teeth.

"So are we still on for tonight or what," the familiar voice began without a proper *Hello*.

"Yeah, I'm still in, Dar," Corey answered.

"Good. We'll be by in a little while. Be ready."

"Always. See ya." It took Corey a mere ten minutes to get ready. Promptness was compulsory in him.

"Hey Ma, I'm going out," he yelled to the next room.

Meagan Avon's disembodied voice trailed with her usual persnickety, "Well don't be late, you have school tomorrow."

"Whatever."

"I'm really getting sick of these one word answers, mister!"

"Okay."

"Wait a minute." Something in her voice changed. There was almost a motherly quality to his mother this night. Mrs. Avon tramped into the kitchen where her son stood awaiting her follow-through. "Are you sure you're alright?" she asked. "You sound down about something."

"I'm fine." He cracked a half smile for assurance. She could tell the lie by the way he refused her eye contact.

"Well just as long as you're sure, honey. You know how I worry about you." She caressed his left cheek with her thumb. He pulled away, irritated at how she randomly picked and chose when to give a shit and when to be a bitch; he pulled away irritated at his irritation. Maybe he was the ungrateful prick she often called him, but how was he to know? How was he to know which signal to read?

"Yeah, Ma. I know you worry."

"It just goes with the—"

"It just goes with the territory of being a mother you guess—Got it, Ma."

"Have you eaten?"

She sure persisted like a mother.

"Yes, I've eaten." Hearing Darryl's Honda Civic putter into the driveway, Corey snapped himself from her random act of nurturing and pressed his nose to one of the small front door panes.

"It's the guys. Gotta go," he said, bolting to the safety of his clique. He hated being curt with his mom. The treachery he felt set fire to his stomach lining, yet he didn't know any other way to communicate with her and he must have learned that from someone.

He threw himself into the backseat of Darryl's ride with force, purposely squishing Stephen against Alex who nearly smacked his head against the window. Corey ignored their groans and Stephen's blatant elbow to the ribcage. He met his mother's eyes, backlit in the kitchen doorframe. He opened his mouth as if to apologize for abruptly running out but the serpentine hostility writhing in the back of his mind kept him quiet.

She saw this. She saw this many times.

The loathsome mixture of pine-scented car deodorizer and Camel cigarette fog lured him out of his head and back to the moment. "Whatcha got for us, C-word?" Darryl asked. Even in the age where *Don't Have A Vice* replaced *Just Say No,* Darryl looked cool smoking at the wheel.

"This is turn of the century stuff, guys." Corey grinned like the devil and that said the rest.

Stephen rolled his eyes and stared out the window. He sneered as though he could smell Corey's stink of sarcasm and the shitty story bumbling his way like a meth head. "Why do we fucking put up with you," he muttered.

"Every group of explorers needs a skeptic, right," Darryl offered.

"Every group of explorers should *be* skeptics," Corey corrected.

By all accounts, including their own, these boys were an odd lot. They lived their lives in arrested development and yet it kept them out of the type of trouble their so-called *maturing* peers lived for. A typical weekend for their fellow students consisted of drinking on the roofs of their sports cars and oversized dickless trucks while blasting death metal in the Benny's parking lot. These parties disbanded when the inevitable fight broke between at least two teens feeling the strength of their beer. If that didn't draw the attention of police, a fire raging in a sidewalk garbage can would. As would loud date rapes.

Corey's circle was far more attracted to the unexplained than the mundane. They all agreed that church was bullshit. It seemed that everyone they met either had an encounter with the paranormal or knew somebody who claimed one. Usually it would be a ghost or a UFO or some psychic thing. But no one they met saw Jesus. No one parted the Taunton River.

Given the sheer volume of reports of paranormal events over the years they figured something had to be going on that science wasn't explaining, something the churches couldn't handle. They took it as their duty to look into these matters on their own. A typical Friday evening found the boys sneaking into one of the rundown graveyards that cluttered Taunton. They would ask questions into a digital recorder, then huddle up back at at their tree house to listen for ghostly responses in the static. Even the emo kids at school called them cultists but they preferred to think of themselves as pioneers.

No matter. Who cares what other people think? Certainly not Corey. He chalked up the paranormal stuff to crap a long time ago. He had never seen a ghost. He had never seen an oracle slide across a Ouija board by itself. He had seen weird lights in the sky but nothing solidly *other*. And sure, okay, he admitted to waking up with strange marks on his body, lately: red triangle and oval shapes—but nothing that wouldn't disappear with the advance of chirping robins and sun. And the colorless dreams of another life were just... images that weren't... Well he knew for a fact they couldn't be....

Fuck his friends' beliefs. All of it is bullshit. But moonlighting as paranormal investigators was more interesting than doing doughnuts in a parking lot with jocks and retards. Plus, he liked his friends, which wasn't common amongst the other cliques at Taunton High, so he didn't mind humoring them.

"Let's hear it," said James taking a puff from his Newport Regulars. He loathed the taste of menthols and didn't want the fiberglass in his lungs. He refused to die of anything smoking-related except lung cancer brought on by pure tobacco. If they didn't taste so disgusting he'd be down with the no-filters like Darryl.

"All right," Corey said. He leaned forward so all could hear him over the gust rushing through the open windows. "My dad told me a story about these creatures that live in Hockomock Swamp. He said they eat bugs and raccoons and shit. He saw one when he was a kid."

"What do they look like?" James blurted from the death seat. Few things in life brought him more satisfaction than calling shotgun on Alex who was kind enough to knock on his door most times when Darryl picked him up. But interrupting Corey's flow was one of them.

"Hold your horses will ya?" Stephen said.

"Yeah, let him finish the story before jumping in. You know the rules," Alex meekly scolded.

Darryl turned down a side street. Stephen adjusted his ass to masturbatory comfort on the rear-wheel drive bump humming in the middle of the backseat. He smiled absurdly broad, teeth clenching tongue, waiting for James to catch him with an icy glare in the visor mirror. James didn't bother with his antagonisms anymore because they were too commonplace to deem funny and riff off of.

"Mightn't I continue, then? Right," Corey said in a deep Cockney voice.

James intoned what he thought was proper English based on movies he had seen: "Please be my guest, me lady." He mimed tipping his hat to Corey. He was notorious for taking a lame gag to the next level.

Corey brought the tone back to serious. "Anyway, small animals they eat—but as appetizers. You can guess the main course. Daddy dearest said they look like little furry people, but not of the cute and cuddly persuasion. They sound pretty ferocious, actually, in spite of their name." He paused for dramatic effect, yet anticipated incredulous guffaws. "Puckwudgie," he stated evenly.

Right on cue, Stephen and James sneered at the goofy name ejaculating from their pal's stoic mouth. How could he keep a straight face like that?

"Puckwudgie," Corey repeated. "Say it."

His audience laughed and said "Puckwudgie" like a chorus.

Corey kept the intensity of a master storyteller on his face and in his voice as he added a layer of justification to make this feel authentic. "Feels silly, right? But think about it. How better to hide your killer appetite than in a name so stupid no one will utter it? You could be a tribe of killer Ewoks and thrive in people's denial. That's what they do, right? That's what all the paranormal do.

"My dad said a bunch of his friends saw them too and then they just vanished. Not the friends, the animals. Well, duh... Anyway, ah, I think the fact that they had like a pattern of sightings that just stopped makes it sound kinda real. "

"Real enough," Alex offered.

Corey went on. "That's what I'm thinking. Also, remember when Billy Loman ran away to the swamps a few years back?"

They all nodded, catching on to his one-plus-one equals whatever's-most-invigorating logic.

"Well they never found him, did they? What if these things hibernated for a little bit like, say, thirty years and now they're back? ... *And they ah fuckin' stahvin'.*"

They cackled at Corey's Boston accent overkill. Darryl added, "The kid's dad wasn't found either, was he? Didn't he like go looking for him or something? And he never returned. Something like that."

"Yeah, something like that, I think," Alex confirmed. "He got stuck in the mud or found his son dead and took his own life. Something. I think I remember seeing that on the news."

"But my dad says these creatures got them both. Ripped 'em to shreds." Corey paused, allowing silence to creep them out then closed his case like a commander-in-chief selling war to the public. "We've all heard stories about the swamp and never gave it a second thought. I mean hell, who here hasn't played on the outskirts or canoed the river down the middle and not seen a friggen thing? A couple deer. A lark, maybe...."

"Bigfoot," James tossed in for their amusement.

"Right, Bigfoot." Corey kept on in the same serious tone. "Who knows? Who among us has ever gone into the swamp—like really into the swamp? Don't you think it's kind of weird that we meet at a tree house at the edge of Hockomock, where paranormal shit is reported all the time, and we talk about paranormal shit all the time, but we've never actually gone into the swamp to find out?"

"Ah. Another paranormal riddle," Stephen deadpanned.

"You had me at 'tree house,'" Darryl chortled.

Corey laughed along but pressed the issue. James bottom-lined it: "Dude, it's simple: we're pussies."

"Well my point is—or it was gonna be, anyway—Who knows what's out there? Maybe nothing. Maybe everything. It's worth checking out." Corey leaned back savoring his own ability to weave a yarn. No one spoke. No one smoked. Wind hissed through the car as Darryl absentmindedly sped up. Finally, Corey broke back in: "I mean, you know, it could all be bullshit— my bet's on bullshit—but who knows?"

"Right," Stephen agreed, staring at James' headrest.

Alex followed the crescent moon with his eyes. James had stopped sucking Newports a good while into the story. He traded them for his fingernails, two of which were now bitten to nubs.

Darryl sighed, regaining clarity. He pushed air from his cheeks through clenched teeth making a weird farty noise. "Gentlemen, it's time to form a plan," he said. He swerved his Honda around a narrow corner skidding a bit more than he had anticipated.

They all knew where they were heading: the tree house. Verbally though they brushed it off as no biggie, each one of them secretly thought there was a supernatural draw to those rickety planks nailed into the maple. They weren't blind to the fact of their age but damn they loved that place like middle schoolers.

Corey knew what it was: they had built it together as kids and repaired it over time. That old getaway nestled in branches meant something to them. It exemplified the word "cherish." At least that's the speech he rehearsed in case anyone at school found out about it. It was an embarrassment but it was *their* embarrassment, damn it! He rehearsed that, too. Thankfully for all involved, he never had to give the speech in all his four-going-on-five years of high school.

The tree house lay secluded behind an abandoned mansion on a gated estate that had its own haunted lore. No one went near it except these boys. Not to break in. Not to throw rocks at the windows. Not on a dare. Not for anything.

It earned the nickname *Spooky Mansion* by the sheer creepiness of its existence. Townsfolk referred to it this way if they referred to it at all. In truth, barely anyone in Taunton thought about it let alone talked about it. Even the boys only mentioned it by way of territorial marker. Let's meet up at Spooky Mansion, they'd say. It was interchangeable with *tree house.*

The boys thought there was something cool in the idea of keeping a treetop shack camouflaged by a sprawling mansion as their getaway. They called it the Reverse Batman because Batman had that unassuming cave exterior camouflaging his palace of high-tech gadgets. James liked to joke, "If only people knew that behind the façade of this filthy rich mansion was our dirt poor bird house, they'd be completely jealous!" That line in all its permutations was always good for a cheap yuck from the boys.

But the people inside the condemned mansion were not laughing. No, they were not laughing at all.

INTERLUDE
Earth Zero

There was a time before man, a time before dinosaurs, a time before time itself. In this time all creatures great and small lived in peaceful harmony on Earth Plane. You didn't need laws and you didn't need currency. Trade was something you did naturally. Work ethic was innate. You were as near to perfection as possible and you didn't know it, you didn't frame it that way, hence it was true.

God, is any of this making sense?

God. There was no need for Deity.

Back then, some species had males and females in body only. There was no gender inside, and no biases toward other races, which there were plenty of. Including dragons, Corey. Dragons!

Dragons and reptilians, praying mantis people, tall, blond elven people, gray wee people, furry giants—all of the thoughtful creatures of folklore lived and they lived here. Language was communicated in the mind and so idle chatter did not pollute the air. Instead, the air filled sweetly with gentle music, which permeated everything and made all of creation hum in the same key.

There was no war here and no strife. Every organism met each other on their own level of understanding. Yes, Corey, things were this Good. Good with a capital G. Even the insect people, red as clay, who lived in immaculate tunnel palaces carved deep within the earth—even they allied themselves with the surface-dwellers.

The good will, the peace, the perfection all lasted un-told millennia.

It could be argued that time didn't begin until the others came. The others were aliens, drifters coasting in the sea of space eking out a new home with an atmos-phere like where they came from, wherever that is, whenever that was. When they found this pearl in the black sea shimmering with such abundance and life, they studied. They waited. They bided their time and they were masters of this for they had nowhere to go.

Eventually, they found the weakness they needed to exploit, to strengthen their numbers, and to over-take Earth Plane's natural inhabitants. That weakness was the secret of the insect people. And that secret would leave Earth Plane in ruins.

Chapter 3

"No icky girl germs! No icky girl germs!"

Alex whipped a pebble off the wooden beam next to James' left ear. "Grow up, James."

"Dude, you almost hit *me*," Stephen bitched.

"I *am* grownup, Alex, and as the adult in this situation you have to do as I say, not as I do—and I do chicks left and right, believe me—but I say no to them joining us and ruining our lives. I do chicks, not hens. Not henpecking chicks and not turkeys either," James lectured.

"Goats?" Corey asked.

"Goats, yes. Goats, absolutely. Give sheep the vote, I say. And I'll fuck a llama 'til it's blue in the face. Hell, I'll fuck the dead Dalai Lama 'til he's bluer in the face. No chicks. That's my final answer. No chicks."

"You're fucking ricockulous," Darryl chortled, mid-Camel-exhale.

"And you throw another rock at me, I'll break your face," James added.

"Oooh! Do it! Do it!"

"Fight!"

Stephen and Corey loved goading James. They all did. James got off on being the black sheep. He was good in the role.

Darryl used his heel as a gavel to bring order to the court jesters. "Gentlemen, gentlemen! Let's put this to a vote so I can take a piss break. Then we'll reconvene and work out the who brings what for our little exploration. All in favor of Alex's squeeze, his flame, his dish, Lina—what's her name?"

"Lina Igasho. And she's not my anything, we're just friends."

"Right. Just friends. All in favor of Lina 'Just Friends' Igasho coming into the club, wrecking all our shit, and splitting us up Yoko style, say *aye*."

Alex's hand sprang up before Darryl finished his proposal. "Aye," he said, "And I object to that characterization."

"So noted. By the way, *aye*. I'm just playin', I'm sure she's cool. Any friend of yours is a friend of mine. I'd like to meet her first of course."

"Of course."

"And so any objections? Show us the *nay*."

"Nay," James and Stephen blurted. They waved both their hands for emphasis.

"Sorry, dudes, you only get counted once. The old *wave and make it look like more voters* trick doesn't cut it when I'm sober."

James raised a finger to interject. "Did somebody say 'cut it?'" He ripped a loud, glorious fart with his ass so firmly mashed into the floor boards that they all felt the reverberations.

"Ah, God!"

"James!"

"Sick!"

"Meeting adjourned," Darryl coughed. Stephen nudged James with his foot. The olfactory-molested crew pinched their nostrils in dramatic fashion.

"Wait, you can't call meeting, Corey didn't vote," Alex reminded.

"Right. Good job, James," Darryl said.

"Don't blame me, blame nature. My puckered shitter is just as God intended."

"Very good, sir. Corey?"

Corey regarded Alex's shy, pleading eyes and then looked to James, that sad sack. Stephen wasn't much better.

"As much as I'd love to say yea, Alex, I'm abstaining."

"How unlike you," James scoffed. Stephen, a huge fan of the 80's revival that was in nowadays, sang the first verse to Madonna's ancient classic *Like A Virgin*, while rubbing his nipples to great laughter from his friends. He came in for some kissy-kissy but Corey shoved him away.

"Whatever, dorks. I'm just saying we shouldn't vote until we meet her."

Alex smiled wide. "Fair enough."

Stephen said, "Yeah, she could be a fucking terrorist like Alex. Is she of the Lebanese persuasion, bud? Is that your thing? Kissing cousins?"

"No, dick, she's Indian," Alex jousted.

"Oh. Dot or feather?" Stephen asked.

"Little of one, little of two."

James broke in, "Nice! Double-dipping—I like it!"

Darryl shook his head while pinching the skin above his brow as if feeling a migraine coming on. "What the fuck does that even mean?" he asked rhetorically.

James answered anyway. "It means Corey will meet her and want to bone her cuz he loves dark meat, and poor Alex won't speak up cuz he's a fuckin' wuss. You'll both end up hating each other and then hate me when you find out I already fucked her. Is that what you want?"

"James, if that's how this ends I will lob off and eat my own balls," Corey assured.

"You have balls? Why didn't you tell us? The only reason I voted *no* is cuz I thought you filled our bitch quota," James fired.

"I did. I filled it when I agreed to let you in."

"That's funny because your mother didn't mention that last night when I was filling her in."

"James, I hardly think my mom finds three inches filling."

"Then explain how you were born."

"That's easy. My dad's hung like an ox. Like father like son."

"Speaking of which, you ever wonder why you look more like me than your old man?"

"Because I'm fugly?"

And so on, well into the evening.

Chapter 4

The next morning was hectic for Corey. Test after un-studied-for test slapped him in the brain. He loved to study, just not for school. Put a book about aliens or remote viewing in front of him and he'd devour it.

By day's end he barely had the self-esteem to slink out of his final class: basic algebra. Sucky as school was, he dreaded the bus ride home even more. If school was prison, the bus was the shower room.

School bus. Yellow and black, the colors of stinging bee. Terrible place. To Corey it was hell on wheels. To the demon spawn who infested it, the bus meant chaotic freedom with little repercussion. It was a place where the id flipped a fuck finger at authority, a place where anything could end up a projectile, including—HOLY SHIT!—including Tommy Almeier!

The bus squealed to a halt on the side of the road home. The students lowered their faces like a shamed seventy-headed hydra. Some quivered with the knowledge that they could be wrongly accused of chucking poor growth-stunted Tommy over five seats and into the aisle where his agape mouth met grimy floor like a whale shark sucking in plankton. The innocents knew, all knew, that were the bus driver to grab one or more of them, the real perps would not have gut check time, would not admit to heaving Tommy like a Nerf ball. No one would rat them out either, including the accused, because you just don't do that.

You just don't do that unless your name is Corey Avon and you've got to speed home and pack for the big campout in Hockomock Swamp.

"What time is it?" Corey whispered to the boy next to him.

"Time to get a watch," the boy goaded. He had no retort for that. It was such an old gag he simply shook his head at the geekiness displayed by his seatmate.

Was Tommy going to be alright? Blood dribbled from his bottom lip but it didn't look so bad. Maybe he chipped a tooth, but that's all. He'd be fine.

Can we get going now? Corey squirmed a little, feeling restless and selfish and guilty for it. He had almost convinced himself that he'd been a culprit in the plan to take Tommy's life for the fun of it. What a way to go: over five seats and *boom!* Gravity serving pain.

The driver consoled Tommy outside the bus. Corey watched the freshman shake his head, refusing to give up the muggers as he swallowed tears. Be strong, Corey thought, but hurry the fuck up.

"Excuse me, you have the time?" he asked the girl in front of him. Her forehead rested on the window so comfortably that she didn't bother to turn around. She knew he was addressing her, though, because he asked it through the space between the seat and the pane and she felt the heat of his breath on her ear.

"Yes. Yes I do. It's time to get a watch," she deadpanned.

"Gee, thanks. I guess asshole is the new helpful these days, huh?"

"I'm only joking," she said. "God, take a pill."

He waited for the follow-up offering of time but it never came. "Then... you do have the time?"

"No," she said. "My atmosphone died. I don't have a watch." She raised her naked left wrist as proof.

"Great. Thank you," he huffed.

"Why? Where do you have to be?"

"Huh? Oh, ahhh... going out. Friends. Camping. I'm like late."

"Was that even a sentence?" she giggled. "Fire. Baaaad. Camping. Gooood."

Corey laughed. "Yeah, I dunno. Sorry."

"What's your name anyway?"

"Corey."

She tensed up and he could feel something change between them. "Corey?" she asked.

"Yeah. Corey Avon. "

She swiveled around, hopped up on her knees and met his
eyes for the first time in one succinct move. "You've got to be
shitting me," she said.

"I shit you not. I know it's a dick name but it's my parents.
It's not like I—"

"No-no, it's not that. But your name really is Corey Avon?"

"Can you believe it?"

"No. But wait 'til you hear—"

"Alright, listen up!" The driver stomped back into the bus
with scary authority. None of the students could point to where
the driver's power began and ended. What could a driver get
away with? They held your life in their hands every morning,
noon, and fieldtrip. Actually, Corey wondered, what couldn't
they get away with? Especially this woman who looked like she
was pushing 300-large through those pleated blue dress pants,
her long curly brown hair squeezed back inside a Red Sox base-
ball cap, her breasts split so wide to the left and to the right that
the buttons on her shirt looked ready to pop. At his angle he
could see the strap of her bra connecting those giant cups, fat
and white, in the crevasse formed by two middle buttons struggling to remain threaded.

When the driver saw that she had every student's attention, she continued. "I am back, alright? Okay?—And as you can
see, Tommy is not. Alright, now I didn't see who threw him
down the aisle, okay?—So whoever did that, shame on you. But
you need to confess it now, okay?—And I promise to go easier
on you than you deserve, alright? Okay, now who did it?"

Corey grew antsy in the drawn conspired silence. This was
retarded, he thought, so very junior high. He knew the bus demons were incapable of finding fault with their own actions.
They'd probably convinced themselves they hadn't committed

the heinous crime, like that football dude OJ Simpson back when.

"That's it! Time's up! Okay, because of the foolish behavior of a few children—and I call you children because that's what you are, alright?—you're all getting a week's detention."

"What are you, the principal?" piped a faceless demon from somewhere in the back.

"Hey, maybe nobody did it. Maybe Tommy knows how to fly," added another.

Oh no. The demons were asserting themselves and the driver was getting that glazed look girls get before inhaling self-righteousness and exhaling a symphony of words conducted by a looping index finger and that side-to-side wiggling Egyptian head dance thing they do. This was bad. This was very bad. Corey was late. He was very late. All of this, the tipping point.

"See the dude in the black shirt with the earring? Him. And the fucktard next to him? Him. And Brian and that other kid directly across from them. 'Oh, who, me?' Yeah, you, douche bag. Them. They did it. Please, let's go. I'm late for something and I don't have time for games so kick them off, assume the position, and drive us home, please pretty with sugar."

It was only after Corey blurted this that he realized he was standing. Alone. The object of astonishment. A bipedal rat. The silence was such that he could hear the blood draining from his face, could hear the quiet sobs of Tommy Almeier waiting for the criminals to exit the bus before slinking back on.

The driver motioned for the four accused to step to the front of the bus. "But we didn't do anything!" the kid with the earring screamed.

And when that didn't matter, "We're gonna kick your ass, man!"

And, "Best watch your back, man!"

And, "I'm gonna fuck you up!"

And, "Dude, I thought we were friends!"

"Alright, if any of you so much as touch that boy and I find out about it, okay?—you'll be walking to school for the rest of the year! Alright?" The driver yelled this as the accused skulked off the vehicle.

'How reassuring,' Corey thought, 'the bus driver's got my back.' He dropped back to his seat. Tommy practically dove into the seat behind the driver and held his head in his hands. He never ever wanted to look at anyone again.

The door squealed shut, the bus engine turned, and the criminals flipped Corey off as he rolled on without them. The boy next to him wouldn't stop staring.

"What," Corey barked.

"Assume the position?"

"Shut up."

INTERLUDE
Earth Zero

All beings of higher mind were connected tele-pathically, and not just on Earth Plane. The aliens were linked, too. There was still individuality, it's just that it wasn't as self-contained as what we experience. It was more like being a rock firmly embedded on the floor of a rushing stream.

But, with the right technology one could shield one-self from the wandering minds of others. Earth Planers had no need for this technology so they never invented it. The aliens, on the other hand, depended on their ability to exist undetected until such time as they were ready to reveal themselves. That time never came with a smile and a handshake; it came with a perfect first strike that was near to the last.

The harmonious peoples of Earth Plane—the faer-ies, the gnomes, the dragons; the reptilians, the tall be-ings of light; the green ones and the blue ones; the shining ones and the insectoids—all of these people lived in agreement. It wasn't verbal. It wasn't written. It was the best thing to do and so they did it. Did what?—You know this stuff already so I don't have to tell you, but I will. Come closer and I shall....

The agreement was to never leave Earth Plane. Never explore. Never exploit. Never go to war. They came to this understanding and decided to focus their attention inwardly. They would master the space they occupied and which occupied them. They would make folds in space and time, creating new dimensions. If the moment ever came that they needed to expand or needed to hide, they'd create a place, a universe within a universe, a bubble in the foam of the sea of mind.

They needed one now.

Chapter 5

Corey booked into his house full of inviting kitsch, absent the parents who adored them. Granted, he was running seriously behind in packing but first things first: he stopped at the fridge, stretched, caught his breath, opened the refrigerator door, and... nothing edible. Shit. Old Chinese food, sure, and ketchup. None in the Avon household recollected how old that forgotten Chinese food was, and ketchup couldn't smother food poisoning, so Corey left it for another victim.

There was a swig of spring water left in its two-gallon jug, which he gladly accepted. As he wiped his mouth on his shirt-sleeve his eye caught a note waiting for him on the table. It read:

Corey,

I'm out shopping, be back soon. Dad is going to be late getting home. Please take out the garbage!!!

LUV,

MOM
XOXOXO

P.S.: Darryl called. He said that it you're not at the meet-up in fifteen minutes they would leave without you. That was at 3:00.

Corey darted his attention to the lame wall clock. It was one of those plastic black cats where the eyes and tail moved left-right to the beat of the seconds ticking away on its whisker hands. *Quarter to four! Shit! That fucking cat—That fucking mocking cat!*

He chucked the letter, stuffed whatever clothes smelled good enough to survive a sweaty weekend into a backpack, and scribbled out a note to his parents telling them he wouldn't be home. Garbage, shmarbage—he was off to the cellar where his trusty bike, Old Faithful, stood worn from a lifetime of youthful adventures but always ready for next.

It was a two-mile ride to Spooky Mansion that primarily involved downhill coasting. When he arrived, he hopped off the bike, still in motion, and ran along side it, ditching it behind some overgrown brush near the NO TRESPASSING sign and Darryl's car. No need to lock the bike up since no one else ever ventured out here. Still running off the bike's momentum, he jumped onto and over the tall jagged rock fence connected to the locked gate. He knew exactly where to aim his hands and feet for this, so many had been his trespasses. The better he got at it the more ninja he felt.

He booked to the marshy area behind the old broken down mansion. Skunk cabbage grew there and the boys got a laugh from kicking it at each other as they waded through toward their tree house.

Tree house. What the fuck am I doing? I'm like an adult and can vote and junk. This is crazy—What the fuck is wrong with us? We should just play with toys and get it over with. You know James still has a blankie. Fuckin' bed-wetter.

Corey wrestled with this idea of growing up and into somebody else. Did he really have to let go the tree house? The bike? The adventures and the laughs? Did he really have to get a job and a wife and pay the bills and raise squirts more irresponsible than he? When he left for college in another thousand years was he leaving himself behind? Is that what it meant to grow up: to morph into this boring older servant of children, wife, and boss?

"Bastards." He broke his own silence. They'd gone without him. Dejected but still game, he followed the footprints into the marsh to find his so-called friends.

'We're supposed to be a team. You couldn't even wait?' He mentally recited numerous questions he would aim at his pals to make them feel guilty. The more he ruminated the less he felt badly for himself and the more he imagined their psychological distress the broader he smiled. 'You couldn't have even waited for me? Think of how you would have felt knowing that your best friends didn't care enough to wait a few more minutes—especially since I'm the one who came up with the fucking expedition!' Just one or two of these gems would force shame upon the group.

Corey snapped out of his head when his ear caught the unusually loud noise of rustling bushes ahead on the path. From the brush, a streak of bright color... laughter... "Hey, guys!"

"Corey?" his pals asked in stuttered unison, chased by Stephen's, "How did you find us?"

"I followed your footprints, douche bags. Why didn't you guys wait for me?"

"How long were we supposed to wait? We didn't know when you'd show up if at all," Stephen explained.

"Dude, get an atmosphone," James muttered.

"No! Fuck you," Corey spat.

James shrugged. "All right. Then suck it." He turned to Darryl. "By the way, oh captain, my captain, how far into the swamp must we trudge?"

"As far as it takes," Darryl answered.

"Great. We don't know where we're going, we don't know what awaits us when we get there, and, shit—!" SLAP! "God damned mosquitoes are gonna eat us alive!"

"James?"

"What?"

"Quit bitching."

Stephen handed James some Deep Woods Off from his bag of necessities. James applied it liberally to his neck and cheeks. "Darryl?" James asked.

"Yeah?"

"Blow me."

"No thanks, Jimmy, I don't eat baby food."

"Don't call me Jimmy, you know I hate that. Did anyone else bring bug spray?"

Darryl glared at him like he was the biggest asshole alive. "Yeah, dude. We're in the woods. We also brought flashlights, a compass, a change of clothes, some fucking sleeping bags, a fucking tent—You think I'm carrying this gear for fucking gym class?"

"You guys really brought all that stuff?"

"I swiped some waterproof matches from my dad's handy drawer just in case," Corey offered.

"Oh cool," said Stephen.

Darryl raised an eyebrow knowing he was in for some dumb shit before he even lobbed James the volley. "Why? What did you bring?"

James emptied his pockets. "A candy bar, some Trident, and a penny."

"Oh," Darryl said straight-faced. "Sucks to be you."

"Kinda does. But it doesn't have to. I mean... I suppose we'll all be sharing everything... right?"

"No, Jimmy, I don't suppose we will. That's why we had a fucking meeting to discuss what the fuck we needed to bring. 'Member that?"

"Thanks, Dar. That's the sign of a great leader: don't keep the troops satisfied; don't show them any dignity or respect; make fun of them; call them names; don't supply them with the least bit of confidence let alone the bare essentials for the wilderness. You're a fucking hero, dude. No, seriously, you are gonna share with me right?"

Some people have great poker faces. Some don't. At that moment, Corey thought Darryl was a stone monument. His expression, his breathing, his posture—nothing changed with the verbal punches and when he finally opened his mouth to address James it was like he wasn't opening his mouth at all. Like a ventriloquist act. "Seriously, I believe you already asked me that. The answer remains the same: no. Jimmy."

"I said don't call me that."

"Why? It's your name isn't it?"

"I don't care, I hate it. Why don't you give me a code name or a nickname or something."

"Jimmy is a nickname, douche." Corey's reminder was chased by Stephen's taunt: "How's about Dick? Sergeant Dick B. Cumming. He can be your right-hand man, Darryl." All but James laughed.

"Are you a right hand man?" Darryl asked. "I mean when you're alone in that Febreze-stink kennel you call a home and you get that urge—You know the one. You're in the bathroom. Alone. Nothing but a mirror and your own echoes, and you whip it out, right? And you do a little rain dance maybe with the shower on or maybe the sink because even though you're alone you're embarrassed by your own panting and groaning."

Alex turned away. "Blecht. That's friggen disgusting."

"True. But only because it's Sergeant Dick here and nobody wants to picture him being intimate with himself even though clearly that's the only person he'd ever be intimate with—and so the question: Are you a righty or a lefty?"

James giggled as he scoffed. "Really, after all that, that's the question?"

"You got an answer?"

"Well it depends."

"On what?"

"On whether I'm doing Alex's chick, Lina, or your mom, Mrs. William Malone. Proud mother of two; husband status: deceased. Wait—shhhhh! That's right. Feel the cold! Ooooh, brr! We're not supposed to say stuff that hurts cuz that's over the line. But seriously, Darryl. We're both single so it's kinda fair."

No one had ever seen Darryl lose his cool. If anything, he grew more distant when his father passed. Cancer gnawed his old man's bones from the inside out. It was shocking to Darryl how awful and slow and godless death came to his father, a good man, a great dad. In the end, greatness did not matter. Love did not matter. He did not matter. That much was clear. Darryl stayed analytical to stay sane. Some inner thing clicked and evolved him into someone much stronger. He stayed like that for his mother and sister who did all of the crying he barely allowed for himself.

The boys hung on the longest moment of their lives expecting the tension to end in the type of unstoppable beatdown only the repressed can deliver. What James had going for him was the power of zero positive expectations regarding anything that escaped his mouth. Every clique has their jackass and James was theirs. He suffered the kind of social retardation where if you ribbed him he'd rip out your guts and feed them to you raw. His brain had no gauge for the sort of moderation needed when joking lightly. This was taxing on his pals but they found him funny most of the time and appreciated his straightforward nature. *Most of the time*. Not now. Now was completely painful.

Darryl's eyes locked onto James' like periscope crosshairs. What he fired stunned more than his victim.

"You know I feel bad for you, James, I really do. I could waste you right now and nobody would give a fuck but that wouldn't prove anything. Everybody knows you're a wimpassed turd, so that's not the issue. I mean it's not like this is a stage you're going through that a good old fashion asswhooping will cure, make you see the light, or whatever. No. I believe, and I think I speak for everyone here, that you are a born asshat. That's why you're in our group. You're such a vile, grotesque shit of a thing that nobody else talks to you. Nobody.

"I felt bad when I first met you. I said, 'Hey, guys, you see that pathetic fuck kicking rocks at the flagpole? Let's be good Samaritans and take him in.' Like a fucking dog, James, because that's what you are. We always wanted a mascot and Baby Jesus delivered. You're our bitch."

Corey toyed with the idea of peacekeeping but figured he'd be snapped at to stay out of it by Darryl who continued his roll in so few breaths it seemed rehearsed.

"They tried to talk me out of it but I walked up to you anyway, extended that hand in friendship, and you know what? I've regretted it ever since, because—and I hate to repeat myself but I can't stress it enough—you are an asshat. A dickhead. You're common. Think of all the derogatory remarks you've heard girls giggle about you as you walk by and multiply by the ones you missed. That's you.

"Now, we've got a cool weekend ahead of us. Please, let's not ruin it, please. Don't talk shit to me. Don't even respond to this. Just—for once in your life—take it like a man, swallow that lump and let it go. In fact, new rule: don't talk to me unless it's an emergency, okay? Do this and remember how I didn't fuck you up just now like I have every right to."

By the end of it James' eyes were trained on his sneakers. This marked the first time he ever felt embarrassment and didn't block it out with smarm. Instead, he nodded slightly, quickly, ashamed even to apologize.

"Now let's get moving," Darryl ended. "There's lot's of exploring to do and not a lot of light to do it."

The crew forged deeper into the muck of the swamp than they'd ever ventured. For a sufferable while none uttered a word. They were two parts shocked, one part impressed by what was easily the longest uninterrupted insult any of them had ever heard. Corey thought even James had to be impressed. Fighting tears, sure, but impressed.

And pissed that he was the only one wearing sneakers out here, which now looked like they were made of mud. And he couldn't ask the group to stop while he wiped them off. And he couldn't bitch about it.

***

The Art of War had nothing on the Art of Darryl. As urgently as he wanted to, Corey couldn't take over the squad, not after that show of strength. If he had been Darryl and James himself, what would he have done? Hauled off and hit him? Burst into tears? No, he could now see that Darryl was the real deal. After that bitch slapping, Corey could only hope to one day be that cool.

One minute he wanted to lead, the next minute he was just glad to be in the group. How long would that feeling last? He hoped long enough to get through the weekend. He didn't want to try and pull rank in the middle of the expedition. He might end up looking like James.

"Smart move, Jimmy," Stephen whispered, the first to break the curse of post-argument shock.

"Fuck off, Stephanie," James sneered.

"Awe, poor baby got his ass whipped, Serves you right for shitting on Darryl's dead old man."

"What part of fuck off don't you get? Why don't you go bug Alex or Corey."

"What? And leave you here all alone with your conscience? Never. I'm a giving guy. It's not like anyone else is gonna talk to you."

James rolled his eyes, sighed deeply. Stephen kept at him undeterred. "Know what's funny?" he said. James ignored him so he repeated, "Know what's funny?"

"That you're a dipshit?"

"Nope. That 'Jimmy' is slang for 'dick.' I just thought of that now. We could have avoided this whole fiasco if I'd remembered you already have dick built into your name. You're a built-in dick."

And that's the way things were: kick a man when he's down because you knew if the roles were reversed he would do you the same. None in the group admired the receiving end but then none had a choice. When their time came, it came unrelenting. Cry? Retaliate? Nope. Take it like a man. Ignore it and it might get bored, might go away.

Please, God, make Stephen go away! I've learned my lesson. Make him walk into a fat tree branch or something. Quicksand. Bees. Anything.

***

Corey didn't mind all the hiking even knowing he'd have to double back eventually; however, dry clearings were becoming a commodity the further into the woods they traveled. "So Darryl, when do you think we should stop and make camp for the ni—"

"Shhhh!"

"What is it?" Corey perked.

"Did you hear that?"

"No. What?"

"Alex, did you hear it?"

"No. What is it, Dar?"

"I don't know. I thought I heard something loud on the wind."

"Loud on the wind, Tecumseh? Maybe it's a squirrel," Corey joked.

"Yeah, right. The well-known Bristol County flying squirrel," Darryl chided. The trio laughed and Corey added, "Hey, it could happen. We got those snow owls now."

"Yeah, well not in this lifetime. Not in this swamp, anyway." Darryl looked far over his left shoulder and rolled his eyes. "Hold up, kids. The dipshits are falling behind." He unrolled a pack of Camels from his shirtsleeve and lit up. It amazed Corey how a smoker could chug along at this pace on a long hike without huffing and puffing and on so few breaks. He was faring infinitely better than Alex whose breathing was a wheeze and face a puddle mess. Alex was short and chubby but it didn't bother him, so no one picked on him about it. Out here, though, his limitations were obvious and he felt kind of guilty about it. Hiking was much easier in videogames.

The trio plopped down on a fallen rotting maple and waited for the slackers to catch up. Annoyed with Stephen and especially James, Darryl shouted, "Hey, assholes! Hurry it up! We want to set up camp sometime in the near future!" The forest was mostly still after that, broken only by sawing cicada legs and the occasional wind trickling through needles and leaves.

"Darryl?" Corey asked tentatively.

"Yeah," he replied without so much as a glance at his friend. It was as if he expected this conversation.

"I just wanted to say that you handled James good. He can be a real fuckin' asshole sometimes and I think if it was any of us in your position he'd be dead."

Darryl had no reaction. His eyes were trained on James and Stephen klutzing their way around a mud hole. Corey considered ways to draw an emotion from him, a sign that he was paying attention to what he had to say and that he cared. He settled on, "I feel like I should apologize for what he said, you know? It was like that deep."

Darryl broke trance and looked Corey straight in the eye. "Don't sweat it, Coronimo. His problem isn't that he can act like a real fuckin' asshole, it's that he *is* a real fuckin' asshole. A real-life authentic Grade A twat in a ball bag."

Alex forced out a nervous laugh. The word *twat* was still taboo to him.

"It's true," Darryl continued. "And the sad thing about it is he doesn't even see where he's wrong. He had tears in his eyes cuz I embarrassed him in front of you guys, not cuz he felt bad about what he said."

Before Corey or Alex could respond, the duo had caught up. Stephen dropped his backpack triumphantly. "Well we're here," he announced. "Where do you want to pitch the tent?"

"You're pitching a tent, Steph? What were you two doing back there?"

"Ahrrrrt! You're a funny guy, Corey," Stephen mocked.

Darryl stood, surveyed the land. "See that clearing over there?" he asked pointing toward a distant birch tree.

Stephen bobbed his head around and squinted. "No."

"Me neither. How about you and James go over there and make one?"

"Oh, fuck off! You may be the leader but we ain't your slaves! If you want a clearing you're gonna have to help us."

Darryl eyeballed him in disbelief. "Don't argue with me, Stephen, just do it."

But Stephen held his ground. "Not unless you help!" James stayed uncharacteristically to himself while they settled their tiff.

Darryl did an about-face and switched into calming mode. "No need to get upset. We'll help. I just wanted you two to start it, that's all. Us three are gonna go set up traps around the camp so that if one of those Puckwudgies tries to get us in the middle of the night we can turn the tables on it."

Stephen scanned Darryl's face for a trace of the lie but found nothing. "Smart thinking," he found himself saying. Darryl nodded.

"Yeah, smart thinking," James tried. Darryl ignored him.

"Now let's get to it!" Darryl saluted them like a drill sergeant. They stood at attention and returned the gesture, calling, "Sir, yes, sir," in unison. It was geeky but they loved it.

Darryl, Corey, and Alex trudged into a thickly wooded area away from the other boys before Darryl plopped himself down on a large smooth rock.

"What's up?" Alex asked.

Darryl lit another Camel, unconcerned with the question.

Alex scratched his nose. Allergies made the tip itch. "Traps, dude?" he inquired.

"Hmmm? Oh, you didn't really think we were gonna set traps did you?"

Alex shrugged.

"Come on! If we booby-trapped this place one of those jackalopes would set 'em off. No, I figured we would rest here for a little while. Get my smoke on."

Alex cocked his head, shot that *You can't be serious* look. Half of Darryl's mouth grinned while the other managed the cigarette. "They need the exercise."

So the truth comes out, Corey thought. Cool though he is, Darryl Malone is capable of lying to his own friends. Be that as it may, Corey and Alex dropped ass to rock and enjoyed the— "Ouch!" SLAP! "Mosquito."—great outdoors.

Chapter 6
Henry

Henry didn't dress in black unless he needed to fit in. A corporate setting, say, or a goth rave. Most of the Man In Black legend originated from FBI showing up at the front doors of rural Americans in the fifties asking questions about their UFO sightings. Top to bottom, from sighting to business suit, this was so foreign to the farmers that it all appeared alien. Sci fi writers and their readers with a need to believe took it from there. Someone even managed to tie Bigfoot to aliens and a sub-subculture was born. Henry called this the fringe of the fringe and he totally understood them for he, too, was alone. Fringe of the fringe's fringe, he'd say, would he were allowed to talk about it.

Henry knew more than any other human ever had. In America, there was the government, there was the secret government, there were pockets of secret cabals within both governments, there were secret societies tying them all together, and there was Henry. The chain of command went: corporate interest, politician, military. But the chain of power began and ended with Henry. So vastly far above top secret was that fact, it wasn't even classified. Nobody grasped the extent of his reach except him.

Henry wasn't his real name. Few knew his real name, not that it mattered, for he hadn't a family and he'd burned off his fingerprints years ago. He called himself "Henry" because he figured that if he had to live the life of a pseudonym he'd liken himself to his favorite mystery twister, O. Henry. It was that or Fulcanelli. Too obvious.

When he got the call to rush to the broken down mansion at the edge of Hockomock Swamp he was not surprised. It came sooner than he expected but only in the way that a volcano might explode sooner than expected. What "expected" really means is "hoped for."

2012, the year of the great Mayan prophesy, had come to pass and uneventfully so. There would be consequences. Like the various takes on the prophecy itself, these were promised but not detailed leaving a bit of a mystery. A bit of a mystery like, what will happen to mankind? What had Charles done?

He found it comical how so many millions of people knew about the prophesy and not a one reckoned its meaning.

According to some scholars and pseudo-scholars, the Mayan shaman kings had pegged December 21, 2012 as the end of the final age. Having an end date to an age with no explanation of what that means, how it comes about, or what comes next tickles the imagination to torturous lengths.

Some thought the end of 2012 meant humanity would experience an upgrade in consciousness, a mass enlightenment. Others believed it pointed to natural cataclysms, a pole shift, extinction. Some melded the two concepts: first comes a species dieback and the remaining survivors go on to rebuild civilization in spiritual harmony. There was a vocal minority assuring everyone that the 2012 believers had it wrong, that they were misinterpreting the Mayan count by nitpicking the Dresden Codex to sell fear. 2012 would be nothing special after all.

Henry had been amazed at the number of people who had plotted their lives around whichever ignorant opinion best reflected their disposition. His favorite, of course, was the fringe of the fringe lore that on the magical winter day, energy would shoot from the center of the Milky Way to Earth during a rare galactic alignment. This would be the cue for aliens from the mysterious Planet X to infiltrate and take us over. He liked that best because the details were clever, yet the big concepts involved were deceptively vague. Also, it was closest to the truth.

Or it would have been closest to truth had Henry's predecessor, Charles, not given mankind the greatest gift in history: 2013. So thankful were the dozen shark suits with a need to know that they would thank him every day of their lives with loyalty and secrecy and they passed that inheritance to Henry. These faceless men of old wealth had the kind of permanent, legitimate power required to make that mean something. Everything. Whatever Henry wished was his.

"M-Site 5 in haste."

When he heard the man on the other end of his atmosphone calmly state that then the line go dead, he excused himself from the slow grind he was performing on the Ukrainian college hottie to whom he had been rapping for the better part of 20 minutes. He could sell ecstasy to her some other day.

He pushed his way through the morass of sweaty club kids to the locked exit in the security booth behind the two-way mirrors. A hefty man dressed as a bouncer greeted him. "You didn't close the deal," he said, more surprised than anything.

"A thousand of her slide through these doors every night. This can wait," Henry replied.

He leaned his forehead into a molded cup by the door. A horizontal red laser gizmo straight out of a spy thriller scanned his retina. He always got a kick out of that part. The exit unlocked and he jogged up the winding staircase on the other side to a second retina scan. That door released, too. Nobody followed him.

"Hi, baby. Daddy's home," he uttered with a grin. He walked briskly to the unmarked black chopper waiting for him on the roof of his Lower Manhattan techno club, Glow Styxx. How he loved to fly that elegant monstrosity. Any excuse was a happy excuse, even the end of the world.

He ignited her and revved up the whisper-quiet blades, then navigated her to Pease Air Force Base in New Hampshire. There an entourage of soldiers escorted him to the mouth of The Worm Hole, where they left him to buckle into the pressurized seated elevator nicknamed *The Worm*. The Worm, predictably, dropped him deep into the earth via The Worm Hole.

Even at forty miles per hour the descent felt like it took forever. The elevator doors finally opened and his seat wheeled automatically into a shuttle tube ride so fast that if it were a Disney rollercoaster, Six Flags Amusement Park would go out of business. He squeezed his head into the tight-fitted helmet and checked for any systems glitches. There were none. Ever. He radioed command that he was set.

Two hours by car, ten minutes by this, Henry surfaced through the underground elevator beneath the dilapidated mansion at the edge of Hockomock in Taunton, Massachusetts. The men who worked here called this place *The Castle In The Tank* for it reminded them of the plastic gray castles pet owners set in fish tanks. Only in this castle, the fish watched you.

A crumbling mess on the outside and inside, the mansion provided cover for the military installation tucked underneath the basement. The heavily classified base housed a slick organization of computer banks, surveillance equipment, and that unassuming Orwellian thing: a four-foot-long coiled black antenna encased in blast-proof glass named the Tesla Dream Machine. "What have we got, gentlemen?"

"We've got a light up, sir. Extensive."

"Do you know all the details?"

"Sir, I have been stationed here for the last five years. I have internalized all of the available data."

"Very good. I will take that from you now."

"Yes, sir."

Henry tapped a Morse code sequence on the palm on his left hand like Spider-Man shooting web. The officer paralyzed where he stood, his body rigid, his head numb, full of pressure and energy so immense that if he didn't know better he'd think he were about to explode. His superior had briefed him on what to expect but that explanation didn't match the real deal.

Everything of the officer's brain came alive in Henry's mind. He took only what he needed. Documents, reams of them, downloaded into his brain. He finished quickly, thanked the offi-

cer, and relieved him of his post. Henry now knew every important fact the officer knew. He knew about the fluctuations in the
swamp. He knew what was happening on the ground there. He
knew a group of local boys were being drawn in by a force so
hungry it had bypassed the powers of suggestion emanating
from the Tesla Dream Machine. He knew the campers would
not be happy for long.

He knew they'd not be alive much longer than that.

Chapter 7

Corey felt bad leaving Steph and James to do all the work but not badly enough to offer help. His mind churned out excuses proving why this was fair. *They'd be sitting here if they'd thought of it first. It's not like it's work, it's… it's… quality bonding time. They're probably growing real close working together. Too close. Butt sex. Then again who wants to bond with James? Oh well, they'll live.*

"Hey Alex, what happened to that Lina chick?" asked Darryl.

"I don't know, I couldn't get in touch with her. I guess it was for the best, though, cuz everyone seemed to be opposed to letting her in."

"Hey, man, I wasn't opposed. In fact I believe it was me who wanted her to join, but I think James and Steph would feel intimidated if we let a girl in the group."

"Yeah," Corey added. "Especially if she's any bit as smart as they are. You know how apes get."

"Now there's a hard chick to find—dirt is smarter than the two of them combined." Darryl kicked up soft earth for emphasis.

"You know, isn't that sad? It's like, we're almost out of high school and that stupid sexist stuff never ends," Alex fumed.

"Nothing ends, it just changes," Corey said.

Darryl realized he was down to the last cigarette. "Fuck a duck." He left it in the soft pack, inhaled deeply the aroma of raw tobacco, then rolled the pack back into his sleeve. "Well, great pontificating with you young Yodas, but you wanna know what I think?"

"You think that you shouldn't be calling me young when I'm a year older than you?"

"Close, Coronosaurus Rex. I think that Stephen and James may be more alike than they want to admit."

"Oh, no question," Alex pounced. "I don't think James real-izes it but I think Stephen does, sometimes, and I think it scares him."

The three seized on one another's psychological profiling in quietude. Corey broke first: "Then maybe we shouldn't have left them alone with each other."

Alex offered to go back hoping his friends would catch his meaning: they should all go together. Darryl looked up at the darkening sky then rolled his head around cracking his neck ten-sion. "Might as well," he conceded.

The trio headed back after a three-minute jogging in place. They worked up the light sweat they imagined people setting up traps would have accumulated. As they approached the site Darryl called out, "Well, chitlins, we're back! How does it... look?" He turned every which way but could spot neither James nor Stephen. He cupped his mouth with his hands and yelled, "Hey, assholes! You didn't do anything!"

"Well isn't this some shit," Corey said.

"I don't think they're here," Alex stated cautiously.

"Of course they're here. They're fucking with us," Darryl assured. "In fact I'll bet you a thousand dollars James—"

"Jesus mother-fucking—!"

"What? What is it, Alex?" Darryl knew to be alarmed. Alex rarely swore casually and he was shaking something fierce. He didn't want to stand perfectly still speaking in clips, he wanted to run screaming, but when fight or flight instinct kicked in, he did neither. He froze. Darryl snapped his fingers close to his friend's eyes. "Dude, say words."

It took everything but Alex got enough of them out. "Blood. Tree. Look where I'm looking."

Darryl and Corey pivoted around sharply, following their friend's gape. Corey fell back a few steps like an unbalanced toddler and squeezed Alex's left shoulder. Darryl inhaled a deep relieving breath. "Wow, that scared the crap out of me," he admitted.

"It's still scaring the crap out of me," Corey said faintly.

"What? It's just paint. Dudes are fucking with us." As if taking his own dare, Darryl abruptly marched up to the lone birch, its white bark freshly coated red. The liquid oozed down like a thick sap covering half its length. The closer he got the more his calf muscles twitched to sprint the opposite direction. There were diced meaty chunks in that red and when he stood an arm's length away, he heard a squishing sound underneath his feet.

He stopped. Crimson gunk swallowed him at the ankles. First he heard his heart and then his breathing and then he was aware that there were no other sounds. No forest critters. No wind. He dislodged his boots from the leaves and the twigs and the chunks and hair and from the mixed wet colors of death, with an enormously loud suction sound that filled the stillness. He regarded his friends, huddled statues, who looked to him to lead. But who was he? This was ridiculous. They were teenagers, almost out of high school, still playing army, still playing Columbus, still *playing*. He wasn't a leader; he was a kid. And right now he wanted Mommy.

Corey scanned Darryl's body language, read the Clift's Notes of everything reeling through his mind: *We will die here.* He called out, "What is it?" because playing dumb was all he could do not to vomit.

Darryl soldiered toward them, his poker face tightly wrapped over the scared child he just was. He split them as he marched past. The boys just watched. Darryl went to his backpack, dropped to his knees. The boys listened to the sounds of furious rummaging, the tearing of cardboard package, and a series of lock and load clicks. Darryl swiveled around and stood up at the same time. He faced the boys with as much angry smile as he could muster.

"We're finding our friends and getting the fuck out of here."

"Where'd you get a gun, Darryl?" Alex asked, his nerves only slightly less frenzied.

"It's not a *gun* gun, it's my dad's flare. He used to keep it in the glove of his truck."

"I got a weapon," Corey said almost to remind himself. He pulled a small Swiss Army knife from his fanny pack and yanked at all the compartmentalized metal until he found the blade.

"So it's not paint," Alex said.

Darryl blocked out the statement. "You got something to fight with?"

Alex nodded toward his bag, which his body was not prepared to move toward. Darryl went to it. "Where?"

"Front zipper. The larger pocket."

Darryl tore at the zipper, pulled out a stun gun. He checked it out having never handled one before. "Really?" he asked.

"Yeah. I have a stun gun. I stole it ages ago, when I was a kid but it still works."

"You steal? Really?" Darryl was momentarily taken out of the grim situation.

"I don't steal, I stole. I was a kid. It was like eighth grade or something."

"Well, Alex, we're going to have to have a talk about this when we get home."

Much as Darryl tried, he could not lighten this. Corey drifted to him and Alex followed.

"Good, let's get out of here while there's still some light," Corey commanded.

"How can we do that, Corey, our fucking friends are out here."

"Our fucking friends are on that tree, Darryl! God, I knew I should have lead the expedition!"

"All yours," Darryl enthused.

"Guys, shut up! This is not about you, okay? There's no time for this and it's totally disrespectful to our friends who…." That was as much speech as Alex could choke out.

Corey owned it. "You're right. Sorry."

"No need," Darryl said.

"Stephen had mace," Alex recalled.

"He did?" The surprises never stopped for Darryl.

"Yeah, but look where it got him. He probably lived as long as James with no weapons."

"And we didn't hear a fucking thing," Corey added.

Darryl darted his eyes around the trees searching for a big evil surprise. "I know. And we were close. They should have screamed. Something took them before they screamed."

"Or maybe not. Maybe it only got one of them."

"Take a look at his boots, Alex. There's enough blood over there to make a moat." Alex looked at the boots, then at the blood feeding the roots of the birch tree. Again, he froze.

"So it's settled: we get the fuck out of here as in right now," Corey continued.

Darryl patted the air in front of him as if to say, *Keep your voice down, they might hear you.* But Corey kept on at the same level. "You don't think they know we're here?"

"I don't know, Corey. But let's use our time wisely here—"

"And do what? Build some real traps? Make some Ewok missiles out of dead wood? They weren't much more than a hundred feet away and we didn't hear a struggle. Obviously any defense they made was in vain."

"We don't know that! We don't know that it was in vain!" Darryl squeaked when he yelled without yelling.

"Look at that tree, Darryl! It ain't stage makeup!"

The three turned as one and regarded the sap of their friends pooling at the base of the tree, a mystery of smears and entrails glistening in the faded day. It was an ungodly memorial. Corey thought of it not as blood but as the agony of defeat. He wondered if the remains were of Stephen or of James, or maybe both. There was so much splay that it was impossible to tell if only one had bared his soul to the tree. If so, where was the other? Why was the gore confined to a single birch? Why were they three spared?

And why the fuck didn't they scream for help?!

That one question alone enraged Corey. He was confused and scared, for sure, but that pissed-off feeling was beginning to overtake his better senses.

They should have made a noise—should have cried out in agony. Something. Anything. But there was no struggle. How is that possible?

What burned him most was knowing that the impossible became possible, a twisted evil miracle, mere feet away from him and at the expense of his best friends' lives. It was as if the answer to all their prayers came and killed and went. The Lord gaveth and he tooketh away in one swift cut and it was fucking bullshit. Somebody evil and powerful was laughing right now. Laughing at them and waiting to strike again.

Corey got that and when he got it he realized that, in a way, Darryl was right. They might as well look for their friends because this force or being or whatever it was would surely not let them leave in their skins.

"Guys," Alex said. "Why are we still here? They're dead. We'll be sitting ducks if we stay much longer. Let's go get the police."

"We don't know that they're *both* dead, like you said," Daryl pressed. "But you're right: we are sitting ducks. Let's find the trail and kill this motherfucker. It's probably a bear and it's full. Whatever it is, it's eaten."

"Jesus!" Corey spat.

"I know, dude, I'm just saying! It's full and lethargic and we can get it. We owe it to Stephen and James and again, we don't know if it dragged one of them off for later. One of them could still be alive, you have to believe that."

"This isn't movies, Darryl! We aren't going to save the day! One or two of our friends is mutilated. I don't want to be third, do you?" Alex asked.

Darryl shook his head not believing the cowardice he was hearing. He retorted, "Well what do you plan on telling the cops? 'Hello, officer. Nice weather we're having, eh? Say, I was just wondering if you would go into the middle of Hockomock to fight a yeti so we may confirm that, yes, our friends are dead…?'

"Great plan, Alex. If you're lucky you might not get locked up for murder. At least if we track it, we might clear our names. We might find one of 'em alive. Maybe it saved James for dessert or something, we don't know. But if we don't try… if we don't care enough to try…. Don't cry at their funerals, boys."

Alex tried to turn away but Darryl kept on him. "We all knew there were dangers here but we ran the risk anyway. What for, Alex, a myth? The thrill of the hunt? Who knows what draws us to this stuff but whatever it is it draws us together. What kind of guy leaves his friends behind? I say we came into this together, we leave together. No *ifs, ands,* or *buts."*

Darryl dropped his hand softly on Alex's shoulder. His friend regarded him expressionlessly. "I'm glad one of us ain't afraid of no ghost." He shrugged Darryl's hand off then scuttled urgently to his backpack and began rifling. "Help me out here, Corey. Am I right or am I right?"

Corey stared into the distance. "I'm sorry, Alex," he said. "I think Darryl is right after all. We came in together, we leave together or—"

"Or die trying, that's just great." Alex found what he'd been fishing for. He stood and waved his compass at his friends as if to say, *Got it.* What he actually said was, "You kids go off and play superhero; I'm going home. And I *will* cry at your funerals, gentlemen." Not waiting for a retort from either of them he began retracing his steps out of the stygian marsh.

"Don't go, Alex," Darryl said firmly. "There's strength in numbers. You leave now and you can kiss your ass goodbye."

Alex wasn't interested. He kept his eyes trained on his compass and on the path before him as he abandoned the security of friends.

Darryl raised his voice: "It'll get you too! You'll be a stain on the tree! This is a mistake!"

Alex stopped in his tracks. Slowly he raised his head but did not turn back. Loud enough for them to hear he said, "It's mine to make. And look what you're making, Darryl. Jokes. Really. You're messed in the head." He again concentrated on the compass and on the path home.

"Hey, wait a second," Darryl huffed. He caught up with his friend—his brother since early childhood—and maneuvered in front of him, grabbing his shoulders for attention and emphasis. "I'm not gonna try and force you to stay, I just don't want you to get hurt, is all."

"You sound like we're fighting a war," Alex said.

"We might end up there." Uttering those words flipped his stomach but Darryl kept his composure. Alex's lips formed a thin smile. There lay a bond underneath the hostility that wanted greatly to impose itself. Darryl reciprocated. He looked defeated and relieved and on the verge of a new wind. "Look, I don't want you to leave on a bad note in case we... you know."

"If anyone can pull this off it's you," Alex said. This time he didn't shirk Darryl's consoling hands from his shoulders. "Good luck, man. And stay cool." He said this and immediately felt like a jackass, as if lamely signing off on Darryl's yearbook.

Darryl saw in Alex's eyes something he'd never noticed before: strength. He answered, "Always. You watch your back, cuz I don't want my best bud to end up in a stew."

Alex laughed nervously. His green eyes welled. "Me neither," he said. "Look, you better get moving while the sun's up."

They hugged, then Alex waved adieu to Corey who was sitting on the ground Indian-style rubbing his temples. Darryl was amazed that quiet little Alex was secretly a tough guy waiting to birth. Certainly they had all underestimated him. And most certainly, his newfound strength would lead him out of the swamp and back to civilization where real help awaited. That assurance and a flare gun were the tools of Darryl's courage. The only tools of Darryl's courage. He left his brother to his travels.

With a dogged stride he raced to his backpack and stripped down. "If we're going to do this we'd better do it right," he said.

Corey sprang vertical. "What gives, Dar?"

"Here. Put this on." He tossed Corey matching black shirt and pajama pants. "They should fit."

Corey handled the clothes quizzically. "What are you gonna wear?"

"My extra change of clothes are camouflage. And when you finish getting dressed... here." Darryl scooped up some mud, caked his face with it. "Do that," he said.

Corey tore off his outfit and slid on the elastic waist pj's and shirt, a perfect fit. "Smear mud on my face?" he asked, hoping he'd heard wrong.

"Yeah. See I have a theory that this creature or creatures didn't see us because, besides being covered by trees, me, you and Alex were wearing neutral clothes. Tans and browns. James was wearing florescent green and Stephen's got that bright red shirt. Maybe when the sun sets we can't be seen."

"I hope you're right," Corey replied. What he meant was, I think we're dead already and we're too dumb to know it.

"Better to be safe than sorry, right?" Darryl said. He meant what Corey meant.

Corey nodded and rubbed the floor of the swamp into his delicate skin. He was the rare teen who never broke out in zits. Surely this mudpack would change that.

"I'm ready when you are. Let's find the trail before the sun takes a nap," Corey said.

Darryl tossed him a bottle of Poland Spring water as he took a swig from his own bottle. "Okay, here's the plan: We'll find the trail. You get a long branch and every ten feet or so press into the ground with it. I don't wanna drown in quicksand because we're too busy looking for them to check the ground.

You be the trailblazer and I'll be the surveyor. If we go on too long and get tired we'll switch."

"Fair enough," Corey agreed.

"Good. Only take the shit you need. This could be a long night and—"

"Know what? I don't really want to touch my stuff. I feel like it's tainted. There's something... *ick* about it."

"All the better. Just bring water and your knife. Let's get our friends back."

Corey was amazed at how quickly this all came to Darryl. If he was this set to hunt the hunter, what adversity wasn't he prepared for?

They searched out leads near the blood-soaked tree. Nothing. Not one clue.

"The only thing I can think of is maybe it rides the wind," Corey offered.

"Like a bird?"

"Like a god."

Darryl rolled his eyes. He said, "Uh-huh. Keep searching."

They wandered around seeking out footprints, broken stems, a sign of struggle, a sign of fleeing—a sign of anything, but to no avail. Whatever this thing was it knew what it was doing, knew how to cover its tracks. This was no animal. This was not a human or a cult of them. The boys had no reference point in reality for this but that didn't mean it hadn't been imagined somewhere.

"Hey, Corey, you ever seen *Predator*? The old, old one?"

"Yeah, why?"

"I don't know, I was just thinking about it. I mean what if this thing can make itself invisible?"

"Like in *Predator*?"

"Like in."

"Then we're in deep shit—Look, we aren't finding anything, what's next?"

Darryl racked his brain a moment. "Well we could make it come to us. Build a campfire, hide in the trees. Wait it out."

"Yeah, right, like that almost might work too."

"Alright, smart ass, you think of something."

Corey paused to relieve himself on a nestle of thick tree roots. He couldn't talk and whiz at the same time. As if an exclamation mark, an epiphany came to him the moment he snapped his waist band back in place. Startled at the simple brilliance of it, he rushed over to where Darryl stood like an excited child about to beg parent for toy. "Let's just go," he said.

"What do you mean, 'Let's just go?'"

"I mean pop out the compass and continue in the direction we were headed before we stopped to set up camp."

"What if it bumps into us?"

"It's the price we pay. Heck, anything's better than this. You game?"

Darryl weighed the options and that did not take long. Perhaps all they really had left was the renewed sparkle in Corey's eye. "Why not," he shrugged. "Good a plan as any."

They followed the direction of Darryl's compass due east. Corey stuck the ground with a long branch every ten feet or so. Darryl commented that their heading ran a straight path from the tree of blood and their equanimity built from this clue but so did their caution. They spoke rarely and in whispers and tread lightly, snapping as few twigs and dead branches underfoot as feasible. They didn't stop to rest save for the occasional piss break.

The sun was down now and a canopy of tree leaves blocked the light of moon and stars. The boys didn't have their eyes but they still had their ears. And their ears told them there was movement ahead. And it wasn't a flying squirrel. And it was coming at them.

***

Alex backtracked swiftly damming his tide of fears with a mission: run to where his atmosphone gets a signal just beyond the Spooky Mansion property line, call the police, lead them back to the tree. It was so straightforward yet so deeply unnerving.

Just do it. Don't turn around. Nothing is there. Just keep moving. Why me? Why fucking me?!

He trained his flashlight on the ground, monitoring only his compass and his busy feet. He didn't want to look up, didn't want to jump at shadows or animal eyes that might glint in the light in his hand. *I left my friends to die.* And he had to block that out too.

He had to but he couldn't. It skipped over and over in his mind: *I left my friends to die... I left my friends to die....* It became its own engine he couldn't turn off.

Screw it. I'm going back.

He muttered, "I'm coming, guys. I'm coming" under his breath and turned and was obliterated before his pivot foot landed. What had done this he neither saw nor heard. At the end of his short life he was brave and mature and that did not matter. Not to the thing that had swiftly finished him. Not to the nearby tree covered in moist warm blood.

***

There was not a blasting wind but a gentle breeze carrying on it a low, consistent human moan. "That ain't no god on the wind," Darryl whispered.

"What do you think it is?" Corey asked.

"I think it's the thing I'm aiming my gun at." Darryl pointed his flare gun straight ahead. Corey dropped his walking stick and fumbled for his blade. He gripped it tight and similarly pointed it in front of them at the invisible sounds of agony growing bolder in the night.

Darryl leaned in to Corey's right ear. "Don't move," he whispered. "Don't even breathe."

The boys froze in postures Darryl imagined would become etched in monuments celebrating their valor for the coming battle fought and lost. The moaning grew and receded, grew and receded like the crescendo of tide. Soon, the rustling took form. A shadow. A silhouette. Three.

"What the fuck is a family doing out here?" Darryl was so shocked and relieved he barely choked out the words. A Black man flanked by his two sons stumbled out of the brush holding hands.

"Maybe they're looking for the boogie man too," Corey said. Whatever the family was up to they still hadn't noticed the boys.

And what they were doing was drooling.

INTERLUDE
Earth Zero

The red insect people were a simple race with a complex mind. Their secret was that they weren't individuals, they were a singular female hive intelligence acting through her many bodies. The Hive Queen buried herself underneath a layer of individuality that mimicked how the surface-dwellers thought and behaved. There she hid like a sociopath acting the role of average neighbor, except she was not sociopathic, she was queen. She was queen and royal subjects in one. This was her natural state of mind. Hiding as multiple personalities within countless bodies was what a being like her did. It was her greatest survival mechanism.

Imagine if that secret got out to the enemy. Imagine what you could do if you got rid of her, replaced her mind with your own. You would have a kamikaze army of millions at your disposal.

Imagine a time when there was no enemy to anyone's knowledge, yet there the enemy sat. Lurking. Watching. Figuring you out. Your neighbors out. Your friends.

Imagine that, Corey, imagine it.

Chapter 8

"Holy shit, Dar! What the fuck is that thing," Corey blurted. The loudness of his voice jolted Darryl but it didn't faze the group closing in on them. The man and his children ambled like zombies in no particular direction, their mouths a foamy mess, their chins dripping long strings of saliva, and that moaning. That awful, awful moaning belching from the father.

"Maybe he's a re-re or a mental case who escaped the hospital."

The hospital. Corey remembered as a kid hearing "true" stories about patients escaping from Taunton State Hospital, stealing children and dissolving forever into the landscape. When Massachusetts shut down the institution some of the patients returned. The demented ones. It was home. Kids were food.

Of course those were camp stories from sixth grade, obvious confabulations. Like swamp monsters.

"It doesn't see us."

"Go talk to them, Corey."

"No way, you talk to it!" It. He heard himself say that word and wondered if, when in shock, the truth comes out and the truth was he was a racist. He didn't feel like one consciously... but, *it*? Clearly there were three people—humans—lost in the swamp together and at least one of them was hurt. Did they struggle against what took Stephen and James? Did they win?

Darryl tucked his flare gun into his pants.

"What are you doing?" Corey asked.

"Taking your advice."

Darryl stepped out of the shadows and waved to the family who, at this point in their circuitous ambling, had their backs to the boys. "Hello, sir." No response. "Hello," Darryl said louder. "We're looking for our friends. Something happened to them."

The family completed their random circle. They faced Darryl and Corey who stayed motionless, waiting for an acknowledgement. Nothing, still.

"Look, Corey, we're standing in front of them and talking to them and they still don't know we're here. What's wrong with this picture?"

The man moaned again, his salivating mouth perpetually open, his eyes slightly crossed and lifeless.

"Dude, maybe they're blind and deaf and sick. Maybe they're lost. Maybe they won a shit lottery," Corey said. Part of him was bursting with sick laughter, anticipating a film crew who, any minute now, would jump out of the bushes to explain the joke. Another part wanted to piss down his leg while he bolted. They both chuckled nervously and that was enough for Corey to feel comfortable stepping out of hiding. He started toward Darryl, his right hand still clutching the Swiss Army knife. With his initial step the children grew furious. The drool snapped from their chins as they screamed so loudly that if they had not killed the monster, it now knew their location.

The children flailed, thrashing their free hands like claws. They tugged on dad to let go. They found in Corey the fix to a senseless bloodlust. Dad moaned louder as if the tugging on each arm yanked the nerves inside. Darryl saw then the nature of his agony: they were not holding hands. They were joined at the wrists.

Or rather, they were joined where the wrists should be. There were no hands there. It was as if some mad doctor had lobbed off their hands and melted their arms together.

When Corey stopped walking the kids quit their tantrum. Darryl backpedaled until he caught up with his compadre. He refused to take his eyes off Franken-family. Each of his steps triggered their same spectacle and when he stopped they stopped.

Corey reached a hand to Darryl's shoulder. "This is some *Twilight Zone* bullshit," he whispered.

"They don't have hands. They don't fucking have hands!"

"Yeah I see that now. Ewe," was all Corey could offer. The father moaned and the trio again staggered obliviously, mouths agape.

"How the fuck did they get dressed," Corey barked militantly. Laughter exploded out of Darryl from so deep down he thought he might throw up.

"Dude, you're right! How do they have shirts?"

They both screeched uncontrollably in the face of the nightmare. Darryl unrolled his pack of Camels and tapped out his final smoke.

"Seriously? Now?" Corey asked. He cackled harder at the thought of the scene that was their lives.

Darryl teared up trying to suppress his belly laugh. He lit the cigarette, inhaled deeply, held, then blew out the smoke. With it, all emotion. He sighed and felt stable again. He flicked the empty pack onto the floor of the swamp and said, "Give a hoot. Don't pollute!" Both boys erupted in laughter again but they didn't move their feet. The zombie children remained docile.

Corey couldn't catch his breath he was laughing so hard. He stammered, "Wouldn't... Wouldn't it be awesome if Hootie The Owl swooped down right now and grabbed... and grabbed that thing?"

"What's a Hootie The Owl?" Darryl asked.

"What do you mean?—You just said its catchphrase."

"Yeah, but I don't remember what it's from."

"Don't you remember that stupid thing I showed you on Youtube?"

Darryl lit with recognition. "Oh right! That thing from, like, a thousand years ago that was supposed to teach us not to throw shit on the ground. How'd *that* go?"

The boys erupted again. As they did so, Darryl drew his gun and clicked the safety off.

"What are you gonna do, Dar? Signal Hootie?"

"No." Darryl puffed his cigarette. "I'm gonna slay it."

"Slay it? You can't slay Hootie, he's an endangered bird!"

Darryl doubled over in hysterics. His laughter infected Corey with the giggles and they both put fingers to lips, trying to shush each other at the same failed time. "Seriously, I'm taking that thing out. I have to. It killed our friends," Darryl said, almost out of laughs.

Corey came to his disciplined senses as if a switch were thrown. "I don't think it did, Dar. I don't think it could. I think it's got to be a victim too," he offered solemnly.

Darryl pondered a moment and saw it. "Yeah, you're right. That thing doesn't know we exist unless it's looking at us when we walk. Whatever killed Steph and James is on the other side of it. We've got to be close, we just need to go around."

"You willing to bet your life on that?"

Darryl puffed the last of his cigarette and flicked it away. The fire of it sizzled to death in the mud. "Yip," he said before pushing the smoke from his lungs. He did an about-face and began his arc around the human oddity. The kids lashed out. White foam on their angry shrieking mouths had them looking like evil circus clowns. The father moaned his special moan. Darryl maneuvered behind them, no problem. "Come on, Corey," he hollered. "Let's get moving!"

Corey chortled to himself about what a crazy fucker Darryl was. He followed the curve his leader had jogged and caught up without a hitch. They scrutinized the conjoined males from a safer distance where their movements were no longer detected. "Nazi fucking experiments," Darryl concluded.

"You think?"

"What else?"

"Jesus, if that's true...." Corey let it hang in the air. They turned around and shined a penlight on the compass not wanting to give their new positions away with a bright flashlight. They orientated themselves due east. It was uphill but not treacherously so. They walked it in silence. Corey didn't stab at the ground for mud holes because fuck that. They both ran on the bravery of people who knew they didn't have long to live. They never spoke this to each other but they had no further illusions about making it home alive.

When they reached the pinnacle, Darryl again shined his penlight on the compass. As if on cue, a light shined back. From all around. They were trapped in it. They were it. They were it and the wind blinding them, overwhelming them, becoming them.

"Jesus!"

"Corey, where are you?"

"I can't see my arms!"

"I can't see anything but I can hear you! Can you hear me?"

"Darryl!"

"I'm here! Where are you?" Darryl's voice pinged like a surround sound echo.

"Darryl!"

"I'm here!"

"Darryl, where are you?!"

"Here!"

And it was over. The boys collapsed side by side. Corey vomited. Darryl almost shit his pants but didn't. They lay still for a minute catching more than their breath, catching their souls. Corey felt rearranged. Something in that blinding wind tunnel dissolved his body and put him back together again the same but different. The difference was he knew that had happened and in knowing understood that he was more than his body. This wasn't guesswork. This wasn't belief. This was experience and it was instantaneous.

Darryl blinked hard a few times like he normally did if he woke up with sleep gunk in his eyes. There was still light but it wasn't consuming. It was…. "Daylight."

Corey wiped his mouth with the back of his hand and rubbed it into the…. "Grass."

Both straightened and sat back to back. They were now in a meadow underneath the sun in its aqua heaven. The field was a perfect circle carved into the swamp, which remained nighttime dark. They could see the swamp, see the nighttime and, in fact, Darryl's shoes nearly touched the lightless woods they'd just passed through.

Corey patted Darryl on his left shoulder and when he did a splash of colors pooled into Corey's sightline. He blinked hard a few times to purge his eyes of the hallucination. The liquid rainbow quickly recomposed into Darryl's shoulder and Corey gasped in astonishment.

"What is it?"

Corey ignored the meaning of his question and redirected him to a greater concern: "People," he said.

"Where?" Darryl scooted around with his hands, too fragile to stand. They squinted to make out the group of people mulling about a large metal something at the furthest curve of the meadow. Something in this felt like safety and yet... What was all of this doing in the middle of Hockomock Swamp?

"Why does this feel okay?" Darryl asked this rhetorically. Corey bequeathed the answer: "It doesn't. It feels familiar."

Corey fell as the boys grappled each other for balance attempting to stand weakly on trembling legs. "Shit! Did my hands just pass through you?" Corey asked.

"I still don't feel right," Darryl said.

"You look blurry," Corey told him.

"You don't. It's just your eyes," Darryl said.

Once standing, they shook out the meekness, regained their balance.

"What are we doing here, Corey?"

"We're going with it."

Chapter 9
Henry

When your superior hands you a vial of murky white substance and commands, "Drink this," you drink it. It's not for love of country that you do, nor is it cheap curiosity. It isn't because you've been strip-searched, nor because you've come too far to turn back now.

You drink it because you will be killed if you do not.

You will be killed and your history will be erased. These words are never uttered, never hinted at. You know that after the liquid come things unseen by all but the chosen and you know you've never heard of this checkpoint before. You surmise that the reason you've never heard of this checkpoint before is because no one has ever turned back and lived.

Truth is, you don't know these things and your suppositions stem from the self-made illusion that you do. Like the world of espionage, the world of military science is so compartmentalized that the only thing you wholly know is you won't wholly know.

Such was the case until Henry.

When Henry was told, "Drink this," he did not hesitate. He unscrewed the lid and threw it back like a wino tossing a shot. He relinquished the vial and stepped through the hermetically sealed door when he was ordered to do so. If he gave a whit about unidentified flying object lore he would have instantly recognized the vehicles parked inside that vault. In fact, he would have known precisely the location where his higher-ups had whisked him blindly. He paid that UFO junk no mind and so it took a few for the scene to register: he was staring at a storehouse of alien spacecraft.

"Is this what I think it is?" he asked his escort.

"What do you think it is, Dr. Metis?"

"Is it aliens?"

"How would you feel if I told you *yes?*"

"I'd feel... wow."

"Please. Follow me. You can look but don't touch anything."

Dr. Metis, who was Henry before there was a Henry, did as instructed. He lagged behind in awe of the science fiction museum they were snaking through. All kinds of round and triangular craft sat in this underground lab. Or was it a hangar? Did the U.S. have an alliance with aliens? He dared not ask. Perhaps when they reached the tiny white office in the back corner he would receive a full debriefing. Perhaps not.

In fact, not. His new career, should he accept, would have nothing to do with aliens. And he did accept. No real choice in the matter, but he didn't want to say no regardless. "We will contact you when we're ready," he was promised.

He left and heard nothing more. Three years passed and nothing more. In those years he studied ufology, became familiar with its most notorious characters, many of whom claimed to be scientists who studied alien ships that had crashed and been retrieved to an underground facility in Nevada called Area 51. Alternatively, there were those who claimed to work hand-in-hand with aliens at Areas 51. They couldn't prove it, of course, because their histories had been erased, they said, and the only thing keeping them alive was their public testimony.

Henry read as much of this UFO material as he could sink his greedy eyes into. Conducting a basic job interview in that conspiracy theorist's wet dream was beyond peculiar, it was downright ridiculous. He had to know why and yet he never—not in one conversation—even hinted that he had been there and laid eyes on craft about which the stars of UFO conferences lectured dizzily. For three whole years he kept this to himself and went about his mundane life as a university professor in Tucson, Arizona. He taught computer science until the day he received that promised call.

He was vacationing in the Peruvian rainforest at the time. Most professors took real breaks from work. Not Henry. He preferred to dive into other fields of study most people would consider work. Ethnobotany was one of his more intense hobbies and this day found him examining the effects of a legendary shaman's brew called *Ayahuasca*.

Stale academics labeled Ayahuasca a hallucinogen and left the issue there. However, hitting the specific combination of plant life it takes to make the brew work is like hitting the winning combination of lottery numbers. When asked how they figured out this recipe, indigenous shamans invariably stated, "The plants told us." Henry found this answer less preposterous than hitting the lottery, so he quested for more information directly at the source. But that quest was snipped short. Too short to satisfy. The secrets of Ayahuasca would have to wait.

Henry gathered that the call was timed this inconveniently to prove they could find him anywhere anytime they wished. A lesser man would have grown paranoid, especially after reading all of those books he had absorbed about CIA spooks faking the suicides of military engineers who "knew too much." Dr. Metis was not a lesser man.

Soon he would be the greatest mind ever committed to an organism.

Chapter 10

Corey and Darryl chased through the meadow, playfully an-
tagonizing each other. They didn't understand why they weren't
quaking in fear but the riddle lurked so far back in their minds
that they didn't care. They went with it.

It was utopia here in the middle of this swamp. The colors
of the sky and of the grass were oversaturated like cartoons, yet
this is where their lives made sense. They understood what it
was to be conscious animals, a beautiful freeing feeling. Darryl,
the tough guy, was floating, and that amused Corey enough, but
something about that glimmering metallic contraption in the
closing distance beckoned them. It was a nonverbal calling but it
was tangible. It was there.

The people by the object came into sharp focus as the boys
approached in joyous bliss. They were human. Adults mainly.
They milled aimlessly with the blank stares of the welded three-
some roaming the swamp, but they weren't agonizing, weren't
lashing out, and were not conjoined. Still, the boys discerned
that they were not people in the ordinary sense. They were a
herd. This realization stirred the boys from their high.

"What the hell is happening to us?" Corey giggled.

"Aha—I don't know!"

It was as if they were waking from a profoundly gorgeous
dream into the realization that they had been sleepwalking
through a zombie apocalypse the whole time.

"We're going crazy. We're going fucking nuts." Darryl
sighed as if the fact were no big deal.

"I give up. What is this place?"

"Don't know. Someone's toying with us. Slap me."

"Do wha—?"

"Slap me, Corey. Make me your bitch. Wake me the fuck
up."

Corey patted him on the face. "Did my hand just go through you?" he asked. It felt that way but he couldn't tell if he had actually touched Darryl because he kept pulling in and out of focus like he were partially trapped in another spectrum.

They both chuckled and Darryl said emphatically, "No, I'm serious, dude. Wake up. Wake me up. You gotta—"

Corey slammed his face hard, open-palm. Darryl came alert. Corey fell onto his shoulders laughing and spent. It took copious energy to remain sober. "Sorry, dude, but you said—"

Darryl whacked him stiffly across the left cheek. He came to.

"Ow! Gah—Fuckin' A," Corey slurred.

"You out?"

"Yeah, I'm out! I'm awake. What the fuck just happened?"

They shook out the listlessness, intuiting that their circulation had been slowed.

"You good?" Darryl asked.

"I'm good."

"Let's check that thing out."

"I suppose running is out of the question."

"I'm all adrenalined out, Coronimous. I just kinda wanna fuckin' die now."

"Yeah."

"I'm not afraid, you know?"

"Yeah, me neither. I'm just waiting," Corey said.

"I wonder if this is how my dad felt when he found out he had cancer."

"Jesus."

"I know, I shouldn't think like that, right?"

"I don't know."

"You falling back asleep?"

"Yes."

"Me too. Let's move."

The scintillating construct was hard to get a bead on. From afar it looked like a metallic orb. Close up, however, the thing went mercurial. It appeared to shape-shift with the slightest change in perspective. One step it was an orb of quicksilver, the next it was a cylinder. Move left, it's a dome; move right it's a diamond.

Is it black? Is it gray? Is it metal? What the hell is it?

"A UFO, Darryl! In the middle of Taunton! This rocks hard!"

Once again the boys were possessed by a consuming giddiness. Darryl mouthed something about aliens and a dream come true. Their surroundings blurred. Words and actions worked through them in slow motion as they bobbed between oblivious zombies, closer and closer to the craft.

The meadow spun. Corey's mind raced with everything and nothing, the same jumbled mess his body had become. He suddenly felt weighted down, like an unseen thumb was pressing him into the ground. He was losing consciousness and he knew it. He turned to Darryl. The last thing he remembered before fainting was seeing the terror and confusion betraying Darryl's smile and thinking, 'You're not unbreakable after all.'

An idol smashed. Terrible feeling. It faded with everything. The pettiness of it never registered.

***

Tranquility. Lovely, lovely tranquili—"Shit! Where am I?" Corey bolted upright on the gray rectangle molded seamlessly in the round gray wall. Was it a wall? He didn't know what to call it. It was more like he was lying on a bed on the inside of a gray ball. No windows. No doors. No Darryl. No telling how long he'd been out.

He wondered if he hadn't been drugged and this was all a bad trip. He'd heard about that from friends who'd done acid and 'shrooms. He felt worn down, depleted, but he had to get out of there and find his friends. This, he was determined to do… after a brief nap.

INTERLUDE
Earth Zero

The Hive Queen was no mere formless intelligence drifting about in virtual space taking command of bodies as she saw fit. She had a body of her own but it never died. It shed itself every thousand years and formed a pool of slime around her from which she drank.

She lived in a chamber carved specifically for her. She never moved from there. Actually, she never moved at all except to contract the muscles that squeezed out new drones when the old ones stopped working and to osmote nutrients from slime every few hundred years, give or take. She didn't have eyes or ears or any useful appendages. If you saw her you'd mistake her for a mutant grub, but you would never see her for no one ever did.

She was asexual but she produced male and female drones to keep up the ruse that her bodies were a race of unique beings. They looked unique. Had arms and legs and genitals. They were bipeds. Had personality quirks. Even so they were a bit stiff, a bit robotic compared to the real races. It wasn't the type of problem that raised suspicions, though, because who would suspect that they weren't real? Who could?

There was a day far, far distant, before the Great Enlightenment, when the Hive Queen needed an army and an air force to fend off the surface dwellers. After the brutal warring ceased, she buried her craft but didn't destroy them just in case things fell apart. Back in those polluted times she had the brilliant idea of creating a series of chambers exactly like hers that gave off the same vital signs as she. All were booby-trapped. If anyone did make it past her drones they would still not find her, not easily. She wasn't that worried about it, though. Her fortress was all but impenetrable and she could reproduce drone soldiers at will.

The surface dwellers had the technology to capture souls at death and return them in cloned bodies, but their means of production was nowhere near as efficient as the queen's birthing process.

The aliens, monitoring everything as they did from their artificial planet drifting two suns from Earth Plane, figured this out. Figured this all out. Themselves master hunters they were adept at plundering the defense secrets of any species they engaged. Imagine Einstein working a crossword puzzle? They were like that, Corey. And it brought a damaged smile to Leader's deeply scarred face when he saw that the Hive Queen hadn't considered ground-penetrating frequency beam technology that could hit her palace and bake whatever organism it sought, unnoticed.

He happened to have such a beam. Make that several.

Like Earth Planers, the aliens had perfected cloning technology and the means to vacuum souls at death. Because they were a homeless race, they devised a way to run their computerized world on the renewable soul energy of the defeated. During his five hundred eighty-six year reign, Leader changed the meaning of the word "enemy" to what was for his people a neutral term. These races of beings he destroyed were not adversaries, they were obstacles and their souls were war booty. War wasn't for malice it was for survival. And yes, pleasure. It was just what they did and it was never personal. Their computers, called *etherputers*, didn't run on electricity, they ran on souls. Souls were oil.

The invaders set coordinates and launched a camouflaged city carrying war machines and soldiers, the things of brutal endings, from their hidden planet. Leader captained the ship. His first orders after parking in a concealed space between moons was to light up the suspicious subterranean chambers they had discovered when they X-rayed Earth Plane. They didn't shoot one at a time, they shot all of the chambers at once, leaving the Hive Queen no chance to escape or warn the surface dwellers. The impact of the beam paralyzed her brain and then cooked it, but the pirates were quick to snare her essence and jail it within their etherputer system before she had a chance to die properly. To the outside world, anyone interacting with her insect people would have noticed them go silent, as if in a trance or caught in a day dream for a second, and then back to normal. It was an odd hiccup to be sure but one that was so brief everyone collectively ignored it like change blindness.

The invaders had never encountered a being such as her, never tried to pull off an attack such as this. They needed her society of vessels alive and behaving normally but they didn't know if any old soul would bring the right type of energy to the task of controlling them, so they had to use her. Her energy would run the etherputer program that would instruct those bodies living underground and in the large cities of Earth Plane, but she would have no say in their actions.

And the first instruction the etherputer program gave was ingenious: Dig up those insect air fighters and get her air force back online.

Chapter 11

Corey stirred once more and rubbed his groggy eyes. Through blurred morning vision he spied Darryl asleep on the parallel wall of the bubble. He, too, lay on a gray bed-like furnishing that was molded into the dome, yet hadn't been there the first time Corey endeavored to rise.

He stumbled over to his friend and collapsed onto him. He shook him ferociously, yelling in his ear, "Darryl, get up! Get up! Come on, Darryl, wake up!"

Through haze and half-shut lids Darryl barely made out the figure bearing down on him. He attempted to swat at Corey, an annoying fly of a friend. "Uh...g'off," he slurred.

"Come on, dude, get up!"

"No, you get up. Tired."

"Come on! We have to find Stephen and James and get the hell out of here. Now... Get. UP!" Corey slid his hands under both sides of Darryl's back and jerked him upright like a flick of spatula. Darryl pulled away, slamming his head back down on the hard surface where he lay. The stab of pain in his skull was enough to jolt him to a sitting position on his own. "Ow, shit! I'm up already!"

Darryl still moved like a blurry prism but Corey ignored it. He was all urgent business, smacking at the walls looking for some give. "We have to get out of here!"

Darryl pressed the back of his cranium checking for lumps. It was tender but he wasn't damaged. He stretched and yawned and squinted and sighed a heavy sigh, then stated the obvious: "But there's no door."

"Where were you?" Corey asked.

"Where am I now is the question—What do ya mean?"

"I mean I woke up before and you weren't here."

"I don't know. Maybe you were dreaming or something. Maybe I am. Am I still asleep?"

"Not if I'm real."

"Are you?"

Corey curled his lip. He didn't know how to answer that anymore.

Darryl knocked on his own forehead with his fist, which helped restore his wits. "Alright," he said, "What do we know?"

Corey spun around, assessing the barren cell. "We know we're in a gray bubble that's bright but has no light source, no way to enter or exit, and I'm guessing the walls are amorphous."

"Good word."

"Yeah. Thanks. But seriously, how else was there no bed there and now there is?"

"There wasn't a bed here? But the thing is coming from the wall in a smooth... right, it's amorphous. Stop looking at me like I'm a doof."

"You *are* a doof." Corey plopped down next to his friend. "What now?"

"I don't know. We wait."

"Don't you want to get out of here?"

"There's no door."

"We can look for one. Press on the walls. Maybe there's a pressure trigger—"

"—Also a good word—"

"I can't believe you don't want to leave this place, like, yesterday," Corey snapped. He glared at Darryl who shot back his own fierce stare. "Go right ahead and look," he said. "But me? I don't see a door. I don't see the outline of a door. All I see is a room with two freaky-looking beds and morning breath. You want to press on the wall I'm not stopping you. You want to ram it with your shoulder be my guest. But don't shit on me because I'm a realist. This place wasn't built with an escape hatch. Clearly we're in a jail. I'm going to sit in it until a cop enters—however the fuck he enters—and tells us what we're being held for. That's it. That's me giving it my all."

Corey shook his head more at himself than Darryl. "You do have a point," he confessed.

"Yeah. Cuz say we even do escape—what then, Core? We don't know where we are. We don't even know what the game being played is."

As Darryl spoke, three dwarves in beige tunics abruptly floated through the wall and stood before the boys like solid ghosts. Who were these circus freaks? Darryl couldn't make out any of their faces, hidden, as they were, in the shadows of long hoods.

You have nothing to fear. You have nothing to fear....

Corey shrieked and threw himself into a fetal position as far away from the beings as he could. "The bug men are back! The bug men are back! Don't let them get me, Mamma!"

....You have nothing to fear. You have nothing to fear....

"What the fuck is this, Corey?! Don't go nuts on me now, man!"

....You have nothing to fear. You have nothing to fear....

"Mamma! Mamma! Make them go away! They wanna eat me!"

....You have nothing to fear. You have nothing to fear....

"Dude, get up! I'm scared too—get up!"

....You have nothing to fear. You have nothing to fear....

In fact, that was an extraordinary understatement. Darryl had never felt terror this cutting in his life, including his father's death; including the time he was trapped in a fire.

....You have nothing to fear. You have nothing to fear....

It was a robotic voice repeating itself in Darryl's head. It was male and cold and he knew it wasn't his own brain reassuring him. Corey shivered against the wall where he'd fallen. He was kicking the air trying to propel himself through the wall if he could. Darryl didn't know enough to call it posttraumatic shock, he just knew he was on his own. On his own but not alone.

There were aliens. Just like he'd seen on TV, *aliens*—four feet tall, smooth gray hands, the color of this room. Almost human hands but the fingers were long like dangling spider legs and the thumb was also a finger and it was in the wrong place, nearer the palm. One of these vicious, solemn things jerked its head straight up at Darryl, exposing itself and making eye contact for the first time. Its eyes were large pools the blackness of space, slanted up at the temple. The forehead was hairless and he thought it was bald but with the sandy cloak draped over its head he couldn't really know. Was there even a nose?

Daryl was transfixed, out of the original surrealism and trapped in a daydream where this wasn't happening and he had all the time in the world to study this exotic creature. He detected a slight smirk on the thin line this being called a mouth.

Was it toying with him? Were these grotesque David Lynch characters getting off on their fear like intergalactic sadists? Darryl thought this, thought the worst, and then immediately retracted as if some other piece of him knew what they were and knew that these negative projections were his own and were a defense mechanism because fear is the unfortunate first wave of emotion when in contact. He thought, 'Being in their presence is a hero's journey every time.' And then he didn't know if he had thought it or someone else thought it into him.

He snapped out of his daze and saw that they were all three peering at him now and all looked the same, like balloon-headed robots, but very definitely were alive.

….*You have nothing to fear. You have nothing to fear*….

He didn't know if that voice was communicating from one of his captors or some hidden device somewhere. The absurdity of the message caused him to shout, "The hell I don't!"

He thought about lunging at them and with that thought found his body unmovable.

Knowledge was out. Forming a plan was out. Corey was out of it. The only option Darryl saw was to fight, to break through the paralysis and nab one of them, beat the shit out of the others, force them to let him escape with his friends.

'Move,' he yelled internally at his fist. 'Move, God damn it, move!'

....You have nothing to fear. You have nothing to fear....

He would have yelled at them to fuck off but his jaw refused to unhinge. And they weren't really in front of him. Or were they? The room was spinning and this wasn't real. How could it be? It was only a... only a....

Darryl floated back gently onto his gray amorphous cot. Everything was okay. He had nothing to fear. Only a dream.

The shit in Corey's pants smelled real enough and told a different story. One they'd both forget.

Chapter 12

When Darryl awoke the second time it was of his own accord. No one shook him and there was not a sound. There was a light, a bright white spot beaming on him from an unseen source above.

Where was he? An emergency room?

He discovered that he could once again move his body. He opted not to, save for turning his head left and right to get his bearings.

He lay naked on a gray slab not quite rock, not quite uncomfortable, same as the prison cell, but sprouting from the floor instead of a wall. A standing-room-only crowd of nonhumans encircled him. He wasn't anxious. All things considered, he was fine, physically fine, and didn't mind being the nude center of attention. He grasped that he should care about these things, as it wasn't like him not to, but this analysis was outweighed by an unnatural urge to feel at ease with everything going on.

"Somebody want to dim the lights?" His voice cracked but he tried like hell to sound authoritative. "I said dim the fucking lights!" He felt the piece of him that wanted to cry surge momentarily, but it receded and he was glad. He didn't want them thinking they could break him.

The lights dimmed a bit. He could see clearly the faces of his captors, about a dozen of them perfectly still all around him. Black, blue, gray, emerald green; mostly short like the grays he encountered with Corey, but some taller. All slender but the stocky blues. All hairless and insect-like save for the hot emerald-skinned elf couple to his right and that furry Bigfoot thing looming in the back. That massive creature looked ridiculous in stature compared to its friends.

"Chewbacca?" Darryl asked giggling. Then he thought, 'Fucking Nazi experiments.'

A female voice answered his thought with her own: *We are not Nazi experiments.*

He darted his eyes to the elf figuring it must be her in his head. "You're perfect," he said. He didn't know why that slipped out but he meant that her skin was perfect and her features so finely chiseled that she could be a super model if her skin wasn't green and undulating and if being in her presence didn't feel so... off.

He imagined this was what it felt like to be surrounded by the dead in purgatory when you're not ready to die: creepy but also a part of you. Then he went back to maybe this was a hospital. Maybe his body lay in an emergency room after all, being pumped and shocked to life by frantic doctors, while in this dimension his spirit was being kept company by the people of limbo. And maybe those people looked like creatures of myth because they were, because they used to live on Earth, but now physically extinct they existed here and in the remembrance of Man.

A perfect male elf approached him. Darryl smirked at his one-piece outfit. 'Toilet paper,' he thought.

The robe is not made of that material, a male voice thought back. Darryl assumed it was the voice of the bald elf stepping forward.

'Can't you use your mouths to speak?' Darryl thought at him.

That is a waste of energy.

Darryl sat up and hung his bare legs over the smooth rim of the gray table. This close to the elf guy he noticed his skin wasn't green; it was translucent and contained an ocean of pulsing emerald light. The being was extraordinary to behold and yet Darryl found his mouth blurting questions that upon exiting him immediately seemed irrelevant. He was like a child oblivious to where he was and who he was addressing. He was just... saying things.

"How do you read minds?" was the first. Even as he said it he felt like an adolescent asking mom and dad the dumb stuff only those filled with love for him would tolerate without frustration.

All is mind, the green Adonis answered.

"Are you aliens?"

What is an alien?

'You know all my other words but you don't know *alien*?' That thought was from Darryl to himself but the being answered anyway: *One knows what you mean by alien, but that is not a word that signifies anything.*

"I always thought telepathy would be cool, but you know how much it sucks that you can read my mind?"

All is mind.

"I don't know what that means…. Where are you from?"

Everywhere.

Darryl rolled his eyes and cracked his neck. He wished he had a smoke.

Why do you wish that?

"Cuz it tastes good."

Why does it taste good?

"Cuz I'm addicted."

Why are you addicted?

And now Darryl was the parent and this guy the kid and Darryl didn't have the patience for his questions. He blurted out, "Because I am—Look, I've been to hell and back tonight. I think I deserve some straight answers from you people. Like, what am I doing here? Where are my friends? Why haven't you cooked and eaten me yet? Anything. Answer any of those."

The green elf's stoic face didn't register humor or hostility. Nothing undulating beneath his skin fluctuated or signified mood change. *One has not lied*, he thought into Darryl.

"Where is Corey, the guy I was with?"

He is well.

"Can I see him?"

He looks no different, the man assuaged.

Darryl's anger at the communication gap was overtaking the emotional inhibitor they used to sedate him. Were these ultra-intelligent beings or not? They spoke English. In his head. They had technology so fundamentally different from anything he knew that it didn't seem to exist in the first place. What he perceived as bland open spaces and source-less light had to be the product of a science so grand, it resembled nothing like the imagination from which it sprang. This implied to him that their imagination had fallen away with time. These beings had no need for frills, for bright shiny objects, and external art forms. No need for anything. They created forms that followed function, spaces that shape-shifted at will like putty. In a sense, everything was art, but utilitarian art. They were the artists and the art. The scientists and the science.

They were mind.

All is mind, including matter.

'Oh my God, I'm not thinking this, it's being thought into me.'

Yes it is.

'I'm being uploaded.'

Yes you are.

'Am I a robot?'

Not anymore.

Darryl needed a break from this flow. He had so many questions, so many pedestrian questions in the face of what he was being given that it was hard to remember what he wanted to ask or who was asking. "What were those people outside?" he blurted.

Experiments. We herd them.

"Like a fucked up Noah's Ark?" The second he spoke he scolded himself. 'Fucked up? Is that the best you can do? Real mature, asshole. Maybe they don't know what bad words are. They won't know.'

The man ignored Darryl's self-flagellation and answered his question: *Nothing like that.*

"Where are my other friends? Stephen and James?"

They are safe. They are happy. They are new.

"What do you mean, *new*?" Darryl stared at the man, whose cold responses took a turn. Darryl had seen enough *Star Trek* to wonder, if this wasn't an elf or the dead, was he an android or an alien/human hybrid?

The man never answered Darryl's last question or any of his concerns as to their origin. Instead, he communicated, *Come with us.* It wasn't a demand, it was an offer. Darryl assumed he meant fly away with them. Forever.

"I can't do that. I have a life back on Earth."

We are on Earth.

"We are? Well my Earth, with my family and friends."

Are you happy?

Darryl hesitated. The elf's poker face was a million times better than his. Was this a trick question?

No trick.

He contemplated a moment then looked the man square in the eyes. "Yes I am," he said confidently.

You lie. Come with us.

Those eyes did not lie. They were not quite human, not quite like the grays', but something. All of these beings had it, wherever they were from. They had something utterly foreign and breathtaking in their gaze. A clarity and depth, perhaps stemming from their telepathic connectivity.

No, not telepathic connectivity, that's not what they had. They were not linked like computers, individuals that could function on their own or as part of a hive mind. This ran far deeper than that. This was what Mind looked like outside of separation. No interior/exterior; no conscious/subconscious; no species/individual. No connection, because connection implies a divided thing being connected and there was no divided thing here, but forms like paint on canvass. They were the paint and the canvass and we will be them one day if we survive. If not, we die on the vine, a species unfulfilled, a teardrop in the eye of eternity, gone but not forgotten—'My God,' Darryl realized. 'I'm not thinking this, either.'

The emerald man in the white tissue garb possessed all of this information in his stare. Not just the information, but neediness or a craving or... compassion. There was a compassion, most definitely, and that compassion had its own needs. They needed Darryl and Darryl needed them. He could see it now, sharply see it, and this seeing uncorked a block in his being so absolutely that his eyes reflexively poured the tears of a newborn.

He felt all of the hurt and agony of his past, all the repressed guilt, all of the things that made him cool and manly and highly regarded by his friends, feared by enemies—he felt everything that he just was pour out of him and into the silence of this crowded place. Somehow these austere feelings converted to bliss as they fled his body and he knew what these beings needed. He knew the nature of their sadness and their wisdom. He knew why they thought at him as awkwardly as they did.

He knew what they were not and what they were not is anything he had imagined.

"Yes," Darryl sobbed. "I'll go with you."

Those were the last words he ever spoke through his mouth. They were the last bit of him that emoted from the disintegrating tulpa that was his brain-created self.

INTERLUDE
Earth Zero

The ground trembled ferociously all over the plane. Enormous swaths of land caved everywhere from the majestic cities of bde 'byung to the hidden recesses of Dragon Isle. The sinkholes ate buildings and trees and people and beasts. Red insectoids, too, were among the casualties, which cast a spell of confusion over the surface dwellers as they gawked at insect warships ascending vertically out of the wormy depths into the debris-filled air. These death ships hovering above them were of a bygone day, a whole other confused era everybody granted was obsolete.

As the people wee and giant froze, mouths agape, their insect friends drew concealed laser guns and blasted any living thing that was not their own kind where it stood. Panic washed over the masses in waves. No one had weapons except the insectoids, who were marching their armies up the sinkholes in heavily populated areas.

The people ran. Everyone. Every direction. And when they ran, the ships waiting above tore into them with ferocious cannons. Energy bursts cut the people and the buildings that looked like salvation in half. Those species in the populace capable of doing so screamed. It was the first time in untold generations they had made a sound and that sound was unbridled terror.

Of all the creatures on Earth Plane only dragons were prepared to fight. Their bodies were protected by a thick layer of tough scales that could withstand copious amounts of torture. They shot to the skies in flocks, their massive wings beating air like war drums. When they swooped down in formation they looked like one shimmering nimble colossus darkening the sky with its massive presence only to light it again with volcanic fire.

The dragons blew on the hulls of insect fighters that were laying waste to cities, prairies, marshes, and mountains. They tore at the craft with mighty razor talons.

The ships were impossibly fast and could maneuver in ways that defied physics as we know them to bind us. So could the dragons. However, their natural abilities were no match for the ships because at the end of the sky ballet, the insects' ray cannons could blow through the bone plate of any dragon, even the blue elders who were practically made of stone, Corey.

Watching their own drop from the sky in genocidal numbers, their titanic bodies raining innards over the people, the dragons knew the dogfight was an unattainable win. The most they could do was scatter the ships, keep them busy, while the people below found shelter. Not good enough.

They decided unanimously to do the best thing they could do, even if it meant sacrificing their entire race. A handful of the younger, aerodynamic red and adolescent yellow dragons played chase with the ships as a diversion while the older blues swooped down into the cities, into the prairies, marshes, and mountains, blowing over insectoid ground troops with the flap of their mighty wings.

There was a halt to the action that felt longer than it was. In that moment, the ancient blue dragons inhaled oxygen deeply, past their lungs and into the organ that converts air to fire. At last they blasted their bright blue flames into the sinkholes from which armies continued to pour and scurry and kill. Thousands of bug people were incinerated in one dragon sigh, but more importantly, their escapes to the surface were soldered shut.

The dragons piled over the smoldering earth with debris from tumbled buildings and let out a mighty roar to let the world know what had been done here. To the people of Earth Plane it sounded like a triumphant exclamation mark signaling victory. To the dragons it was a heartbreaking cry signifying the final brave act before the collapse of their valiant species.

And indeed it was.

Chapter 13

"Good morning, rock fans! It's a cool fifty-eight degrees out there. I'm Dave Sambargo and you're listening to 'Davie In The Morning,' on WQCL the coolest, *killingest* station in town! Up next we have—"

Corey blindly slammed at the generic morning DJ with an arm windmill to the clock radio, internally begging God to make one of the victim buttons the OFF button. He dragged his carcass into the strengthening heat of the shower, lathered up, woke up, and was bored instantly by the fact of routine.

Get up. Take shower. Get dressed. Do hair. Eat food. Ride bus. Fucking bus. Sit in class. Bell rings. Run to class. Bell rings. Skip gym. Bell rings. Run to class. Bell rings. Go to lunch. Out to lunch. *My school is out to lunch!*

He hated when he arose pissed at the world, but he felt like Pavlov's dog the way everything was patterned in his life. He longed for something more. Deserved it. What more, he didn't know, just more. Different. Better. *Fuck you.*

He smelled the next part of his unwavering routine on time for his appointment in the kitchen, where Mom leaned against the range stirring a vat of apple and cinnamon oatmeal, Dad's favorite. Dad's favorite because he never did the dishes. Let oatmeal sit too long and it turns into paste and then barnacles that can't be scraped from the pot without a drag-down water fight. If he had to struggle with that mess he'd never fill up on the gunk again.

Corey trotted downstairs and into the kitchen, hitting the one creaky floorboard so loudly he thought the wood must be rotten. He imagined a day when it would cave and his ankle would snap in the hole, one on a list of "See?—I told ya so!" fantasies he had lined up for his parents.

He plopped down in the nearest chair. Dad inched his nose over the top edge of the *Boston Globe* spread in his hands. That was as much "Good morning" as Corey got.

James loved to poke fun at how stereotypical the Avon family was, eating meals together, good old fashioned dad with the paper—never a blink-click tablet—mom with the cooking, a few choice words tossed out to make it seem as if they were holding a conversation.

"How was the camping trip, Dear?"

"What camping trip?" Corey was only half interested in her question. He was eagerly reading the ingredients panel on the side of the Cocoa Puffs box. Screw oatmeal—Cocoa Puffs were the shit! He loved that cereal, that chocolaty, nutrient-fortified corn syrupy legal high.

"What camping trip? The one you've been gone on all weekend. By the way, what time did you get in last night? Your father and I went to bed early. We didn't hear you come in." She let an index finger gently graze her husband's neck as she sauntered to the cupboards for a glass.

Translation: *Your father fucked me raw last night. Thank you for not interrupting.*

Corey shuddered at the hideousness of it. He looked up a moment. "I didn't go camping." Then back to the cereal box, which also had a maze on the back he could trace with his spoon handle.

"You most certainly better have, mister. That's what you left in the note. Your father and I would hate to think you were lying to us, right, John?"

"Mmmm." Dad was exponentially more invested in his paper than Corey was in the cereal box. Anything she said would be answered by a sound that didn't involve opening his mouth or paying attention.

"You see?" she said, equating her husband's guttural noise with agreement. "Now tell us where you were."

Corey gave up on the Cocoa Puffs. "What'd you say, Ma?"

"Why do you never listen the first time?"

"Sorry, Ma."

"You said in the note—"

"What note?"

"The note you left us telling us where you'd be this week-end. Honestly, Corey, it's too early for these games."

Corey thought his mother was losing it. Early onset Alzheimer's for sure, and then diapers. He'd refuse to change her filthy diapers. It's not like she'd know.

"I didn't write you any note," he said.

"You most certainly did." She flicked it from underneath the magnet sticking it to the fridge like a magician yanking a tablecloth out from under fine china. "Is this not your handwriting?" She held it to his face. He read it quickly then swatted it away. She hung it back on the fridge.

Corey was baffled and for reasons unknown to him, felt angry. He recognized his own writing. Still, "Ma, I didn't write this."

"Then who did?"

"The boogeyman, Ma, how do I know?"

It was all Mrs. Avon could do not to holler at her petulant son. Who raised this kid, anyway, she often wondered. "Okay," she said through clenched teeth. "Let's try this: Where were you for the past three days?"

Corey searched a moment. He couldn't remember. Perhaps he was the one with Alzheimers. Shoot, it was only a couple of days, nothing to get excited about. "I don't know. Look, I've got to go, I don't wanna miss the bus."

"You haven't touched your breakfast."

"Not hungry."

"Alright," she decided. "But be home tonight. Your father and I need to have a talk with you about house rules."

"Mm-hmm," Mr. Avon grumbled on the way to the sports section. He thought he heard his cue to affirm something.

***

The trip to school was pleasantly mellow. It was like this Monday mornings, so Corey didn't hold out for a serene ride home in the afternoon. Better appreciate what he had now and enjoy it. Except that he couldn't. He couldn't relax, couldn't relish the tranquility. He felt so damned bitter and hostile, pointlessly cranky. He imagined this was how James felt on an average day.

'Did you forget something? A book, maybe?' Corey rummaged his bag but everything was just as he'd left it Friday.

'What did I do this weekend? Not homework.' He laughed into a yawn. Even for 8:00am on a Monday he was preternaturally exhausted.

The bus stopped for its final pickup: Tommy Almeier. He looked fine. Not a scrape on his pimply mug. The weekend must have done him some good. The weekend—where did it go? Corey tried numerous times to focus on that question but was immediately distracted after each attempt.

'No bus demons today. Must have been suspended. Either that or skipping school. Fucking tired. Jesus. Sunday was fun. What did I do Sunday? What's that on the ceiling, gum? ... Tired, tired, tired! Tired little beaver! I love you, Ma, but what a stupid saying. What was she saying about a note? Did I write a note? What for? What was the point? Was there a point like a pencil? A number two pencil? Don't forget that for SATs. Yeah, like I'm gonna get into college anyway. Of course you are, dude. Basic Studies program for fuckups like me. You're not a fuckup, you're bored. You don't work to your potential because school bores you. Thanks Mom and Dad for that shining excuse and for fucking this weekend while I was away. I was away, wasn't I? Wait, where was I? I... I... Aye yi yi yi! Aye, a bread and a but-ter!'

He sang nonsense in his head until the bus pulled up to the school.

***

"Hi, Corey!"

"Hey, Becky." Bitch. Keep walking.

"Corey, wait up!"

"What's up, Dave?" Halt. Turn. Listen.

"Not much. Have a good weekend? Mine was awesome. Oh, by the way, if you see Darryl, tell him I need my tennis racket back. Anyway, Friday night was so opposite of the suck, you would not believe. I can't believe you guys skipped the party; it was legend. So how was your weekend? What'd you do?"

Respond. "Huh? Oh. Ah, you know. I dunno. Stuff. Do we have a math test or no?"

"Today?"

"Yeah."

"Nope. Thursday. You still didn't tell me what you did."

"When?"

"This weekend. You high, man?"

"Tss… come on."

The warning bell rang.

"Shit, I don't wanna be late. We'll catch up later, man."

"Right, Dave." Walk away. Nod at acquaintance. Punch preoccupied friend on arm.

"Hey, Jeff."

"Hey, Corey."

Get to class. Prop head on hand. Stay awake. Don't lash out. Don't look angry. Everything will be fine.

You have nothing to fear… You have nothing to fear… You have nothing to fear… You have nothing to fear…

***

Corey endured all of his classes. No Darryl. No Alex. No Stephen or James, either. He found it completely out of character that his buds would skip school and not invite him. Were they all sick?

Where's Darryl, where's Darryl? If one more fanboy inter- rogated him he was gonna hock loogie in the fapper's eye so they could share a teardrop over the loss. Fuck, how should he know where Darryl was? They were friends, not eating each other's assholes. Corey's only concern was making it through the school day without fainting on the way to class or in his plate of fries at lunch. He hadn't been this tired since he pulled an all-nighter for Santa Claus at age nine.

Even in line for the bus home acquaintances asked him stupid shit like, "How are you?" and, "Whassup?" and, "Dude, you got Brian suspended?"

Brian. Right. Demon of the bus. They all got suspensions. It would be a much-needed peaceful ride after all.

"Hey, Corey, is this seat taken?" Another stupid question. You see anyone in it?

Wait, the girl. It was the girl he had almost met on Friday. She wanted to sit next to him? Well amen to that!

Corey imagined that underneath her frumpy vintage dress was a crazy hottie squirming for the opportunity to rip off those clothes and come sexually alive on his dick like a porn librarian. She smelled nice. Like flowers. He put his bag over his lap.

"No, you can sit here. Hey, you remembered my name."

She cocked an eyebrow. "It's a pretty specific name."

"I guess."

"My name is Lina Igasho, by the way, thanks for asking." She extended her hand with a giggle. He shook it. She felt soft like flowers, too. "Sorry I didn't introduce myself last week but with the catapulting accident and all...."

"Yeah, I understand. You're Alex's friend, right?"

"Alex Zaiter? You know him?"

"Yeah, we're buds."

"Oh, right on! He was the first boy brave enough to talk to the new girl. I just moved here from LA."

"Wow, sucks to be you. Taunton's a shithole."

"It's not bad."

"What's LA like?"

"Hectic."

"Miss it?"

"Not yet. We move a lot. My dad's a contractor."

"What does he do?"

"I don't know. Contracts?"

"What about your mom?"

"You'll laugh."

"No I won't."

"Yes you will."

"So what?"

"She's a stripper."

"Seriously?"

"No, she's a psychic."

"Come on, don't be ridiculous."

"Well, that's what she does. You know you were pretty brave last week. I mean if you hadn't been there those bullies wouldn't have been caught. Hell, Tommy wouldn't have the guts to squeal. Not that you squealed or anything."

"So wait, your mom's a psychic or a stripper?"

"God, I hope not a stripper!"

"So she's a psychic, then?"

"Yeah. It's weird, I know."

"Cool!"

"Really?"

"Hells yeah! What's cooler than that?"

"Huh. Well I dunno. I usually get the opposite. Kinda freaks people out you know?"

"No, that's awesome. Are you psychic too? You got that psychic gene?"

"See, now you're making fun."

"No! I'm not! I'm really not—this is the most excited I've been all day."

"I don't even want to know what that means."

"Can I meet her?"

"I don't want to know what that means either."

"Sick! I'm serious. Come on."

"You got a thing for psychics?"

"I got a thing for a lot of things."

"Well...What are you doing Friday? You wanna like go to the movies or something? You could meet her then."

"Serious? Huh. Well. Alex."

"—Is a friend. You think I have a thing for Alex?" She rolled her eyes.

"What? He's a cool guy. And sexy. He's a sexy, sexy young man."

She laughed. "Is that right?"

"So right it's wrong."

"Are we doing this or what? I'm not saying bring me to a chick flick or anything. But let's go out."

"Wow, man, they must do things differently in LA. Chicks here aren't this... whatever the word."

"Forward?"

"Yeah."

"I move around a lot. I can be forward or I can be reclusive. I choose forward. I like people and I don't know if I have time, you know?"

"Yeah."

"So, yeah?"

"Yeah. Huh? Oh! Yeah! Friday. Let's do it. I mean... go out. Not *do it,* do it. Although if you wanna do it cuz... you know, time is of the essence... we can skip the movie and just—"

"Yeah, why don't you skip whatever's coming next out of your mouth and thank your astro chart I even asked you on a date in the first place?"

"So this *is* a date."

"What did you think it was?"

"Awkward."

Chapter 14

Corey hated to nap. Napping made him feel really old or really young, he couldn't decide which. Still, he couldn't help himself. When he got home he threw down his sack-of-rocks book bag, tore out of his shirt, pants, and socks, set his iPod to *Best of The Doors* and climbed into bed. He had plenty of home-work to keep him busy, but screw it. Sleep.

His eyeballs shifted into high gear underneath those heavy lids. He didn't review his day or dwell on the fact that he'd just scored the new cutie's phone number. He didn't want to feel angry, didn't want to feel aroused. He didn't want to *feel*. Didn't want to think. Didn't want to answer the fucking phone—why won't it stop ringing?—God, what is this?!

"Okay, I'm up! Shut up," he scolded the thing before an-swering. "Hello?"

He heard a clicking noise like static but not quite. "Hello," he tried again, this time firmly. Still static. Still nothing.

"Oh for Christ—Hello!" he yelled at the receiver. When no one spoke back he slammed it down hard with a, "Fine! Good-bye!" and it rang as if uninterrupted by his having answered the call in the first place.

He grabbed the receiver, shoved it to his ear. "Oh, dude, what?!"

"Hi, Corey?"

A grownup. Fuck, what'd I do wrong?

"Yeah?"

"Hi, this is Mrs. Malone. Darryl's mother."

No shit.

"Hi."

"Hi. I was wondering if you've seen Darryl at all today."

Great, another one. When did Darryl turn into Ferris Buel-ler?

"No, he didn't come to school today."

"Well he didn't come home last night either. Do you know where he is?"

Yeah, he can't come to the phone cuz he's coming on my cock.

"No, sorry."

"That's okay—Listen… Did he say anything to you about where he might be when you kids were camping last weekend?"

Come on, lady! Tired! What am I magically supposed to pull a 'yes' out of my hat?

"No."

Wait, what camping trip?

"Wait, what camping trip?"

"Don't tell me there was no camping trip."

"If there was I wasn't invited."

"Huh. Is that right?"

No, bitch, I'm lying.

"Yes, ma'am."

"Great. Well thank you, you've been a big help. If you hear from him tell him to get his tail home, he's got quite the grounding coming to him."

Yeah, there's a reason to run home, dummy.

"I will, Mrs. Malone. See ya."

At my gelato stand in hell.

He hung up and unplugged the phone, then set his alarm clock to wake him in a couple hours at six. He had second thoughts about maybe doing some homework tonight. Meantime, he settled in as Jim Morrison crooned about people being strange to a stranger and snored his throat dry.

***

"Corey, come eat!"

His mom's shrill caw beat the alarm by two minutes and he was okay with that. He was famished. Did he eat lunch today? Couldn't recall. This afternoon existed light years in the past.

"Dude, shake it off," he scolded himself as he patted his face. *Whoa, déjà vu*.

"Do I get an answer or what?"

Corey found himself asleep sitting at the table forgetting how he got there. Wasn't he just in bed? He hoped he was coming down with the flu so he could skip school tomorrow.

"Corey!"

"What?"

"Answer me!"

"I dunno, Ma, what's the question?"

Mrs. Avon sighed, wiping her hands on her apron. She shook her head in dismay.

"What?" Corey asked, frustrated.

"You didn't even hear a word I said, did you? Maybe this is your problem in school: you just don't pay attention."

"Whatever."

"Yes, *whatever*. There's the answer of a generation. What your father and I want to know is what happened to you boys this weekend. We've been getting calls all day from concerned parents asking if we've seen their kids." She hesitated, eyeballing her son as he steam-shoveled Rice-A-Roni down his gullet. He peeked up from his trough and caught her grossed-out face. His cheeks were puffed up with grains and meat. He laughed his way through, "It's the San Francisco treat," spewing rice bits onto the kitchen table. He scooped at his mouth with his cupped right hand so as to not laugh-vomit any more dinner. It almost choked out his nose. Mrs. Avons' eyes darted like a horizontal REM state, like she was yelling "Does not compute" at him with those brown, dark eyeballs.

"Don't talk with your mouth full," was the only wisdom she could squeeze out because, truly, what was so funny about this?

"What are you boys up to?" she asked.

Corey twiddled his fork. "Why we gotta always be up to something? Maybe they are but I don't know about it."

"They didn't say anything to you?" she pushed.

"Not a word, I swear."

"When did you last see them?"

"I dunno. Friday? Maybe? Last Friday, I think."

"You don't know?"

"No, I don't—Why would I lie?"

"You tell me," she said, raising her voice noticeably. A quiet settled on the household that was interrupted only by fork scraping plate and the occasional muffled auto puttering down the street.

Corey wished his father wasn't working late so he could break the foul mood with an absentminded non sequitur retarded enough to force his mom and him into a shared knowing chuckle.

Mrs. Avon wished her husband wasn't working late so he could break the foul mood with an absentminded non sequitur retarded enough to force Corey and her into a shared knowing chuckle.

Mr. Avon broke foul wind in the bucket seat of his new hybrid as he sped home slamming the roof with his palm to the beat of Foghat's lone classic, "Slow Ride." He didn't at all mind working late.

Chapter 15
Henry

Dr. Metis' was the perfect background for the project to which he was assigned. Beyond computer science and ethnobotany he was passionate about biochemistry, neurology and physics, though he only held doctorates in computer science and neurology.

He appreciated advances in modern medicine but maintained that they were unnecessary. Every cure we needed to survive disease appeared in nature. If we just knew where to look and would stop obliterating rainforest we would discover them. About this he was outspoken.

He grew up orphaned, too old to adopt by the time each parent died. His father, an obscenely wealthy hoarder, had twenty years on his mother and three hundred pounds on the average obese man. A heart attack took him at fifty-two. Henry inherited Father's height, an intimidating 6'3", but not his weight.

Mother was a sharp, creative woman but always felt incomplete. Felt it hard, like her soul hadn't finished cooking before birth. The passing of her husband crushed that soul. She slipped into a coma-like depression, which paved the way for her suicide on the third anniversary of his death. She struggled every last day not to overdose on red wine and Percocet but the grief was too much. Her final toxic months alone in her chemically altered head smeared her perceptions of herself, her family, this life, and her in it.

She had stayed with that selfish fat fuck through thin, thick, thicker, and thickest, and what did she get in return? A gangling shit of a son and bills. This, because he'd left everything to his one and only, the bearer of his namesake, his darling prodigy. He loved that parasite suckling her gut for nine consecutive months and she didn't. Period. Now she more than didn't, she loathed him as a symbol of her good years wasted on a gamble that didn't pay. As soon as she squeezed him from her loins the game was rigged for failure. She could not live in that failure.

Those obsessive, dark thoughts were foreign to her. She knew not where they came from but her guilt over them faded with the days. It was easier to give in and be that darkness. The suicidal chorus swelled in her mind with each glass of wine, each bottle of wine, each swig, chug, pill swallowed, until finally, like the irreversible curse of a dark arts magician, it became her mind.

Henry was an orphan but he was a rich orphan. When he blew out his eighteenth birthday candle the wealth of his father transferred into his Bermuda account. Looking forward to this from a young age gave him a taste of inevitability. He was going to be rich. That was his destiny. He may not have had love but he had this substitute worth to counterbalance the devastation of parental losses and mental abuse.

He was a naturally bright kid to start, but the sense of having a role to play once he got that money sculpted his neurotic perfectionism. He imagined rich men were all well-educated and dapper and righteous, like his parents, and so he groomed himself to be those things. His motives changed with time and maturity but he clung onto the perfectionism. If he received less than an A+ on homework assignments he threw primal scream fits into his pillow at night. That wasn't often, though, because he grew to love school, love learning, and evolved away from the egomaniacal fat cat he believed was his fate.

As an undergrad at Yale University he pledged to the notoriously secretive fraternity, Skull and Bones. He was cut from the short list of hopefuls soon after he answered some interrogation questions with honesty.

"What would you do if you found out we stole Pancho Villa's skull?"

"Return it."

"You would snitch?"

"I would return it. It's up to you to take responsibility for your indiscretions."

"You don't consider yourself in league with the group, then? You're not a team player?"

"I'm not an amoral criminal."

"What would you do if you found out we had the skull of an alien?"

"From another world?"

"Yes."

"Return it. Just kidding."

"This is no time for jokes."

"Well I'd say, 'That's neat.'"

"Would you bring it to the *Times*?"

"No."

"Why not?"

"Because some secrets need to be kept."

"Who are you to keep them?"

"I'm the guy who knows them."

"But you wouldn't keep a secret for your brothers."

"I'd do what's right. What I think is right. I hope these are trick questions or else I'm not making it to round two, am I?"

"That will be all."

Metis knew he was a disappointment to them mainly because his wealth equaled status, which they craved. He had failed big but he didn't scream into his pillow. He wondered if they really did stow Poncho Villa's cranium in the tomb and if so, what sick stupid shit did they do to it for "fun"?

He didn't get in but he didn't feel like a failure either. Not to himself and not to the bearded gent watching all the pledges behind a two-way mirror. This man was never seen by Metis or any of the pledges. He was barely known by Bonesmen, that's how they knew he was important.

There were rumors, lots of rumors. He was the man who culled presidents from their numbers. He was just some old kook, a has-been member of the brotherhood. He was a some-body. He was a nobody. They didn't know who he was but he made them laugh with his old-timer stories and they were for-bidden to turn him away by senior Bonesmen.

***

Graduating summa cum laude, the job market was an open door for Metis. He settled on a computer science profes-sorship at The University of Arizona mainly because he liked the arid climate. This uncharacteristic decision was his way of easing out of the perfectionism that had come to define him. He had the money. He had the "Doctor" prefix. It was time to relax and settle into a life of fulfillment. For a man like Dr. Metis, teaching at a university in his favorite state was like early retirement.

By all accounts Metis was an affable charmer. He turned stuffy colleagues into good friends, like a magician, by pulling humor out of them—even that hardened poli sci wonk, Carl Michaels. Students knew him as Dr. Michaels, the boring pro-fessor with the sneer. Metis referred to him as the one man alive keeping the bow tie trade a thriving enterprise. He once asked him in the faculty lounge, "Hey, Carl, what are you a doc-tor of again? Political science?" Dr. Michaels pried his eyes from *The New Yorker* on his atmosphone. What was this belligerent toad going on about?

Metis smiled at him and whistled pretending to be im-pressed. He said, "Man, that's something. I'm a doctor of com-puters, you're a doctor of politics. Lynn over there is a doctor of the English language. That must have been a hard degree—It's the thing we all speak, right?"

Lynn laughed with abandon while some of the others in the room giggled nervously. Dr. Michaels remained stone.

"My only question is, with all these doctors in the house, which one of us is going to defibrillate the first fat kid to drop from eating the genetically modified garbage that passes for food these days? We're like doctors of nothing. How the heck did we grift our way into tenure?"

Lynn laughed again and then the rest felt comfortable enough to do the same. Except Dr. Michaels. He looked back down at his electronic magazine and after a dramatic pause whiffed out the side of his sneer, "Hand me the paddles, I'll see what I can do." The sneer became a smile and they all cracked up at the fact that Metis had done what no professor had done before: tamed this man.

More than tamed him, after that Carl and he became fast friends. On a random afternoon luncheon, instead of the usual chitchat about classes and foreign affairs, Carl invited him to join a secret fraternity. His dry tone made it sound more mysterious and life-altering than if he'd been excited.

"Once you say 'yes,' you can never go back," Carl stated flatly.

"Why me?"

"One of the members has an interest in you."

"You mean it's not you?"

"We're friendly but no it wasn't my idea. Will you join?"

"This is an impulse buy I can't return. What am I supposed to say to that?"

"Will you join?"

Dr. Metis requested time to mull it over. Granted. After a week's deliberation he said yes. Given the caliber of friend asking him this could only be a good decision. Also, he wanted to know on whose behalf his colleague made the offer. Was somebody watching him? For how long? Why?

Carl gave him a time, a date, a location, the instruction to be punctual, and nothing more. This cloak and dagger routine thrilled him, he presumed, because he denied himself so many childhood adventures. He showed up early, waited sheepishly in the corner booth of the Meet Rack on West Drachman, as instructed. He felt filthy just sitting in a bondage bar like this, run by a man who had his name legally changed to "God." He kept his head low, nervous that if one of his students caught him here it would cost him his reputation or worse, his tenure.

"Dr. Metis," a thickly bearded wizard in a black trench coat declared as he slipped into the bench across the table. The man was tall and frail-looking, yet he had an energy about him. Metis guessed by the lines on his face that he was in his early eighties and had lived a full life he was not keen on giving up for social security benefits.

"Yes. And you are?" Dr. Metis extended his hand and the anonymous graybeard shook it firmly.

"I'm the one who asked you to join our... club, shall we say. I've been following your work since Yale. You remember pledging Skull & Bones, yes?"

"I didn't get in."

"No you didn't, Dr. Metis, no you surely did not." The man giggled through his words.

"So what's this you want me to join, The Faculty Club for Second Best?"

"No, no! Nothing to do with faculty. May I buy you a drink?"

"Kind of you to offer but I'm good with my friend Sam Adams here," Metis said, tapping his full stein.

"Very good. You know if you have the name of God branded onto your buttocks you get fifty cents off beer for the rest of your life here."

"Wow. Can't believe I didn't discover this place on my own!"

"Weeeeell you're in for a lifetime of discoveries far greater than that. Far, far greater." The twinkle in the man's eye practically winked at Metis.

"Is that right?" Dr. Metis dug the old man's jovial Merlin act. He was one of those unassuming elders whose eyes betrayed him if you knew how to look. They hid a youthful, keen intellect full of remorseful secrets. He was the personification of "duty." This man had a duty to be who he was—an upbeat character actor, a grandfatherly chucklehead—because under-neath it laid fire. He was friendly but not your friend. He'd probably killed more than once and in service to something—but what? Why did he need Metis?

The man read Metis' facial expression and gleaned that he'd already figured this much out. Two doctorates meant he was a quick study. As he methodically chose his next words, the elder dropped his smile. "What do you know about the inter-net?" he asked.

Metis laughed. "Everything. I teach computer science. I'm a tech geek. What do you want to know?"

"Not I, Dr. Metis. What do *you* want to know? *You*... want to know?"

"I'm not following."

"The Information Age is here, Doctor. For the average per-son that means gaining access to anything one wants through the internet. Not what one needs, mind you, but what one wants. Mainly pornography and UFOs."

"UFOs? Really?" The laughs kept coming.

"That's what people want and give it to them, I say. The corporate entity wants information, too. Wants to know peo-ples' buying psychology and impulsive habits. Wants to know what the competition knows."

"And the military industrial complex wants information on terrorism, right," Metis butted in.

"No. The politician wants the appearance of the military wanting that so as to maintain the appearance of a never-ending war on terror. These wants become quite the tongue twister!"

"Well...when in a bondage bar...."

The man's eyes lit up again and the mirth returned. "Yes! When in a bondage bar! Good! That's very good!"

Metis knew he was humoring him and now he felt like a dolt. He cut to it: "So okay, where is this leading?"

"In 1962 we figured out how to download documents into people's brains. We created an internet of mind."

Metis almost coughed Sam Adams through his nostrils.

"I know, I know. It sounds crazy and that's what this conversation is for now, alright? A crazy old coot spinning yarns in a bondage bar. Who will believe this? Nobody."

"So don't bother telling anyone, is that the warning, Mister...?"

"Ooooh, rude of me. Very rude of me. You can call me Charles."

"All right, Charles. Let's say I believe you. You work for some top-secret hush-hush op and you want me to work on this human internet thing. To what end?"

The old man leaned in conspiratorially and whispered, "We've gone far beyond where we were in 1962, Doctor. Far, far beyond. We used to abduct people in the night and implant them with crystal deposits that could transmit and receive signal. The old way limited our human resource pool to Americans. We tested it out on institutionalized schizophrenics. We even learned how to control their voices so that not only did we have human computers, we had patsies."

Metis shifted in his seat uncomfortably and scanned the bar as subtly as he could for exits. The old man picked up on his language.

"Dr. Metis, this is not evil."

"This sounds like some mad scientist bullshit to me."

"Yes, yes—*sounds like* is not *the same as*."

"So you're using your evil powers for good, is that it? And the tax payers float this or are you private sector?"

"This is means to an end. Nothing more."

"To whose end?"

A Cheshire Cat-like grin swept up the old man's cheeks. "I can't answer that until you say yes."

"What am I saying yes to?"

"You will take the program to its next phase. Currently, we implant people globally with ingestible nano technology. Youth, mostly, and drug addicts. They want designer drugs, we sell them designer drugs. Ecstasy laced with access, Dr. Metis."

"That's unacceptable."

"I agree. We don't know the long-term effects this has on the body. The implants were more work but at least they were stable. This is almost unconscionable."

"Almost," Metis chided.

Unruffled, Charles went on. "Almost, doctor. And so, you see, we need that next step to happen now. We need to be able to implant and extract files, memory, instruction, what have you, with a more, shall we say, hands-off device."

"Like a satellite or an antenna?"

"Yes, Dr. Metis." The man chuckled condescendingly. "You're good at this catching on quick business. We already have something like this in operation. It's called the Tesla Dream Machine. Dramatic, I know. And basically all it can do is beam suggestion over small populations. There is no better way to hide a secret base than right in front of your neighbor's eyes with the suggestion not to look. Is any of this interesting you?"

"I'm still here."

"So you are."

"*Why*... am I here? What about my profile leads you to believe I'm the man for the job?"

"You have the intelligence for it, no question about that. But you've also got something else few men do: you will not be compromised. You would run to the press if you thought this was an amoral operation, yes?"

"Of course."

"But if it was not, you'd never tell a soul."

"Yes. I see."

"Now I cannot convince you that this is the right thing to do unless you agree to more, shall we say, theatrics."

"Why don't we say what we mean instead?"

Charles stiffened. The curving lines of his face melted out of smile mode leaving no trace of the mercurial grandfather. He leaned in and whispered, "You will be transported to an underground military installation where we will meet for further discussion. You will do this and everything will change. There is no going back, Dr. Metis. That's the gamble. I assure you it is worth it. What we're discussing sounds criminal. It is not. Let me prove it to you and in return you get to be the man who saves the world."

"From what?"

Charles leaned back in the calculated manner that punctuated all of his movements and excused himself from the table. "Good day, Doctor. We will be in touch." Briskly, he went.

"Well that was dramatic," Dr. Metis muttered to himself. He again became keenly aware of his surroundings and chortled. "Bondage bar."

He paid his tab to God and left.

INTERLUDE
Earth Zero

Reptilians were a clandestine race. They were not shy but they kept to themselves, chiefly because they breathed the methane-rich air of Dinosaur Chasm where they lived in tribes. To stray from there into the world of oxygen was an ordeal involving air-conditioned suits with clunky filtration helmets. They were the hardest species for the invaders to eliminate because their tribes were comprised of small, unassuming clans spread throughout the valley. Much of their housing was camouflaged by dense swamplands and they were further concealed by the free-roaming giants stomping all around them.

The dinosaurs' sentient ancestral grandchildren, the dragons, hadn't died in vain. They'd bought Earth Plane elders time enough to unite as a council. Reptilian chiefs declined the invitation to join, content to wait out the hostility from their homeland. The council understood and respected their decision.

If you're reading this intently, Corey—which I highly recommend—and not just drifting along thinking about other things, you have to be asking yourself why it is that a council would need to come together in the first place. After all, isn't everybody psychically linked?

Well, yes. But remember that although the insects were really bodies of a hive-minded queen and not autonomous people, nobody knew it except the space invaders. The council thought they were a race that had to be cut off from the telepathic link. This meant passing written notes and resuming oral communication where that was possible. Some species' vocal chords had atrophied through lack of use, the ones who didn't sing.

It also meant awkward, stilted communications because they were used to showing not telling. Their natural language was one of pictures and now those pictures had to be converted into words, which created a slight delay in interaction. The speaker had to properly formulate the words and the recipient had to interpret them. With pictopathy there was no hoping someone understood you, for whatever you were relaying was immediately apparent. With vocal and written speech... not so much.

***

Earth Plane was in disarray. Nobody knew why this was happening or who could be trusted. They only knew the insects from underground couldn't be. Cutting them off had been first suggested by the mantis elders.

Although they looked similar to the insectoids with their bulbous heads and elongated black eyes whose gaze suggested eternity and malice, mantises were in no way genetically linked to the sub dwelling hive. Perhaps they stored their predatory nature in their eyes the way good people bury their worst impulses in the unconscious. What we know for sure is the mantises never acted on impulse or instinct. They were thoughtful and they had been pacifists longer than any other race. No matter what story their eyes told, they had nothing but love and trust for the insectoids until this attack. It pained them as much as anyone to suggest cutting the psychic tie and going dark.

The psychic connections had their on/off switches between species and also between individuals. The Earth Plane Council, as the elders officially named themselves, agreed it was best for now to flip those switches off and resume living in separation. This meant that faeries could only relate in oneness with other faeries, mantises with other mantises, shining ones with other shining ones, and so forth throughout the realm. Elder representatives from each race came together in a location so secret I can't even tell you. It was there that they resurrected the universal written and spoken dead language. It was there that they conspired to take back their planet.

***

The insects hadn't been the only race with defunct airships ready to go online in case this day came. Elves had them and the grays had them, too. Every race bore secrets of the ether that were peculiar to them. They all had their tricks to quarantining information from the trans-species collective mind.

These weapons were their bleakest suppressions. Exposing them within the council produced an odd sense of relief, for as much as it chagrined them to see that there hadn't been full transparency between races, they were thankful the deceit meant they now had a viable means of defense.

The council agreed to take action. They held a moment of silence for their fallen allies, the dragons, then resolved to avenge their deaths with the bloodiest sky battle Earth Plane had ever seen. They granted their forces would be exponentially outnumbered but maybe they could scare the terrorists off by hammering them with merciless resolve. They hadn't a moment to salt away. The insects in the ground were fervently chewing through the soil that buried their hordes and their sky ships made death nonstop.

Soul capture wasn't an option in this chaos. This was a war in which death meant death. The illusions of safety and enlightenment had been blown away like wisps in a meadow. These old races had to gain their footing on the pendulum that swung between good and evil decisions once more.

Oneness died in a day.

Chapter 16

John Avon sucked down two Alka-Seltzer to relieve the failure burning a hole in his gut. He was a master at containing his guilt, keeping it from himself. That's what the workaholism was for. But every now and then it flared up in physical symptoms. That's what the heartburn meds were for.

He managed all aspects of the Taunton public access television station. Sometimes this took him well into the evening, sometimes not. Sometimes he stayed well into the evening with nothing to do. It was that or return to the family—and he was not a family man. He loved his son but he wasn't good at fathering. He tolerated his wife, Meg, because he had the ability to recall a time when he did love her and live in that memory. He loved loving the woman she was before the vows and the union, the softness of her in his arms, the way she smelled just for him, the kinetic poetry that would flow and was meant. The woman she'd grown into was a hard, crabby shell of her former self and, while he accepted partial blame for that, he didn't dwell there. Too busy.

The ordeal with his son's missing weekend presented a need for him to respond as a firm yet caring paternal figure, which would undoubtedly act as the catalyst for his Meg to remember why she married him those long twenty-three years ago. He pictured a giant eraser wiping out his past like a Tex Avery cartoon correcting his years of obliviousness. He saw their love growing from the seeds of a few actions and it terrified him. What they had together now was what he knew. Could he be a better man or was that man lost? The idea of *better* was foreign, yet what they had was so broken that it couldn't last and he knew it. Underneath the denial, he knew.

He hesitated until Corey said goodnight much to Meg's consternation. It was easier to fall into the pattern of arguing with her than solving Corey. It helped that arguing came with the hope of make-up sex, the only sex he got hard for.

"Mrs. Miller called twice today looking for Stephen. I just wish I knew what those boys were up to," Meg sighed.

"Maybe they aren't up to anything. Or don't you believe your own son?" John shot.

"Hey, don't make me out to be the bad guy here, Mr. Sarcasm. I can't read their minds. I just want to know the truth, is that so bad?"

"Cut the kid some slack. He said he doesn't know anything."

"And you believe him?"

"I have no reason not to."

"What about the note? John, Corey was gone all weekend!"

John rolled his eyes condescendingly as he always did when she made more sense than he. Often times Meagan's logic didn't register with him and in his embarrassment he played it like she was the dummy. In times like these it was all she could do not to kick him in his oblivious face.

"Fine," she huffed. "You sit here in your little world playing perfect dad to a perfect son. Nice lesson, John."

"What lesson is he learning by not being trusted?" John struck back. "Meg, you're his mother. What's he supposed to think if you don't trust him when he tells the truth?"

She'd heard enough. "I'm getting him help. He needs a psychologist."

"Oh come on! That's slightly overboard don't you think?"

"Look, John," she snapped, "You don't understand what's going on here! He's protecting his friends. Are you too blind to see that? And you need—don't roll your eyes at me—you need to go talk to him. Just talk to him, John."

"The boy is eighteen. He doesn't need me telling him what to do."

She threw up her hands. "I give up. You do whatever. I'm calling a doctor in the morning. If you don't care about your family at least care about the other families whose sons are missing."

"Oh don't pull that guilt trip crap on me. I'll talk to him, okay? But not because of that."

Of course it was because of that. She was right. He knew it. She knew it. Corey heard it through the thin walls and knew it. Dad was a giant pussy when it came to the things that mattered and Corey knew how to play him just like Mom.

***

Dad's gentle rapping came expectedly.

"Come in."

Corey's bedroom door creaked open. Hall light sliced the dark where Corey lay waiting under covers. Waiting to manipulate his dopy father with the innocent tone that always made Dad forget he was dealing with a young man old enough to vote and drive and not his baby boy.

"Hi, Dad."

"Hi, pal. You asleep?"

"Getting there."

"Sorry about that. Listen, your mother and I still need to know what happened to you last weekend. Where did you go, Corey?"

"You know it's funny. I've been asking myself that all day long but I really can't remember."

John walked in and scooted him over. He plopped down on the edge of the bed. Corey was glad. Something about seeing his father backlit in the doorway gave him chills. There he was a shadowy gargoyle. Here up close he was Dad.

"Corey, you're eighteen years old, this is unacceptable. Come on, talk to me, pal."

"I hear ya, Dad. I know. I got nothin'."

"Nothing?"

"I think... nothing. That's weird. I don't remember anything. What's wrong with me?"

"Look, I was your age once too you know. If there's anything you want to tell me, anything at all.... Your friends are missing, Corey. You get a free pass on this one. Just tell me."

"I don't know. Dave said there was a party—"

"Who's Dave?"

"Kid at school. He was asking why we missed the party, me and Darryl and Stephen, James and Alex. We didn't go to it. Where were we?"

When Corey confronted himself with that question an emotion surged up from the depths of him so great that his eyes erupted with tears. He made it a policy to never cry in front of the folks. It staggered them both that he could not control this reaction pouring forth from the abyss that trapped his memories. This was no longer a manipulation.

"Where were we, Dad?"

John rubbed Corey's mop of hair back from his wet cheeks. "I don't know. But your mother and I are gonna get you some help, okay?"

"Okay."

"Okay." John closed with a peck on the forehead. "Love you, pal."

"Love you too, Dad. Goodnight."

"Night-night."

John reported back to his wife. She wasn't buying the tears. He was. He argued his way to a night on the couch.

***

Corey fell comatose in record time. He dreamed of red roses in a gray house designed in wall-to-wall hieroglyphic writing. Then Lina Igasho entered through one of the walls and gave him head. He felt himself about to cum with the intensity only wet dreams accessed, when a blinding white light that seemed to be shining on his face antagonized his closed eyes.

A high-pitched tone hummed in his right ear. He heard the bedroom door squeak open and he bolted to sitting upright in bed, eyes wide and searching for prowlers. Some vague one, a shadow of a person, slipped into the room, but the room was still dark after all. The brilliance was emanating from behind Corey's eyelids and as intriguing as that was, he fixated on the creature at the door. It talked at him and its head bobbled as it spoke. He couldn't make out the words but the sound was clearly there.

"What, Ma?"

Even as he spoke it he knew this wasn't his mother. It wasn't a dream but it wasn't real, either. It was a failed com-munication. He smiled at the notion and sank back into his sheets.

"What's wrong, assholes? Jammed signal?" he slurred.

The shadow babbled on like a prerecorded message. Corey conked out.

Chapter 17

... Wish you were
just like a Christ
Think it's selfless
think it's nice
All them books
keep you enticed
But you refuse
to pay the price....

"Jesus, shut up! Shut up!" Corey slammed his alarm clock hard. Like Stephen, he dug the retro 80's scene but couldn't stand Pooh Dot. He untangled his legs from the web of sheets and thumped into the bathroom. School. Again. *I'll bet Pooh Dot never had to get up this early,* slogged through his misty brain.

He examined his face in the mirror. Dark skins of restlessness hung under his eyes like a basset hound's jowls. He picked at a tiny blackhead buried outside his left nostril. "Awe shit, a zit." He never got those. This was embarrassing. He popped it and moved on to the scale. Nope, no weight change. Still thin. Time to rake soap over skin in the beading hot water.

Showers were an odd responsibility for Corey. He hated taking them yet once he was in he didn't want to leave. And once in, time no longer existed, like playing in the ocean. Was there a connection between water and timelessness?

Humans are what? Like eighty percent water? So why aren't we timeless? That's retarded. Everything's retarded. God I hate school.

He dressed and lumbered downstairs wondering if Mom was still mad at him. *Of course she is. Probably saved up all her hate for this morning. Go ahead, bitch, try and ruin my day.*

He conjured up a dozen worse-case scenarios that would play out when he entered that kitchen. From the latrine he could smell her dragon-lady eats burning so he knew she was there cooking. Lingering. Waiting to strike. What choice did he have? He barged in and took his seat at the table. "Morning," he said.

"Good morning, Corey," John answered, glancing over his newspaper. That was more rise and shine talk than he was used to hearing from Dad.

"Sleep well, Honey?" his mother asked.

Honey? Uh oh. This can't be good.

"Fine I guess. Not really though. Actually, I'm pretty wiped. Ma, did you come into my room last night?"

"No. I know your father—"

"No, not that," Corey cut her off. "Later. Like at three-ish?"

"No. Why would I come into your room at three?"

"I don't know... Dad? You?"

"No. I wasn't even in my own room at three." John winked at his boy, which made him smile.

"Okay. Never mind. I thought it was a dumb dream. Pass the brown sugar?"

"Wow, you'll actually be eating your food this morning?" Meg asked, pleasantly shocked.

"Yeah. I'm hungry."

And that was it. No fight. No hard questions. No tense expectations fulfilled. No more words 'til class and he was glad for it.

***

"Psst! Corey!"

Corey nodded in the boy's direction.

"You seen Stephen around?"

"No."

"His dad called my mom last night looking for him. I guess he's been missing since Sunday."

"Yeah, I know. Seems to be a new trend."

"What do you mean?"

"I mean Stephen, Darryl, James, and Alex—they're all missing."

"Alex Baxter? I saw him at homeroom."

"No, Alex Zaiter. My friend Alex. Lebanese."

"Oooh. Shit. Did they say anything to you?"

"No. It's weird. Everyone and their grandmother asked me where they went. My mom thinks I'm covering for them, my dad thinks I have a two-day hangover, and I honestly don't know what to think about it."

"Corey and Doug, would you like to teach the class?"

"No, Ma'am! That's an honor beyond my capability," Corey blurted.

Caught. Corey hated that especially when it was important like this. Twenty-two bored, smirking faces were on them plus the teacher, Mrs. Callahan, with her faux anger. Corey knew she was full of shit. She didn't care about this class. She was cool, as teachers go, she just didn't like being ignored. She said, "Perhaps you'd like to share with us what you were so eagerly whispering about, hmm?"

"Doug was just telling me how beautiful you look today, Mrs. Callahan, and I concur. That's all."

The class snickered. Mrs. Callahan was not thrown. "How sweet of you two. Doug, is that true?"

Doug stared at his pencil doodling something fierce on the flap of his paper bag book cover. "I don't know."

Oh come on you worthless sack of shit!

"I guess so. Is that a new dress?"

Yes!

The backup... the twenty-two giggles... the kindhearted nature of a woman who wanted desperately to relate to and not be upstaged by teens.... They were going to transition this right back into normal class mode without detention.

"I know history isn't the most interesting subject at your age but we have to learn it. It's a part of life. Get used to it," she told them and the class.

"I'll try my best. We all will. Won't we everybody?" Corey shifted in his Formica chair every which way pretending to look for support. The students laughed. Some rolled their eyes. Everybody loved a clown.

Corey didn't play funny for their amusement, though. He made jokes for himself and if anyone wanted to come along for the ride they were welcome. In this way he didn't feel obligated to entertain others, it just worked out that way. He rarely overextended like the twerps who never got why people thought they were lame. "But I'm saying the same stuff you are," they'd whine. "Why aren't I funny?"

Because you're a d-bag, he'd think as he explained something gentler.

***

The bell, which sounded more like tinnitus than a bell, rang and the students, more like coked up maze rats than students, ran to lunch. Corey brushed past friends in the hall with a singular purpose: Must. Beat. Lunch line. He hated waiting in the back of the line because all the good food was taken by the time he got served. He wasn't about to settle for meatloaf and an apple.

He rounded a corner at high speed and accidentally slammed into Brock Duwarte, the bus demon with the earring. "Hey, fuckhead! Watch where you're going!" the bus shit screamed in his face.

"Oh, sorry," Corey muttered. He squatted to pick up his book bag, which thankfully was zipped and so did not plaster the hall with loose papers.

"Yeah, fuckhead? You wanna start? Come on, man, right now! Come on! I'm begging you! Take a swing!"

Corey couldn't believe this retard just got back from a day's suspension and he was already picking up where he left off. At this, a small crowd had encircled them with no teacher, no hall monitor in sight. Corey gathered himself and stood up. He felt like he should be embarrassed but he wasn't. The child ape with the ridiculously thick Boston accent shoved him so hard he thought his chest was going to implode.

"Come on, punk! Fight me! Fight me!" Brock was red faced, aching for revenge. It didn't matter that Corey was older, this kid was tough, crazy, and full of testosterone. He was muscular and unafraid to wear an earring in his top lip and stretch his lobes with opal gouges. Still, Corey was drunk on tired, starving to death, and was in no mood for this bully shit. He should have been quaking but instead found that the adrenaline pumping into him balanced him out.

"Leave me alone," Corey commanded more than pleaded.

"Yeah! That's what I thought, pussy. Next time you'll think twice before ratting me out you fucking cunt!"

"No, douche bag, you got yourself in trouble! You shouldn't have touched Tommy!" The crowd was silent and unmoving. They weren't yelling, "Fight! Fight!" – weren't goading this on. They were just there. Staring. Gawking. As if the car wreck had already happened. From this, Corey deduced he was toast. He wasn't going to verbally assault this kid until some teacher waded through to break it up. No, this shit was going down and everybody felt it.

The bus demon clenched his southpaw. Corey watched it like a batter trained on the pitch. Before he jerked back for the swing a female voice in the crowd shouted, "Hey asshole!" It came from behind the bully. Brock spun around and without thinking Corey made his move. He'd never been in a fight before, not a real one. He didn't know the first thing about throwing a punch so he swung his book bag like a sling and launched that instead. Actually, it launched itself. The fabric strap snapped off in his hand and what felt like a hundred pounds of textbook shot at the back of Brock's greasy head. At that exact moment the bully whipped back around to face his victim and his head became his nose, which became ground zero for Corey's scholastic missile.

An explosion of blood painted Corey's bag. The bus demon knocked back and out so fast that he took a couple of kids down behind him. This soft landing was the best of his luck as his shattered nose demonstrated. Corey's luck extended to the fact that the one teacher who did finally wade through the crowd, Mr. Bezrah, witnessed the bag snap on its own.

***

"I'm sorry, Corey, but whenever there is a fight we call the parents."

"I know, Mr. Perez, but couldn't you make an exception this once? You know that dude pushed me first and I was defending myself."

"If I make an exception for you I have to make one for everybody."

"No you—What?—Why?"

"I'm not going to engage you about this. Rules are rules. You broke them. These are the consequences."

Corey hated the principal's office, hated the principal. His was a stuffy office built of mahogany everything floating in a sea of gray cubicles glowing under fluorescents that buzzed more than they emitted light. Cubicles for the guidance councilors and clerical chumps, but this dick gets an office with porcelain lamps and a window? Corey felt strangled meandering through on the occasional shortcut from A Block to C Block; he couldn't imagine what it was like working there.

***

Meagan Avon didn't ask for much, just a hint of respect and a wee bit of courtesy. Corey wasn't a little boy he was a young man. Still a teen, yes, but old enough to know better than to cover for friends and pick on kids at school. If John could separate himself from his job for five blasted seconds he'd see that his son was headed down the wrong path.

She remembered eighteen. It was an awkward age where she was almost over the embarrassment of being seen in public with her parents but not quite. Felt guilty about that but then still didn't want to be seen with them. It must be awful for Corey, she thought, because he had a stay-at-home mom in the age of divorce. Where could he escape to? She was extra mindful not to infringe on his bedroom space or poke around too much in his life. She trusted him not to drink, not to smoke, not to do drugs, and maybe that was a mistake. She was as angry with herself as she was with him. She was angrier with John for smiling through not giving a shit.

She knew he felt love for his family and remorse over not expressing affection the way dads should but he seldom acted to right his wrongs. If it didn't come wrapped in a sports score he didn't care for discussion. She held the family together for Corey's sake but if he was turning on her then what was this for?

She still had her MILF looks; she could go to Surly Johnsons, score a trophy boyfriend and he wouldn't even need beer goggles. She knew this. Because she knew it John must have known it and so it was doubly insulting that he didn't do everything in his power to make their marriage stick.

But then why should he? She was the glue, always the glue, and there's no point in him making an effort when that was always going to be the case. Maybe she did have to assert herself, test the waters with the threat of separation. Maybe she would tonight after their inevitable fight over what to do with their delinquent son.

Their son. Look at him there, his smushed cheek humming against the passenger window, eyes glazed and groggy and scared, anticipating the punishment she had yet to dream up. Truthfully, she thought the seven days of suspension Principal Perez doled out was punishment enough because that meant a week stuck in her care. Mommy's care. He was eighteen. This would be torture.

"Mom, it was self-defense, I swear."

When he swore that before the principal, the man shot her a look of, "probably true knowing the other kid involved." And Mr. Bezrah testified that the book bag slingshot was an accident. Still, where are those missing boys, Corey? Where the hell are your friends, Corey? It may be too early for police involvement but she was going to get that answer from him, damn it, even if she had to drag him to some freaky New Age psychologist.

***

'Home is where the heart is? Bullshit! God this is fucked. This is fucking nuts. What am I doing suspended?—Suspended! Only assholes and retards get suspended! *Corey Avon: Fucked By The System*. I should write a book. Or a porn. A porn book.'

Corey ruminated while scraping demon blood off his bag with a sponge in the bathroom where his mother couldn't hover over him. Although by now he would have accepted hovering, because she hadn't spoken to him since they scuttled out of Taunton High. She didn't hover, didn't lurk, didn't say peep. Ignoring ate at him more than hovering.

He heard her clunking around downstairs. 'They say a picture's worth a thousand words,' he thought. 'Maybe she's drawing me a little something.'

This brought a smile to him but not for long because where was Dad? Where was the old man when shit went sour? Does he even know this happened? Does he care? Is he proud? Proud of his fucked up son in the unspoken machismo way some dads get when their kid pounds on a bully?

'No, no, no. Dad doesn't care. Last night was just for show. For Mom. For the fucking dragon queen that is Mom. Dummy ended up on the couch so what's the point of reenacting the caring dad routine? Only Ma cares and she's a psycho. She fucking hates me and is gonna kill me. By the way, idiot, did you really agree to see a shrink last night? Smart move, nimrod. Now you're gonna look like a baby when you say forget it. You should just climb out the window right now and see if you don't sprout wings, cuz that's the only way out of this mess.'

"Corey, get your coat, we're going out," came the holler from downstairs.

"Where we going?" he yelled back.

"Just do it!"

Chapter 18
Henry

Dr. Metis didn't care that he had lost his identity and was now and forever "Henry." Learning secrets was addictive. He thought he could manage the vaguely titled *The Interconnectivity Project* and remain his professorial self, but he wanted more. Obtaining more meant leaving everything.

He wasn't just in the club, he moved into the clubhouse. He was a lab rat living a barely-alive existence locked thousands of feet under Earth's crust surrounded by, sustained by, artificial everything. A lesser man would have gone mad. Perhaps a lesser man did.

Henry adored Charles at first. Trusted him. Had to. Charles was his live-in boss, but the truth of Charles came swiftly apparent: he wasn't a deep and mysterious old man; he was broken. The work he taught Henry was his work. The life he groomed him for was his life. Charles was a tired graybeard who needed to pass all of his information, his agendas, to a fresh apprentice. To do that, he needed to mold the apprentice in his image. To do that, he needed to drive the apprentice crazy.

Now and then during technical conversation Charles would slip in some nonsense by accident and Henry would steer him back to the point.

Now and then during casual conversation Charles would slip in some Above-Top Secrets he was not permitted to share by law.

Now and then Charles would forget where he was.

Would forget who he was.

Would talk to invisible people.

Would yell at them.

Would not recognize Henry as his friend.

As his apprentice.

At all.

Now and then.

Henry saw this and saw this was his future unless he could create a means to keep secrets that would not burn him inside out. How was he to drink acid and not corrode? Or was it not just the secrets but the secrets and the years spent fermenting underground that turned Charles' brain into a perfectly aged Swiss cheese? He imagined this was what it would be like to live in a barren Vegas casino minus the winning sound effects.

He had to get out of Area 51 but there was no way, so he would invent a way. He would do this and he would not feel remorse because these bastards set him up from the start. He learned this one night (or was it day?) not long ago, or maybe years ago, when he asked Charles, during a short-lived bout of lucidity, how long the U.S. military has been in possession of those spacecraft he witnessed that first time he visited the base.

"Hmm? What spacecraft?"

"The... you know... UFOs. Or whatever. Don't tell me those are ours!"

"You mean after you drank the vial of liquid?"

Henry thought back a moment. "Yeah, I did, didn't I? Drank a liquid and stepped through the vault and there were these ships. Huge, some of them. Looked like what people report seeing all the time."

"Yes they do, don't they?"

"What are you telling me here?"

Charles laughed heartily. "Henry, come now! What do you think was in that vial?"

"Nano bots so you can read my mind?"

This gem also tickled Charles. "I'm afraid it was more old-fashioned than that, sir." He tapped Henry's left temple as he whispered, "And you've got a ripe pumpkin so I'll wait."

"Drugs. You drugged me."

"Hallucinogens coupled with props and special effects, my boy. Yes. Quite successful. Quite, quite successful."

"But why?"

"Oooh don't take it personally; it's part of the weeding out process! You take that vision to the media and we know you can't be trusted. And if you can be trusted with that, you can be trusted with anything. We were monitoring you all the while you were waiting to hear from us. We know you didn't run at the mouth all those years. You were exactly what we were looking for. Those other clowns you see on TV—"

"Were high."

"Were recounting the trip we gave them based on popular images of aliens, yes. Everything for a reason, Henry. Nothing is amoral here."

Amoral. That was the buzzword for Henry. Whenever he grew suspicious of the why of everything, Charles loaded up his mouth and shot out "not amoral" in rounds. They profiled his psychology. They used it against him. Charles never even told him the greater good end they were working toward and he'd long forgotten to ask. The access to new knowledge, the freedom to explore anything and everything down here, mesmerized him. His entire time in this perfect dungeon had been one hypnotic mind fuck.

Get him to do the work.

Get him to live the life.

He is a rare breed.

Charles is a dying act.

This soft torment must only work now and then.

Chapter 19

"Okay, Corey, where would you like to begin?"

The boy fidgeted a while, scraping the heel grooves of his sneakers against the chrome legs of his swivel chair. If he were home he'd have been spinning himself dizzy in the chair but in this place it felt like a trap, a way to squeeze out his nervous habits. He chewed at a thumbnail and flipped his soles on the chair absentmindedly teasing out an answer in his head.

"Wherever," he eventually said.

"Would you like to tell me what's bothering you?"

"Nothing." Corey spit a chunk of nail out the side of his mouth like a sunflower shucking. This tête-à-tête with Dr. Olif was a nightmare for him. He had agreed to see a shrink for Dad but that was then. This was now. Now he was a different person. Harder. Guard up. In shock from battle and suspension. This was too soon.

"I see," Dr. Olif continued. "How would you describe your relationship with your parents?"

"Which one?"

"Both."

"Fine."

"I see, I see—Tell me something...." He paused as if he were going to lean in to create an air of extra privacy for the serious question he was about to lay on Corey but then didn't. He remained relaxed and un-doctor-like, slouching in his seat, even. He continued, "Did you ask to come here or were you forced?"

It was then that the spectacle of the man questioning him came sharply to Corey—so sharply that he belched out a laugh, rude and honest, then bit his lip in embarrassment. The humorous tapestry of hobo art the alleged doctor Olif wore with zero concern for public image, let alone basic fashion sense, was preposterous enough to be camouflaged this long by Corey's own expectations of how another human being could dress. The psychologist had on a warm smile and an even warmer thick wool sweater—argyle, the color of Checkers—green corduroy pants, and flip flops. His glasses were a nerdmare: beady-eyed coke bottles fastened at the left hinge with neatly cut electrical tape. And Corey was the crazy one?

"The question was funny?" Dr. Olif asked.

Corey imagined his eyes came off with the glasses like a Muppet. He held all of this in and had to jog his memory to even get back to the question. It came to him and he answered, "No. Ah, forced, I guess."

"You guess?"

"Yeah, well, I mean… yeah, forced." Corey composed himself in the mature way he expected of the doctor and leaned in. "Look, here's the deal," he confided. "I agreed to come but that was to keep my father out of hot water with the mom. We both know I was forced to come here by my mother cuz she thinks I know where my friends are and I don't."

"Why do you need to know?" Dr. Olif asked.

"Because. This is going to sound fu—I mean stupid, but—"

The doctor interrupted, "It's okay if you swear, Corey. I'll remind you that nothing you say in here will be relayed to your parents unless you indicate you might harm yourself or others. Then they hear it and the police hear it and it's a mess, okay? Them's the rules."

"Okay, good. Thanks."

"So you were saying?"

"Oh, yeah. Anyway, apparently my mother found a note telling her where I'd be all weekend."

Corey paused while Dr. Olif busily scribbled on his notepad. He assumed the doctor was jotting quotes so he gave him time to catch up.

"And that would be where?" the doctor asked.

"Camping with friends."

The shrink nodded. He already heard this from the mom unit. Had to have. Corey explained anyway if only to clear his name. "I didn't know anything about it but she didn't believe me when I told her that."

"Why do you think that is?"

"Because the note is in my handwriting—but I didn't write it, I swear! Plus, and my friends have been missing since, like, Friday or something."

"Does that concern you?"

Corey shrugged.

"Do you like your friends?"

"They're my friends. Of course I like them."

"I see. So let me ask: What *did* you do last weekend?"

Corey ran down the bookcase to his left. Too many books to catch a specific title.

"Corey?"

"What was the question?"

"The weekend—"

"Oh. Right. I don't know."

"You don't know what you did? Where you were?"

"I have no idea."

"How does that make you feel?"

"Like my fucking grandfather."

"Do you understand your parents' concern?"

"Not really. My mom doesn't believe me and my dad thinks we all got smashed and they're puking in someone's tub about now. So really neither of them trust me, he's just cooler with it I guess, so that's good, right?"

"Do you drink with your friends?"

"Dude, I don't drink, I don't do drugs, I don't smoke. I don't do any of those things. I'm a fucking angel, okay? I mean at heart. I'm a sailor by mouth an angel by heart."

Corey cracked himself up but the shrink wasn't biting. "How many of your friends have disappeared?" he trudged.

"Let's see, there's Darryl and Stephen and Alex and James. Twenty."

Nothing.

"That was a joke."

Still nothing.

"When was the last time you spoke to any of them?" Dr. Olif asked.

"Friday, maybe? In school."

"What did you talk about?"

"Dude, that was a long time ago. What did *you* talk about Friday?"

Dr. Olif looked at the ceiling and adjusted his glasses, then back to his client in that same unaffected manner, his smile indubitably a mask. "I'm going to ask you one more time. I completely understand how unnerving this all must be for you, but think Corey. Where did you go last weekend that got your parents upset? *Think* now."

Corey's eyes darted back to the shelves. "Oh, *Of Mice And Men*? I had to read that one last year." Turned out he *could* make out some of the titles in the doctor's collection. "Aaaaah, I'm thinking, I'm thinking…. Let's see, I know Thursday we went to the tree house—and before you say it, yes I know. We have a tree house, okay? Just deal with it. Ummmm… let me stop… ummmm…. Okay, look, we talked… we talked… something about Alex's girlfriend who isn't really his girlfriend. And then James was an asshole. That's…. I dunno, that's all I got."

"That's all you remember?"

"Yeah. Thursday night. And then I know I saw them Friday too but I don't know what we talked about. 'Hi' and 'bye,' maybe. It was brief I think. Must have been." Corey giggled nervously and shrugged again.

"Okay, Corey. You did very well here today and I appreciate it, especially considering that you didn't want to come."

"No offense."

"Believe me I get that all the time. None taken. So what I'm going to do now is ask you to step into the waiting room for a few minutes while I consult with your mother."

"Okie dokie!" Corey sprang to his feet and extended his hand. The doctor shook it with a smile. Corey, too, wore a smile and he knew he wasn't the only one faking it.

His mom and he traded places. The waiting room was cold and damp. Boring. Too much air conditioning. Felt like a morgue. 'So this is what it's like to be a stiff,' Corey thought.

They were taking longer than the doctor led on. A lot longer. What had it been, a half hour? Corey squinted around looking for a clock. He found one by the water cooler practically hidden in the leaves of a rubber tree.

'Five minutes. How is that possible? Dude, I am not reading *People Magazine*.'

The main entrance swung open with immediacy. From his vantage point, Corey could only see chubby brown fingertips wrapped around the door's edge. He heard "Go, go, go!" and two cute little African American boys ushered in, trailed by their father who let go the door behind them. He nodded to Corey, mouthed "Hi," then sat his boys down across from Corey and rummaged through the magazines on the glass table. Two ragged issues of *Cricket* would satiate the tykes.

Corey glared at them. He didn't mean to and they didn't see it, but they looked familiar to him, offensive in some way. Who were they? They'd never met before. The kids were adorable. They were just kids.

Were they?

He didn't know why he'd question that. Racism, perhaps. Something latent. Something—some *thing* about this family made him want to jump out of the chair and drive on home right now.

'Hurry up, Ma.'

Another door opened. Corey whipped his head around. To his great relief Dr. Olif was finally escorting Mrs. Avon out of his private office.

"Corey, can I see you a minute?" the doctor requested.

"Sure." He was nervous about the horrid things he imagined his mom told the shrink but he'd rather get lectured in there than sit peacefully out here with that nice family.

He scurried in past his mom without any acknowledgment and sunk back into his familiar chair. Meg followed, sat next to her son, and Dr. Olif reentered after some pleasantries with the dad in the waiting room. Corey beamed his eyes straight ahead but from his periphery noticed his mother was oddly calm now.

"Corey," the shrink began as he took his seat across from them, "your mother and I have discussed it and I have explained to her the procedure...."

"Procedure of what?"

"Well we feel that you would benefit from some relaxation techniques to try to find out what happened last weekend. Of course the final decision is up to you. We won't force you to do it but I think it is for the better that you do because your friends are missing and you're the only one who knows where they went. Potentially. Maybe not. But we'd like to find that out for their sake at the very least, right?"

"I dunno, dude. What's it—like hypnosis?"

"It's like a very peaceful state of calm. You will feel relaxed and I will guide you into your memory. It's not foolproof and it might not work at all. For some people it doesn't. But it's quick and harmless and worth trying."

"You won't make me quack like a duck or program me to kill the class president will ya?"

The doctor chuckled more out of courtesy. "No, no, nothing like that. It isn't hypnosis. Hypnosis doesn't work for memory retrieval. It's a nightmare. There's nothing voodoo about what we're going to do, I promise you."

Corey leaned back practically being absorbed into the puffy foam of the chair. He pushed off with his feet, spun a 360 and stopped the ride after one rotation. "What does Dad think?" he asked Mom.

"Actually, your father and I discussed it before I brought you here. He's not keen on the idea of you even being here in the first place but whatever you want to do he supports your decision." She smiled at him assuredly.

He thought, 'In other words, you brainwashed him like you always do and now you want this guy to brainwash me.'

"How well are you trained in this?" Corey blurted.

"Corey!"

"No, no, that's a very good question," Dr. Olif intervened. "I've ten years in the field, Corey, and a lifetime of breathing. What I'm talking about are some breathing techniques older than any of us that aid in relaxation and concentration. They de-stress and focus the brain."

"He's good at what he does. You can trust him."

'Shut up! You don't know what you're talking about! God I hate it when you do that!' The words sliced into Corey's mind like ninja stars, but he edited them into, "Okay. I'll do it."

They settled on Thursday at 3:30pm. Corey thought, why not get it over with sooner? It's not like he had to take time off school. But if 3:30 worked for them, it worked for him. Shit, maybe his pals would turn up by then and he wouldn't have to go through with this nonsense.

He was relieved to see the African American family wasn't there when he left. 'Must have had an appointment with one of the other therapists. Thank God,' he thought.

Feeling this relief, he vowed that even if his friends did re-surface he'd visit the doctor again about this new, irrational prejudice.

Chapter 20
Henry

Dimethyltryptamine - DMT. The psychedelic chemical compound found in most Ayahuasca brews, elixir of South American shaman. Also the active hallucinogen produced by the human body in the pineal gland, known in Eastern traditions as *the third eye.* Henry had absorbed all of the research on DMT ever published. He knew well the term "hallucinogen" was a misnomer. DMT didn't cause illusions it acted like a radio tuner. His guess, and the guess of others, including Charles, was that it tuned one's perception to various dimensions that the basic five senses could not detect, the way one switches broadband stations. Discovering how DMT achieved this was one of his assignments.

Another assignment was to distinguish between this authentic perceptual shift and psychotic hallucinations. His research required a holistic approach. He read not just scientific journals and secret military-sponsored finds but also studied ancient religious texts, shamanic testimony, transpersonal psychology—he had to dive deep and swim in many directions. Mainly what he did, though, was sit quietly in the middle of the lab's recreation of rainforest. There amongst the magic mushrooms and Ayahuasca ingredients he meditated. He listened to the plants. He felt voices in him that were not his own. They attached themselves to his intuition and guided him.

His intellectual eureka moment came when the one story that nagged him—a story he'd heard many times before—finally made complete sense.

The year was 1967. Famed American Flower Power spiritual seeker Ram Dass traveled to India to see if there was anything new to learn there about LSD. What would happen if a spiritual master took acid, he wondered? He found out when he gave Indian guru Neen Karoli Baba an unfathomable 900 micrograms of LSD at his behest. The effects were as astounding as they were repeatable: no effects. Zero. None.

How was that possible? In examining the data of various fields with this story in the back of his mind, Henry solved the riddle.

Neen Karoli Baba had spent his life in a state of meditation, he was a clear vessel, a clear mind. He'd dealt with the unconscious clutter that influenced most humans. He didn't suffer any fears, any illusions that manifested in average trippers when the pineal gland was activated. Therefore, his perception of these other realities wasn't filtered through layers of personal and cultural psychology, which Henry determined was the root of hallucinations that comprised most trips.

Henry scribbled this analogy in his journal: *If the pineal gland were a faucet and the vision it produced water, one's psychology would be the filter that adds taste. One never tastes the water as it is.*

Because Neen Karoli Baba had no filter he accessed the hidden dimensions as they actually were and he did this at his leisure. Drugs did nothing for him because he was in control of his brain, or, as he might say, he could open and close his third eye on command. He drank in the pure waters of reality on their own terms. Henry granted that there could still have existed in him physical limitations of the human organism but the psychological problem had been solved. The fact that LSD amped up serotonin levels in the brain, creating topsy-turvy vision in the average person, wasn't an issue for the guru.

Still, that didn't answer how DMT worked. This was the trickier question and it took some months or maybe a day for Henry to find the answer in his expansive underground cell. Shortly thereafter he asked Charles, "Are you ever going to let me go?"

"You can go but you can never leave," came the reply.

"I'm not asking to break my contract, I know that's impossible. I'm asking why you get to go to the surface and I'm trapped here. I didn't sign up to be a prisoner."

Charles' cheeks radiated with the active smile that meant he was joking but not and said, "Prisoner? Henry, we've brought you everything from your home—recreated your home down here for you. We've even given you a jungle in which to vacation. You're hardly a prisoner."

"That's not the answer I wanted to hear."

"I know that. I was you once, remember this. First you feel elated and free. Then the newness of your toys wears off and you feel trapped. But rest assured you will be let out, set up, and compensated handsomely. You will be set for life, believe that, Henry."

"Do you feel compensated, Charles? Where do you live?"

"I live here."

"Why?"

"Because it's home. It's timeless. I like it down here. If duty didn't retrieve me to the surface I'd gladly drown here beneath the mud of other people's busy lives."

"Charles, I never took you for a poet. Do I need to like it as much as you before I'm given the keys to the gate, or am I supposed to hate people, too? Which came first for you?"

"I don't like what I'm detecting in your voice, Henry. Trust me. That is all I ask. Trust me."

Charles turned to make his exit when Henry's voice stopped him at the archway. "Oh, by the way, I've solved that little DMT problem, Charles. Thought you should know. I'll be writing up my report today."

The old man turned back. He had long ago given up on the notion of surprise. This brought him to it.

"It's true. And once your crack staff of technologists engineer this thing to my specs, I know the perfect guinea pig to test it out on."

"Oh?"

"Me. Me, Charles. I take full responsibility." Henry stepped to his mentor emphatically. "No more secret human experiments. No more drugging kids. I need to be a part of this to feel right with myself. It's the moral choice."

Charles looked impressed. Henry told him trust was a two-way street and the old wizard concurred. Silently, but it was there.

Also there... escape.

INTERLUDE
Earth Zero

While the Earth Plane Council dusted off their old warships, one reptilian geared up her breathable suit and trekked out of Dinosaur Chasm, careful not to attract insect attention. She met at a predetermined rendezvous point in what used to be a mainland haunt of the dragon with a friend, a tall, regal shining one who had seen better shine. His phosphorescent skin glowed dully underneath the grime of battle.

They felt safe dealing in the open here as they were unlikely to bump into enemy among the ruins. She handed him what looked like a polished stone flattened on one side. He held the curved end in his palm and squeezed it gently. A hologram sprouted from its center showing an object beyond the sky, an object that did not belong there.

***

I said before, Corey, that prior to this war all races agreed to stop seeking more out there in the universe. This was the notion of Absolute Contentment. If aliens stumbled into them or called out to them in a friendly manner, okay. Welcome to Earth Plane. But none felt the compulsion to reach out or to explore, opting instead to radiate bliss from where they resided.

None except the reptilians, that is.

Reptilians evolved up from an aggressive animal. They had ruthlessness written into their DNA with only a modicum of compassion. Every race had something dark encoded in their fiber that they had to transcend. Coarse anger was the reptilians' shadow side. Through many, many long generations (the average reptilian lifespan prior to the mastery of soul transference was about 800 of our years) they had learned to live in true harmony with their neighbors by not acting out and not repressing. Like all beings of Earth Plane they learned to pay homage to their genetically encoded lesser impulses, celebrating them publicly through art and ritual.

Privately was a slightly altered affair. Privately their collective best-kept secret was that they did monitor the galaxy for incoming beings. They refused to get blindsided by hostiles simply because everything on Earth Plane was peaceful. They did not, however, take any further measures like training a secret army or storing functional warships and caches of weapons the way you might expect. This wasn't really preparation for the worst; it was homage to the dark, as I said.

The reptilians didn't really think these dark days of assault would come nor did they want them. In their heart of hearts they wanted peace. In the recesses of their genes they carried a nearly vestigial yearning for war. This faint echo of the reptiles they used to be was more than satisfied with cosmic voyeurism, but they would only admit this to other species if it were a dire emergency leaving no decent choice. Like today.

***

The shining one stared at the hologram, twinkling eyes unbelieving. Out there, floating between the fourth and fifth moons, was a ship the size of a small asteroid. How long had it been there? Were the people onboard involved somehow or just watching? They had to be involved, covert allies of the insectoids waiting their turn to strike.

The shining one thanked his reptilian friend for this vital information and urged her to have her people join the coalition in this fight. She explained that her people couldn't afford to travel that path, stating, "If we fight now, we may never stop. It is in our blood but not in our hearts. Best kept from beating there."

"What will you do?" the shining one asked.

"We have exploded a new universe. We will terra-form a planet there so that it is suitable to our needs. There we will live in seclusion with our dinosaurs."

"Will you come back?"

She beamed at the shining one with intense love in her eyes. "When we are ready. Do not come looking for us, dear friend."

Chapter 21

By Wednesday afternoon Corey could see why his mother was so frantic. Parents kept calling and calling and the conversations evolved from polite questioning to flat out accusation. These were people he grew up knowing and they suspected him of covering for their sons.

The police refused to get involved yet, which was great news for Corey. Surprising, he thought, given the pact suicide fresh on the town's mind, but protocol is protocol. His protocol was going to change to hanging up on James' mom if she called asking, "Are you sure?" one more time. He felt betrayed by his friends and now by their parents whose trust he thought he'd earned over the years. Sure, he'd cover for his pals if they were in trouble, but not for days. Not this long. In fact, now that he thought about it, he was pissed that their parents and the school and the police and the town at large weren't more concerned than this. What the fuck? If he had kids and they vanished into thin air he'd be kicking doors down to find them. In fact, he'd be kicking his own door down, not just calling to bitch and hurl accusations.

No, fuck it. When his mother stepped out to run errands he unplugged the phone and sat in glorious quietude. It wasn't enough to turn off the ringer because it would go to voicemail and they'd fill it up with their concerns. He was sick of their concerns. Mom forced Dad to lock away the videogames so that his suspension meant something. He didn't care. Just keep the other parents away from him. If they weren't worried enough about their kids to act, why should he bother with them?

Plus, they're gonna show up anyway, right? They're just screwing around. Without me. Thanks, bastards!

Suddenly Corey wished he had videogames to take his mind off his anger. Whatever he was angry about. His head was such a jumble he couldn't remember.

***

9:00pm was beddy-bye time. Doing nothing all day tuck-ered Corey early. He didn't understand how that was but it was. His parents had been both warm and distant at the same time over dinner. For once his mother didn't know what to say to him. Saying nothing was Father's normal M.O.

The night air was chilly and he liked it that way, liked to huddle underneath sheets while the room turned to ice. He opened a window, tuned out his anger and depression; tuned in crickets chirping in shrubs. He could barely hear an audience cheering on the TV downstairs, some God-awful reality show, no doubt. Mom loved those. And then he didn't hear anything. And then he heard his door open.

What time was it?

'Time to get a watch,' he slurred to himself. The door didn't creek slowly, it swung wide and in poured light, bright, blinding, and alive. He wanted to scream, a piece of him, but he couldn't and mostly thought he was dreaming. He controlled the fear with that belief until a familiar bobble-headed avatar scam-pered in.

"You! You fucking get away!" Corey thought he was yelling this but he couldn't be sure. His mouth didn't seem to move, nor did his bowels, which he felt he'd released. If he was yelling no one heard him. No one except the thing at the foot of the bed.

A hint of thought swam steadily in the undertow of the rapids that were his fears: 'Every time it is like this. Being born. Every time.' It didn't sound like something he'd think but it felt like his. It was in there, in his brain, splintered off and observant and whispering.

Next instance—and there was no discernible transition, just the next instance—Corey was fine. The scare, the hurt, the adrenaline, all of it gone tranquil. He could move again and that was good but it was too dark to see. Incidental light sources from outside his window, under the door, and the alarm clock's LCD display rendered his room dim but not invisible. Not like this. His bedroom was incapable of achieving darkness this absolute, which is how he knew he was no longer in it.

Was this still a dream? He was lying down on what felt like a bed, just not *his* bed. Where was he?

You know the answer to that! Came a man's booming voice.

"Who said that?" Corey demanded. He sat up and patted the air around him with his hands like playing pin the tail on the donkey. If someone or something was near him he wanted to have a handle on it before it grabbed him.

"Where are you? Where am I? No, scratch that, I don't care—just bring me home," he called out.

You are home, child, a female voice assured.

"Let me see. Let me see who I'm talking to!" God, this was scary. Most vivid dream he'd ever had.

If that is your choice, the passionless woman intoned.

The lights came on. Corey saw he was sitting on a platform in the center of a large, crowded room.

He scanned the place. Creatures everywhere. Looked like bugs. Giant, miserable insects, ants and mantises, the stuff of a Burroughs novel. Ogling these creatures gave him the distinct feeling of déjà vu. He wasn't terrified in the animal way he had been back at home and he wasn't normal, everyday scary situation scared. He actually felt pretty good about this. Unnaturally good, though, and he recognized that and figured he'd been drugged.

You are not drugged. We sedate the fear reflex of the body by suppressing the amygdala and then we interface with your consciousness. This room is a thoughtform construct. One with which you are familiar.

Corey said, "Isn't the amygdala the queen in *Star Wars*?" Then he waved to the furry ape-man in the back. "Hey, Chewie," he said with a nod and a giggle. "Now I know this is a dream. Yup. A fucked up nightmare where I don't feel scared. That's a new one!"

Two tall, slender beings made of blue radiance flitted over to him in broad sweeps. Their angular faces were completely featureless but they shimmered when they communicated. *Hello, Corey. How are you doing?* One of the beings nodded at him acknowledging that it was his voice in Corey's head.

'But that's impossible. You sound just like James,' he thought.

I am James.

"What are you doing in my head?" Corey scolded.

This is how I talk in this form. Is it not wonderful?

"No. Where's James? Get out of my fucking brain!" The impulse to punch this being in its light face surged and receded before his muscles twitched involuntarily for such a move. 'Oh well,' he thought. 'That's how dreams go.'

This is not a dream.

'That's exactly what a dream would tell me.'

Remember the camping trip. James didn't ask him to remember, he demanded it and on demand, he regained full recall, as if James had waved a magic wand with that sentence. Corey flashed on that gray room Darryl and he woke up in at the point when bug men floated through the wall like hungry ghosts. The experience remained startling, but with his fear suppressed he was better able to observe the images of memory like pictures in a photo album and wonder, 'Huh. Was that really me crying like a baby?'

Stephen and I died on that camping trip, Corey, James explained.

Another voice, that of the light being next to James— Stephen's voice—chimed in: *In death there is life. We learned that. You must come with us soon. There is so much to do.*

"So much what to do? Where's Darryl?"

He is away.

"How did you guys die?"

Hockomock is a portal. In the portal is a subspace farm for experiments. Some of those experiments escaped. When they crossed the barrier they mutated. We bumped into one. We felt no pain, James explained.

We shall never feel pain again, Stephen remarked.

"*Shall*? Really? Death turned you douche? Where's Alex?" Corey asked.

Same as us, he is alive in a new body. The Watchers grabbed his soul before it left its imprint. Same as us, Corey. We are all happy. We are all connected. We are one.

"Okay. That's good."

Join us. James and Stephen extended their glowing blue hands welcoming Corey into their fold. Something about their voices appealed to him. There was a sincerity there, a compassion—even from James—but the robotic elocution left him skeptical.

Corey thought, 'Wait, how did I not see them glowing when the lights were off? Is this a trap?'

It is not a trap, James thought back.

"Your parents are worried about you. You ought to let them know you're okay."

They are no longer our parents.

"There. That's the James I used to know!"

No reaction.

"What, too soon?"

Humor is necessary to a point. This is that point. Come with us when time is aligned. Only Stephen said this. Everyone else was stone. Dozens of heads of varying shape, color, and hue stood in perfect mannequin freeze. James stood likewise. How is this even James, Corey asked himself, and there was no response. It was as if the program had ended and the next one could only start when Corey gave his decision.

"Guys, look: I can't go with you. That's just not something you decide on a whim."

Are you happy? That disembodied female voice asked.

Corey shrugged. "I don't know. Am I happy? Uuuuh.... Is anyone happy? I don't know. But I'd like the chance to figure it out."

Corey's friends lowered their beckoning hands. James said, *You must go back now. You will not remember. We will come for you again.*

"No. I need to remember. I need to tell your parents what happened."

The room shocked to black. Corey jumped up to piss something fierce. He caught himself in the bathroom mirror, a sweaty pale mess. He looked like he'd suffered a night terror but he didn't remember one. That wasn't what woke him. His full bladder did.

For some reason he had that line, "It is Queen Amidala herself," from *Star Wars: Episode 1* looping over and over in his head. It was annoying but he was able to quiet it and fall back asleep in no time.

Chapter 22
Henry

Henry kept what he knew must be the most unprofessional freestyle journal in the history of science. He had listened to the plants—for many hours had listened—silently in a rainforest recreated without the march of insect, screech of bird, or cry of monkey. He listened and he heard.

At first he heard them growing physically, pushing out of the nutrient-rich designer earthen floor toward the artificial sun and precisely timed rains that created a perfectly humid climate. Being so quiet that he could hear the growth of the plants made him giddy. Unprofessional. Meditating brought him out of routine, out of structure, and widened his focus, which had been narrowed by rationalism, professionalism—the humorless trappings of Western thought. This growth in him—his growth with the plants—blended into his writing like a weed and he didn't care. He didn't care because it worked.

After weeks of hearing their physical emergence into the world he began to hear them talk inside of him. They didn't use words, they used feelings speaking through his intuition, and those feelings bubbled to the surface of his consciousness as thoughts, words, and actions that he knew were not his alone. He was not under plant control, but he was under their influence. He blended with them and they guided him like impeccable teachers.

Henry was in school again. The thought made him loopy. He giggled a lot to himself in that rainforest, high on all that life.

The flora talked to him about his own growth. They told him what he must do to regulate and control DMT, to make it purposeful and functional within himself. His Western intellect rendered useful again when time came to parse out the biotech the boys and girls in lab would need to engineer a regulatory device that could accomplish what the plants said was possible. He would give them the shadows of the thing, the specs, and they would turn those specs into the object he would merge with to become... what? The world's first human super computer? A librarian of mind? Virtual time traveler? God?

Henry ignored these vital issues. Whatever form this giant leap for mankind was destined to take would happen because of one small step taken in blissful ignorance. His notes reflected that. Their wunderkind style looked like somebody else's writing, as if the carefree inner child of all mankind had been playing peek-a-boo behind a controlling adult veneer this whole time and that's what adults were. That's who Metis was when he wasn't blocking out awe to playact maturity.

Still, the act of writing linear notes helped him come back to his rational adult self. This depressed him for a spell, but the kid in him was soon forgotten like a great dream. His notes were his only proof that he'd been another person happy with being tiny and more alive than alive.

When Henry received what he needed from his green teachers he kissed his favorite Psychotria viridis on the leaf and moved off campus. He translated what they'd given him into pseudoscientific jargon and later into useful scientific terminology.

Final Entry - Notes for Report

Physics tells us there is such thing as particle/wave duality.

UNTRUE!

- there is only consciousness, which manifests particles. The so-called "wave" is no more a singular thing than the finger that connects nail to hand. - It's all hand!

- "wave" is a description of the distance from oneness to particle.

- *"distance"* means the stretch of information that gives particles structure and inherent action. It's the information superhighway, if you will. (And I will!)
- at root (no pun intended) the wave, the particle, the distance—all maya. Forms represent formless consciousness imagining. We are being imagined. (Imagine that!)
- DMT is chemical that moves the brain to perceive—not waves, but—the one whole consciousness. Normally, brain only perceives the stuff of the world by its sensory organs.

Experience of subjects "under the influence" of heightened DMT appear chaotic and dreamlike to untrained eye.

2 reasons:
1.) Subject's experience is filtered through personal psychological and psychosocial mechanisms that lead to interpretation and hallucination.
2.) Average subject untrained in the art of focus.
- *"Focus"* means picking a place/time to observe & interact in. [Analogous to

staring at random fibers on a patchwork quilt unable to choose which one and unable to make sense of the larger picture of which the fiber is but a fiber (tee-hee).]

Although the above do not apply to shaman & other spiritual adepts, these people are complacent in their vision quests, having settled on interacting in a mere handful of dimensions. Or, sticking to the quilt metaphor, they have seen and culturally claimed some of the pictures and settled there in isolation from the rest of the quilt.

If we are going to up/down load information as thought construct in humans we need to devise a way to:

1.) Focus on target ~~like fiber on quilt in the human patchwork~~ [over-extending metaphor!]

2.) Stimulate target's pineal gland and ~~superimpose~~ divert their "trip" with our signal.

Note: work in Tesla findings here. He didn't die for nothing!

Telepathy is not one brain reading another, it is the chemical switching from particle to "wave" thereby recognizing the one lake of which it is. [watch wordy metaphors!] Information exchange is nonlocal, is instantaneous.

DMT, not hardware, should be mainstay of biotech. [More bio less tech!]

~~We invent things that mimic those capabilities in us we've yet to unlock. Here's one of those discoveries, boys and girls.~~ [Henry: King of Hyperbole!]

Chapter 23

Both Avon parents accompanied Corey to Dr. Olif's office. Dad took off work to support his son and Mom was in high spirits considering her pride-joy was suspended from school and refusing to squeal on his irresponsible friends. All told this wasn't a bad family outing. Corey almost felt good about it like there was a family bond he had long ago dismissed making itself apparent.

Corey took hold of the brass handles to the office building and flung open the doors with might and pleasure. Air rushed at him like a timeless Michael Jackson video. Even though he didn't care for shrinks the essence of the place appealed to him. It had the pasty smell of a new building. The wall-to-wall carpeting also smelled new and muffled the echoes of Mother's clanking heels. Something about the Rosewood Lacquer color scheme felt warm and cozy.

All of that was a nice change for a Thursday afternoon yet Corey wanted out of here as soon as possible. He felt like he was going under the knife, like it was brain surgery, and though he got a kick out of the doctor's goofy style he didn't really know him and didn't trust his ability to relax a sloth let alone a client.

'Should the shrink be more laid back than the patient?' he wondered.

He didn't have long to find out. Dr. Olif saw them to his office not minutes after their butts met seat in the client lounge. He brought them to a different, roomier office that looked more like a den. There was a couch, three chairs, and book shelves filled with tomes, journals, and awards—the knickknacks of professionalism.

The doctor gave a prelim, answered concerns from the folks and from Corey, then asked John and Meg to leave. Come back in an hour. It would be more comfortable for their son.

Secretly, John was giddy for this. It meant lunch with his wife and maybe a reconciliation of sorts. In other words, his own prelim to a long-overdue and passionate course in make-up sex. Hell, if they could fit that into the hour, all the better. He'd bring her to a fancy restaurant with a large, secluded individual bathroom just in case lunch went well.

***

"Now Corey I want you to lie back. Relax. Breathe in deeply through the nose…. Hold it…. Enjoy the moment of fullness…. Exhale through the nose until your lungs are completely empty and really cherish that moment when your lungs are empty. Stay with it for as long as you feel comfortable. Allow yourself to be that emptiness. When you're ready, breathe again through the nose. There's nobody here but us. You are safe."

Corey giggled under his breath at how Olif shed his nonchalant baritone for this soft, condescending tenor. He closed his eyes and breathed as he was told. Olif's vocals drifted into the background and old random thoughts floated to the surface of Corey's mind.

That time he and his pals built the megalithic tree house. He could smell the maple again, hear the hammers and saws.

That time Jenny Shay let him feel her up on a double dare. First time he'd touched a girl. Not much to feel but it was awesome.

That time he wanted a monkey, begged for a monkey, so Dad got him an expensive monkey puppet as a joke. Pissed him off.

The first time he rode a bike with training wheels. Cool as it was, he longed for his Big Wheel with the pull brake.

"I want you to relax and hear my voice, but turn it into your voice. Be present in the moment and talk to yourself. Ask yourself my questions as if they were your own," the doctor instructed.

Corey's memories sank back into the depths as he assumed the doctor's voice internally. There was a visual, too. Or rather, a distinct lack of one. He pictured himself not in a happy place like he assumed he'd be brought to, but in a blank room. Not a room, even, a void.

The doctor's voice felt like his own internal voice but soothing and nonjudgmental. There was no guilt in him. "I want you to go back to last Friday. You wrote a note to your mother. Do you remember writing a note?"

"Yes," Corey slurred.

"Good. What did you write in the note?"

"Going camping. That I'm going camping. With my friends."

"What happens next?"

"I get on my bike and ride out to the... to where my friends are. To meet Darryl and everybody."

"Where did you meet them?"

"They aren't there. Those bastard left me! It was my idea. Can you believe that? They went without me."

"Where did they go without you?"

"Camping."

"Yes, camping. Where? What part of town? Or was it out of town?"

"Just camping. I don't know. I'm not supposed to say. That sounds weird. I can't believe I'm remembering this, or.... No, actually I can't believe I lived this and didn't remember it. How's that possible?"

"Just relax. Don't get caught up in trying to figure that out. We will figure that out later."

Corey heard this instruction in his own voice and giggled out, "The royal *we*."

"You are safe here and you can say anything you want to, okay? Do you understand that."

He nodded a little. "Mm-hmm."

"Good. Now let's walk through it. Just relax and if you can't remember don't force it. You don't need to search your memory or try to fill in the blanks, you understand? Just allow your-self to recall what you can and that's good enough. No pres-sure."

Corey blurted, "I do remember. It's all right here," like a lit-tle boy surprised with himself.

"Excellent," Dr. Olif responded. "Where did they go camp-ing without you?"

"No, they didn't! I found them! They left without me. Why would they do that? But I found them and now we're going camping. All of us."

"Who is there with you?"

"It's Darryl, Alex, James, Stephen and me. James is such a prick. He's talking shit about Darryl's dad. We think he's gonna kill him but he doesn't. And we keep walking. For a long time just walking. You can hear branches crackling in the wind cuz no one wants to talk after James got bitch-slapped."

"It's quiet?" the doctor asked.

"Mmm-hmmm."

"And where are you?"

"Camping."

Dr. Olif's inflection never changed, never showed frustra-tion. "Corey, you said a minute ago you're not supposed to tell where you went camping. What did you mean by that?"

"They don't want me to tell. Not my friends, the people. Voices. I don't know who. There's a woman. I think she's a woman. I can't see her. I'm not allowed to see her but she's there. Talking. I don't remember her from any of the other times. Her voice is weird. I don't know how to put this…. It's everywhere."

Corey intoned the female voice as he relived bits of con-versations. *"You will not remember, child.* But I have to remem-ber. Somebody has to remember. *When the time is right you will remember. Not now….* They're full of shit all the time you know what I mean? They just lie. It's never the time to remem-ber. They just want me to go with them. Fuck that. But she sounds so nice, you know? Like, honest. But still, they harass me in my... in my dreams sometimes. Or at night, or... they come. Somehow. Through a light. They stand in a light in my bedroom in my head, but it's not real. It is and it isn't. Why the fuck do you want me to go with you so bad? *We need you. You're special.* Ah, bullshit. Then just take me already. Fuck."

"Okay, Corey. I'm a bit confused. Let's back up. Who is the woman talking to you? Is she camping too?"

"No. You don't know her. You wouldn't understand."

"What wouldn't I understand?"

"Gaaaah!—Aaaaaaah!" – Corey bolted up grabbing his ears. "What the fuck?!" His head felt like a factory of tiny circular saws chewing through his brain.

"It's okay, Corey. What is it?"

"It's not okay, Doc! There's something else in here! It's inside me!"

"It's okay. We're breathing in—"

"No, Doc! It's something else! Something just fucking jumped into my brain!"

"Are you in pain?"

And just like that the pain was gone.

"Not anymore but this is fucking nuts! Did you do this?" Corey snarled.

"No! No, I wouldn't cause you pain."

Corey paced the length of the couch. "Well someone did," he said. "More than pain. This is fucking nuts, dude... holy shit! You're not gonna believe this but someone just... it was like someone beamed documents into my head. But I mean that happened. I don't mean like I'm crazy. I'm not crazy—which is what every crazy person says, right?—But I'm not! I'm fucking not."

"Okay, okay. Let's focus on calming ourselves. Whatever it was it's over now."

Dr. Olif sat Corey back down and brought him a Dixie cup of water from the cooler outside. Corey gulped it in one shot.

"Better?" the doctor asked.

"I guess. But... why did I see documents?"

"What did you see?'

"It was like Russian or something. Hieroglyphics, maybe. I don't know, I don't understand. They were black and white photocopies. I mean literally documents! Is that normal?"

"No. I don't know what that was. Are you familiar with Philip K. Dick?"

"No."

"He was a writer. He claimed something like that happened to him."

"Was he crazy?"

"Probably. But that doesn't mean you are."

Corey chuckled. "Thanks," he said.

He stared at nothing in particular for an awfully long time. Dr. Olif sat patiently with him. At last he related, "I feel like my memory—what I just said—it's going away. Like seeping back out of me. Christ, what the fuck is wrong with me? Should we try it again?"

"No, that was good for today. You did very well. Why don't we just chat until your parents come back?"

***

"Miss? Excuse me, Miss? Are you okay in there?" The muffled groans fighting against the loud ventilation fan in the women's room at Benjamin's Restaurant sounded like utter pain to the ears of the eighty-five-year-old patron waiting her turn. She shook the door handle a few times but it was locked.

"Just a minute!" a breathless voice hollered from inside. "I'm coming! ... I'm coming!" And then a two-toned primal scream of great relief, his and hers. Quick shuffling. Buttoning. Zipping. Water faucet.

"Sorry about that," Meg Avon told the old woman, barely looking at her as she slipped out of the bathroom, John scampering behind her. They ran out of there laughing before the old lady could form a question.

John thought, 'Sometimes a day off work pays better than the job.'

Meg thought about how good it could be again if they made these little outings more often.

Then they thought about their son's predicament. They left their smiles with the check at the table.

***

Corey's folks didn't know what to make of Dr. Olif's take on the session. How could Corey not remember the camping trip? What horrible thing scarred his psyche? He didn't seem scarred. Seemed normal. Actually, yes, too normal. The daunting truth again gnawed on Meg that these were his best friends missing and something happened and he was there and he seemed way too okay with all of this. The same thought crossed John's mind yet neither vocalized it.

They drove into Raynham to the nearest surviving Friendly's, bought hot fudge sundaes to go, and gorged on the ride home. "You know, Corey, we've been trying to calm your friends' parents and not get the police involved because we don't want this to turn into a media circus but I don't think we can do that anymore."

"I know, Ma. It is what it is."

John shot a glance in the rearview mirror to his precious son who was innocently licking chocolate off the back of his plastic spoon. It was an off-guard moment that brought him back to when Corey was a boy and Daddy was king. "Son," he said.

"Yes, Father?" Corey mocked.

"Do you think it's a little... I don't want to say weird but... a little weird that you're so nonchalant about this whole thing?"

"John, I was just thinking that!" Meg interjected.

"Wow. You two are really on the same page. Glad to bring you together like this. Even shit grows a rose, am I right?"

"Seriously. And watch your language," John reprimanded.

"Yeah, I don't know, Dad. I mean they'll turn up. Come on, it's the guys. I think we're going overboard a bit don't you?"

Meg cut her husband off before he could formulate— "No! Corey, come *on*! These are your best friends! It's been almost a week, now where are they?"

Corey calmly lapped up the sugary goodness clinging to the sides of his cardboard sundae cup. "Didn't the shrink tell you not to yell at me?"

"I'm going to kill him. John?—I'm going to kill him."

"Come on, Meg. He doesn't know. You wanted to bring him to a psychologist and even he says he doesn't know, okay?"

"Pardon me, Mr. I Don't Give A Shit, but why am I the only one in this family who gives a damn that our son is complicit in a fucking crime?"

"Ma, language," Corey deadpanned.

"Listen, you shit. This isn't funny anymore."

"Meg!"

"Tough love, Dad. Let her vent."

"I can't... I just can't. Let me out." Meg scrambled for the door lock.

John swerved to the curb as he slammed on the brakes. "Whoa-whoa-whoa! What the hell do you think you're doing?"

Meg unbuckled and managed the door open. "I'm walking home. I'm done with you boys for now," she said.

John rolled his eyes, tapped a nervous beat on the steering wheel with his finger tips. "Meg, get back in the car."

She slammed the door closed and power-walked away. John paced her with the passenger window down. "Meg, this is ridiculous—get back in the car, come on. You're on Route 44. It's dangerous."

She stopped, turned and leaned into the open window. "John. Listen to me. I'm walking. You know me. You know that means nonnegotiable. I'll deal with you tonight."

And that was that.

"Bye, Ma!" Corey waved to her as John reluctantly drove away. "What a bitch."

"Yeah, but she's our bitch, pal." He drove the length of two mini malls to a stoplight in anxious silence then turned to his son. "I didn't mean that," he confessed. "Your mom's not a bitch. She's concerned. This whole thing is putting her on edge. You would be too."

"Are you?"

"Yes. Of course. But I handle things differently."

"Less bitchy?"

John's laughter cued Corey's. "Something like that," John said. He made a left. "Tonight's going to suck, huh?"

"Not for me, I've got a bed to sleep in. You better make friends with that couch, old man."

They shared another laugh outwardly as they drove by Taunton High. Inwardly Corey churned a stomach full of writhing snakes and John felt lost. He wondered if Meg's volatility was the adult response.

John dropped his boy off at home then doubled back to pick up his wife. He pulled up in front of Meg and opened the passenger side door. She stopped in her tracks and huffed the exhaust fumes of Route 44. She gathered herself and reluctantly climbed in. They both stared straight ahead as John chauffeured her back to the house.

***

"You in jail yet or what?"

"What?"

"Jail?"

"Who is this?"

"Lina?"

"Igasho?"

"Duh. Yeah. Corey? … Corey Avon?" she mocked.

"What are you doing calling me? Isn't that breaking some sort of chick protocol?"

"What? Were you going to call me? Because my phone hasn't been ringing and I think we still have a date tomorrow but I can't be sure."

"Yeah, I have a date tomorrow. With your mom. Is she around?"

"Ass. She's not even going to be home. You'll just have to make do with me unless you can't handle the pressure."

"That, young Lina Igasho, is all I've been handling."

"Oh. Yeah, I guess so. You want to talk about it?"

"Not really. I'm all talked out. But tomorrow, maybe."

"Good. I've got to give you my address. You're coming over. I have something to show you."

"What about the movies?"

"Forget the movies, that was a ruse."

He laughed, figuring she was kidding, and asked, "What time?"

"Seven."

"No, later than that. I'm grounded. Like, nine? I can sneak out at nine."

"Wow, you really are in big shit aren't you?"

"Dude, I was suspended! My parents aren't crack-heads; of course they're gonna punish me."

"Nine-ish, then, or nine-thirty or whatever. Looking forward to it."

"Yeah. Should be good times. Let me get a pen…. What's your address?"

She hesitated a moment, then, "First I need you to promise me something."

"Anything."

"Not with your dick, I'm serious."

"I'm serious too! Name it!"

She paused again to release a heavy, burdened sigh. "You won't freak out?"

"I won't freak out, just name it."

"No, that was the promise, not to freak out."

"Oh. Okay. Whatever it is I promise not to freak out."

"Cool."

"But you're not gonna tell me what it is are you?"

"Tomorrow. Hope you like surprises. Hope you like big ones."

'Hope *you* like big ones,' his penis thought. His mouth continued with small talk.

INTERLUDE
Earth Zero

One advantage Earth Plane had over the invaders was its size. You cannot imagine how long this roughly rectangular mass was. It was practically a galaxy unto itself. Even with all the bug people in the world—and the aliens *had* all the bug people in the world!—no one could expect to execute a hostile takeover in a handful of battles. This was the type of challenge the aliens lived for.

The aliens weren't a hive-minded race like the insects, though they might as well have been, such was their loyalty to Leader. No one fought for control, not even conspiratorially. In fact, if enemy ever caught Leader, his people would fight to the last to get him back. No one would rest until that mission was accomplished. No one would jealously steal his rank and leave him a prisoner of war.

Leader enjoyed the powers of a dictator but didn't suffer the same ego needs. He didn't have a god complex and nobody starved under his rule. He got things done, that's all. He was his function, which was another trait in common with the hive mind. Perhaps this is why he remained in direct contact with the disembodied Hive Queen stored, as she was, in a cylinder infused with the wall next to his bed.

***

Earth Planers cloned their own but they also pro-created through natural biological processes. These aliens only cloned. They had polluted their organic home planet so abhorrently that the males lost their active sperm count. This was ironic given the cultural demand that they live in giant families, but by the time sex stopped producing babies, they had developed cloning and just didn't care.

A good many eons later found the masses continuing to divide themselves along gender lines even though their genitalia had atrophied. Their appetite for larger and larger family grew when they choked themselves off their own planet and into the colossal war machine they constructed for planet hop-raping, but by then, functioning sexual organs were lawfully deemed a privilege reserved for the elite.

Leader was the pinnacle of the elite and was most definitely attracted to the Hive Queen's energy. Not a day passed when he didn't talk to her through the clear glass that housed her. She, too, was now her function, her essence running the etherputer that killed her people, her friends, her planet. She had grown fatigued and depressed, saddened by the energy she had become and the evils she was forced to do. The last thing she wanted was to converse with this pirate but it was her only hope of escape. She thought maybe she could convince him to stop his crazy war and live with them in peace. When it became clear this wouldn't happen, she thought maybe he'd slip up and she could flee, get word to the people of Earth Plane that the insects were not to blame—she was not to blame—the true criminals hid between moons by another sun.

If only there were a way to break free. If only there were a way to regain control of her precious bodies. She waited for an epiphany while the energy of her gave life to killing machines.

Chapter 24

On Friday Meg became the reluctant informant on Corey telling his missing friends' parents everything she knew (more like everything she didn't know), realizing the implications for her son, for her family, for their town. If these boys didn't stumble home tonight, there would be a media frenzy by Monday.

Missing teens. The boy who was there. What does he really know? Did he do it? Of course he did. He killed them and his parents covered it up. And then when the police figure out that's not what happened, there will be no public apology from the media. They were just doing their job. Their job was not to investigate; their job was to tell a story that garnered ratings for their advertisers. If they could tie it in with the school jock death dive of yesteryear all the better.

News was money, nothing more. Meg understood this.

Corey blocked out the feeling that these were his last days of freedom. He didn't contemplate jail, but pictured hours of grueling good cop/bad cop power play in a smoky office tucked away in the police station. There would be one yellow light bulb dangling from the ceiling above the metal table to which he'd be handcuffed. A pair of blue collar moustaches would take turns extracting information from him while suits recorded the whole thing behind a two-way mirror. Television and movies played the scenario so often that it had to be right.

Certain this was his future he felt no remorse sneaking out of his house at nine. He hadn't done this since he was a kid running from home, tired of being strong-armed into doing chores. It was run or put his toys away. But eyeballing the apple tree out his window, he recalled that its soft branches had elasticity against his tiny body. He wasn't sure they would now support his mature frame.

Regardless, he leaped from his second-story window to the tree with lemur grace. He landed safely on a thick branch and scaled his gnarled old friend to the bottom. He brushed himself off and checked his elbows and forearms for scrapes. Nothing major so he tiptoed to the cellar's bulkhead and gingerly yanked it open—the hardest part of the crime. That thing was wobbly and noisy and almost impossible to secure in the open and locked position without accidentally letting go and slamming it shut. He did make a bit of a clang but not enough to hear inside the house.

"Where's my bike?" he muttered under his breath. His glorious rusting Scwhinn Rocket wasn't where he always left her but he couldn't risk fumbling for the dangling light cord to search the basement. What if he tripped on something or cut himself on a jagged edge waiting for a victim in the dark? What if he found the light but Mom or Dad noticed it on underneath the door in the pantry?

Fuck.

He squeezed his hands manically unsure what to do. Yellow from the moon and streetlamps beamed on something reflective by the tattered leaf bags of musty winter clothes enough to cause a red glint in his periphery.

'My bike!' his inner Pee Wee Herman exclaimed. He grabbed Old Faithful, wheeled her up the concrete steps, and inched the bulkhead back into place with master stealth. Then he pedaled to Lina Igasho's in the black and blue night, obsessively ruminating over the fact that in all his years since training wheels he'd never put his Rocket in that corner where he just found it. He didn't remember doing it this time either. He didn't remember when last he had ridden Old Faithful. He didn't remember a lot of things and like those things, he shrugged this off in due course.

Chapter 25
Henry

Final Entry - Notes for Report

3rd eye opens Everything/everywhere is available.

- Pineal gland siphons every-thing/everywhere to a manageable few things/locations, sometimes superimposed over each other. That information pools in the right hemisphere of brain.
- Observer's thought interferes, collides, and creates a logical or illogical picture.
- Reverse feedback loop to subvert interference and control vision.

***

Henry's body accepted the prototypical implant and it worked flawlessly. The unconscious collective of Man was one pressure point away from becoming the ultimate information field inside of him. This nano instrument literally in hand, he could also transfer and retrieve data with other human brains just as the project demanded. Mr. Lab Rat was prepared to run his scientists through their maze.

With a few taps to the left palm he activated the energy channel of his subtle body—a chakra—that flowed to the brain where energy pooled in the right hemisphere. That energy was like a pure will to seek without intention, like a bloodhound that received its scent track from the left hemisphere—essentially whatever Henry focused on—then sniffed out its answers through the pineal gland. The pineal received instant, precise feedback from the underlying continuum in which all memories of all people who ever walked Earth pulsed and churned and begged for a receiver to know them again.

Experiences lived wanted to be relived again and again. He used the pineal gland like a flashlight, shining it on whichever memory moth he desired, causing it to fly into his light. The life experiences of the people he concentrated on played out in his mind's eye and stored in his brain as if his own memory. He was the super computer at the center of the human internet but he was so much more.

***

Henry knew the next phase of the official project would be to invent a quantum computing system that could mimic the brain/chakra system he had exploited without evolving into a sentient machine. It would nevertheless supplant Henry and the need for a human controller. He knew this because he extracted it from Charles as he slept.

Henry made other plans.

He compiled a list of secret society names throughout history, of famous, infamous, and untold figures; of popes of monks of lamas; of chieftains of shaman of gurus; of messiahs of biblical writers of mystics; of artists of alchemists of scientists; of politicians of warriors of dissidents. He stole what they knew. Their secrets lived in his brain. Secrets of post modernity; secrets of antiquity. The secrets of Charles.

Charles' greatest secret—the one that kept him an alive and vigorous rat chewing through the corridors of power—was a real mind-fuck for Henry. He saw that there truly was a UFO crash in Roswell, New Mexico in 1947 and that Charles, about a decade older than Henry assumed, had been a young military doctor at the time called in to autopsy three alien corpses. And the aliens really did look like diminutive gray people with bulbous heads and outrageous eyes, just like what marginalized citizens reported being abducted by.

He saw Charles' frustration with keeping the alien secret, how he turned to booze and sex, and eventually gave those up for an addiction to power itself. If he couldn't spill the secrets he would become the embodiment of secrets. Not just their guardian but the man who walked into the room and you knew he knew something great and terrible by the shiver you felt at what lurked behind his gentle smile. This was a conscious act on his part. Charles owned this alien mystery and he tried everything he could to learn about it. He tried open contact and failed. He tried aiding the beings by monitoring their activity on American soil and cleaning up after them. Still, no olive branch and no declaration of war.

Then—ah, the true origin of the human internet—Charles tried communicating with the aliens via messages implanted in the minds of abductee. No answer. No answer until a few years ago.

The first ever communication from the gray beings came through an African American man, a Tauntonian, with a lifetime of abductions. One night after his military handlers fished him out of Hockomock he spoke to them. They would normally find him lying in tall grass unconscious. Then they'd deliver him to local mind-controlled intermediaries waiting by the gate of Castle In The Tank, whose job it was to tuck him back into bed. He'd arise in the morning with no recollection that he had been abducted by aliens and returned by humans. But this night his eyes were open and he had a message to deliver to the one in charge. To Charles.

That message?—Bring us Corey Avon at midnight on December 21st 2012 or suffer untold consequences.

Henry watched this play out and felt Charles' vexation, but also felt his own feeling of betrayal that the aliens were real and he never shared this. Of all the secrets Charles did leak, this one never spilled out of him. The military-industrial complex used aliens as a smokescreen for secret projects and as the ultimate recruiting tool. During the Cold War, they disseminated false stories about Area 51 and other previously unheard of facilities to ferret out Russian spies who might take an interest. Henry saw that an associate of Charles—a crafty psychologist, a Company man—devised a room full of cabinets at Langley Air Force Base said to house UFO files. This room was strictly off limits to anyone without a need to know and yet everybody knew about it. It was the ultimate temptation. It was the ultimate loyalty test.

Fraudulent alien stories were utilized as cover for everything else and yet underneath that surface... there were aliens. Son of a bitch, there *were* aliens!

And that? That wasn't even the mind fuck for Henry. The really confounding piece of it, the part that made him wish he could take off virtual reality goggles and shake away what he'd learned because it was just a game after all, was that at midnight on December 21st 2012, Charles did not deliver the young boy named Corey Avon as instructed by actual aliens. Did not deliver the boy to the Grays because he figured they had to be bluffing or else they'd just take him themselves. In fact, Charles realized their impotence early on when he learned that these beings never extracted anyone from their bedrooms or vehicles—the abductees showed up at portals around the world of their own volition.

Or was it their own volition?—Because they never remembered going anywhere in the morning. Entire swathes of an abductee's life were cut down to weird dreams and sleep paralysis.

Charles hypothesized that the aliens could exert an influence on their subjects but not blatantly pluck anyone from their lives. Obviously this Corey kid was immune to their mesmerizing call, and if they couldn't retrieve the boy they needed, then

Charles had an upper hand. In what, he did not know—but if he could take The Interconnectivity Project to the next level then perhaps he'd never have to find out. Perhaps he could exert his own influence over large populations, counteracting the alien thought virus.

Did a tiny lie have wings like a butterfly? Could he stave off a hostile alien takeover by agreeing to deliver Corey Avon to them and then not doing it? Given the obviousness of the date for delivery, there must be a window of opportunity for these aliens to do something here in a few Earth hours, or perhaps even minutes, on December 21st, 2012. What if he kept them waiting? What if the window closed because the Gray people arrogantly assumed the goods were coming?

What if Charles took a gamble with the fate of humanity for our own good?

And so he did and so he was correct and so he would never tell anyone about this. Instead, he disinformed the right people with a beefed-up truth about his heroics in solving and counter-acting the alien agenda that sounded like an action/adventure plot wherein he bought humanity at least another hundred years. With that lie as momentum he received funding for his black budget experiment, The Interconnectivity Project. with the aim of permanently staving off the alien influence.

Of course the hundred years projection was as much a lie as his heroics. He still didn't really know what these beings were capable of, but nobody else needed to know all of that. They just needed to know they would be ringing in the New Year with their friends and family and their political system safely in place thanks to Charles.

And when next the aliens got word to him through the same man in Taunton, Charles would learn one more thing that no one else needed to know: humanity was being given a sec-ond chance. They still needed Corey Avon but not at the portal in Hockomock. They needed him in a sensory deprivation cham-ber on the roof of the human lookout post, Castle In The Tank.

They needed him in the wee hours of the morning. They needed him for a new deep space planetary alignment.

Who the hell was this kid?

Charles had surveillance on him twenty-four seven. If there was anything overtly special about the Avon family it was impossible to detect. One thing that stood out about Corey, though, was that the Tesla Dream machine had no effect on him and he exerted greater influence over his best friends than the coil. He brought them to Castle. They played near there. They built a tree house there. Why couldn't the aliens scoop him up on their own?

None of this made sense to Charles and he was really good at making sense of things. Knowing this, he needed to tell someone. He needed a worthy partner. He needed Henry. But even then... even then he held onto his secrets like a miser. He had subsumed them as his identity. They were what made him the respected and feared enigma, the invisible hand guiding not the destiny of one nation but of all mankind. No, it turned out Charles didn't need a partner. He'd been wrong on that count. What he needed—and needed soon—was an impeccable replacement. He was getting on in his years and there was no conquering death.

Now, having learned all of this, having experienced Charles' journey through his own eyes, Henry rendered the old keeper of secrets obsolete. And then the good doctor ended him.

Death came to Charles swiftly and expectedly. He had groomed Henry, guiding him to this day, but did not factor in how crudely his apprentice would end his life: a pillow to the face in the night, smothered like *Cuckoos Nest*. No goodbyes. No apologies. No majestic final soliloquy. Just the inhalation of fabric, orthopedic foam, and dust mites; the feeble screams and weak struggle of a frail old man's body wanting to live in spite of the soul inside who welcomed final release.

Charles' body shut down in under four minutes. Henry did not consider this murder, he considered it checkmate on the king by a pawn.

Just as Charles had planned.

***

Henry's brain collected thought data of people living and expired, as intended. But, his mind collected the emotional pollution of the people whom he had stolen. This was an unforeseen consequence of viewing lives. You don't view them, he found out, you relive them. You osmote them whole and they become you in layers.

He internalized the contemplation of the Buddha and the compassion of the Christ. Equally, he internalized the sick fetishes, the repressions, the tortures, murders, and rapes, the guilty unconscious begging and the psychotic indifferences of some of his other subjects, like Genghis Khan, Josef Mengele, and the Zodiac Killer. Their intelligence writhed in him. So did their demons.

The changes in Henry were instant, new and alive and real. Each life he plucked from the flux of human story became a layer of his personal self. Reliving and becoming people was not the dry psychic data transfer he and Charles had hypothesized. Storing documents in human brains was as mechanical and predictable for the person receiving them as for a desktop computer. They'd feel pressure in the skull, often a short-lived thunderclap headache, and the strange hallucinatory visual of files flickering through their mind's eye, which would often make them fear for their sanity. Memory transference, on the other hand, was actually *experience* transference. It entailed reliving the visual and emotional content of the moments retrieved—and not in real time. In the hair of a second. It was a punch to the gut every time but each punch made Henry stronger.

Such an intelligent beast was Henry that the only thing he could not understand was his new nature. Neither could his keepers. Without Charles there to overrule them they released him back into the world of the normal to work on a series of new Interconnectivity Project-related drug-tech schemes targeted at the Eurotrash discothèque scene in Lower Manhattan—projects he had rendered moot by his new supreme existence. He did as he was told, biding his time until the new deep space planetary alignment. His military handlers would never know this.

Still, some of the higher-ups suspected he was too dangerous to let live but too complete to destroy. He was the heir apparent to knowledge that would keep humanity safe from alien invasion. Keep him happy but monitor his every move twenty-four hours a day.

Henry knew his freedom was more like a mobile cage and so he acted with extreme grace. He acted like a team player. He acted like a charming vampire living in a world of angry food and this was easy to pull off because ultimately he and the shadow establishment he worked in had the same goal: to preserve the global status quo through the delayed coming endgame. They only differed on who would be master when gravity yanked dust back to Earth and slow evolution carried on. And only he knew that this difference of opinion existed. And only he saw pawn taking king again.

Checkmate.

Chapter 26

Corey's heart thumped faster than his feet pedaled when his eyes caught the dull yellow lamp glow illuminating Lina Igasho's living room from the street. She lived in the front apartment of a converted Victorian house. The exterior held nothing special for the eye: white with black shingles, could use a fresh coat of paint. What was special was the silhouette of the girl walking in and out of window frame inside.

Was this really a date? No car in the drive. Were they going to make out while her folks were about the town? Or were they already too familiar for that? Too jokey? Too friendly? Had they prematurely crossed the line into "just friends" before giving something more a chance?

Dread.

Closer and closer the lighthouse drew his vessel, its siren playing peek-a-boo and singing a tune meant for him. In all likelihood, he thought, she's still getting dressed, a manic flurry of clothing and makeup and last minute decisions. She must have been as nervous as he—more so. She was the one with freaky secrets.

A flash of embarrassment exploded from the gut and consumed him. What kind of eighteen-year-old rides a bike to his first date? What mature older man sneaks out of his room and jumps a tree to make that date? How could this be anything other than a night of galling disappointment for either of them?

His brain ordered him to turn around while his feet pedaled furiously toward the light. For a moment he lost his balance and nearly wobbled into a parked Buick but he reflexively cleared his mind and gut, conspiring, as they were, against his heart. He made his arrival at the stoop of his new fascination, popped the kickstand, straightened himself, tucked his shirt, took a breath, and went to the door for a knock. It opened before knuckle met oak and there Lina stood, these words vibrating on her perfect, bare lips: "Don't be so nervous, dude. I'm just a chick."

"Hi, Corey. Welcome to my home," he immediately countered.

"Oh right. Welcome, Dracul. Won't you please come in for a bite?"

Corey stepped into her living room and plopped down on the couch. It felt like the least firm thing on the planet and nearly ate him alive. He had to pull himself up and resettle just to not bend funny.

"Make yourself at home."

"Thanks."

"Tea?"

"What?"

"Would you like some tea?"

"Would I like some tea? Are you serious?"

"I like tea."

"I'm a dude."

"Ah. I see. I don't have any O'Doul's."

"Blaaaaah—that stuff's ass."

Corey wiggled out of his jacket. "I'm actually fine, thanks. I'm not big on liquids," he said.

"Plastic sheets?" she asked.

"Something like that." He half smirked at her, a repressed sexual thing. It wasn't often that he made such a fast laidback connection with anyone let alone the hip new cute girl.

Lina swept into the kitchen and poured steaming water into a mug with soothing chamomile. No milk or sweetener. Spoiled the purity.

"You want anything at all?" she hollered.

"No thanks…. Neat house, Lina," he hollered back. She came out to the living room with her tea. "You like it?" she asked, unsure of his sarcasm.

"Yeah. It's very… Victorian." He pulled the word out of his ass but he really did admire the place given what he'd scoped from the couch. He even liked the smell, which surprised him. Normally he cringed at the scent of other friends' homes, but not this one. This one smelled faintly like the rose bushes his aunt grew in summer.

"Victorian? Hmm… yeah, I guess it is. My mom's kind of into that look," she said admiring the place herself.

"Cool. So whatcha wanna do?"

"My, aren't we impatient? You have somewhere to be?"

"No, I was just… I didn't mean anything, just asking."

She glared at him an uncomfortable few seconds. He saw the contemplation in her eyes. She had an agenda for him but didn't know how to approach it or if she should. Her face darted forward in a micro impulse, her mouth about to speak, but she held back, clamping teeth the white of dentist dreams on her bottom lip.

He found himself urging her softly, attempting to put her out of her struggle. "Just tell me what it is," he said.

Her eyes met him. "It's not that simple."

Nothing came next and he didn't know what they were talking about, but in case he missed the point he didn't admit this.

"You like board games?" she asked.

"They're okay."

"Yeah, everything kind of sucks with two players."

"Not Ouija boards."

"I don't have a Ouija board."

"What do you have?"

She hesitated, fighting one last time not to blurt what she inevitably did: "I wrote a book about you. There, I said it."

Corey chuckled uneasily. "Okaaaay…."

"I haven't finished it yet."

"You seriously wrote a book?"

"Yes."

"About me?"

"Yes."

"You do see the impossibility of that don't you?"

Lina drew a sip of tea. "Most men would be flattered or creeped out."

"Well if I believed you that'd be one thing."

"You think I'm pulling your leg, Mr. Avon?"

"I hope so."

"Come on over to my bedroom, I want to show you something."

"Let me guess: a book?"

She stood up, grabbed his hands and tugged him to his feet. She said, "Just come on," and led the way.

She didn't let go the fingers of his left hand. They remained weakly locked as she guided him upstairs. Her elusive touch made him feel comfortable. It was as if getting to know each other would be a mere formality because, really, they already knew, already had been with one another for so long that the memory had disintegrated. Seeing her again kicked up dust and that was love. Whether true or not, he felt this strongly and knew she did, too. That should have freaked him out— especially the L word. It didn't. And *that* freaked him out but he played it cool.

Corey scanned the family portraits and various framed photos that papered the walls and hid on end tables throughout her home. He took that scene in then trained his eyes on Lina's firm ass just in time to stop at her door, have her turn around, and catch him. He knew he was caught, so did she, but she didn't call him on it. She smiled a little, puffed out a one-breath giggle and was flattered but on a mission.

"Here you go," she said. "Welcome to the palace."

She opened the door. Corey stepped through first. She followed, closing the door behind her. The light was already on and it was bright in here. Lot's of pinks and yellows—far more girlie than he'd expected.

"What do you think?" she asked.

"It's nice. You're actually clean."

"Go figure…. Have a seat."

He dropped down and bounced on the creaky edge of her sharply made bed. "You mind if I take my shoes off?" he asked.

"Have at it." She rummaged through a pile of papers and journals on the bookshelf framing her desk.

He kicked off his sneakers and flopped backwards onto the queen-size mattress, legs dangling off the side. "Yup," he said, staring at the ceiling, "this is comfortable."

She found what she'd been hunting for and told him to make room. He scooted his torso over so that he lay properly, lengthwise, on the bed and she pounced onto her belly next to him.

"You've got a lot of books," he noticed.

"Well this is the one you should read. I didn't just write it about you, I wrote it for you." She almost handed it to him but yanked it out of his grasp. "One thing: This is completely embarrassing for me. I mean this is a big deal. It's off the top of my head. I mean I didn't rewrite it or anything, obviously, so…." He thought her trailing off was his cue to reach for it again but again she snatched it back—"Please don't freak out, Corey. That would totally fuck up my day."

He smiled and nodded and mouthed the word *okay* like he understood the pressure she felt. With that she relinquished the voluminous notebook to him. He opened to the first page, the introduction, and couldn't believe she'd written an introduction to her personal diary about him, who she'd obviously had a major crush on since Monday. Maybe earlier. Maybe Alex told her all about him before they met.

Corey laughed as he critiqued. "'Do your job?'—Are you serious?—'Pay attention. Be the hero. Die to live.'"

He looked up his nose at her. "What's 'liminal' mean?—You sure you got the right guy?"

"Oh, it gets better," she said.

He thumbed through what at first glance appeared to be a science fiction fantasy tome written in longhand with his name peppered throughout. He closed it and turned on his side facing her. "So when you said you wrote a book you meant you wrote a *book*."

"That's what I meant."

"And it isn't finished."

"No."

"How long is this?" He flipped through the pages to the end but there was no indication.

"It's just a journal so I don't have them numbered yet, but when I type it I will."

"Well take a guess. What would you say, like a hundred and fifty?"

"More," she said.

He stopped talking and skimmed a random page. "You know a lot of big words," he said, truly impressed.

"That's really not the point," she huffed under her breath.

"We met like a week ago, right?"

A sparkle flickered in her eyes. "It's coming to you," she said.

"So you're telling me you wrote over a hundred and fifty pages about me—not like a love thing but just a story—in a week? Why would you do that?"

"It's not coming to you."

"So you're telling me you wrote a hundred-and-fifty-page story and you left the hero's name blank until you met me. So I'm like your hero or something."

"Getting colder."

"So you're telling me…." He sighed deeply, feeling stupid, unable to decode her riddle. "What are you telling me?—That your mom, the psychic, knew me in a past life and is dictating to you a story about me from then? Plus I'm your hero."

She winced. "Warmish but colder."

"But I am your hero, right? Damn, at least give me that."

"You appear to be, yes. Book's not finished."

"So I can turn. Like Vader. Dude, I'm totally Vader! This is awesome!"

"You still don't get it do you?"

"You wrote a book about me! That's totally fucked up!" She punched his arm. "In a good way! Not like you're a psycho! ... Are you?"

She sat up and spelled it out for the nitwit. "I wrote a book about you before I ever met you—before I even moved here—that's the fucked up part!"

"Oh. Well that's not fucked up, that's not possible."

"There it is."

He sat up, put an arm around her shoulder. "Okay there it is but that's not possible. I mean you could have been writing about—"

She shrugged his arm off and chastised, "Dude, shut up, your name is Corey Avon, no one else's name is Corey Avon, the book is about you, deal with it." She muttered this at such velocity that he recoiled and laughed. She gave up the angry pretense, laughed with him, and followed his lead back to lying side by side, heads propped on elbows, journal betwixt them.

"Is your mom really a psychic?" he asked.

"Yes."

"Then you are, too."

"I didn't think so. But this is... I mean if this qualifies then yeah I guess... I guess I am."

"You sound like you're gonna cry."

And she did cry. Not a faucet of tears but enough to admit *I'm vulnerable with you.*

"Am I a freak?" she asked.

He moved the journal behind him, inched over to her, rubbed her back and held her, this comfortable stranger who had written a book about him. "You are a freak. You're totally a freak. But you're my freak."

She laughed through her tears and thanked him. He went to kiss her on the forehead but she moved so that their lips met.

He trembled then, nervous that this was so right so fast. She pulled back and gazed into his eyes, fishing for what he wasn't saying.

Her face practically glowed with that perfect smile. She leaned in and breathed into his left ear, "I know. I'm right there with you."

She kissed him more and he her and their tongues danced to the rhythm of their hearts.

He whispered, "I will protect you." The words came out of him like an involuntary spasm.

"Why did you just say that?"

"I don't know."

Corey internally cursed himself for ruining the moment. Lina reached behind him, grabbed the journal, and opened it to the final four words of the last page where she'd left off. She pressed her thumb to the part she wanted him to read and held the book aloft:

I will protect you.

He huffed in disbelief like she had performed a magic trick. "This is insane," he said.

"It's our lives," was all she could come back with.

In the ruins of the previous moment evolved a new one more passionate and less scripted than the last, filled with kisses and touch and anything to erase the dizzying confusion. Anything to express the truth that had become them.

They were for each other.

INTERLUDE
Earth Zero

From the blackest pits of the ocean they rose, scattering mers, amphibs, and their fish flocks every which way. Out of the frozen mountaintops they blew into the sky forcing lion gnomes and long-haired squatch to abandon their territory indefinitely. From the grainy dunes of striped deserts they shimmied to the sky, congesting the atmosphere with sandstorms for miles around. Oval shapes, diamond shapes, and giant charcoal triangles. These were the death tech of a treacherous era no one wished to revisit, yet here they all were, armed to the teeth with beams and cannons that could open up those insect craft like sardine cans.

Though they were grossly outnumbered by the insectoids, their craft were nearly identical in maneuverability and firepower. They were steered by thought and could bank right-angle turns, could stop and accelerate on a dime, could shoot off at breakneck speeds without breaking anyone or anything inside the craft. None were remote controlled, for eliminating deadly consequences drained war of its meaning, which inevitably generated the lazy mistakes that spelled loss.

The Earth Planers were not going to devolve into warring people despite this fight. They swore oaths not to let what must be done now become them again. To that end, they relented on their original take-no-prisoners agreement and equipped as many of their fighters with soul catchers as they had manufactured, an act of compassion their ancestors would never have performed. They would do their damnedest to capture each and every insect they murdered and give them new bodies when the inevitable truce came.

It only took one dogfight to see that the insect people had no souls. At first the surface dwellers thought their equipment was malfunctioning but after a few of their own were killed and rescued the clear fact was these insectoids they thought they knew were not alive. Epiphanies fell into place from there.

Why was this attack from the insects so precise and unforeseen?—Because they were the drone bodies of one mind.

What happened to that mind?—It was either compromised by the intelligence on that alien craft or it was allied with the intelligence.

Well, the reptilians didn't speak of the craft until the battle was raging so it must have just arrived here. Therefore, the aliens must have compromised the hive mind.

Ah, but wait a minute. If the reptilians saw this craft sooner would they have spoken of it? Searching the heavens for potential enemy was their quarantined secret. What if they had another deeper secret? What if they wanted war to come to Earth Plane? What if they were the ally of these invaders? Is that why they refused to stand by their fellow Earth Planers?

Yes, that must be it.

Earth Planers didn't have enough resources to fight this war and hunt down answers from reptilians cowering in their artificial universe. They resolved to wait until they destroyed the alien menace. After that they would agree on a solution to the reptilian question. Complicity begot serious consequences. Sometimes, eternal ones.

Chapter 27

Corey didn't stay to finish the book and Lina wasn't lending it to him until she completed writing it. He wanted to devour the thing but he didn't pester her about it as she clearly felt shy and exposed over the ordeal. He just thought it was cool. He chalked it up to a psychic thing. Lately it was all too easy to brush off the strange.

She asked him about that—about how he could just go with the flow like this in the face of not only the book but his missing weekend and his missing friends and the probability that cops would be on him soon. He shrugged and said, "They'll turn up. It's the guys. They're fucking with us," as if that answered it.

"You're so laidback you should be the one from LA," she told him. And then she admitted that she had been the disembodied voice who yelled for the bully's attention in the hallway at school, setting Corey up to knock the bastard into next week. He rolled his eyes, laughed proudly and thankfully, and kissed her. He kissed her without concern for whether she'd mind. He knew. For once with a girl, he knew.

They explored each other's mouths again and were intimate in ways neither of them had ever been. They weren't physical ways, necessarily, though some of them played out in the tickles of the flesh. Warm waves of spiritual craving pulsed from the cores of them in beats. It was as if this union were the right and perfect answer to questions unspoken and perhaps unspeakable.

Who was this girl in his arms? Why did he feel such affection, such great and sudden love for her?

On the bike ride home Corey's brain was so jumbled with these thoughts he couldn't think at all. He decided instead to take in the night. He loved gliding in the cool breeze like this up and down vacant streets. A checklist of the oddities that had become him flashed through his mind: 'Let's see: suspended, hot girl psychically writes about me, and by this time Monday I'll be a prison bitch for murdering my friends and dumping them in Hockomock.'

"Hockomock!" he blurted to the crickets. He stopped gliding and pedaled fast, realizing he'd finally remembered where they went last weekend. Not just the swamp but roughly the path they took. He didn't care if his folks caught him sneaking back in—this was new and vital information. This was his salvation and hopefully that of his friends.

As he rode he felt a pressure building in his head. Was it his skull or his brain? He didn't know but it felt like a head cold ballooning in there. He squeezed the hand brakes, skidded, and hopped the sidewalk. He turned down Church Street and fell off his bike to someone's cold lawn. He lay there fetal, mashing both of his temples with his palms but the pressure grew worse. He felt like an aneurysm was going to explode in his forehead and he was going to die.

Images flickered behind his eyelids, which were sealed tight from wincing. The images were documents like those he'd seen in Dr. Olif's session, except they were not being loaded into him, they were peeling out of him. He tried to focus on the content and not the knives in his skull. In so doing, he realized they weren't documents at all. They were memories. His memories. Memories of his friends and that horrid, sunny day in the middle of the night in the center of the swamp.

The images flew by at such a rate that he didn't have time to feel anything about their revelations. There were his friends. There was death. There was a monster. There were aliens. There he was back in bed.

Corey's face ran flush and he might have vomited had he not forced himself to splinter off from the pain, and from the experiences being vacuumed out of him, to execute a task: get to the door. He thrust himself to unsteady feet and staggered to the decrepit entrance of the unlit house where he had crash-landed. He needed to pound a fist on the old wood paneling but the screen door was locked, so he slapped at the wall until his hand found the doorbell. He kept it pressed and a light came on. A dark figure approached and eyeballed him through the peephole.

"Can I help you?" an elderly man's voice wheezed.

"I... I'm having a problem. Can I use your phone? Please. It's an emergency."

"Oh, my. Please, come on in!"

Corey heard several locks unfasten before the door creaked open and he was nose deep in the white chest hairs of a withered elderly Irishman wearing striped boxers, blue slippers, and mauve bathrobe. "Watch your step," said the old man, pointing to the fact that Corey had to step up to get into the house. "Phone's around the corner on the left-hand side of the dish cabinet. You on drugs?"

"No," Corey said brushing past the man to the phone. He doubled over, squeezing his head as hard as possible while debating momentarily: Call 911 or call home? Was this a *Get me to the hospital* situation or a *Mom will fix this* situation?

"Who are ya calling?" the man inquired.

Corey turned to answer and as he did, the pain went away. So did the room. So did the man.

So did consciousness.

PART TWO

Merrily, Merrily, Merrily, Merrily

Chapter 28
Henry

'Oh, I'll bet those little Gray bastards were just dying to scoop you up! But they couldn't, could they? No. Not physically. Not until the alignment.'

Henry delighted in the rush of memory pouring into him. It must have been hell for those boys last Friday but the more of their experience he gained, the more complete he felt. It didn't matter if the experiences he leeched out of people were joyous occasions, moments of boredom, or gut-wrenching tragedies, when they entered him they became him, good trip or bad, and the trip was the thing. Obtaining, possessing, knowing. This was the ultimate high and a high only he understood.

These other beings, the... whatever they were—they had the power to block his ability to view their victimization of human subjects, but it wasn't foolproof. They could suppress abduction memories, yet they could not erase them out of the abductee. The best Henry could deduce was that abduction events were nonphysical and so the experiences did not imprint as memory on the brain, but the emotional trauma of being ripped from normalcy did. He extrapolated from this that the victim who wonders what's happening to them, why there are chunks of time missing from their lives, why they have recurring nightmares of something entering their home and taking them—that curious participant retrieves a partial answer from somewhere.

Perhaps emotion contains a fractal seed of the memory to which it was attached. Or perhaps the memories flit to life in the mind's eye of the terrorized from the hidden alien dimension. Was something in the abductee connected to this parallel world? Anchored there but living here? Henry had no firm answers so he held open all possibilities.

Whatever their advanced modus operandi, these beings were more efficient at this abducting people business than were the U.S. military. Nevertheless, Henry could extract those rogue trickles of memory that leaked naturally as flashbacks. In this way did he try to piece together the agenda of the aliens, or whatever they were. That part eluded him as well for they never gave abductees a realistic origin of their species, never shared useful or practical information at all.

***

Henry learned early on that when he absorbed the memories of people, he wasn't taking the objective, pure experiences (if such things even existed)—no, he was taking the experiencer's subjective interpretation of the world around them. When he gazed at the seas through the eyes of Capac Yupanqui, an Inca worker alive in 1527, he didn't see Pizarro's ships sailing in. He suffered the same change blindness Capac Yupanqui suffered and saw only the crashing waves and blistering sun.

When he watched fiery flying shields pacing Alexander The Great's trek through India, he didn't see high-tech flying machines in the sky, he saw fiery shields and experienced their presence as an attack. Alexander's historian describes flying shields because that's what the soldiers actually reported. It was what they could conceive of in their time and culture.

On June 24, 1947, pilot Kenneth Arnold described the movement of nine objects he witnessed in the sky over Mount Rainier. He told a newspaper reporter that they flew erratically like "a saucer if you skip it across water." The reporter brilliantly truncated that into "flying saucer." However, this was not a literal description of what Arnold saw, it was a metaphorical description of how they moved. They did not look like sandwiched tea plates; they looked like craft, like air transport of the future.

The ancients, with an eye on the past and reverence for the knowledge of their forefathers, saw what they knew. The moderns, looking toward the future, anticipating what science would bring them, saw what they imagined they would achieve. Arnold, a forward-thinker and a pilot, witnessed futuristic piloted technology. The ancients, with veneration for the past, saw old technology, the only technology they had. Neither saw what was really there.

This was a quick firsthand lesson for Henry in how language and culture affected perception and it followed suit when the nonhumans interacted with people. The gods of old really did appear to be gods of old. The aliens of now really did appear to be aliens here now. Compounding the problem was the fact that these creatures did not just speak in human languages. They spoke in a holistic language more closely related to shamanism. They seemed to have the ability to manipulate the environment to communicate in physical metaphors that subverted the conscious mind and spoke straight to the unconscious. They used the literal, the physical, the waking state, the abstract, the dream state, the psychedelic state—all states—to speak to humans intersubjectively. It was as if there were no *them* and no *us* but this *we* that has been here forever, but which humans broke down into *them and us* relative to culture and psychology. But maybe that was an illusion, too.

Henry wasn't completely baffled by their agenda. He knew from feeding on the memories of a great many human secret keepers that something transformative had been slated and rescheduled to alter humanity again and again through the centuries. The anointed ones from peoples as distant in time and space as the Mayans from the Tibetans were given dates by astral creatures claiming to be gods in which they promised to physically manifest on Earth and bring peace and harmony to her. Different cultures were given different dates for this new beginning, but nothing ever came of them. The latest and the last had been December 21st, 2012. Perhaps coincidentally that one turned out to be real. Coincidence was a bit much for Henry to swallow, yet he found no link between the alien ultimatum to

Charles and that fabled date. What the aliens promised wasn't Man's spiritual evolution, but extinction if Charles refused them Corey Avon. When Charles sat on his thumbs in 2012 and the year uneventfully ticked off the calendar, the only thing that went extinct was end times prophecy.

Well, except for the new one involving Corey. Recent discoveries from the James Webb Space Telescope confirmed the astronomical portion of what Charles was warned would occur if their demand wasn't met:

On March 25th at 3:33am, Eastern Time, a galactic alignment in deep space that connects the Milky Way to the epicenter of the Big Bang will tick into place with stopwatch precision. The aliens say that when this happens energy will shoot through the planet, charging ancient and modern structures built on key centers along Earth's energy grid, commonly called *ley lines*. These structures were erected by human masons from instructions given by inter-dimensional beings posing as gods. There really are rare galactic alignments that open doors between worlds and although the Grays weren't able to step through before, well, now they are. And they will. And it will be the end of us, not a new beginning, unless Charles gives them what they want: *Bring us Corey Avon alive on March 25th and this all goes away. Trick us again and be wiped from existence, a teardrop in the eye of eternity.*

Corey Avon who lives and plays near one of the rare energy centers that isn't harnessed by Masonic design.

Corey Avon, the alien abductee.

Corey Avon, just some goofy small town kid.

Charles acquiesced.

The ultimatum didn't make sense to Henry, not on any level, so he didn't trust it. In fact, the whole range of mythos so carefully preserved from antiquity by the secret keepers could be—slight chance—bullshit.

Of course if it was true, Charles couldn't be there to make good on his promise. But a little thing like murdering Charles wouldn't stop Henry from delivering the aliens their boy, pro-vided he was there to oversee it. Provided he could bait them into stepping out of their bubble to retrieve the boy long enough to steal their minds.

Provided he was the one in control.

Chapter 29

Corey opened his eyes and met the dark. So dark it was as if he never opened them. His hands were cuffed around a large pole and when he moved to check the swelling lump on his cracked head the handcuffs tightened.

It hurt. Bad. The musty air was choked with dust, which made it hard to catch his breath. He was so groggy and in shock that he didn't know to be frightened. This, only, was on his side. He listened intently for signs of life in the space around him. He heard a creaking sound, steps on a floorboard, perhaps, coming from above, but that was it. He wanted to brush this off as a nightmare but the intense pain in the back of his skull assured him it was not.

He cried then, involuntarily and hard. Tears and snot mucked his face, which created an itching that was almost as unbearable as the injury. Across the room a brilliance struck down from above like salvation, only this was not salvation. First a sliver, then a rectangular swath of pure white light came in a beam through which Corey watched the thickness of the air dance with no partner.

A shadow materialized at the source of the display. Slowly it descended in the stream of light, step at a time. An old man's voice boomed authoritatively, "Hello, boy. Enjoying your stay?"

Corey sobbed at the words but tried to gain composure. If he couldn't think he wouldn't live much longer. Everything in him told him this. "Yes, sir," he said politely.

"Liar!" The voice shot into his ear as a flexible stick came hard, smacking down on the top of his head near the bleeding wound. He wanted not to cry out but he had to. He wouldn't risk accidentally biting his own tongue off just to save face.

One wet eyeball glinted in the light as the profile of a man emerged. The old creature spoke calmly as if the yelling and whipping hadn't occurred. "That's the problem with little boys, they always lie and they think they can get away with it."

The silhouette stepped forward and Corey lost sight of him again, but he felt him. Oh, he would feel the power of him, punctuating each word with an increasingly strong caning. "They. Think. We. Don't. Know. When. They. Are. Lying." Then shrieked in Corey's face, "We aren't stupid!"

Corey felt the man's angry saliva spray into his mouth joining the gunk that had already accumulated there. His face no longer itched. He could feel nothing other than the trauma in his skull.

"Are you ready, boy?" The man asked this back in silhouette in the light. Only that eye and his foaming pink lips shown in the radiance.

"Sir, my name is Corey Avon and I... have to get home."

"I didn't ask you that question. Perhaps you misunderstood. I asked if you were ready."

"Ready... for... Ready for what, sir?"

"Never answer a question with a question, you fucking idiot! Boys are so fucking stupid!" He cracked Corey's left cheek. Corey felt woozy, expected to pass out. He didn't scream, though. He endured the blow and went numb. He felt nothing anymore.

"You and me, we're going to dance with the gods tonight. You ever dance with a god, Corey?"

"No. No, sir."

"Oh you'll enjoy it, it's very... liberating. Yes, liberating!" He punctuated the brilliance of his own articulation with a cackle and a whipping to Corey's left temple. Corey cried again wondering where his parents were, where Lina was, where God was—anyone. Anyone good and kind. Why was this hell unexpectedly his life? How could he die here just like that, by an accidental twist of shit-rotten luck? Was this penance for abandoning his dead friends? Was it for knocking out the bully?

What great and universal hatred produced this situation and said, "All yours."

"Crying is for the weak," the man said in a new gravelly, soothing tone. "And you mustn't be weak, Corey. The gods don't care for the weak and neither do I. Do you hear me, boy?"

"Yes, sir. I hear you."

"Good. At midnight of the Sabbath we ride. If you try to get away... well... Don't try to get away, hmm? We'll leave it at that. Can I have something?" The man wiped away the blood and the tears and the mucus from Corey's lips and chin with his bathrobe sleeve, which reeked of gin. He pressed his forehead to the teen's and nuzzled him, breathing, almost humming, on his face in ecstasy. Before Corey could pout, Old Man Death jammed his tongue into his mouth and sucked a kiss from him. Corey fought the instinctive urge to clamp down and bite off that wriggling worm of a muscle invading his throat but he knew that would be the last act of his life and at this point he wanted deeper revenge than to die here choking on tongue.

He took the kiss and thanked his captor. "Bullshit!" The man yelled. "And you taste like shit!" He backed up and swung three more whacks to the gut. Corey puked on himself. The pain was so intense he finally, mercifully, passed out.

When he regained consciousness he had no reference for time. The trapdoor was shut and the room lightless. He didn't hear anyone else breathing so he assumed the man wasn't gawking at him from some far corner. He struggled with the handcuffs again, which tore into his wrists something awful. He tried to stand. Couldn't. He didn't know if he was bound to the pole in such a fashion that he wasn't able to gain his vertical base or if he was just too weak and injured and drained. He had pissed and shit himself, that much he knew, and the stink of it was as brutal as the withered man's cane.

He had a hard time picturing that kindly old man he'd barged in on as the terrible, crazed monster to whom he'd fallen prey, yet here he was. There was nothing in that humid basement cell for Corey to feel good about, no spark of confidence that he might escape if he could only will himself to reach X. There was no X to reach, no Y and Z to work through once he reached X. There was nothing but the stillness and the dark and the dust.

An image flashed in Corey's mind of him breaking free, lighting a torch, and casting flickers over decomposing corpses all around him that were responsible for the swirling phantom of flesh particulates. The prospect trembled his belly and he had to hold back from heaving again. There was nowhere left for him to go physically and mentally he had no happy escape, but suddenly he had no compulsion to fear either. It was as if his brain recognized that no emotional reaction would spark the adrenaline or the insight coveted to solve the riddle of freedom despite its seeking self. He was for the first time in his young adult life completely still.

There. Was. Nothing.

The brain had stopped. Stopped imagining. Stopped struggling. In that moment of calm the brain fell silent, transcendentally so. It was no longer Corey's brain for there was no Corey being projected by it. It was just a brain existing in steady silence open to instruction should it come, but not awaiting any.

This moment was complete freedom.

This moment was timelessness.

This moment was nothingness.

The timeless empty moment spontaneously became self-aware and when that happened, Corey was back again except his personal self-awareness had receded. He was purely a witness to the visionary event unfolding and this event was more him than he was.

First, he saw blackness so dark that it had to be space devoid of stars. He not only saw this, he was this. He felt it as if the void were his own body.

Next, he saw and was a clear yet tangible circular something, like a two-dimensional water droplet spreading out evenly over the blackness, forming all directions by its very presence. The brain felt as if it was expanding with the invisible circle. It had elasticity, and if it snapped the brain feared it, too, would snap and die. This fear surfaced as a background emotion unable to swim to the fore of the experience.

The perfect circle reached its limit and it did snap and from that snapping, at the center of nothing, a tiny three-dimensional light blipped into existence and from that light shot everything. Hot rock and solar wind; stars and planets and bacteria; all the things of the universe great and small burst to life, bringing with them the advent of time. Spirit danced there, in all things, tasted of time from Its royal court in the now and Corey not only saw this, he was this. There was no Corey, really. That young man was a shallow façade inching his way back into existence as the scene of everything unfolded.

Corey was that hot rock, was those planets, was the wind riding on the ocean of Earth and the ocean itself. He was the breeze and the trees it whipped. He was the frenzied molecule and the tired elk. He was the sun, an immense self-aware organism, alone and alive and content with giving life to the nearest rock that could take it. He was all of these things and the Spirit that danced through them.

He was all things. He was nothing. He was human and alien. These fractured points of view settled into one and that one was cell division—one round cell snipping off of one long— only the cells were full of the stars and planets and life that he also just was. He heard an androgynous voice say, "This is you for there is no you when you slough off he who knows."

Then, with a drastic perceptual thrust, Corey the witness zoomed into one of those planets in one of those universes. It loomed huge in his awareness and he was *that* and *that* looked suspiciously like Mars, only redder than any picture on NASA's website.

The genderless voice carried on about something but Corey found it increasingly difficult to pay attention to the words. He was becoming aware of himself again, of the pain in his skull and the itching everywhere. Those physical sensations forced him to climb back into normal bodily awareness. The pain came rushing to the fore and he lost track of what was being told to him. Something about him being one of them hidden here but ultimately everything was one thing and that one thing was nothing. Meanwhile, a second voice, that of his inner thinker, repeated over and over, "It's an illusion. It's an illusion. It's an illusion."

The situation made so little sense to him that he feared he was dying. He concentrated on the throbbings and stabbings of his injuries and in so doing pulled himself completely to the here and now dank hell of a leathery psychotic overlord.

Recomposed, he immediately chastised himself for wanting to live. Why the fuck did he want to live here in this place of torture when death was so sweet and God-alive?

"Fuck!" he spat. "Shit, shit, shit!" He screamed a primal, desperate scream while pulling on the cuffs. Only the skin of his wrists gave. "Somebody help me! Help! Fucking help me!"

The absurdity of all this caught him off-guard and he laughed, which made it more absurd, which made him laugh harder. Then light from above shone down again and again the shadow man descended into the rotten pit, the new home of the human blood clot, Corey Avon.

The man squatted nose-to-nose with the boy. Corey could feel the heat of the beast, feel its acrid breath bouncing off of his face. "So, boy, are you well-rested?" the man snarled. Every hard consonant sprinkled Corey's mouth and chin with alcoholic phlegm.

"Yes."

"Good. That's very good. Tonight, then. Tonight we ride to a better life. The Heavenly Father told me. Told me what you want, precious angel. A better life. A better life. That is what you want, isn't it?"

"Yes."

Corey heard the old man wheezing but mercifully couldn't feel his breath on his flesh. The man coughed a spell then just breathed. Dried snot whistled from a tangle of nose hair. Corey suspected his one-note affirmations were throwing this guy off and he wasn't sure how to react. Was Corey goading him? Was he telling him what he wanted to hear? Or was he being forthright?

Corey heard a crinkling sound followed by a dull tap. "They told me about you, Corey." There was a flicker of match light, then the ripe smell of fresh pipe tobacco. "They requested you, said you'd be coming around the house about the time you did. They instructed me not to kill you, but if you try to escape, so help me, boy, I will do just that. Is that understood?"

"I understand. Do you know the gods well?" Corey didn't know if his question would be met with suspicion, with a lash of the switch, or if he was making a connection, endearing himself to the abuser. Making a connection was all he had for hope.

"They are the ones who create all. Time, space, flowers, trees, us…. They are the princes and princesses of our one and only Lord Jesus The Christ and they have chosen me as their apostle. Their only apostle. I am the divine, boy. You will see that. I know them like no other alive."

Corey braced for a whipping but it never came. Instead the man asked, "Tell me something: have you ever heard the saying, 'You cannot simultaneously prevent and prepare for war?'"

"No, sir. I haven't."

"Of course not. You're young and a fool. Albert Einstein said it and he was correct. You cannot have your cake and eat it."

"I guess not."

"They believe that, the gods do. They don't want peace though, so it isn't a matter. They want war, for only in war may lasting peace result."

"How do you figure, sir?" More inquiries, more talk, longer life. He imagined his wounds mending with every precious second stolen from that human death machine.

"You ask too many questions, boy." The man whacked him lightly on the knee with his cane. Corey watched the profile in the shaft speak between cob pipe puffs. "After the destruction of all that is, only then will there be true peace. We, the species, can start over again. From scratch... from scratch, from scratch, from scratch. We'll appreciate what we've got a helluva lot more after it's been taken from us for a while, like a child missing his toy. Like a starving man lost in a desert. Give him a loaf of bread and some water and see how damned grateful he is. It's a beautiful thing, death is." His glistening left eyeball darted in Corey's direction. "I'm glad you're here to share the experience, boy."

The madman furrowed his bushy white brow slightly, the need to beat his captive surging to the fore. Corey honed in on this and kept him talking, holding his cruel impulses at bay. "Meaning what?" he boldly asked.

"Whatever the gods want! We will both see, you and I. We'll enjoy it; I was promised. That was the promise. They won't lie, not to me."

"I believe you."

With delicate method the old man put out his pipe, rolled it in something—Corey couldn't tell what—and stuffed it in his shirt pocket. "You believe me," he said. "That is cute." He moved and was swallowed by darkness only to reemerge back in Corey's face with the unchallenged power of a sniffing bear. "I don't believe *you*!" he roared. "I know what you're doing! I promise you greatness and you mock me! I know what you're doing!"

The man stepped back and revved up. He slammed his cane into Corey's shoulder. Again and again he hauled off muttering, "I know what you're doing... I know what you're doing."

Corey cried out. The pain was sharp and deep as if his collarbone was now floating in shards like icebergs beneath his skin. The man coughed and wheezed and struck a final blow, this one to the cranium, where Corey had previously been split. He heard a squishy tearing sound as the watery clot reopened. "I'm sorry! I'm sorry!" he shrieked.

"Stop! The! Ly—! —ing!" Each syllable punctuated by pain.

Corey screamed until his vocal chords gave. He wailed, he kicked, but nothing worked. When he shut his eyes he saw the cane slamming into him. When he opened them, he saw the rage had stopped and his tormentor was standing perfectly calm, readying his pipe again. He lit it. Corey watched the exhaled smoke waltz with dust of the dead in the shaft of light. The man turned, ascended the stairs, and dropped the hatch back in place.

Shock took Corey's body, then. Sweet, numbing shock. He knew only one important thing and it brought him no comfort: the gods in the man's head needed him alive. For now. That could change on a whim. Corey tried to think about something else. Something happy. His mind went to Lina Igasho and he felt something of love boil in him like a saccharine aphrodisiac.

"Find a way," he pleaded to love in the dark. "Find a way."

Chapter 30

"Find a way," he pleaded to love in the dark. "Find a way."

Lina stared out her bedroom window caught in a daydream of self-pity. She had been wondering why Corey didn't call. Was it the folks? Did they catch him coming in? Was he ignoring her a few days, playing it cool? Or was it that she was crazy to him now? Yes, definitely that, she decided. He loathed her and would start rumors about her being a slut when he got back to school. She should never have shown him her journal or taken his mouth to her breast so soon in their burgeoning relationship.

She broke the spell and looked down to see her pen scribbling furiously in her journal. This wasn't her book. This wasn't her writing. It was as if her mind had drifted and someone took control of her hand, like a spiritualist parlor trick.

She flipped back, read the pages she'd scribbled while drifting. No, that definitely was not her expression jotted there. It was Corey's. He was trapped blocks away, suffocating on the agony of an abuse no human should endure.

It didn't occur to her to call his home, check in with his parents.

It didn't occur to her to call 911 and scream into the phone to help her.

It didn't occur to her to tell her own folks.

It didn't occur to her to wait at all for anything. He was telling her where he was and she needed to get to him right now, so she ran. Ran past her folks vegging on the sofa in front of the tube. She thought maybe her dad got out a "Hey!" before she slammed the door but she couldn't be sure and wasn't looking back. Ran breathlessly down the street, following the path of Corey's bike and her heart.

'How do you know this? This isn't psychic, this is more. How do you know this? How do you know this?' she quizzed herself.

She turned down a side street she'd never been on and stopped at a lawn of a house she didn't know. She caught her breath there but didn't allow time for rational judgment to take over and confuse the situation. She didn't know the house number but she knew where she was: this was the nest where evil dwelt—the place where Corey sat trapped and bloodied and passing.

This wasn't how her story about him ended. She hadn't finished it yet but she knew it wasn't supposed to lead here. She sneaked around back, surveyed the dark interior from all available windows. Nobody stirred inside but she didn't trust that.

A chilly wind nipped at her but she couldn't feel it. She darted her head about, frantically looking for something to use as a weapon. She found a small rusty spade half buried in what must at some distant time have been a quaint garden by the back porch. She grabbed it. It was dull. It was everything.

She crept up the back porch steps and inched the squeaky screen door open just enough to try the handle of the thick wooden door. Locked. Boldly pressing her face to a side window, she cupped her eyes with her hands and peered in. Blackness and objects but no movement. No struggle, certainly, no shadows of people. With as much stealth as her shaking hands mustered, she wedged the spade up between the loose, old windowpanes and popped the lock clean off. It dropped to the kitchen floor with a slight clank that was amplified in her fear. She paused, statuesque, listening for anything, anything at all in there. No response.

She slid the window open but it wouldn't stay propped. She didn't care. She hopped through right leg first with that heavy pane dropping onto her back and then scraping the length of her left leg until she was partway in. Childhood ballet lessons paid off here. As she balanced meticulously on her right foot she lifted the window off her left and furtively lowered it into place, all the while shimmying in. Mercifully, there was no décor in front of the window hindering her break-in.

She tiptoed in the dark, with a mime's care, not daring to move fast lest she bump into something and alert the owner. The layout was fresh in her mind. It was as if she had written it and maybe she had in those sad daydream moments that beckoned her here. There was a basement door on a steep wooden staircase that led down to the laundry room. Once descended, a dirty Japanese throw rug lying inconspicuously before the dryer hid a trapdoor to the special chamber of horrors and tortures and insane gratification.

Lina skulked to the basement door. Unlocked! Finally, a break!

She handled the door cautiously, opening it slowly so none of its old parts in need of oil alarmed. She felt her way down one step and shut the door behind her. She wouldn't risk fishing around for the beaded light chord.

Step at a time she descended, patting the filthy wall with each drop down. She stopped at the bottom, listened for footsteps or breathing that were not her. Nothing. She bit her lip willing herself not to hyperventilate, breathed deeply the stale air, and psyched herself for phase two.

Lina dropped to her knees, then crawled around the rug hunting for a lever or something to pull the trap door. She couldn't find it but discovered that the rug was glued to the door and there was a notch or something on one end. She imagined the monster slept with the handle underneath his pillow and screwed it into the hole to open the hatch when he was ready to inflict more punishment on his victims. His victims: how they cried to her now. She didn't have to be psychic to feel their pain etched as it was into the walls of this demon-haunted cave. Corey wasn't the first but she would make damn sure he was the last meal for this ogre.

She felt for the seam of the hatch and began chipping away at it with the spade until it fit. She jammed the spade in there and pried with adrenaline-fueled strength. The door popped up an inch but the shovel handle broke and the door careened back into place with the head of the shovel still wedged there.

The force of her momentum flew her skull-first into the white metal drier. She reflexively blurted "Shit!" then slapped palm to mouth, horrified that she'd made a ruckus. She hoped—prayed—the old man of her imagination and this reality lay two floors up in his bed fast asleep and hard of hearing. She hadn't written where he was and had no intuition warning her. She again stopped everything to listen.

Just her heart. Still nothing. Still lucky. Still alive.

'Okay, think! Think, Lina!'

The immeasurable stupidity of this prison break dawned on her now. What the fuck was she thinking? She should have called the police when she had the chance. The second-guessing was so unhelpful now that she shrugged it off and went back to work.

She swept around the floor for the broken shovel handle and gurgled with nausea when she realized that it might not be just everyday floor grime building underneath her fingernails.

She whacked the handle with her right hand, which sent it rolling underneath the dryer, so she flattened out onto her stomach and shoved her arm under there. She could brush it with the tips of her fingers, almost within reach. She could also feel cobwebs, muck and hair.

'Ignore it. Eyes on the prize.'

She squeezed her thin arm under there until she had the handle firmly in grasp. Withdrawing her arm was another ordeal because the lip of the dryer curved inward and its rusty edge threatened to cut like a used razor blade.

'Now is not the time to be a girl. Do this, woman. Do it!'

With that, she jerked her arm out fast and left some of her skin behind. Her arm stung fiercely, more of a gash than a scrape, but she turned the pain and the anger that it caused into strength. She pressed the wooden handle horizontally across the splintered off piece of itself attached to the spade wedged in the trapdoor. She shoved it with everything she had. The door tugged up and then tugged up again and finally she had enough leverage that she could force her fingers under it.

Lina stood and lifted the gate to Hades. Not waiting for accomplishment to wash over her, she jogged halfway down the rickety stairs and whispered, "Corey? Corey Avon! Wake up! Where are you?"

She heard shuffling in front of her but couldn't see anything in this abyss. "Corey! Is that you?" she rasped.

She descended all the way and stepped toward the sound. She accidentally kicked someone's foot and tripped and fell onto Corey's chest, which woke him up with a loud groan. She immediately smothered his mouth with her hands. "Shhhh! Sh-sh-sh! We've got to get you out of here but you have to shut the fuck up," she said.

"Lina?"

"Yes."

"I'm handcuffed to a post," he slurred.

"Shit."

"You've got to get out of here."

"I am as soon as I get you free."

"No, I mean you gotta get out of here. There's a guy."

"Help me find a key or... fuck you can't help me find anything. We've got to get you out of here."

"There's a guy."

"Yeah-yeah-yeah, I know all about it."

"I don't think that you do," an old voice wheezed.

On instinct, Lina whipped around to destroy the man but was met by a searing heat in her stomach. She looked down but couldn't see what it was. The old man lit a match for his pipe. In the dim flicker she saw the hilt of a serrated hunter's knife stuffed inside her belly, dripping her blood. She met his face, her eyes choked with tears. She fell backwards into Corey's lap. She felt failure and regret but nothing of the blade.

"Lina? No! No!"

"Finally awake are we, boy?"

"You mother fucker! I'll fucking kill you! I'll fucking—"

"Shut uuuuuuup!" Something familiar slammed into Corey's blood-puddle cranium and silenced him. The old man sighed and dropped the cane overtaken by the limits of age. He gathered himself and cleaned up the messy rag doll spilling more red onto Corey.

The girl tried to speak but her mouth didn't have words. The old man scoffed at her, more put off by this feeble rescue attempt than anything. He twisted the knife in her soft belly and pulled up until he heard a crunch. A half-formed joke about Eve and the rib flitted through his mind, but *oh well* if he couldn't come up with a punch line for this in time for her to hear it.

Lina gurgled with death and then her lungs released her last breath into eternity. The gods had warned the old man of her coming but now neither they nor he had anything to fear. Not that he knew how to fear.

INTERLUDE
Earth Zero

Bloody as the fighting in the sky became, the ground battles were even ghastlier. The night raved in a laser display from crystalline assault wands hot off the factory floor. These were simple devices conventionally used to balance atmospheric energies to one's personal comfort that very easily converted into a type of focused beam gun. Daybreak showcased the results. The streets of the big cities, where most of the fighting broke, were smattered with blood and scorch marks crisscrossed like a sadist's game of hopscotch. Bodies piled up, rotting and stinking and waiting for friends. They never waited long.

The aliens watched their opponents' reaction to this first wave attack. Unimpressed with resistance efforts, Leader ordered the second wave—his own fighters—to swoop in and finish them off. Hundreds of pristine fleets ejected from the city in the sky. The aliens were fantastic pilots and perfect marksmen. They knew where to strike. They had long ago mastered when and how to do so flawlessly.

If they had a weakness it was defense. So sure were they that this was going to be a quickie joyride, some of them would get caught off guard and find themselves divided from the others by a triangulation of resistance fighters. The alien pilot would concentrate on shooting the bait craft in front while two in the rear took him out. It was rare that this tactic worked, but when it did it told the Earth Planers that these invaders were vulnerable and, unlike the insectoids, had souls to capture. They caught as many as they killed. Perhaps the souls could be used as bargaining chips, they reasoned, forcing a line of communication to whomever was in charge of this sick race.

***

Leader gave the Hive Queen frequent updates like he was phoning in the score of the World Series to a friend. She feigned enthusiasm and cheered him on through the robotic voice modulator built into the etherputer apparatus that jailed her. Soon, he assured her, they would land and enslave whatever was left of the resistance. They would eat up the resources and overpopulate in however many millennia that took. Then they'd move on, leaving billions of their own to suffocate in squalor—such was their custom.

The queen played along, pretending to understand. After all, she told him, it was she who ruled the underground—not just one landmass but all beneath Earth Plane. Leader was falling for it, falling for her. Was it possible to love a woman from another planet? From a planet you were in the middle of conquering? From a fallen race you were utilizing as first wave battalions in a war against her friends and fellow earthlings? From a soul slave firing up the death machine you were using to destroy every form of intelligence in your wake?

She never once begged him for release from her etherputer prison. Conversely, she never once hinted that she would stand proudly by his side for all eternity in cloned body after cloned body if he so chose. What she did do was agree with him in similar astonishment when he'd go on about how much they had in common.

They thought alike.

They commanded alike.

And in their autonomy they were alone alike.

Yes, finally somebody who understood what it was to be peerless, to be without real and equal partner. Finally, somebody to love—only this somebody had no body. He killed it, replacing it with a clear jar where in precious random moments he caught a glimpse of her essence fading in and out of the visible spectrum like a wisp of smoke made of light.

He would fix that. He would clone her a fine organism in the image of his people. If she couldn't adjust to controlling the one, he'd make her several to occupy at once. Whatever it took, for he saw that she was special, was different, and did not deserve the hellish chore he'd foisted upon her. Leader only had compassion, such as it was, for his people, and this was how he was rapidly coming to view Hive Queen.

After a few days of mulling he decided to take a risk. He switched out her soul with that of a random peasant from who-knew-where kept in storage. The soul came from some planet he'd overtaken eons ago. He didn't keep track of the details. Not important. If an ordinary soul couldn't control her hive bodies, he'd have to put the queen back until this war was won—and this thing was just shy of won.

No big deal. She would understand.

***

The conquerors gave Hive Queen a sleek organism to wear but it didn't fit. Something about her hive nature required insectoid DNA. No problem. The aliens gene-spliced insectoid with their own and voila! The perfect hybrid!

Queen of insects was queen once more—queen of her Leader's heart and other sensual parts, in her suit of flesh genetically sculpted to his taste.

The body felt loose over her like corpse on ghost. Walking and coordinating gestures took some getting used to. Having spent her life as an appendage-free globular organism she had no experience living in her own moving parts. She depended on Leader to teach her basic movements. The nurturing further strengthened their bond.

***

Remember when I told you that planetary take-overs never took longer than three waves of battle for the aliens? Well, the third wave was upon them. Earth Plane was by far the largest territory they had ever attempted to claim but the three-wave rule was compensated for by the fact that their first wave battalion was insectoid. Technically, they could fight this in four waves and not count that initial surprise attack since the insects were not their own warriors and they had done most of the barbarous warring.

Custom required that Leader ride into battle flanked by his Royal Guard on the tail of the third wave to pick off the remains as a symbolic gesture of triumph to his adoring people. But this time, for the first time, Leader was in love. He did not want to leave his lover's side but he surely was not taking her into battle.

He toyed with the idea of calling this the second wave based on the insectoid technicality, so that by the next there really would be no resistance left and he could take his dearest with him. But he couldn't risk looking weak to his people.

Mustn't be selfish. Love can wait. Time to assemble the Royal Guard of ace pilots and gallop, as it were, onto the battlefield.

Reluctantly, his queen agreed.

Chapter 31

11:00pm. Corey woke, gagging on his own blood. It tasted better than the shit in the dog bowl this man once held to his lips. His ears rang like tuning forks and he'd pissed himself again. He had grown accustomed to the various wretched odors of the damp cellar and the dust no longer congested his lungs. He could feel the slits in his wrists scabbing around the steel cuffs constricting his circulation, but he paid that agony no mind.

'Lina. God damn it... Lina....' Corey's stomach convulsed as if it were sobbing in the way his eyes no longer could. He was so desperate and angry and feeling like he had killed his true love by simply meeting her that his emotions collapsed. His ability to feel had been replaced by a creepy calm at odds with the twitches and pain in his body.

The ceiling opened and light beamed in. The old man hollered from the top, "Ready, boy? The time is now."

"Yes, sir. I'm ready. The question is, are you?"

The man stood dumbfounded a second then trotted down and into Corey's face. "What?" he snarled.

Corey met his eyes and spoke with unblinking confidence. "The gods are dismayed with your actions here. You have killed an outsider. That was not part of the plan."

The man's face corkscrewed. He couldn't believe what he was hearing. How dare the gods leave him in charge and then question his judgment? "She was trying to take you away from me! What was I to do?"

"Not that."

The man thought a moment and his face contorted into an angry, revving motor. "You don't hear the gods."

"Of course I hear them! You think you're the only chosen one? You think I'm here by accident? The gods don't want just anyone, they demand me! Now stop acting naïve and take these fucking handcuffs off me before I lose it!"

The man eyeballed him waiting for the façade to crack. "If you're lying to me, boy…."

"If you do not trust me then you do not trust the gods. If anything happens to me that was not in the original plan, great and eternal tragedy shall be your destiny." Corey assured this with nary a tremble in his voice.

"Why did you not speak of this earlier?"

"It wasn't to be. I probably shouldn't have spoken up now but you've gone overboard in your beatings. The gods do not want any further harm to come to this vessel before the great arising."

"Great arising?"

"Yes. Tonight. You shall know all tonight. Ask me nothing further of it."

The old man's eyes rolled back in his head with ecstasy. Corey expected him to speak in tongues or kiss him again but he did neither. He just smiled a blissful, orgasmic smile. "If what you speak is true, then… then we must prepare. Come…." The old man fished around his back pocket for the cuff keys. He went behind Corey and freed his damaged hands, then un-locked two thick chains that glued the boy's thighs to the floor. Corey didn't even know his legs were chained until they came undone.

The man was quick to cuff Corey's hands behind his back prior to standing him up. Corey wasn't about to press his luck on the issue. The man helped him to his vertical base and pa-tiently observed the boy's limbs come to their senses. It was difficult and for a while Corey was dizzy. He couldn't feel his legs and feet. The numbness gave way to pins and needles and then he was able to limp weakly. He felt every movement in his bruised collarbone but he didn't cry out. He was beyond that now.

The old gargoyle was gentle with Corey, hoisting him up one step and then another and another until they were out of the dungeon and onto the basement stairs. The man helped him through the kitchen, through the pantry, into a tiny bathroom with no tub. He sat Corey on the toilet and sponged off the dried blood and assorted other gooks caked to his face. Then came the rubbing alcohol, which stung like a motherfucker but he took it. "There you go, boy. Good as new." The man beamed with pride.

Corey stood and twisted to the wall mirror above the sink. What he saw revolted him. He looked like he'd been run over by a Mack truck and then kicked in the face for good measure. His head... was his head even there? The top of it was a casserole of meats and blood and hair like the tree where his friends had died. He remembered that now and was glad that he had a second chance at not ending up a crimson pool of the things inside a body.

"You wait here while I get my coat. I'll only be a minute. We must hit the open road before midnight." The man abandoned him saying, "Cannot be late," as he scurried off.

"Yes, hurry back. We mustn't be late," Corey found himself agreeing. He immediately chastised himself for it. What if the man did hurry back? He needed all the time he could hoard for his escape.

He heard the psychopath's feet thudding up the carpeted staircase to the second floor and immediately dragged his broken, tired carcass to that kitchen door. He knew he had less than a minute and if he were caught he'd be killed, simple as that. He put his back to the door and felt for the handle with his barely accessible hands. Everything he did stabbed knives in his shoulders but he sweated it out instead of yelling in pain. He found the handle, twisted it and pulled. Nothing. Pushed. Nothing. Jiggled it. Nothing.

'Fucking locked!'

The knob to the deadbolt was built into the door handle so this was less problematic than he feared. He unlocked the door and yanked it open. A little. Chain lock. He fumbled desperately with the chain but it was too high on the frame for his hands to reach and he assumed he'd already made too much commotion. He ended the scramble and listened. The man was thumping back down the stairs. Corey silently cursed himself. So close to freedom and yet he now had to hobble back to the toilet and pretend this never happened.

But... but... so close!

He was paralyzed with indecision when he heard the man stop in the middle of the staircase. "Oh, toot. Keys." The man again ascended the case.

Corey took that as his cue to whip back around and crunch down on that brass chain-lock with his teeth. He clenched it with his incisors and carefully slid it up and out of its socket, but it snagged and fell back into place. He tried again. It was harder the second time, slippery with saliva, yet he managed it off. He regarded the dangling gold-colored chain as a thing of beauty, a sign that he would live through this exhausting nightmare. He pivoted back around, turned the knob with his bound hands and opened the door.

The screen door was locked, but no problem. He flicked that open and a gust of wind caught it, smacking it against the side of the house. He heard the man shuffling down the stairs, this time with alacrity. "No!" the devil howled.

Corey hobbled down the back porch, through the driveway, and back to the street. He ran as fast as his limping broken organism permitted. He was closer, way closer, to Lina's house than his own so he ran in her direction. Rather, her house's direction.

'Lina...'

A lump scraped into his parched throat so big that he thought it might close like that time he suffered an allergic reaction to strawberry yogurt. He felt the love-hurt for her screwing in his stomach like blender blades and he swallowed it down like the worst damned repression he still couldn't afford to express.

What happened to Lina's body? What did that lunatic do with the remains of his love? Did she stare at him in dead quiet from a corner smeared in shadow? Did she watch him leave the catacomb, as she never would? How could this be the end of a girl so daring and beautiful and sweet?

He thought of her parents. What would he tell them? What words could describe *this*? Would they blame him? Would they end him themselves? Would they be wrong to?

The streets were abandoned and he would never trust another stranger's house again, not even to get away from this vile reaper. Not ever.

He prayed for a cop car but no patrol rolled his way. He was confused and dark of night added heavily to his confusion. He'd only been to Lina's house once. He thought he remembered where she lived but found himself at an intersection he didn't recognize.

'It can't be this far down. Shit, I must have missed it!— Fuck!'

He turned back, stooping and dodging between parked cars and across lawns and driveways where he saw no fences separating homes. Anything to stay off the main streets. He decided to take a risk and a breather, stepping out of the shadows to catch the name of a street sign so he could get his bearings. The street lamps were few and it was nearly impossible for his swollen eyes to make signs out from afar.

A dot in his periphery zoomed into a fat black van squealing toward him. He began to hyperventilate. He was too tired and too hurt to run. Defeated, he waited there on that anonymous street corner, cold wind chapping his open head wounds. If he gave up perhaps the devil would go easy on him.

The van caught him in its headlights and sped up. He expected the old man to jump the sidewalk and bulldoze him into the next neighborhood but instead the van peeled by. Relief. Drunk teens, likely friends of his who didn't recognize him. Probably looked like the living dead to them and they weren't that far off.

But he did have life and the second chance of a second chance gave him a third wind. His lungs calmed down and he breathed normally again, too exhausted to reflexively cough out particles of decay from that hell place. The breeze felt gentler now as he watched the red taillights of the van fade down the road. There was peace in this moment, an unprovoked connectedness with all things that felt so tranquil Corey thought he might pass out.

He got moving again. He stepped off the corner and into the street. A rusty white Oldsmobile puttered to the stop sign on the adjacent avenue. Its blinker went on but Corey had the right of way. With a big overdue yawn Corey began to cross. Something in him screamed to get help and he impulsively turned to the car to flag it down. His hands were still bound and it hurt to talk loudly let alone shout for help, so he nodded furiously in the direction of the driver who was obscured by headlights and tinted windows.

The driver's electric window hissed as it lowered. The Olds lurched and turned sharply. Corey stood in the middle of the street letting the coughing auto glide to him. 'Thank God,' he thought, smiling at the clunker. The car slowly chugged up along side him and rolled over his feet. He squealed in pain and when the front tires were off him, he collapsed forward onto the open window frame.

"You should never have done that, boy." The old man jerked the gas, nearly decapitating Corey. He flailed, reflexively fighting not to stumble backwards, and the old man crushed his feet again with the back tires. The boy's agonized screams were ineffective as his vocal chords gave out mid shriek. His meager noise reminded the man more of a baby bird than food worthy of the gods.

The man stopped the car. He rolled up the window while Corey tried in vain to inch his body to the sidewalk. The man threw it in reverse and drove over his legs. Corey felt like he was yelling at the top of his lungs but only a flaccid croak trickled from his throat. The man stepped out of the car and opened the trunk. He bent at the knees and heaved Corey's flesh and blood sack up and into it.

"Fuck you, mother fucker! I'll fucking kill you, fucking bastard!" Without his voice box, Corey's protests were pantomime.

"Shut up! You shut your mouth before I rip it off! You lied to me, you little prick—you! Lied! To! Me!" He slammed the trunk closed. A mutt in a far off yard barked manically, which triggered other dogs to do the same, but no porch lights came on. No nosy homebodies wondered what the fuss was about.

The man muttered to himself a frenzied speech about always being late as he got back in the car and pulled away, carefully following the speed limit. Shortly thereafter a police cruiser scouted past doing its normal rounds.

It was a humdrum night for crime in Taunton.

Chapter 32

"Where is your son, John? Where is your goddamned son?"

"Oh, we're in that mode are we? When he's bad he's my son, when he's good—"

"When was the last time he was good?"

"Ouch, Meagan."

Meg Avon loved her son, she really did, but right now she wanted to kill him. How dare he run away at a time like this? How dare he run away at all at his age?

"He's eighteen. Maybe he didn't run away—maybe he's left for good."

"Oh, bullshit, John! You don't believe that!"

"Fine."

Meg shook her head at this load of a husband she'd wasted life with. "You're so fucking weak, it's painful," she said evenly.

"Know what? Be an asshole alone. I'm going to find *our* son." John stormed past her to the closet for his coat.

"Great. Where you gonna look first, the cable station or the pub?"

"That's cute. That is cute, but you know I was thinking more along the lines of the tree house because that's where he hangs out. They're probably all there having a laugh. Don't know why I didn't think of that before."

This triggered a rare moment of self-reflection for John. The hectic drama receded into the background and the importance of the question came bubbling true: "Yeah. Why didn't I think of that before?" And what he meant was, why didn't anybody?

Meg shoved her way to her coat in the same closet. "Where are you going?" John asked.

"With you. That's the first sense you've made all week."

***

Corey cursed the fact that he'd completely lost his voice and broken everything useful. Every time the Oldsmobile stopped at a light he wanted to scream out and kick the roof of the trunk, but he couldn't feel his legs never mind lift them. All his body was good for was wincing and tearing up when they hit bumps in the road, and lately it was all bumps. The man must have turned down a gravel drive. Corey could hear the small rocks sifting through the treads of the tires, pinging off the undercarriage.

The car squealed to a halt. He listened to the man get out and walk away, then something like a wrought iron gate swung open. The lunatic got back in the car and drove on causing more agony to his captive bouncing in the trunk. The car drifted for not even two minutes before it came to its final stop.

The man abandoned his car. For a long restful while Corey couldn't hear anything but the wind bristling through crevasses in the Olds, then something squeaky and dawdling rolled into his audible range. He listened to it close in then heard the man fumbling with keys above him.

The hoary animal popped the trunk and regarded his prey. "Come, boy." He lifted the human offering as best he could. He may have been elderly but he had a youthful strength to him when he needed it. Still, this was too much dead weight, so he planned to drag the boy headfirst out of the car and into a wheelbarrow.

Corey bit the man's arm. Like an obdurate grizzly he seemed unfazed as he methodically smashed the boy's face into the rusty barrow. Corey unhooked his jaw and the man dropped his legs in next. The pitiful child lay there fetal and helpless but, importantly, breathing.

"Come, boy—come, come. It's past midnight. No time for games, the gods await us. No time for games, no time for games." He shut the trunk and whistled to pass the time as he wheeled his sacrifice to the land of the gods.

***

"Where is that old mansion? I don't want to miss the turn-off," John said. He squinted at every dirt road they passed.

"There. That's the one," Meg blurted, pointing to the next right.

"You know… you're going to kill me for this… but I just remembered something."

"If it's important, yes I *will* kill you."

"Okay, I ah… I think it was last week. You know how Corey loves ghosts and that?"

"Oh no."

"No, no! It's nothing bad, it's just… I, ah, seem to recall telling him a story about these monsters that live in the swamp. In Hockomock Swamp. Last week or thereabouts. And so—"

"And so that's where they went camping. They went monster hunting and now they're missing and you didn't think this was vital fucking information?!"

"Meg, I did!—I mean I didn't remember until just now. But I do! I see that that's stupid, okay? I'm a fucking moron, is that what you want?"

"Just. Drive. The car."

They puttered along not wanting to blow a tire on a sharp rock or invisible trash waiting for victims on this lightless, foreign stretch. Meg tried to break the hot silence with optimism— "Maybe they wouldn't go camping out there anyway"—but even she wasn't buying it.

"Yeah, why would they want to do that? It's just a cool swamp to explore. They only hang out there."

"John, do not try me! Not now! Corey told me they never go in there, they just hang out by Spooky Mansion. And they don't go in there either."

"Right. Teenage boys don't go in the abandoned mansion and they don't go in the cool swamp with the monsters in it, they just play in their tree house," John scoffed.

Meg's jaw dropped but nothing came out of her mouth. All she could do was shake her head. Responses raced to mind and clogged like traffic until finally, "I don't know who I'm going to kill first but one of the Avon men isn't long for this Earth, I promise you."

"Feel the love," John muttered under breath.

"Shut up!"

***

"Sir, live drop has arrived with actor outside The Castle."

"Good. When they arrive at the door, allow them inside. I will handle them from there."

"Sir, that's a no-go. Live drop has moved actor past The Castle."

If it was one thing Henry loathed more than work interrupting Vivaldi, it was confusion. This was both.

"Where are they moving to?" he asked the voice on the intercom, his mouth full of vodka and crushed ice. His temporary living quarters took up an entire subterranean floor of Castle In The Tank. This was the first week he'd ever utilized them. Everything in there smelled new and annoying. He had hoped that would be the extent of his troubles.

"Sir, they appear to be on a trajectory heading to the anomaly."

Henry lay back in his leather recliner, shaking his face in his hands.

"Sir, we await your orders."

"Look, that's not possible! We very specifically programmed him to bring Corey to the door. Not to the anomaly, to the door!"

"Yes sir. We did do that, sir."

"So then there must be another sphere of influence jamming our signal."

"That is a likely interpretation, sir."

"Which means the Tesla Dream Machine is a hunk of useless shit—like I've been telling Command for the better part of a year!" As much as Henry didn't trust the weak powers of frequency influence on the human brain, the real issue for him was the name *Tesla Dream Machine.* Any billion-dollar black op with a name that fancy never worked properly. It was as if the contractors who produced these wonders thought they could hide their malfunctions behind an intriguing title.

"I have no information on that, sir."

"Oh, fuck you!"

"What are your orders, sir?"

"My orders are for you to sit tight and monitor the situation. I will take care of this presently."

"Understood, sir."

***

The wheelbarrow was a bumpier ride than the trunk but at least Corey could breathe real air. He lay curled on his side, left eye closed underneath smushed face, right staring at the dirty rusted wall of the barrow.

"Tonight we go to a better place. A better place, a better place. To the outskirts of perception. To reality. The core of it, boy. To destiny."

Corey couldn't look up, nor did he want. Didn't want to see those psychotic wide eyes lording over him, brimming with excited nonsense.

"Last stop. Everybody out!" The man tipped the barrow to one side and sent Corey rolling on the ground. All of it, silent agony. The man crouched to face level. "Now boy, this is as far as I can wheel you but we have much farther to go. You can't walk. I'm going to have to drag you. This may sting a little."

The man produced a frayed rope like an evil magician. He tied Corey's busted feet at the ankles, threw the rope over his shoulder and towed him through the woods. Even from this strange angle, looking up at the canopy of trees and stars, through the crackling fire in his nervous system, he recognized where he was: this was the path he and his friends took through Hockomock last weekend.

'Jesus, is this what happened to them? Am I gonna be a blood stain on a tree?'

Corey considered the impossible strength and endurance coming from the frail elderly beast dragging him. If he weren't the swamp monster, if there were others out there, Corey wouldn't be the only loser of the next fight.

***

John crossed the open gate onto private property. "Whose car is that?"

"I thought nobody came out here except the boys."

"Any of their folks drive an Olds?"

Meg wanted to retort that she didn't know her own son at all, so how could she possibly know what his friends' parents drove, but she opted to stay mum. They parked next to the black car and gaped at the dilapidated old-wealth structure before them. "Spooky Mansion, huh? Even spookier in the dark," John said.

"Why don't you knock and see if anyone's home?"

"No one's home. No one's been home in years, look at it."

"We should bang on the door anyway."

"You want bats to fly up our asses? I'm going to go around back, check out the tree house first."

"Chicken."

"No, that was always the plan."

Meg arched a brow.

"Plus I'm chicken. You?" John said with a smirk.

"Cluck, cluck," she responded.

"So let's go."

"You bring a flashlight?"

"Of course not. That would be smart."

Meg patted him on the cheek. "There's one in the glove," she assured her man-child.

John went back to the car, fished around for the light and found it. He clicked it on and after a few whacks from his palm the double D batteries kicked in. "Got it! … Meg?"

"Come around!"

He followed her voice around the side of the mansion, where she was already feeling her way to the tree house in the dark.

***

"I used to live out here, boy, back before you were born. Course people call it Spooky Mansion now but I called it home. It'd been in the family for generations. My great grandpappy built it himself."

The old man leaned back against a tree, caught a breather. He'd taken off his boots and was massaging his gnarled feet through filthy wool socks. Corey stared helplessly at the sky. Jagged tree limbs made it look like a cracked painting. He focused on the terrible beauty there and not the man's voice.

"Imagine my surprise when the gods told me I was to come back here to deliver you. I haven't seen the place since I left in... what was it, seventy-nine? Seventy-eight, maybe? Yes, nineteen hundred seventy—nineteen seventy-eight. The state took it from me. Those cruel, fucking... they locked me somewhere. I was freed in nineteen hundred and eighty-six and I just walked. Got a job at Trucchis bagging groceries. Made a living out of it. Kept to myself. Oh, I've had other friends like you but they don't count anymore."

He looked down at Corey's prone body. "You're what I've been waiting for. Waiting for my whole life."

He squeezed back into his shoes and crawled to Corey's face on his belly. "You ever wait for something your whole life but you don't know what until you get it? That's what you are to me," he confided with a breathy whisper in the boy's ear.

He brushed Corey's hair back, his rough, calloused fingers digging into the boy's scabs and bruises. Corey quivered a bit and winced but he didn't take his eyes off the sky. This creature would never know his eye contact again.

"Come along now. Time to get moving." He slung Corey's towrope over his shoulder and prepared to sally forth when snapping twigs alerted him to someone in the brush. He dropped Corey's legs and pulled a thick, serrated hunting knife from inside his blue jeans. It was the blade that took Lina. "Sounds like we got company... Might as well come out! I know when I'm being tracked," he hollered to the wind-kissed trees.

A man in black stepped out of night and glided like a shadow toward them. "Hello, Nelson."

The old man grunted and demanded more than asked, "Who are you? How do you know my name?"

"I know all, my child, I know all," the shadow said in a compassionate hush.

Nelson stiffened with shock and relief and atonement. He dropped his Bowie knife. "Jesus," he whispered. "I knew you'd come!"

"I am the keeper of promises but you did not keep yours. I commanded thee to bring the boy to my mansion."

Nelson's eyes burst with wild confusion. "No! No, you said bring him to the shining spot in the darkness."

The compassion of the shadow snapped, revealing an unwavering sternness. "You contradict your Lord?"

"No! No, Jesus! Someone... the gods... the other gods—the lesser gods—they must have said the wrong thing! They tricked me!"

"They speak on my behalf!"

The old man's face writhed with angry intentions and his eyes flashed with predatory hunger on the Bowie sticking hilt-up in the ground at his feet as he spat, "Then you are not Jesus. You're an imposter! I know what the gods—!"

A silenced bullet cut through the air, through Nelson's forehead, and into the pine tree behind him. His ancient body crumpled like an accordion, its manic energy released. The lower torso fell across Corey's legs. He frenetically wiggled his way out from under the twitching corpse of his dead captor.

He tried to scream at his savior a series of *thank yous* but his voice was still missing. The man in black shushed him, told him to save his energy and heal. He went to the fresh kill and searched his pockets for keys to the handcuffs. He found them hidden deep inside the jacket, having slipped through a hole in the lining of the front left interior pocket. He pushed Corey gently to his side and unlocked the manacles.

"Can you stand?" the stranger asked.

Corey shook his head gently, not wanting to disturb what was left of his collar bone.

"Okay, too much of you is broken so I'm going to knock you out and carry you. It's the fastest way out of here. But Corey, remember me. Remember my face. My name is Henry and I am real. I'm telling you this because when you wake up you might think you're in a dream or that you've gone mad. It's neither. You've gone with me. I am your protector. And I am going to get you to safety."

Henry doused a white handkerchief with chloroform and wrestled it over Corey's nose and mouth. Corey's protests were meager and over within several short breaths.

***

"Anything?"

Meg dangled half in the tree house, bent at the waist, her feet precariously balanced on a small wooden foothold that needed its loose old nails replaced. She steadied herself by grabbing either side of the opening and spit out the flashlight she'd been biting on the whole climb up. She scooped it up with her right hand and clicked it on in time to see a daddy long legs running on all eight cylinders toward her open mouth. "Aaaah!" she screamed.

"What is it?" John yelled up.

She frantically smashed the startled arachnid into the floorboard with the butt of her torch. "Nothing! Spider."

"Oh. Hey, Meg?"

"Yeah."

"You still have a great ass."

"Not now."

"I'm just saying."

"Good to know, thanks. Whelp, the boys aren't up here. And actually I can't believe they'd ever want to be, it's disgusting."

"That's called nature, Meg."

She grabbed the top of the opening, stood up and leaned back. "Well I call it gross."

"Meg, don't do that, you're gonna fall."

She tossed him the flashlight, which he caught. "I'm not going to fall. Light me."

He spotlighted her rung by rung until she made it safely to the ground.

"See, tough guy?" She swiped him playfully on the butt and grabbed the flashlight. He felt appreciative that their arguing had turned to playful banter but before he could keep it going he saw something had caught her eye.

"What is it?"

"There." She nodded to what she was illuminating: a snail trail of blood leading away from a tipped wheelbarrow into the swamp. It was some distance away but they both recognized what they were seeing.

"Fuck ... Fuck!" John stomped in place, accentuating his curses.

"I know."

"This is not good."

"I know."

"Get your atmosphone, we're calling the police. Now."

She remained tightlipped.

"Shit, you didn't bring it."

"No. You?"

John patted himself down reflexively. "No," he admitted. "I wasn't thinking."

Meg continued staring at the Christmas-red sheen on the dirt path. This can't be happening. Not to her family. No, this was not the blood of her son. That resolve held back her tears as she weakly peeped, "Okay. Let's go have a look."

They jogged over to the barrow, Meg training the light at their feet so they wouldn't trip on roots or get caught in a thicket. There was blood in the thing and smatterings of it leading into the woods, no question now. Guilt overtook Meg and she broke, crying in her husbands arms.

"My God, John, what is this?"

"I... I don't know." His eyes welled. His throat felt like it was asphyxiating. Don't hyperventilate, John. Not now.

"What do we do?" she asked.

"We pray. And we follow the trail."

"This is not good. Do we need weapons? I mean this is not good!"

"We don't need weapons. If anyone's hurting Corey, I'll kill them. I won't need a weapon, it's a done deal."

Meg hugged him close. In this moment she knew she didn't want to lose her husband, certainly not her son. All of the wounds that had become their relationship healed in the face of annihilation.

"Maybe you should go back for help. I think that makes more sense," he suggested.

Meg stiffened. "Bull. We're in this. Let's go."

Discussion over. They followed the winding ribbon of their son's blood.

***

Henry slung Corey over his left shoulder like a sack of rice. He half wished he'd kept the boy's ankles tied so he could drag him. He kept himself in decent enough shape but even so this was eighteen-year-old dead weight through tricky terrain at night. He nagged himself to call in to The Castle In The Tank for a medivac, while at the same time chastising himself for even considering it. He didn't need help, he needed resolve. Even though the boy was out cold, he could unconsciously be picking up the fact that Henry was his hero. Henry alone saved him and he'd need that deep bond if he was going to rapidly win Corey's trust.

His trudge through the swamp was a mercifully short back-track. He didn't want to rest, didn't want to lose his momentum and lazily call for backup because he knew he shouldn't. The boy was his. The moment was his. The future would be his, too. The deep space alignment was just five short months away and somehow this sack of tortured meat slung over his shoulder was involved. Would he end the world or would he save it? Was he the key to seeing what comes next? There was little of this world Henry didn't know and those things ate at him.

Loud yammering up the path in front of him broke his day-dreaming. He'd lost focus and had no time to hide. He'd gone radio silent. If anyone from The Castle tried to warn him of a breach it was his fault they couldn't.

The jabbering voices were on him. He knew they weren't soldiers from The Castle, but who were they? He rounded a bend and there they were, one man and one woman. The couple halted their chatter with a startle.

"Hi there," Henry said. He squinted hard and recognized them as Corey's parents. The gravity of the scene immediately came to him. "Oh. No-no! I can explain!" he stuttered feebly as John lunged at him.

Henry dropped Corey and pulled his Sig Sauer from its holster. Undeterred, John charged full on. "Shit," Henry squeaked. He blew two holes cleanly through John's chest. John slid on his knees, stopping of his own momentum at Henry's feet.

Meg slapped hands to face and covered everything but her eyes while shrieking in horror. Slasher flicks were real. Horror movie clichés happened. This was their lives. And yet....

"I'm sorry," Henry told them. "It didn't have to be this way. But there is a greater good and you're serving it now."

A third silenced bullet ripped through John's skull sending a splay of blood, bone and brain in the direction of his wife. She wanted to run but... but Corey. Her boy. Her poor, poor boy.

"Why are you doing this?" was all she could think to say. It barely came out and was distorted by the shock and tears and shaking frantic vocal chords. Nevertheless, Henry understood. He walked slowly toward Meagan Avon, gun in hand at his side. The hot acrid stench of its discharge stood out from the rootsy smells of swamp.

"Look...." Henry searched for the right words and there were no right words. "I didn't do this to your son. I rescued him from a serial killer."

"Oh, God!" Meg could feel the blood draining from her cheeks like she were going to vomit and fell to a tree for support. Time slowed and actions slowed and the murderer's words sounded faint and muffled like he was talking to her through water. If he was speaking truth, John died needlessly. But then why did the bastard shoot John a third time? Was it a mercy killing to shorten the agony of a prolonged, inevitable death?

Meg resurfaced and it was just like that—like emerging from a blurry, stifling depth that would drown her if she stayed long. With a frustrated scream she regained her strength and brushed past Henry.

"Corey!" she exclaimed as she closed in on her precious boy. She dropped to him and was momentarily stunned and confused by the amount of damage impacted on her son. She cradled his mess of a head and just rocked there like that, kissing his gashes and regarding the lifeless corpse that was not moments ago her husband. She lost it there, lost everything, and cried to God, pleading for a why of this night. John's body discharged electricity making him flop like a fish on ice. The sight threw Meg into a raging fit of despair.

Henry stalked behind her. Corey's lids opened and his eyeballs rolled down for split-second recognition. "Mom?" he slurred through the haze of drug suppressing his ability to come conscious.

"Mommy's here, baby…. Mommy's here." She rocked her baby, she kissed him, she cried on him. Her tears washed away the grime of her boy's ordeal.

She heard that psychopath cock his gun behind her head and she knew these were her last words. "Corey? Corey!" She patted his face anxious for his attention but he was again out cold. "Corey, I love—"

Bullet said the rest.

INTERLUDE
Earth Zero

Leader's cruiser streaked into Earth Plane's atmosphere like a blazing comet. He was flanked by his two best royal fighters with two pulling up the rear, but his real strength stemmed from them being the last to enter the war in this, the third and final wave of battle. They ripped through the sky surveying the carnage and picking off damaged insurgent fighters wobbling in retreat. It was great fun, this. Always great fun. Shooting down enemy on their home turf had been the only time he felt truly alive. Then he met his queen. Now she, too, did that for him.

As queen she had no real power. She could not, for example, waltz into the machine room and smash the etherputer that controlled her insects. While Leader was away, she was confined to her royal quarters, which were humongous and immaculately decorated in the finest jewels of several galaxies untold. Still, beauty with guards is a jail and she was living in one.

But she had to do something, damn it! A planet was dying! *Her* planet! What could she do? Nothing. So nothing is what she did. No action. No thought. She evaporated into a quality of stillness she had never fathomed possible. That stillness felt expansive, like it was going to explode, but she did not fear it. She noted it and let the description drift.

As if in reaction to the thought and the letting go, the stillness did explode and she found herself back inside her many and precious insects. In that state of nonlocality she overrode the etherputer program that had replaced her, and not a moment too soon. She saw through the eyes of a brigade that had stormed a resistance stronghold and were on the cusp of murdering several important Earth Plane Council members.

The insects, wands raised, sticky hair-like fibers itching triggers, stopped in their tracks and lay down their arms at the feet of their victims just like that. In short order, Hive Queen explained herself to the resistance through the mouths of the many, while at the same time turning her air force on the real enemy. Weary Earth Plane pilots cheered from the decks of their ships. They were told which craft was Leader's and were instructed to blow it up and capture his soul while the insectoids held off the third wave strike force. They did as coached and it worked. Perfectly. No single being in the entire universe has ever been—not even now—more astonished than Leader was the moment he felt his own golden royal cruiser exploding around him.

Back in the space city the aliens were frantic. Something must have gone wrong with the etherputer or the old soul running it. The queen couldn't have had anything to do with this for she was lying in her chamber bed fast asleep. Fast asleep yet wider awake than she'd ever been. She knew she couldn't maintain this state forever but the fact that the aliens took their etherputer offline to fix it meant her insect bodies would drop and die when she released them from her charge. This was a tart pill for her. She swallowed it with a smile. Still smiling, the Hive Queen let her foot soldiers fall to extinction.

When she was informed that Leader had been captured and the strike force chased into retreat, she landed her remaining insectoid ships safely. This stopped cold the cheering and celebrations erupting on the ground. Imagine an entire planet struck quiet in nervous anticipation of the unknown like a flock of chirping birds unsure of the beast crossing below their treetop. That was this very moment, Corey.

The queen's bodies hopped out of their aircraft and stood at attention. Every small movement echoed in the silent anticipation. This held for seconds that felt like lifetimes until every insect was in position. What came next was an unimaginable sound. Every insect opened its mouth and sang a note. The rippling musical tone created a wave that washed over the Plane like a tsunami. It was an apology. The apology heard 'round the world. It was heard and it was felt and it signaled the queen's final release of insectoid drones from the breath of life.

When the last of her bodies dropped, Earth Plane cleanup began, also in silence. There was no celebrating this. Celebration was shown to be the immature reaction that extends from war mentality.

There was only gratitude here. There was only moving on.

Chapter 33

Blipping machines regulated him. Fluorescent tubes lit him. Adjustable bed hugged him. White walls sheltered him in the antiseptic room where he lay.

A sound emerged from the depths of him. A voice. Or was it there all along and he was the thing emerging?

"He's coming to. Call Henry."

He came to only long enough for the nurses to see that he had, then he slipped and fell into deep, deep nothingness, different from the coma he'd just woken from, for in this nothingness there was a trace of him. In this nothingness Corey Avon was alive.

Suddenly, a pinpoint of light manifested and expanded in front of him. Corey flashed to the creation event he witnessed in the serial killer's dungeon, but this wasn't that. Although he was immersed in nothingness, he was neither the nothingness itself nor the light materializing within it. He perceived the brilliance out there, in a location within range of his normal ocular sight. The glow was expanding but not like the Big Bang, which happened in an instant. This was a slow opening, as if a struggle to make it happen, and the luminosity was as distinct as it was familiar. This was the diffuse light that preceded aliens. This was technology.

Aliens. Corey balked at the idea. Thanks, Johnny Come Lately. If they were so interested in him why didn't they rescue him? Why did they leave him to rot and die in a dank basement of trapped children and claw marks? He asked himself these questions fully grateful that he could; grateful, that is, that the intolerable agony, which had overloaded him in those murderous hours, had delivered him to normalcy. Well, not quite normalcy. There was still the matter of a coma and a hospital and the creature stepping through the portal in his headspace or wherever he was in this moment.

Hello, Corey.

He recognized the telepathic voice and the face. Darryl. Darryl was here. Now he knew this was a dream.

Not a dream, Corey. I don't have long. It was Darryl but it wasn't the friend he knew. This incarnation wore the same body and clothes, but the face, something... in the eyes... something murky there and he couldn't tell what but they were nearly impossible to regard. It was like they reflected what Corey was at the deepest unconscious core of himself and whoever was in there reflecting that could swallow him whole. All of this in the eyes.

"Are you with the aliens too, like James and Steph and Alex?"

There are no aliens.

And that provoked a tantrum. "Oh. Okay, great. That explains why nobody came and helped me out! Where were you fuckers?! All you do is take and take and give me fear and you left me to die! You left me to die! Say something! Have an emotion, Fake Darryl! You left me! One of your best friends, tough guy!"

We did not leave you to die. There was nothing we could do.

"Bull-fucking-shit! You could open up a portal like this and take me the fuck out of there! Put me back in bed like you do so I'll forget. Or however that works. However that works, you could have done it!"

We do not physically take you anywhere.

"Looks physical to me!"

Appearances are appearances.

Corey regarded his friend with suspicion but he calmed down, aware that he might be wrong. "Then what is it?" he asked.

In the woods we take your soul.

Corey rolled what he felt were his eyes and balked, "You do. And if he'd killed me you would have what? Given me a new alien—excuse me—not-alien body?"

If we found you in time we would have hid you in another human.

"You what?"

These are complex issues and we do not have time.

"Make time! I want some fucking answers, Darryl! You didn't know where the fuck I was? I was locked in a fucking basement of a fucking serial killer! Pretty specific fucking location, I'd say!"

Darryl glared at him silently with an infinitesimal smirk on his lips. Against his better instinct Corey stared his dead friend in the eye. Darryl's pupils were black and dilated. Corey saw now that that's what was different about them: they'd lost their whites and their brown irises. "Shit!" he said involuntarily, startled by the find. Was this a demon?

I am sent to warn you. Beware the one who knows. He is not what you think. He did not save you.

"What *do* I think? Hold on a second. Something's coming to me here, Dar. You guys didn't rescue me and that fucking monster was dragging me into the woods toward *you*. *You* did this to me! Someone else rescued me but you did this to me! You did this to me, you sonofa—!"

Corey, we are through here. Remember one thing.... Suddenly the black drained from Darryl's eyes and they became the eyes of the friend he loved and missed. He looked momentarily flustered and Corey somehow knew that he had let an entity speak through him and the tactic failed as Darryl cautioned the being it would—but there was no time for fluster, no time for *I told you so*. His voice, too, was Darryl's when he spoke through his mouth and said, "You went to them, Corey, the people you think are aliens. And you brought us with you. *You* felt drawn to the swamp. Nobody abducted you. Work this out; it's important and there's no time. The answer is only true if it comes from you. You can argue explanations from me but you can't deny yourself, bud."

***

"He's coming around again, sir."

Henry smiled like a proud father at Corey, whose comatose body writhed, trying to wake up. His lids lifted now and then, exposing his rolling eyes like a hoodoo priest full of Spirit. His eyeballs stopped rolling and Henry saw the life struggling to fill them. He bent down and whispered Corey's name. Corey's body settled. His eyes shot open. He cocked his head and darted it all around like a paranoid finch. "Where am I?"

"Leave us," Henry ordered the nurses and doctor.

"Sir, we have to examine him to make sure—"

"I said leave us. Now," Henry insisted. The medical staff knew better than to press the only man who could strip them of their careers at whim.

Now alone, Henry pulled up a plastic chair to the right of Corey's bed and stroked his spiky hair. It had been shaved off when he was first rushed here so that doctors could staple his head shut. Henry thought it was growing in nicely.

"Who are you? Stop touching me!" Corey hissed. His throat felt raw and sore and clogged. He hadn't spoken in... he didn't know how long but his voice was so hoarse it was like hitting puberty all over again.

Henry chuckled a bit at the rebuking. "Sorry about that. I thought you might need a loving touch right about now."

"Where am I? What is this?"

"You're in a military hospital, Corey. You're safe."

"How did I get here?"

"I brought you. I saved you from an unimaginable— Well...." Henry shook his head as if to speak it was to relive a trauma. He said it anyway. "He was a serial killer, son. Do you remember that?"

Something about that rang true but it didn't trigger the visual memory.

"Where's my mom and dad?"

Henry frowned and dropped his head in a moment of silence for the departed.

"Where are my parents," Corey reiterated forcefully.

Henry squeezed Corey's wrist and regarded him with compassionate eyes. "You've been through a lot. There is no good way to tell you this...."

"No...." Had he not been so physically depleted, Corey would have cried then sensing the ultimate bad coming next.

"I'm sorry, son. They died trying to protect you. They were heroes."

"No!" Corey waded through the fog of amnesia searching for images, attachments to the person he had been before waking up here. He found *her*. The face on the school bus. Just the face, smiling. "What about Lina? I saw her. I saw her...."

"She didn't make it. Police found her in that monster's basement. It was a huge blow to the town. Everybody mourned her loss. The mayor named a street after her."

"Jesus, fuck...." Corey pounded the bed with his left fist and that's when he realized his arm was hooked to an IV bag. His throat choked on a breathing tube and he saw that's why he could barely speak.

"You've been out for a while, Corey. A long while. It's a miracle you're back."

For the longest time he stared at the ceiling while Henry sat rigid, waiting for him to say something first.

"Why am I here?"

"Well, that's a long answer, son. I think we'd better wait on that one until you're back on your feet. The short of it is, your country needs you, strange as that sounds. But before we go any further let's get these tubes out of you and get you rehabbed, hmm? I'll be with you every step of the way."

Corey rolled his eyes and huffed.

"I know I'm not your parents, Corey. I know this is all com-pletely—let's be blunt here—completely fucked up. But I am here for you so if you need anything at all just ask the staff to get me, okay?"

Corey sealed his lips tightly and glanced back at the ceiling, but he nodded an affirmation.

"Okay...." Henry patted Corey's knee reassuringly. He left the doctors to their jobs.

***

The medical staff took Corey off life support in short order and within a week discharged him into Henry's care. Henry brought him "home," to a place that was decorated just like his real bedroom. He knew Henry meant it as a comfort but the reminder of all that he'd lost disgusted him. He kept that to himself.

For the first couple of days he confided in Henry like a friend, blabbing animatedly about everything he could recall happening to him. The shocking unreality of all that had tran-spired overwhelmed his emotions. He never once cried for his losses. Having everything ripped from him in a single fierce tear, he endowed none of it with meaning. He felt numbness in the once-sacred place in his heart where he connected to the peo-ple he held dear. They were just—he was just—gone. The peo-ple who defined him—gone. Loved him—gone. All gone.

Physical therapy began immediately. Corey loathed being tethered to a wheelchair. If getting back to normal meant em-bracing a boring exercise regimen, so be it. He suspected that walking on his own would be as close to normalcy as he'd ever come again when days turned to weeks turned to whenever. No pets, no phone, no calendar. It grew clear that he wasn't going to be leaving. This wasn't a stint in a safe house; this was indefi-nite. Maybe forever. After that epiphany, he went mute. He only had himself and in his anger about that he kept mum for weeks.

"Why don't you talk to me, Kiddo, hmm? I know you're depressed. You need to talk to someone. I'm here for you," Henry routinely pressed. Every day Henry tried to get Corey to open up but he ignored the man while he played videogames and robotically did as his physical therapist instructed.

Henry often filled Corey's silences with half-truths from his own life. He told him a little about the technology embedded in his arm and how it had changed him for the better, neglecting to convey how the snakes of another man's sins writhed in him with psychotic poison. Corey didn't even flinch to stop himself from examining the man's skin when he displayed his forearm. He had videogames to conquer.

He tried tantalizing the kid with the story of how Charles had bravely staved off the 2012 prophesy, but doomsday was still around the bend, and a pat rejoinder about Corey's importance in this melee. Nothing. No, *Hey, Henry—What's that mean?* Nada.

Finally, one random day before Henry amped up another personal history lesson, Corey blurted, "I'm not catatonic." Sharing this revelation meant nothing special to Corey so he continued button-mashing the game controller as if he'd remained tightlipped.

Henry perked up, clearly thrilled by these few first words. "You're not! That's good! Thank you for saying something finally. I worried."

Corey blasted a wolf Nazi with his ion cannon then paused the game as the howling abomination's guts sprayed the TV screen for more points and an extra life. "Why am I here? I have other relatives I can live with," he said.

"Oh, Corey. I wish it were that easy. We need you here."

Corey turned sharply to face his heroic captor. "I don't even know where *here* is! An underground safe house in Buttfuck, USA? Why?"

Henry sighed indicating he felt as defeated as Corey. "I wish I could tell you where you are, Corey, but the where is the why and we've been over this. I cannot risk those creatures probing your mind and finding you. I need you here. The world needs you here right by my side, Kiddo."

"Well, hooray for what everyone else needs. I need to go home!"

"Search yourself. Do you? What's there? Pain? Memories? How much time do we have left?"

"What is that supposed to mean?"

"You know what it means. There's no use in returning home if there's no home to return to."

Corey changed the subject. "You say you can press a thing in your arm and see people's lives through their eyes, but... I mean why did you invent that? You must have heard of remote viewing? Why not invent a device that gets the whole picture?"

"Oh, I know all about remote viewing. Here's the thing: RV was a psychic spying program developed by the military as a means of seeing what our Cold War enemies didn't want us to. Did they teach you about the Cold War in school or did you sleep through that?"

Corey shot him a droll look that said *Ha, ha.* Henry acknowledged it with a condescending smirk and went on. "The forefathers of RV invented protocols for making it work semi-effectively but they never discovered the actual mechanics of it. They just knew that by focusing on a target they could visualize it well enough to scribble out a sketch.

"And then later they tried to peek into the future and past with the technique, but it wasn't good for that. It was a flawed model. Intriguing? Sure. But weak, which is why I didn't invent around it. If there is a way to see all of everything objectively—that is to say, not through the eyes and memories of others—I haven't found it."

Henry took a breath and saw that his audience wasn't nearly as impressed with himself as he was.

"Well you better get on it before somebody else does and you're outdated," Corey sneered.

"I'm working on it."

"So if I do what you want, you'll let me go?"

"Train with me and you won't want to go," Henry said.

"Oh, I doubt that!"

"Then take the challenge. Stop feeling like a prisoner in your own life. Take it back. Save us all, Corey."

That sounded familiar but he couldn't place it.

"Like I've told you countless times," Henry continued, "I would do it myself but I can't. I have the most filled mind of anyone on the planet and this requires absolute emptiness."

Corey took his first-person shooter off pause and resumed game play. "I know things," he mumbled, dejectedly.

"Sure you do. And one of the things you know is how to shut off thought and be nothingness. Remember what you told me about becoming nothing and then the universe?"

"It was both at the same time." Corey whispered this correction.

"Corey Avon, look at me."

He did so. Henry smiled wide, almost too wide to be genuine. Charles wide. "You have access to the ultimate state of mind, the state saviors are made of. People spend lifetimes trying to get to where you are. Do you understand what you are?"

"A torture victim."

Henry laughed. "No! I mean yes, but... sorry to laugh at that—"

"No, I meant it to be funny."

"Okay, good. Yes, it was an awful, awful circumstance. You went through hell and came out alive. You came out a god and you don't know it."

"The god who has amnesia."

"Something like that, yes."

"Cool. I should do well on my SATs."

"I'm not joking."

"Good. God says, bring me home! I commandeth thee!"

"Can't do that, Kiddo."

"Then the difference between this and the prison you rescued me from is I'm not getting my ass kicked here. Do you see my problem with that?"

"I do, Corey. I do and I am sensitive to this. I just am at a loss to do anything about it until you play ball. And I'm confident you will play ball not because you feel like there's no other way but because you will see it's the right thing to do. It's who you are and you can't escape that. Not anymore.

"People like you and me… people who have seen too much… all we have left is our moral judgment," Henry said.

Corey thought about that a hair too long and was snapped out of it by the increasingly rare game-over jingle that indicated his videogame character's death. "Dude, you just killed me. You got any peanut butter cup Ben & Jerry's around this dump? I'm starving."

"I'll see what I can do."

"What's the training about? Some meditation crap?"

Henry was aglow. He could tell Corey was warming up to this. Finally—*finally*—warming up to it. "Some of that," he said. "And controlling flight simulations with your brain. You like videogames, you'll love this."

"Why do I have to practice everything when you can give it to me? Dude, just click on your wrist and import it to me or whatever."

"Well the thing is I've never done that before. I don't know if you would absorb all of the emotions and unconscious motivations that went into the decisions of the people who learned these techniques or just the techniques themselves. I can't risk it."

Corey stared straight ahead, nervous about asking his next question. Henry picked up on the stiff demeanor but didn't know how to read it. "You do understand why I can't risk it, right?" he asked, graspingly.

"I've had... things. Documents or something. I've had, like, documents beamed into me before." He turned to Henry, scanned his face for betrayal. "Did you do that?"

Henry's brow furrowed, his mouth and chin slowly twisting into a quizzical frown. "I don't know what you're talking about." Then brightly, "Hey, not to change the subject, but do you like those *Use Your Illusion* albums?"

"That's... kinda the definition of changing the subject. Sure. It's Guns N' Roses. Who doesn't like old school?"

"I thought so. I heard you playing them before. Listen to what this sound system can do." Henry clicked on track one, *Next Door To Hell*, and pumped the volume unbearably loud.

Corey shouted, "Dude, you've got to be kidding! My ears," but was drowned out by thumping drums, sliding electric guitar, and Axl Rose's nasal cavity.

Henry got so close to Corey's ear that he could feel the breath of consonants bouncing off his temple. "Sorry, Kiddo, but there are others listening and I don't want them to hear what I have to say. You understand the severity? I'm going to tell you some secrets. I'm going to trust you here, Corey, because I want you to trust me implicitly but I need to earn that. So I'm going to tell you."

"Okay!"

"Can I trust you?"

"Yes!"

Henry leaned in and whispered in Corey's ear. "We know you're an alien abductee. We know this because we've been monitoring you since you were a kid. Well, I haven't. But, you know, other people have. When I say 'we' I mean military. That mansion you boys liked to hang out at, Spooky Mansion? Yeah, that is a beyond top secret military installation."

"Jesus. What do they do there?"

"We monitor this portal the aliens open and close when they come for people in the area. The weird thing is... well, *a* weird thing, I guess I should say, is they never step through it.

Sometimes creatures escape—experiments, or something like that from their world—but they never ever step through it themselves. When things escape we clean up the mess. That's it. That's the main reason we're there. We monitor the workings of an advanced race we know nothing about and do damage control."

"Okay."

"In fact, we're the ones who returned you and tucked you in that night after they left you in the woods. After... after your friends...."

"Okay."

"When the light goes out on their portal we find the people they took just lying there on the ground asleep."

"You're a cosmic nanny, I get it," Corey yelled through the wall of sound.

"Yes, yes—turn off the cynicism a minute. You and your friend Darryl walked through the bubble into their space. That has never been successfully accomplished by anyone before. It's been tried. Gruesome what happens to people. And, in fact, a family of abductees tried to escape it that night you went in. You have no idea—"

Corey cut him off with a wave of the hand. "Yeah, I think I do," he interjected.

"We had to shove them back inside and pray the aliens could make them right again."

"Humpty Dumpty sat on a wall," Corey snickered.

"Corey, your government does terrible things. I do terrible things. I'm trying not to, though. I consider myself a reformer. One of the things we've been heavily invested in is beam technology. Beam technology that can do different things. One thing is how we hide the mansion. There's an antenna, right? And with it we sort of... suggest to the town not to come near there. There are unforeseen side effects, of course. Unspeakable stuff. Your football team taking a dive off the roof, for example."

"Why'd that happen?" Corey asked.

"Don't know. We suspect it had to do with their groupthink mentality colliding with our powers of suggestion."

Corey raised a brow. "Death by conformity?"

"It's an unfortunate but acceptable loss," Henry said.

"It's an unfortunate but acceptable loss? Really? What are you a fucking robot all of a sudden?—Talk that shit to their families. See how acceptable it is."

"Look, we have an unknown intelligence infiltrating that swamp, is the point. And now nobody goes there, is the result."

"I went there all the time."

"Yes. That's it exactly, what I was coming to: you and your friends did. These beings, these aliens, whatever they are—they don't give a damn what we do. They don't care if we monitor them or not. I think by overriding our antennae to lure you boys in they were sending us that message, so we sent one back. We took you and implanted you with our own... well, it's a project we've been working on—the one I'm trying to reform. It's where we take... people. We take people and implant them with—it's like a microscopic computer chip—that allows us to store precious documents in their brains."

Corey burst out laughing.

"That's funny?" Henry asked.

"It's stupid! Why would you do that? We're not robots!"

"No you're not. But some of you are secretly part of a global internet."

"And I'm one of them?"

Henry hesitated and that was answer enough.

"That's fucking lame," Corey said.

"We wanted to see what the aliens would do. Yes, you're one of them. How they would react—"

"—If someone they were abducting was a robot?"

"Not a robot."

"Or a whatever. Cloud storage—a file share. Whatever you want to call it."

"Yes. It was an experiment within a larger project. We sent them messages this way, tried to communicate with them."

"So... what did they do?"

"Nothing. They didn't care."

Corey laughed again beneath Slash's wailing electric guitar and Henry did too.

"This is fucking insane. My life is insane!" Corey said.

"Tell me about it. Before you came along I was implanting foreign exchange students in the Big Apple with this stuff through drugs. We spiked their drugs with nano chips in a night-club to take the experiment global."

"You spiked some Eurotrash douche bag's drugs?" Corey laughed hard. "Dude, that's fucked up!"

"I know! I'm a rotten asshole, Corey, but I'm a recovering rotten asshole. I want to help you change everything."

"Why did that evil fucker bring me to the swamp?"

"I don't know."

"He said he lived there."

"Where, in the swamp?"

"No, in the mansion."

"Nobody lives there. We live there—it's a station—"

"No-no! Before you guys. Like years ago."

"Oh. I don't know. I can look into it for you if you like."

"What do you mean you don't know?—I thought you knew everything!"

"Almost everything I need to know, I know. I didn't think that qualified."

"Well it does. Dude said someone took it away from him when he went to a mental hospital or something."

Henry shrugged. "I don't know."

"How can you not know? He heard voices! He was from that mansion! He fucking dragged me into the swamp toward aliens—How have you not asked these questions?"

"I will. It's an oversight on my part. I'll figure it out and get back to you. Meantime, are we through? Can I turn this shit off?"

"Yes!"

"Remember what I said. I'm trusting you now. Not a word."

"You forget: I don't have anyone to talk to."

"You've got me and you've got yourself."

"I don't talk to myself."

"Well then we're halfway to perfect. Just don't ask me anything about it when I turn the music off and we're golden."

Corey shot him a look like, *Duh*, and Henry turned off Axl Rose's high-pitched whine to both of their great relief. If this was Henry's attempt to get Corey to trust him it worked in the weirdest of ways. Corey still wasn't convinced this guy was being truthful with him—couldn't he even now pull that serial killer's bio out of the ether with his consciousness palm-tapping thing?—but he found the attempt and the story endearing. Some of his best friends had been master bullshit artists, rest their souls. He appreciated the craftsmanship.

On that level alone he was beginning to warm up to his latest subjugator.

INTERLUDE
Earth Zero

The leaderless aliens were irate. They had lost their drone army, lost Leader, but knew the resistors down there had his soul trapped somewhere. They could not by law or custom elect a new Leader and could not afford to blow the resistance off the face of Earth Plane without recovering him first. They called off the third wave and regrouped in their city in the sky.

For their part, the Earth Plane Council refused to release or destroy the souls of the nemeses they had captured, including Leader, and refused to keep them locked away in containers for a torturous eternity. The council agreed unanimously that the best course of action was to pay the reptilian turncoats a visit on Earth Zero, their synthetic dinosaur planet floating in the barren universe of their making.

A handful of volunteer council members donned breathable suits and touched down in the middle of Dinosaur Chasm at the reptilian leadership's abandoned swamp court. The people had vanished to their safe haven but they'd left their portal intact, which implied plans to reemerge here. In the eyes of the council this was further evidence they were in on the attack. They must be awaiting an alien signal that it's safe to return. Wands drawn, a blue dwarf activated the stone chamber and stayed behind while the others walked through to Earth Zero.

The council was impressed by what they stepped into: lush forests, cavernous oceans, thick swamps, spitting volcanoes, and life. Everywhere, life. The reptilians had done well for themselves in record time and were to be admired for their ingenuity. Shame they had to relinquish all and become a penal colony for lost souls.

The council handed the reptilian chiefs their verdict, certain of lizard complicity in the alien invasion. They would confiscate Earth Zero and turn it into a prison rehab planet for alien spiritual evolvement. If the reptilians wanted Earth Plane so badly they had eternity to recreate it here with all ports to their real home sealed until such time as they proved themselves innocent through their actions.

The reptilians protested but stayed true to their time-honored pledge to never again regress into war-crazed lizards. They would manage here as teachers to a cloned hybrid race—part reptile, part alien. These new organic shells would mature the souls of the dead through birthing amnesia coupled with guidance by reptilian masters. It was now the duty of the reptiles to raise this alien strain out of its aggression.

Aggression was as genetically encoded into the aliens as the reptilians, so they already had that in common. But, as the reptilian people found out long ago, any sentient species could transcend its instinct into higher ideals of behavior. That choice is the first free will choice of the spiritually arisen: embrace the instinctual programming that worked so well that it brought you to this moment... or see it for the vestigial holdover that it is and move beyond it. Recontextualize it. Make it a thing of reflexive action in the body but not the mind, not the decision-maker. Not you.

Reptilian influence would be strong but they couldn't force the hybrids to do anything, couldn't delete choice from their genetic code. Besides, incarnating a soul as an automaton could not hold forever. Robots are robots and souls are souls and to make the soul robotic is a prison on the verge of collapse.

But teaching, leading by example, works most of the time.

Most of the time.

***

It turned out the hybrids' respiratory system was incompatible with methane air, but this was their planet now. Their reptilian overlords had no choice but to terraform Earth Zero out of a methane atmosphere, into an oxygen-rich habitat, and bury their dinosaur dead. The ashes of that short-lived age gave birth to an entirely new, smaller set of flora and fauna more suitable for hybrids than reptilians, who must have moved off planet to survive. It was of no concern to the council. After all, it was the reptilians' universe to move around in and even go extinct in if that's what happened.

The observer team marveled in shadow at how quickly the new species, built on souls of the enemy, prospered and expanded.

***

When a universe such as this was created, what exploded into existence came from formless consciousness—mind, Corey. Pure, singular mind prior to and inclusive of all matter and energy.

Mind is the "no" in nothingness, the "one" in oneness, you see?

All of this meant that when a tribe of people gave birth, they added to their population by creating body and soul from pure mind. In this way the population not only reincarnated, it grew. And in a very real way, people were their own universes within the universe. When they procreated new soul energy bubbled in the foam of oneness. They formed crowded empires of themselves over and over, ever-evolving and expanding in separation until they understood oneness or died.

The hybrids' cordoned-off universe was no mere jail. It was a second chance at Heaven—or the free will choice of their own extinction. These were the consequences of whichever path they strolled and they had the will to choose either, like everyone everywhere, but they would never again bring their death arts to Earth Plane.

Observer team protocol required that they destroy the portal in Dinosaur Chasm and create several others at discreet locations in a more tolerable atmosphere for the council and their scientists. On the Earth Zero end, these portals would never show up in the same place twice, thus insuring that none of the felons escaped. At key moments in development, Observer team members would appear and bestow wisdom upon the amnesiac races of Earth Zero. This, unless the reptilians returned to teach again. They never did.

Council presence and that of their miraculous craft in the skies would accidentally give these primitives hope that there were gods in the stars come to rescue them. When they left, these people would toil and eat away at themselves, praying for more outside help to end their confusion—to answer the question that plagued them through life and through death: Why am I here?

No one would come along to answer that, for the universe was likely an otherwise empty construct with rudimentary signs of life spread throughout. This was the common experience of exploding one.

But the hybrids would never know that. Collectively they'd have their memories and those of their forgotten selves, those of their ancestors, and shards of recollection of the "gods" from Earth Plane. They would call these fractured shadows of memory archetypes or collective consciousness, if they believed in such things, or imagination if they didn't.

As for the original enemy souls of the root races cycling lifetime after lifetime of reincarnation on Earth Zero... well... Corey, I don't have to tell you, do I? They would have strange visitors from time to time. These they would call angels or faeries or alien abductors, if they believed in such things.... Or imagination if they didn't.

And that, dear Corey, is the story of Mars.

Chapter 34

"Just breathe like I taught you. It'll calm your nerves. You won't even know we're watching you."

"Oh, thanks. I feel much better," Corey said mockingly. He took to his meditative training exercises like a savant. It didn't feel to him like he was learning anything new these many months, it felt like he was remembering knowledge he'd lost. More times than not Henry needed only lay out a technique once for Corey's body to take to it. It was as if yoga and the various breathing exercises that complemented it were the body's natural language. All he had to do was approach the nothingness state that was now very much a part of him for his body to come alive of its own volition and work out Henry's suggestions.

Initially Henry explained this energy to him as "…. more you than you are, which is why it knows how to move the body in healthy ways even if you don't. But if you do speak the yoga languages, you can tell it what you want and it will perform. It's called 'kundalini' in the Sanskrit."

Henry understood kundalini better than anyone on the planet but that knowledge—all knowledge, in fact—is what blocked kundalini from expressing itself in the first place. Henry was nothing if not the ultimate organic repository of knowledge. Kundalini awakening fell into the category of things he could live vicariously through other people's memories but never have for himself. Accessing it with no psycho-spiritual preparation, no decades-worth of tutelage under a master, was part of what made Corey so valuable, if unique.

Henry guided his protégé to the elevator that would land them in The Worm Hole. At this late hour he felt safe enough to let Corey know where he had been kept for the past five months, just as they were leaving. Leaving for Castle In The Tank. Spooky Mansion. Corey's personal Hellmouth.

"You ever wonder why pyramids hold energy differently than other structures?" Henry asked him.

"No."

"Really?"

"Some astrology shit, right?"

"No, smartass. Never mind."

Corey had grown to trust and even like Henry. He knew the man guarded secrets but he didn't begrudge him those. It was his job and probably the factor that saved him from tossing back an assassin's poisoned drink. Corey had more alone time to dream up these scenarios and reflect on what his life had become than any kid he knew. Not that he was a kid anymore. He was nineteen now and he had buried the child inside with the life he used to call his own. Outwardly he behaved the same, his persona running through the motions of old programming, the boy he was used to living as. Inwardly there was a deadened space like a house haunted by the ghost of a lonely boy who had died too soon and was waiting there for a family to move in—a family to love. And if he caught his eyes just right in the mirror when his guard was down at night before sleep or in the morning when he brushed his teeth, even he could see it— could see who he longed to be underneath this destiny, this puppetry of higher purpose. Could see he'd trapped himself inside himself to maintain the ruse that this life he was forced to live was okay.

But who else was he? Was he really the savior of all mankind? Or bait? He felt like neither. Presumed dead and buried in Taunton, living and training in need-to-know facilities, being under surveillance twenty-four seven—he felt like James Bond. The people who monitored him maintained invisibility so well that he didn't even mind them; they were more of a theory than a reality. He couldn't see them but they couldn't see him either, not really. Not deeply.

Many were the restless nights when he'd mull over his last encounter with Darryl. Was it even real? He had to wonder because so much of it was dreamlike and the aliens let Corey re-member everything this time, which was a first.

What did Darryl mean Corey came to them? Even if that wasn't alien Darryl 2.0, if it was an unconscious piece of himself talking through a mask, why would he tell himself that? What deep thing did it imply? The answer was *so* right there, crown-ing in the thighs of articulation, he felt like he would give birth to it any second now.

"Any last questions before we strap in, Kiddo?"

"Yeah. You viewed my memories from the coma, right?"

Henry's tongue tripped in his mouth, stuttering to form words. Corey stopped him before he squeezed out a lie. "No, dude, hold up. Let me rephrase that and save you the despair. I know you viewed my memories, okay? It's your job. You'd be an idiot not to, that's not the issue. I'm just wondering what you think it meant."

"Which part?"

"The part where I drag my friends into the woods with me."

"Ah. What does it mean to you?"

"It means they weren't sending you guys a message at all. I broke through your dream machine bullshit and found their hid-ing place or whatever it is on my own and something about me... I don't know, maybe I had an influence on my friends too and they weren't affected by your machine either."

Henry nodded, glazed over in thought. "Could be. That's smart. Very smart of you, Corey."

"So why would I do that?"

"You're asking that now? I don't know. Little late in the game for this, Kiddo. I'm a bit preoccupied to work it out. And one thing you cannot afford to be—cannot afford to be—is pre-occupied. Get ready to buckle up. This is going to be one helluva ride."

The elevator doors opened and spit them out at the mouth of The Wormhole. Corey should have been impressed with all of this clandestine gadgetry but he was stuck in his own head full of last minute questions and was on Henry like a yipping puppy. "Well look, at the very least it means they might not be bad guys, right?"

"Corey, they've abducted you your whole life. They invade our space for the singular purpose of mocking our national defense. Now they want to take over the world and we've got a chance to stop them. I know you're scared—rightly so—but you have to do this."

And he knew he had to do it not for himself, not for his country, but for all humanity. Henry did explain everything to him about the repercussions of that deep space alignment during his training, as promised, and it made complete fucked up sense.

"Within seconds, we will be a slave race, Corey. Within seconds. No presidents. No prime ministers. No kings and queens. No videogames. No TV. No sports. No power and nothing to hide in. Our armies... our technology—it's akin to an ape smacking a tank with a bone. There won't even be a summit of world leaders explaining this to us, conceding power to the alien masters. It will be instantaneous, it will be awesome, and it will be the death of us as we have come to know ourselves."

"Jesus."

"No. No Jesus. There is no savior, only you. You will save us and no one will know about it. Life will carry on as if nothing ever happened until the Big Bang alignment repeats itself in another five thousand-plus years. By then our technology will have caught up with theirs. I hope."

"That's just nuts. I can't do shit. I'm a kid for fuck sake! I'm from Taunton!"

"N-n-no. You're much more than that. You've got a whole other dimension to you. These creatures must know that or else they wouldn't be so interested in you, right? So you know this is true and you have to face it right now. Have to face it! We're out of time, Corey. You cannot afford the luxury of processing this and coming to a decision. It's a fucked up impulse buy, Kiddo, but you've got to make it.

"What I'm teaching you is how to brace yourself for that blast of energy and funnel it away from here into the empty dimension within. It's the state prior to all creation and you connect to it in a way I've never seen. I mean it's always been hypothetically possible, but you can do something nobody alive can do. You can be totally aware while at the same time being void of all thought. This is the key to opening the wormhole inside you that extends to the time before time and you can dump this monstrous force there. If aliens try to pull themselves into our world on the energetic rope of the alignment they will fall through you into nothingness. They won't be able to manifest physically, you see?"

"What will that feel like?" Corey asked.

"I can't answer that for sure but I imagine it will feel like a rush of electric wind blowing through you. Blowing into you and out the other side. It might be painful. It might be bliss. It might be a fart. I just don't know."

Corey was smiling to himself taken aback by it all. "Can't just get a Shaolin monk on the horn, huh?"

"Lot's of people meditate, Corey. You're the only one who doesn't have a context for it. Those contexts are thought. They create delusion. If the energy were to hit a man of religious conviction he'd see the archetypes of his belief system play out before him. He'd get caught up in it. He'd be thinking and that wormhole in him would remain closed. You're not the only one with a wormhole—we've all got them. You're the only one who can open it completely."

"Who knows about this?"

"Those who need to. Nobody on this base, put it that way."

Henry's story was too fantastic not to be true. Corey factored the countless experiences of others Henry must have stolen to complete this picture and knew he had to trust the guy on this one. How this gift had blossomed in Corey was a beyond wretched bit of chance but if he could make some good out of it… *all* good. In fact, he'd be saving the human race. "Well how can I say no?"

Henry beamed and mussed Corey's hair. "I knew you'd come around."

"Don't touch me. Nobody touches God," he quipped.

"You're not God, you're the human lightning rod—a circus act at best."

***

The trip through The Worm Hole was like being shot from a cannon. For ten minutes. At first Corey shouted with the joy of a child on his first rollercoaster dip. Two minutes into the unrelenting speed he yelled, "Is this really necessary?"

"Almost there," Henry yelled back. They rode the bullet all the way back to Taunton, Massachusetts. Back to Hockomock.

Corey needed a few minutes to gain his orientation after that shock to his system. He squatted to prevent his twirling stomach from heaving. Henry, lucky bastard, never got motion sickness.

"You have no idea how odd it is to see no suits in The Castle at this time of day," Henry said.

"My popularity precedes me."

"Secret keepers are more efficient than the media leads on."

One more elevator up and they were on the roof of Spooky Mansion. It was a chilly night but the wind was still. Corey breathed in the fresh outdoors so hard that his nostrils clamped shut and his ears popped. "Oh my God, sweet air!" he exclaimed. This was the first time he had been allowed outside since he was eighteen and free. And near death—but he didn't consider that part.

"You don't remember how much you missed it until you've got it again."

He sulked a bit when he realized he wouldn't have it for long, for there in the center of the roof stood a tall circular enclosure made of vinyl and metal tubing like a pup tent. They were heading there and Corey figured the inside smelled like a plastic shower curtain.

Henry peeled back a flap and escorted him inside to a tepee, which Corey thought was cool, and inside of that, a coffin-like sensory deprivation chamber. Corey opened it and glared at the human-shaped pool of water lying still as a mattress. It wasn't the same chamber he had practiced in, but close enough. "This shit better be heated."

He stripped to his underwear and lay down in it. The temperature was moderate; he felt comfortable enough to lie there for hours and he had hours. They had gotten here early to afford Corey all the time he needed to instruct his brain to divert that energy through him and into nothingness before letting go all thought.

"Anything else before I shut you in?" Henry asked.

"Nope."

Henry began to close the lid but Corey blocked him with his hand. "Wait! Yes, one thing," Corey said. "When you told me you thought the aliens were bad guys sending you a message through me by bypassing your Dream Machine thing, was that before or after you sucked out my encounter with alien Darryl?"

Henry did not stutter: "Before. Way before. Do you believe me?"

"Sure. Are you lying?"

"No."

"But then why didn't you correct yourself later?"

Henry rolled his eyes impatiently. "I don't know. Slipped my mind? Nobody's perfect?"

"You're pretty fuckin' close."

"Damn skippy. Now get in the box. See you in another tomorrow."

"Not if this fails."

"Let's make sure it doesn't. You've got time to let go. Don't feel pressured. But hurry up. The fate of the world is in your hands."

They shared a final chuckle then Henry sealed the chamber lid. Corey couldn't see, hear, or feel a thing in that tomb. The sensation of no sensation boggled him anew every time he lay in deprivation. He'd grown pro at calming his nerves and his active mind in short order and at maintaining the nothingness state without launching into an experience of the creation of the universe. Ordinarily he could stay a blank slate as long as he needed but he'd not been able to rehearse directing anything into that blankness. It just wasn't possible to gauge a result. Not only was he Earth's only hope, he only got one shot at being that. Calming his nerves now would take more than a pro.

He told himself, 'Just relax, Corey. Breathe.' But he couldn't. Questions persisted about why he was here, who he could trust, what this was really about. He knew he was just scared and that these questions weren't real. These weren't questions he had ignored until now; they were roadblocks to emptiness. They were a means for his fear to take over and keep him noisy when what he needed to be was silence.

'Okay, if you don't want to breathe then just shut up. Try that one, Grasshoppa.' He giggled to himself but it still wasn't enough. He couldn't joke this away.

'What's irking ya, Corey? Come on, me... deal with this!'

It came to him in sputters of insight. It was the old man who had stolen him into his cellar. When Corey experienced the birth of the universe he saw that ultimately everything happens in the now. On that level there is no time, there's just every-thing always already happening right now and so on that level there is no such thing as chance. But on the day-to-day level in which people live there *is* chance. Therefore, he had little prob-lem chalking up those horrid nights to bad luck and bad timing. The elite dickholes Henry answered to downloaded information into his brain, which caused him to crash his bike on that lawn.

It had to be an amazing coincidence, Corey thought, because Henry made sure the killer didn't deliver him to aliens and shot him dead to boot.

Shit happens and a lot of it to him. Corey wanted to leave it at that, but still... still something... still that word *still*. It would not go away, this feeling like he was processing something wrongly. Was he ignoring an ugly truth or was he amnesiac to it? Could he not process it back then because of the agony and the blackouts?

'What is missing? ... What?!'

He huffed and growled in frustration and then caved. "Fuck it—Shut up!" he yelled aloud, bored with his own questions. That crescendo ended the fears.

He settled in for the hypnogogic light show that always flickered behind his eyelids prior to the opening of that ultimate dimension. As Henry explained it, the human collective unconscious existed like a buffering layer sandwiched between his personal consciousness and impersonal nothingness. When Corey pierced the layers, chaotic hallucinatory phenomena unfolded in predictable sequence. First he'd watch fractal patterns, like mandalas, pop in and out of existence. Next he saw faces, human and alien, for no reason he could decipher. They were just there chattering without voices, a firework of heads manifesting and dissolving at random in his mind's eye. Then he'd be immersed in random scenes like a compilation of movie clips. Sometimes he'd witness a stranger's life through their eyes. Other times he'd witness an environment like a meadow or a forest or the sidewalk of a metropolitan cafe. There was no sound to these visions and he couldn't move his perception. Whatever he was seeing he was stuck there seeing it for a few seconds and that's all.

This time was different. Something in the combination of really wanting to know what happened to him and giving up on that want at the same time sparked a different image behind his lids. More than a random glimmer, it was a flashback. Mom was there… cuddling him in the grime of Hockomock. And Henry, too. Henry behind her staring down… something in his hand… something—a gun. A gun! A GUN!

"I love—"

'He shot her! Jesus fucking Christ, Henry shot Mom! No! No—how can this…? This has to be wrong! It was that crazy guy! Not Henry! How could it be Henry, unless…. He controlled that guy. Nelson. Henry said his name—his name was Nelson! Oh, fuck, I get it. Yeah, he was watching… watching everything. He made me crash into that guy's lawn! He controlled that guy's voices! He did this to me!'

Corey slammed palms against the lid of his watery tomb but he couldn't throw it open. Henry had locked it. "Henry!" he screamed. "Henry, let me out! Now!" He struggled but remembered that the damned chamber was soundproofed. This didn't stop him from crying out, "Why am I here?! Why am I here, Henry?! Why am I here?!"

He sobbed, "Why did you do this to me? What is this?" but there came no reply, not from outside or within.

"Okay…. Okay, get it together. Breathe… like that fucking monster taught you… breathe…. I came to them…. They didn't take me they took my friends…. Why did they take my friends? … I was no good…. I was a failure, maybe, right? … Is that it? … Or am I supposed to—Did they know this would happen? Am I supposed to be here? What is it? … Just breathe…. Breathe in… and exhale…. In… exhale…."

There was nothing Corey could do so Corey did nothing. He had no sense of time in there but knew it had to be nearing 3:33am, the time of deep magic. He centered himself then let himself go, drained of adrenaline and anger and hope and his senses. He drifted aimlessly into oblivion forgetting to harness that energy, when it shot through him, and funnel it into the abyss.

And it did enter him, just as Henry predicted. His body felt it like a jolt. It writhed in him like a snake awaiting the tune of its charmer. Henry taught him that he was like a levee and if he didn't redirect the raging flow it would overcome him and kill him and move through the earth.

Corey saw the lie of his teaching.

This energy had no intention of leaving Corey. He was buzzing with it. It felt blissful and was as if he was levitating on a bed of it. It was affecting the body but the mind had already given in to nothingness. With no instruction to sustain that nothingness, it began to display the creation of all things that was also him. The empty space grew conscious of itself and that consciousness spread out as a clear ball over black just as it had when he was someone else's captive. The brain felt like it was expanding with the clarity of that ball and if it snapped he would die.

It did snap and from the epicenter, a spark of light and from that light came… a female. She looked perfectly human— too perfectly, like a robot with plastic surgery, he thought, but that aura and that eloquent voice were unmistakably alive.

In him she said, *Understand hither-thither and in that understanding be neither swept away nor carried on the seas of time. Come to me now, body and soul. Failsafe closing. Waste not another breath in prison, my love.*

It wasn't merely the lilt of her voice but the very essence of her that spoke in him and as him. There was a connection, no average bond, but a deeply felt thing, as if on some level he and this bizarre goddess melded into one. Was she the love and remorse felt after his recurring nighttime flashbacks of a previous life?

He felt his awareness normalizing in this nothing state and his body evaporating. Her queer first sentence came alive in his mind as an instruction on stepping out of space-time through understanding that the concept of "here and there" is an illusion of boundaries. Came alive as his boundaries of conscious/unconscious were dissolving and as she was coming alive in his being. This woman wasn't just speaking through him she was waking up within him as the instruction to physically step out of the universe through a simple realization amidst this in-credible situation. This ability was the very action of Henry's dreams.

Henry's dreams. Was this Henry's dream?—To deliver him to the aliens body and soul at this final hour? Every time he had an answer another question replaced it and there was no time left for cycles. There was no time. Failsafe closing, whatever that meant. Corey didn't get that one and even though he felt himself evaporating into the instruction of this woman who felt a part of him, he hooked onto the only word that made con-scious sense to him: love. Corey's face smiled reflexively and his lungs sighed a goofy chortle as the essence of Lina Igasho per-fumed the word and captured his soul. His soul, which he now in this moment relearned he had. And into that moment, all of that moment, he died.

Body fading, mind coming sharply alive, this vital force humming and stealing him to wherever he wished to travel in space or time. Anywhere. There was nowhere he wanted to be but with his true love. She pulsed through him like a beating heart and he needed to be with her. For this, for her, Corey let go completely. He abandoned his instruction from the alien goddess blending her essence with his, as he had done with Henry's, and dissolved all trace of himself in this bitter exis-tence. There was a fleeting sadness then in that no-space. The expanding, snapping ball of clarity might as well have been the teardrop of a universe unfulfilled and dying to the whims of free will and the guilt that clenches a man and never lets go until he does the right thing.

All of this, all of this, all of this *all*... Corey Avon.

Coming to his senses.

Regaining his body.

Materializing in an entirely new place.

Same as the old.

But different. It was his. He was self-aware. The moment was his. The future was now. So was the past. The world was right again.

"Excuse me, you have the time?" he asked the girl in front of him. Her forehead rested on the window so comfortably that she didn't bother to turn around. She knew he was addressing her, though, because he asked it through the space between the seat and the pane and she felt the heat of his breath on her ear.

"Yes. Yes I do. It's time to get a watch," she deadpanned.

"Gee, thanks. I guess asshole is the new helpful these days, huh?"

"I'm only joking," she said. "God, take a pill."

He waited for the follow-up offering of time but it never came. "Then... you do have the time?"

"No," she said. "My atmosphone died. I don't have a watch." She raised her naked left wrist as proof.

"Great. Thank you," he huffed.

"Why? Where do you have to be?"

"Huh? Oh, ahhh... going out. Friends. Camping. I'm like late."

"Was that even a sentence?" she giggled. "Fire. Baaaad. Camping. Gooood."

Corey laughed. "Yeah, I dunno. Sorry."

"What's your name anyway?"

He paused and stared a hole through her. She felt the force of it and didn't know what she was feeling. Panic?

Corey materialized within himself then, caught his mouth running through the motions of a conversation from another time, another space, the one he had just wiped away. He searched for new words to end this déjà vu and they came. Horribly they came because although he had always known that he loved her, he now knew the depth of what true love meant.

"I have a girlfriend," he choked out softly so only she could hear.

"And does she own your name?"

His throat swelled and so did his eyes. He searched the stains of the bus window, holding out for another answer, another way, but this was it. This was all he could see.

"What's wrong with you?" she asked, genuinely concerned.

He narrowed his eyes and they went cold like a predator's. He turned them on her and then into her.

"Don't ever fucking talk to me!" he barked through grinding teeth.

Her jaw dropped. She was perplexed but also a tinge scared. The way he growled it with such menace she knew something had changed and they were no longer joking around.

Lina Igasho faced forward in her seat and vowed to never look at this miserable boy again.

PART THREE

But A Dream

Chapter 35

"No, you can't go! I don't give a shit if you're already there—Don't you hop that fence! This was my idea! My expedition! ... Don't tell me to calm down! Listen, put James on the phone.... James! Dude! You didn't bring anything with you, did ya? No, of course not, so why do you even want to go? You're just gonna get bit by bugs and we're gonna laugh at you so what's the point? It's gonna be miserable.... Cool. Cool. Thanks. Okay. Put Darryl back on...."

Corey almost lost reception on the cordless when he stepped into the garage to dump the trash.

"Hello? Hello—Dude, don't hate me, I promise you this is for the best. Drop those guys off at home and get over here.... No, they can't come. We'll meet up with them later. Trust me on this one.... Trust me, okay?"

They said their goodbyes and on the way back to the kitchen Corey dropped the phone and doubled over, slamming palms to temples. The pressure in his head... the copies of memories flickering away.... He knew what this was. Henry was stealing him.

***

Darryl pulled up to the gate of Spooky Mansion for the second time that Friday. The first that he knew about. "I cannot believe I'm agreeing to this," he said. "You better not burn me, Core."

"I won't burn you, Darryl, I just can't tell you what's going on."

"You're lucky I love you, man."

Corey smiled, taken aback.

"Like a brother, bitch. Don't get any ideas."

Corey laughed and said, "I need to borrow your gun."

If he'd been drinking Darryl would have done a spit take. "Dude, are you high? I don't own a gun!"

"The flare gun. It's in your backpack."

"The flare gun. How did you know I have a flare gun? I packed it at the last second. I *know* I didn't tell anyone."

"I know a lot of things. Man of mystery today. Where is it?"

"I don't know, dude."

"Come on, please. I'm begging ya here."

Darryl relented. He leaned into the backseat and rummaged through his backpack for the gun. He found it and loaded it for his friend, then showed him how to take it off safety.

"Thanks, bro. Stay here."

Corey got out of the car.

"Stay here? Dude, are you serious?" If Corey heard his plaintive whining he ignored it, all business striding to the mansion. "Dude's serious."

Corey tucked the gun under the back of his shirt and hopped the fence. He stomped through the dead tall grass up to the door of Spooky Mansion with the confidence of an actor rehearsed. He rang the bell but he couldn't hear if it worked. Probably not, he figured, military would have disengaged it if the old thing worked to begin with. He was tempting to bang knuckles on the door but someone opened it before he could. Henry. Smiling the smile of a man gazing Death in the eye, wondering if a poker face and some fast talk would be enough to sway him.

"Corey Avon! Welcome home. I've been expecting you," he emoted like a long lost friend.

Corey smiled back, a calm dog with bite. "I know," he said.

He stepped inside the mansion. The door creaked shut behind him.

***

Spooky Mansion was enough distance from the perimeter fence that with the overgrowth Darryl couldn't see what was happening. But he heard that door open and close and what sounded like an older man's voice.

What the fuck is going on? What are you up to, Corey?

He knew his friend didn't deal drugs. Did he owe somebody money? Was this a secret mob lair? Was it hoboville in there? Was Corey feeding the homeless? Maybe it was a flophouse. It's not like he'd ever checked it out himself. Maybe Corey had a problem he kept from everyone. Whatever it was, Darryl would be damned if he was just going to sit here and wait.

Wait for what? Gun shots? From a flare gun?

Fuck it. Darryl was a better friend than that. Whatever Corey was into, he had his back. He quietly opened and closed the Civic door so no one would hear it and dug his toes into the scaling sweet spot in the fence.

***

Corey eyeballed the interior scanning for traps. All he found was a dusty living space that he imagined contained in its decay the energy of white-collar spirits stuck in the delusion that this was still the Ritz. And then Nelson flashed in his mind and he cringed. How many monsters called this land home?

Henry read his concern. "What? You waiting for Special Forces to jump out of the walls and haul you away in a net?"

"It's just you?" Corey asked.

"Just me, Kiddo. I sent everyone packing. Half day today. You used to love those."

"You in my head again?"

"Been there. Done that."

"That makes two of us."

"You know it's funny, when you watch high tension scenes in movies there's always bad dialogue that looks clever on paper. You never think you'd say those things in real life but here we are. The ironic thing is, you think I'm the bad guy."

Corey sighed and relaxed a bit. "Well, maybe we're both stalling for time."

"More like stalled *in* time."

Corey shot him a look that said, *enough.*

"Sorry," Henry said. "It's hard to stop once you get on a roll."

"I'm not here for your bullshit."

"Yes. Here to kill me. I get it. You love her. You can't be with her. I killed your parents, yada-yada. A serial killer. All my fault. But the thing is, you're here. None of that happened. In fact, I didn't do all of that. Henry in... whatever world did that. Sorry. I read you while you waited for your friend in the car. Thank God for timing, huh?"

"I felt the pain in my skull. I knew what it was this time."

"I guess I'm out of secrets."

Corey cocked his head, shot him a look that asked, *You think I'm an idiot?* But his mouth said, "No. You're not out of secrets, Henry. In fact you have plenty of those. I just don't care is the thing."

Henry's tone dropped to sternness. "You think I can't take a flare gun from you, Kiddo? Are you out of your mind coming here?"

Corey paused thoughtfully and lowered his eyes to his black Ecco sneakers. "I don't know what I am," he admitted.

Something about Corey deflated in that moment. Henry detected a plea for help there. Perhaps this wouldn't have to end in the kid's messy death with Darryl framed for murder. "Well there I can help you," he said earnestly. "You're the boy who changed the world—literally changed the world. For love."

Henry smiled and cringed at the inherent clichéd cheesiness but his exaggerations weren't lightening Corey's mood. Seeing this, he picked up, "There's an irony here. And this is the important part, Kiddo."

Corey's gaze of a man torn apart drifted slowly from his Ec-cos to Henry's squinty eyes.

"After I read you I read her. I wanted to know what this girl you love so much was about," Henry continued. "Turns out she's writing a book."

Corey began to say he knew all about it but Henry talked over him—"No you don't. Not this one. That one, the one you know about? Doesn't exist here."

Corey was genuinely taken aback. "What are you saying?"

"The book she's writing now, in this timeline, isn't about you. So on the one hand, you just told the girl you love and whose life you resurrected at the expense of your own—who doesn't know jack shit about you or any of that—you just told her to go fuck herself. Not good. But on the other she's a kid, she'll get over it."

"Do you *want* me to use this gun on you?"

"No. What I want, Corey, is for you to go win her back. Go live your life. You're free."

"But I'm that guy. She's that chick. From the story she was writing."

Henry flailed his arms melodramatically. "Apparently not."

"No. No, this can't be right. I'm an abductee. They want me. The aliens, or whatever... they... It's me they need."

"No. See, I don't even know you from that stuff here. I took it from your mind because... Awe Christ, moment of truth time—Look, here in this timeline there is no alien abduction. No aliens, Kiddo. Just delusional people. That... we... that is to say, the people I'm in charge of... make delusional so they won't know about being part of a human internet."

"So that's still happening," Corey snarled.

"Oh, game on, pal. And you're still part of that. Hence, our relationship. I mean... what do you think I'm even doing here? There's no techno club in New York for *this* guy. But again, the good news... and let's focus on that.... The good news is that you saved us. Clearly. Whatever these aliens wanted you for there?

They don't even know you're here. That all died. Poof!" Henry clapped his hands for effect. He thought he heard footsteps behind him and began to turn when Corey dropped the gun, which drew back his attention. For that he paid with a severe crack to the skull by a large chunk of jagged floorboard. The wood was old enough that it split in half on impact.

Henry slammed face first into the dusty grime at Corey's feet. "Poof," Daryl said standing where Henry just was.

Corey gaped at his mentor, the unconscious bloody mess, and then at Darryl in shocked disbelief. "Loose floorboard," Darryl explained. "I found it on the way in a busted window. This place is shit. I'm glad we never broke in here as kids."

Corey nudged Henry's head with his foot to see if he was still alive. No response. "Let's get the fuck outta here," he said, still unsure.

Darryl retrieved his flare gun while Corey opened the front door. Dust and debris rustled up from the clobbering danced there in the stripe of sun, flashing Corey back to a time worse than this in a basement just as murky.

Darryl drove his best friend home in the silence of things gone wrong.

*****

Corey found no solace in the post-industrial town scenery whizzing by his open window but he wasn't ready to look at Darryl again. It was hard enough glancing sideways at him without staring, having met his alien doppelganger. But this? The pressure of having to explain why he might have killed a man and for what? Too much for words and probably Darryl hated him now.

They pulled into Corey's driveway. Corey hung his head and nervously played with the wrinkles in his jeans. He listened to the murmuring engine and tried to think of something, anything, to end this while Darryl lit another cigarette. He'd been chain-smoking Camels to their filter nubs.

"Thanks," Corey finally managed to squeak out. He opened the car door and got a foot on the ground before Darryl clutched his shoulder softly. Corey appeared to ignore that by stepping all the way out beyond Darryl's grasp, but then he pivoted around and hunched in the frame to meet his friend again.

"What we did back there," Darryl said, his voice shaking, "It's okay, right?"

Corey thought a moment how to approach this. At last he said, "That guy was lying to me."

"But he was gonna kill you?" Darryl needed this, needed a clean conscience.

"How much of what we talked about did you hear?"

"A lot. How much of it was lies?"

"A lot."

"So he wasn't gonna kill you?"

Corey climbed back in and hugged his friend at an awkward angle. He said, "No, dude. But trust me, you didn't murder him. He let us go."

Darryl blurted a clipped laugh. "How do you figure that?"

"He saw us coming a mile away. I know how he works. This was theater."

"Now who's lying," Darryl balked.

"I'm not, I swear. The place is a military base. They would have swarmed us if he wanted that. He doesn't. He wants to know what I'm gonna do next."

"Why you?"

"Gather the troops, Dar. Tomorrow I'll explain everything to all you guys as best I can. But we can't meet at the tree house, not ever again."

Corey squeezed out of the Honda Civic. He shut the door and heard the buzz of the electric window rolling down. He stooped in the frame. Darryl stamped a butt in the ashtray and blew smoke out the left side of his mouth away from Corey's face. "Are we cool?" he asked.

Corey made a crinkled facial expression. "You mean me and you?"

"Yeah."

"Yeah! Of course! Dude, I thought you'd hate me if anything."

"No way, Coronimus. Brothers to the end."

Corey smiled. He felt the first nourishing emotions since fading alive here washing through him. "Brothers to the end," he repeated.

"Punch it out," Daryl said. They fist bumped through the open window and Darryl took off leaving Corey to his parents. To his parents whose death he had mourned. To his parents who had been slaughtered trying to find him.

To his parents who were right now surprised to hear their boy coming home in time for dinner.

INTERLUDE
Earth

Heru are an androgynous mammalian race with chameleon skin. On Earth Plane they blend into their natural environment. In their distant past, they meandered about eating leafy greens and large insects under the rule of instinct until grays decided to tweak their brains with the gift of sentience. They remain a chatty people who make perpetual chirping/clicking sounds in their throats even when communicating psychically. They are bipedal now and control when and to what hue they change color. Control this on Earth Plane but not Earth Zero.

Something about entering a parallel universe sets them to an unalterable dark green. They did not know this about themselves until their representative in the Earth Plane Council materialized on Earth Zero—the species' first exploration into parallels. The young heru rushed back through the portal for immediate testing. Nothing was resolved and to this day the change is a mystery, save for the fact that it lasts the duration of stay and does not lead to illness.

This was the sole documented case of physical alteration between worlds but it was harmless enough. There were no cancerous effects from stepping through the portal for any of the council members. That was never a concern. Thus, when next they passed through to check on the evolution of their thriving penal colony and found Earth Zero barren, rampant new disease was not at the top of their list of mortal causes.

***

The council explored the dead world, dusty and red, with minimum caution. Although this universe had been artificially created it was possible, even if unlikely, that new intelligent predators existed here.

All forms are expressions of the singular formless consciousness in which they are embedded. This is as true for artificially exploded universes as it was for the original unmade group of them. More space-time continuums equal more room for expression.

However, the odds of exploding into existence a life form more advanced than any race from Earth Plane was highly implausible. Even more farfetched was the notion that this life form would be hostile. Such had never poofed into existence before. Be that as it may it was still technically possible, for all things must be expressed and an extraordinarily intelligent, if aggressive, race is one of those things.

There is a loophole to the necessity of expression: all things must be expressed but they do not need to be expressed outside of imagination. Imagination is the ability to invest a mental image with emotional content and life for the duration of one's interest. Fantasizing about a race that is more intelligent than any from the original universes winking into existence at the tip of a big bang would have been expression enough. If Earth Planers could imagine it, it need not materialize.

Problem was, Earth Planers had lost much of their sense of wonder, the vrooming engine of imagination. They didn't imagine this scenario of spontaneous perfect intelligence. In fact, they barely considered it. They considered it the way one mouths the words to some truism they don't believe in the interest of fairness.

In other words, this barren red planet might be a trap—and one in which the Earth Plane explorers, for all their hyper-intelligence, were feeling the contours of right now.

Chapter 36

"Wow, our boy is actually home for supper tonight," Meg said with blunt astonishment.

Corey startled her when he came up behind her and wrapped his arms around hers while she busily pieced together casserole parts. "Hi, Mom," he said and he squeezed her tight laying his head against the back of her neck.

She craned around, gave him a peck on the temple. "What's got into you?" she asked.

He let go and rubbed her shoulders for a few seconds. "Nothing. I just wanted to tell you that I love you."

She melted into the massage. "Oh, that feels good. I'm waiting for the catch."

"No catch. Just I love you." He lightly grabbed the magazine his dad was reading at the table and lowered it until John made eye contact. "You too, Dad," Corey said.

John responded in his usual bumbling manner, "Well... that's nice to hear. Love you too, son."

"I know you do. Listen, both of you. I know I haven't been the best kid in the world, but I'm done being a kid. All that... stuff. You know? That dynamic we have. Had. Dynamic we had—that's gone now and there's just I love you, okay? From now on I love you."

"I hate to sound like a dad but, Corey, have you been drinking?" John asked.

Corey laughed. "What? No! No, it's not about that; it's about this." He meshed his fingers together forming a circle with his arms for emphasis. "Us. We're a family. Other families aren't this lucky. I've got two parents. You've got each other. And you've got me. It's time we all remember that."

Meg slid her specialty basil penne casserole into the oven and set the timer, then pulled up a seat at the table next to

John. "Did something happen at school today?" she asked. "Did a friend of yours die?"

"No, Ma." He said this as condescendingly as she'd asked it, but actually felt hurt that he couldn't disclose the grim understatement. He flopped into his usual chair across from them. "This really isn't about anything else. I know it's weird. Weird, right? Sudden. I'm just saying—I had an, um... what's the word?—Epiphany. An epiphany today. You and Dad have this really fucked up relationship—"

'—Corey," she scolded.

"Well it is, let's just be real. It's unhealthy, the two of you, but it's still a relationship and I think it's time we all reflected on that. On... on what makes us stick together even though we roll our eyes at each other and, you know, sulk around and... and hide behind newspapers." Corey shot a look at his dad who shrugged guiltily as if to admit he had a legitimate point.

"We do love each other, right?" Corey urged with the lilt of a naïve plea.

"Oh, honey, of course we do," Meg soothed.

"Right! See? So that's our bond. We genuinely love each other. So... so the surface level that we interact on—that can be like or disgust or distrust, or... you know? We can like each other or not to each other's faces but underneath that? Underneath that is an unshakable love. So I'm saying, why don't we just quit it? Quit the trivial nonsense. Put away the masks and get back to that love because that love is really who we are and how we feel about each other. Let's be that for each other on the surface, too. Then we don't have to just live, we can be happy. We can be with each other again and not just living with each other. Does that make sense?"

The Avon parents sat slack jawed. John secretly wondered if Corey was writing a play. He was waiting for the "Just kidding, Dad!" but it never came.

Meg broke the stiltedness with, "Well, if we're really having this discussion for *real* for real, then yes. That makes more sense than anything I've heard in a long time."

"I can start over," John found his mouth saying to stay in the conversation. But as he said it he sort of willed himself to believe it, to become a better person—the kind of person who isn't ashamed to start over. And he smiled. Sheepishly, but it was genuine.

"Come here you two," Corey said. And actually he went to them and gave them a hug and a kiss before heading to his bedroom.

"Where are you going?" Meg asked.

"I need to make a phone call. I'll be back for dinner. You guys make out or something."

"Yuck," John blurted.

Meg whacked him gently on the shoulder.

"Not yuck, you. Yuck that he would say that. I'd never say that to my parents. I mean the thought is...."

"Don't say yuck," Meg warned playfully.

"Then kiss me, you fool." John pulled her to him. They made out.

***

"Hello? ... Hel-lo-oh?"

Corey had dialed the number but he didn't know what to say. After all that he'd relayed downstairs he was dumbstruck here.

"Giving this one more shot—Hello!"

"Hi," he finally broke.

"Yes, who is this?"

"It's me, Lina. Corey."

"Corey," she stated trying to figure out who Corey was.

"Corey Avon from the bus today."

There came a pause so quiet he imagined he was hearing her hold her breath as recognition yielded to anger and disappointment, which converted at last to droll delivery. "Oh. Corey. The asshole. How did you get this number?"

"You gave it to me."

She laughed at his foolishness. He sensed the hang-up coming and tried to blurt out, "No! Wait! You really did!" but he only got partway through when he heard the click.

He called back and was sent to voicemail.

This is Lina. Leave it. … Leave it to Lina sounds like Leave It To Beaver. But that's dirty. Whatever… Leave it!

"Hi, again. Look, I don't blame you for being mad. Or creeped out. Are you creeped out? I'd be creeped out. Hell, I *am* creeped out and I'm me—imagine how *I* must feel. Shit, is there a way to erase this before you get it? I, ummmmm…. Please just find this cute instead of stalkerish and call me back, I've got something to tell you, okay? I know about the notebook. You're writing a book and… and you're going to wonder now how I know that, right? So call me ba—"

The voicemail beeped indicating that he'd been cutoff and the message sent.

"Fuck!" he yelled. "God damn it I sound like I'm in her fucking window!"

His thumb hovered over the redial button but he couldn't do it. What if she answered? What if she didn't?

During his indecision the phone rang. He didn't even hesitate to pick up the call. "Lina, I'm so sorry—"

"Stop! Stop-stop-stop. Really, who the hell are you? What are you, going through my stuff when I'm not home? Sniffing my underwear?"

"I can explain—"

"I haven't told anyone about that book. Not a soul. I don't write it at school. It could be a lucky guess, I suppose. You a lucky guesser? You a psychic?"

"No, but your mom is."

She shut up, stunned.

"Listen to me. Lina, this is going to sound... I don't know what." He took a moment to gather his thoughts. She stayed with him on the other end. On edge. When he felt his shaking breath steady he inhaled deeply and let it all out.

"There's not a way to tell you this without you thinking I'm crazy except you won't think I'm crazy because you of all people—of all people, Lina—understand what it's like to know something deeply about humanity. Something the rest of us can't get. That book you're writing is about me."

After a pregnant beat she ripped into a mocking laugh but he stayed even. "No, it is! It's about me and it's about you and it's about our love for each other."

She laughed harder, piercingly like a startled chicken bagawk. "Is this a fucking joke? Alex put you up to this, didn't he?"

"You can laugh if you want to but you know it's true. I love you Lina. I always have. It's just taken me this lifetime to find you."

"Oy vey," she sighed. "Is this how you score the chicks?"

"I'm trying to be serious," he whined.

"Try harder! My book isn't about you—are you high? I don't even know you! In love with you? Spare me!"

He knew he was losing her. He grasped at anything he could find not to blow out the flame. "Well I knew about the book, didn't I? And your mom's a psychic. And... and your dad— what does he do? Um... You don't know! That's right. You don't know what he does but he travels a lot. He's a contractor. And you're from Los Angeles. Your favorite color is red sun at night. And you're a great kisser, I can tell you that—"

"Whoa."

"Too far?"

"What did you do, steal the Cliffs Notes from an ex boyfriend?"

"No, don't be silly."

"Yes. I'm the silly one in this conversation. Okay."

"Well…. You're still here so I can't be that creepy to you anymore. That's a start."

"I'm just sticking around to see where this is going."

"Can I see you?"

"Can you see me? Like you saw me on the bus?"

"No, that wasn't me. I mean, that was me—but I was lying. I don't have a girlfriend and I'm not an angry psycho with angry psycho eyes. I just, ah… see this is something I need to explain to you in person."

"Right. And then you kill me," she stated.

"No! I would never, ever—you'd be the last person on Earth. You *really* don't understand and I'm really not helping. Can I just please? Just meet with you? In public if you're scared."

"Huh. I'll think about it."

Corey quietly but emphatically cheered himself on with a *YES!* He asked, "Okay. Cool. Thank you. When can I call you?"

"Oh, you're asking now?"

"Yeah, I'm asking."

"I've got your number in my phone, I'll call you. I'm going to hit the shower now. Try not to be in a tree with a telescope."

She hung up on him a second time.

'Henry was right,' Corey realized. 'I can go on like normal.'

He didn't remember smiling this much in the last world. He smelled Ma's casserole wafting upstairs as he pondered and the thought of eating a meal that she made for him—the quaintness, the simplicity that had been lost on him all these years—morphed his smile into a glow.

INTERLUDE
Earth

Earth Planers were excellent surveyors. Mapping the surface of a planet in fine detail would take us years. They mapped the surface and interior in seconds.

What they discovered was that a barrage of asteroids had collided with the planet killing it in predictable fashion. First the giant rocks "popped" the atmosphere. Second they exploded the land and seas. All that had been, *poof!* Exterminated like they had never existed to begin with.

As I said it was predictable. And slow. Slow enough to see coming. Slow enough for the reptilians to stop it if they wanted. Would the prisoner race have been able to stop it without reptilian assistance? There was no way for the Earth Plane Council to verify. If only they had arrived earlier they could have watched the events unfold. They agreed not to make that mistake twice.

***

Following the trajectory of the asteroids the Earth Plane Council found another small planet, blue as sapphire and alive. Alive with methane creatures. Alive with cold-blooded dinosaurs. Had to be alive with reptilians.

So that's where they fled. Did they observe the destruction of Earth Zero? Did they cause it? Did something unforeseen occur that left them helpless to intervene? Were they able to locate and save any of the souls of the original prisoners? Many new questions came clear to which all the answers lay dead ahead, a quick jaunt through space.

The Earth Plane Council representatives went home for their ships and a portable atmospheric gateway. They would set up shop on that new planet, as they had here, eliminating the hassle of repeatedly flying through space to get there. They would anchor themselves there to see this ambiguity to its end.

They would discover a new and terrible mystery that would give pulse to the atrophied imaginations of races older than time.

Chapter 37

Corey half expected not to wake up Saturday morning. And then when he did he wondered if his life had been an extensive lucid nightmare. He lurched his tired carcass downstairs for rye toast and scrambled eggs. His mom kissed him good morning. His dad tussled his hair. That answered that.

Later, in the shower, he scrolled down the mental checklist of obstacles keeping him from the new normalcy and congratulated himself on scratching off four of seven in half a day:

- Send message to Henry, "Don't fuck with me."
- Convince Darryl this happened so he will back me up later with the boys.
- Recreate family.
- Win back true love.

With Darryl on his side it would be nearly impossible for the boys not to believe him. He had wedged his foot in Lina's door, so if he didn't screw that up royally she would remember their timeless connection through the amnesia of this new time stream. And that left just one alien obstacle and one piece of unfinished business. He didn't have a plan for the alien obstacle but later that afternoon, right before Darryl picked him up, he made a frantic anonymous 911 call that finished the business.

***

James didn't want to hang out; he wanted to slog around his house and watch TV. Darryl convinced him to slog around the movie theater with the clique instead. *Remake: The Movie: A Reimagining* had come out Friday. The original *Remake: The Movie* was a gut-busting send-up of all the atrocious Hollywood remakes from yesteryear.

The boys remembered loving the flick as kids, but who knew if it would stand the test of time? They had planned to

find out next weekend how well Pixar reimagined this live action childhood classic as a 3-D animation, but with the camping
trip called off they now had free time aplenty. Unbeknownst to
three of the four comrades, they would have to wait a week
anyway because Darryl lied. Today wasn't a movie day.

Darryl regretted the lie fairly immediately. *Remake: The
Movie: A Reimagining* was all James wanted to talk about during
the ride. "Dude, I'm stoked. This is gonna be awesome. I heard
the scene where Justin Bieber gets his head lopped off looks
totally real. You know... real for a cartoon chipmunk. Like, the
head pops toward the camera and then splats and smears down
the lens, which in 3-D is like his head is smearing down your
eyeballs. Totally risqué for a kid's film I think."

"Risqué?" Stephen mocked. "Did you just say *risqué*?
What—Is that your word for the day?"

"I know words, asshole," James retaliated.

"You picked it up in a movie review before jumping in the
car, admit it," Stephen said.

"I picked up your mom and jumped on her, how about
that?"

"That doesn't even make sense," Alex squeaked into the
passenger flip shade mirror.

"Your mom doesn't make sense," Stephen retorted in perfect James imitation.

"Dude, I was just gonna say that," James added, faking na-
iveté. He went on, "I can't wait for the day when they can inject
movies into your head. That's gonna be fuckin' rad. Then I don't
have to go anywhere."

Stephen took that as his cue: "Oh, trust me. You're not going anywhere."

James chuckled. He appreciated a good ribbing even at his
expense. "Corey, why are you so quiet?" he asked. But before
Corey could process the question James directed his focus on
Darryl and added, "Looks like we're all not going anywhere.
Dude, you missed the turnoff."

"I didn't miss the turnoff," Darryl corrected.

"You totally did. That's it back there getting smaller. Smaller and smaller like Alex's balls in Lake Sabbatia," James said. Alex flipped him off in the mirror.

"I didn't miss the turnoff because we're not going to the movie," Darryl admitted.

"Well we better be! I got my ass off the couch for this," James lamented.

"Where we going?" Alex asked softly.

"The Cape," Darryl said.

All but Corey groaned in protest.

"This is bullshit," Stephen whined. "What the fuck are we gonna do at the Cape? Ocean's freezing."

"It's too cold for the beach," Alex agreed.

"Fuck that. Movies or we riot," James said.

Corey absentmindedly rapped his knuckles on the window keeping no particular beat and jumped in. "We're not going to the beach. We're going to a restaurant."

"Okay. Does that restaurant have popcorn, Cherry Coke, and *Remake: The Movie: A Reimagining* playing in it? 'Cause that's the only restaurant I'm going to," James spat.

Darryl glared at him something deadly through the rear-view. "Quit bitching—God! Don't you think that maybe, just maybe, there's a bigger reason we lied about the movie and are bringing you all the way to the Cape," he growled.

James thought a moment. "We? You mean you and Corey, then?" Their silence said yes. "Well okay," James continued. "Yeah, I get it. You're taking us as hostages and forcing us to eat stuffed quahog."

Stephen rolled his eyes while shaking his head and chided, "Yeah, that's it."

"No, you fucking moron, just go with it!" Darryl barked.

The atmosphere was uncomfortable then, which was like a breath of fresh air to James. "I'll go with it if you got a cigarette," he said suddenly chipper.

Darryl nodded at his pack of Camels below the ashtray. Alex grabbed it and flicked it at James. "Thanks," he said. "Now hurry up, I gotta take a leak. And turn on the fucking radio for fuck sake."

***

Darryl put the radio on after the boys pledged to one condition: Do not ask where we are going until we are in the restaurant.

James was the last to set foot in the eatery. In perfect sync with the door closing behind him he blurted loud enough for patrons in the immediate vicinity to hear, "McDonald's?! Is this a joke or are we on a scavenger hunt?"

Some of the adults stuffing burgers and fries into their pudgy faces shot him the stink eye.

"Did you know that scavengers won't eat McDonald's fries?" Alex offered. No one acknowledged him.

"No, James, we're here to eat. Go tinkle, get your slime burger, sit down, and shut up. We're going to explain," Darryl said. He moved to the back of the order line.

"We? We again? Corey, you in on this, too? You hate McDonald's," James said.

"Actually, this part I didn't know about, " Corey confessed.

When James got back from the bathroom and everyone had their meals Darryl seized the least spilled upon booth available near as many frantic, shrieking children as possible.

"The torture never stops," Stephen muttered.

Darryl said, "Pull up some plastic, boys. You're in for something bigger than all of us."

"More Puckwudgies?" Alex asked, twiddling a long fry in his mouth. The guys chuckled to make him not feel lame more than because it was funny.

"Not Puckwudgies. Corey?"

Darryl threw it to Corey so abruptly that he stuttered and stammered, mouth in conflict with brain, at the end of which he peeped, "Me?"

Darryl rolled his eyes. "Yeah you. It's your story, dope!"

Corey gathered his thoughts. Remembering every detail was one problem; spitting them out in chronological order was another. First things first he needed them to acquiesce to the disclaimer that as unreal as this is going to sound it is dangerous knowledge. He could be dragging them down a rabbit hole by merely uttering it.

They were numbed to the conspiratorial whisper routine as Corey's go-to story telling device. Because of that and because they were here, not a one hesitated to verbally signoff on the warning received.

***

James rubbed the salty fry grease into his fingers while raising his hand to announce, "I have a question."

"Go ahead," Corey said, his voice swelling with trepidation. His retelling of their impossible history went unforeseeably well. The guys were attentive and at points slack-jawed. Even unflappable Darryl turned a new shade of white as Corey described his torture at the hands of a maniac.

Alex teared up during the death of his new friend Lina and said, "This is better than movies" when Corey revealed it was his mother and father who tried to save him from Henry—big reveal—the bad guy. Alex also felt emboldened hearing of his brave turn in this other life where he walked alone in the woods in the dark of night. He wondered what happened to him out there.

But now James had a question and it was a safe bet that this would be a joke, followed by another, followed by another. Corey presumed that Stephen and he had conspired in sideways glances to save the ridicule for last.

James put his hand down and wiped it on a napkin. He leaned in like he had something important to say but instead froze, mouth-breathing, searching for the right way to put it. Then, "So if all of this is true, what happened to the dead us's?"

Corey exhaled deep relief that this was, miracle of miracles, a serious question. Or it sounded like it might be one. Actually, he didn't get it. "What?" he asked.

"Dead us's. Dead me. Doppelganger James—what happened to that guy when you destroyed the timeline? Can ghosts be killed, too?"

Corey reflected a moment. Wow. Good question, James. Where did that come from?

He answered with a shrug and Darryl saved him with, "You really expect *Dr. Who* here to understand how the fucking fabric of reality works? He ain't Einstein, he's from Taunton."

"Actually, Einstein didn't know how it worked either," Alex noted. They ignored him.

"Yeah, I don't know. All I know is what I told you," Corey affirmed. He slurped the remnants of Sprite off the ice cubes melting on the bottom of his waxy cup.

Stephen finally piped up. "I think we're overlooking the other pressing question, which is why assclown brought us to a McDonald's way the hell out here." He bounced half a French fry off Darryl's chest. James scooped it from the table with the speed of frog tongue and swallowed it whole.

"You're gross," Alex said.

"Five second rule," James replied.

"We came here cuz I didn't know if my car was bugged and Corey said we needed to get out of town cuz of that coil. The dream whatever—"

"Tesla Dream Machine," Corey helped.

"Yeah, that. Maybe they can hear us with it if we're around Taunton, who knows? So we're out of range and it's loud here and even if they wanted to follow us I didn't tell anyone where I was bringing ya and who the fuck would guess this place even if the car was bugged and they knew we were coming to the Cape? So that's why," Darryl said.

James blurted, "Wow, that's fuckin' genius, dude! You don't think they have drones tracking us? Or satellites? Google Earth has satellites up my grandma's snatch by now, surely these fucktards know where we are." He lightly backhanded Stephen's chest on the way to a stretching yawn and said to him, "Dude, we totally could have seen *Remake*. It wouldn't have mattered."

Darryl exploded but tried to keep his voice to a level that wouldn't scare children at other tables. "Okay, asshole! Next time you kill a Man In Black you try protecting us!"

"You didn't kill anybody," Corey assured with the lightness of background noise.

"If you wanted to protect me you shoulda left me at home, happy as a pig in shit," James countered.

Alex, voice of reason that he was, now felt strong enough to settle them. His story in the other life did this for him. Fingers outstretched he patted the air in front of him and said, "Guys, guys—calm down! None of that stuff matters. We're here now. The question is, what do we do with this?"

The boys stopped fidgeting and arguing as if on Alex's command. They pondered their lives, their meaning in this world, for what felt like uncomfortable minutes but was actually less than one.

What were they? Even James was slapped by it. Even he didn't hide from the depth of the question, but he cut the hush with a straightforward point. "I don't remember being abducted."

"Me neither," Stephen seconded.

Alex made three.

Darryl nodded a fourth but said, "No. No, we wouldn't. That's what makes Corey different."

"Corey *thpethial*," Stephen lisped, which translated as an impression of the mentally challenged.

"Not if Henry was telling the truth and there are no aliens here," Darryl recalled.

"No, he's lying." Corey left no wiggle room there. "They implanted me with messages for the aliens, remember? So he wouldn't just know about me and be waiting for me at The Castle—at Spooky Mansion—unless there were still aliens. No, there are aliens. We're all a part of what they're doing, somehow. Maybe I'm that alien leader Lina was writing about and you guys are some of those other pilots. We're prisoners trapped in this reincarnation thing and we found each other." He chuckled and admitted more to himself than them, "It does sound stupid when you say it out loud."

"What does Lina think?" asked Alex.

"She doesn't know yet. She thinks I'm psycho."

"She's got that right," James poked.

Stephen had the look of a man daring himself to speak his truth. "Alright, I'll just say it," he blurted. "I don't know if I'm buying this; it's too much."

Darryl threw his hands up. "There it is!" he cried. "I've been waiting for one of you jamokes to say it!"

"Well, come on! Maybe he dreamed it," Stephen fired.

"And me too? I dreamed it too, right? (*Unfuckingbelievable*, this guy....)"

"I don't know, dude. It's just too much is all." Stephen didn't want to fight about it, just state what he believed was obvious.

Corey finally broke in. "I thought you'd say that. Well... not *you*. I thought James would say that—"

"Thanks," James groused.

"—so I did something this morning to prove it. On second thought, that's not why I did it, but whatever—The point is I did something and you'll see it when it's all over the news: I turned Nelson in." Merely speaking the serial killer's name made him involuntarily wince and that should have been reality enough for Stephen.

"I thought you said you didn't remember where he lived?" Alex asked.

"I don't *know* where he lives but I remember roughly where. I remember the house. I know its secrets. Ugh, I'll never forget that place—Had to do a little acting for 911. Said I'd escaped the sub chamber in the basement but was still trapped in the house—*Oh, God! He's coming!*—That sort of thing. But I got in as much detail as I could in thirty seconds before making the line go dead."

"Finally, you've found a reason to have 'unknown' come up on your phone where, say, a normal human being has their phone number so we actually answer you when you call," Stephen joked. Countless were the times they each lamented not knowing if their friend or a telemarketer was calling because the unlisted Avon name and number never popped up on their atmosphones.

"Shit, dude. They probably nabbed the bastard by now," Darryl said. "Nice work."

Corey smiled with pride. If Darryl was correct there'd be no question in the boys' minds that this was real. How it would shake out for his buds wasn't predictable but that was life. And Corey almost had his back.

INTERLUDE
Earth

Eight Earth Plane Council volunteers—two faeries, three grays, two squatch and an elf—drifted silently over the treacherous black sea of the new planet in their oval ship. A thirty-foot dunkleosteus leaped out from between crashing waves and snapped ineffectively at the giant silver lure. Since dinosaurs ruled all of the land it was a fair assumption that reptilians likewise populated the globe and so someone would spot their ship, would flag them down and welcome them.

Not a soul.

The team scanned the planet as best they could but if they were wrong and a mere handful of clans lived here they would be hard to detect. The problem was compounded by the fact that all of the dinosaurs they'd created here were of the cold-blooded variety, just like the reptilians, and the warm-blooded mammals were tiny. Reptilians obviously preferred cold-blooded life forms to warm. Back home in Dinosaur Chasm they never voiced a preference, yet here it was. Chalk it up to another secret exposed.

The volunteers tracked down the largest population of anapsids they could find and landed in their vicinity. Anapsid eggs were a staple of the reptilian diet. Find one, find the other.

The Earth Planers clothed themselves in breathable suits and touched foot to soil on this familiar alien world. They took inventory of their surroundings looking for classic signs of reptilian life. Nothing. But they had to be here. Had to! So many lumbering anapsids!

Two squatch and an elf, expert trackers by nature, set off to find people while the others hovered above their sky barge and constructed a door back to their own world in the atmosphere. This involved grouping the specific type of subatomic particle the two universes held in common. Particles of all kinds naturally zipped around and appeared to bounce in and out of existence at random. They appeared that way but what they were really doing was flipping randomly between the visible spectrums of the dimensions they conjoined. This chaotic weaving in the visible spectrum of one dimension and out the visible spectrum of the other was what comprised the fabric of reality. Earth Plane science was so advanced that they could isolate and consolidate the particles that married this newly exploded universe with home and control the flip. They could, in effect, make a door between parallels.

The magic of Earth Plane science was its simplicity. Inventing to the point of simplicity was complicated. Gates like these were rudimentary compared to their later discoveries and inventions. This is what made the reptilian riddle so confounding. How was there even a riddle at all to a people this advanced?

***

The squatch and elf returned to their ship empty-handed. No reptilians. But where they returned to was also empty. To where did their five compatriots venture? They obviously built the gate between worlds just fine, but then where did they go without notice? Home?

One of the squatch growled a low baritone of confusion when the elf pointed out their landed ship: it was sinking.

Sinking? Was there a sinkhole here? It wasn't quicksand, they knew that, but how could they have made the careless mistake of landing on a sinkhole? The trio didn't stand around to watch their ride disappear. In the off chance that the other volunteers were trapped in the vessel, they made a dash for it.

Or tried to. All three found their feet stuck to the ground as if encased in cement. This was impossible! The squatch were fur and muscle but they couldn't move their feet any more than the scrawny elf. They began to sink at the rate of their ship.

The two squatch looked to their elf colleague for guidance but she had nothing to offer. They were up to their knees but she was up to her thighs already in solid earth. That solidity was the doubly infuriating problem, for they could not push up with their hands or dig free of the compacted dirt. Touching it glued them to it like fly paper.

Chest deep and sinking. Soon, suffocating. A family of anapsids shambled over and encircled them. They had no problem standing on what for them was soft soil. Statuesque, they followed the trio with their eyes as the Earth Planers sank to their deaths. The last glint of submerging oval ship faded from sight between anapsid shells.

The shock of the impossible kept the squatch and the elf from realizing the severity of their dilemma until their lungs filled with soil and with death. The elf was first to go, and there was no crying out, no primal release in her final moments, for elves did not fear death. Neither did squatch. No one held their breath to stave off the tickling of dirt.

The anapsids gazed attentively until the last hairs on the tall squatch heads were buried alive. Anomaly vanished, they scattered back to their drowsy lives.

Chapter 38

The boys retired back to their individual lives. Corey's revelations were a lot to process and it would be easy to slip into
paranoia. This is where James' and Stephen's defense mechanisms worked to their benefit. James zoned out in front of the
tube for the rest of his evening and Stephen got into several
bidding wars at the online penny auction, Quibids. Darryl had a
posture to maintain as the cool, collected one, but Alex was a
changed man. He was still meek on the outside; inside he had
strength.

Corey played a couple of rounds of Scrabble with Mom and
Dad but his head wasn't in the game. He was obsessing about
Lina, couldn't help himself, and his nagging inner voice told him
to go to her even though it had only been a day since they
talked and she hadn't called him back. He bowed out of round
three to bike to her place. She *had* to be home on a Saturday
night; she barely knew anyone but Alex.

He was so in his head about the Lina conundrum that his
feet involuntarily motored the pedals. They drove him not to
her apartment but to Church Street where lived the demon who
had tortured him and killed her. A swarm of flashing blue lights
snapped him out of his daze. He stopped pedaling and drifted
along the curb opposite the police melee. Neighbors watched
the show safely from their porches and yards as Taunton's Finest rolled out the yellow tape. A man was being dragged from
his apartment in cuffs. The dude looked like a slimeball—short
with a squishy rectangular build, his mullet a matted oil spill,
hazel eyes glazed with meth and confusion. He wore tattered
boxer briefs stained in places a normal man would be embarrassed to wear. Shirtless, of course, his arms were draped in
tattoo sleeves and his chest hair was amazing. He was perfectly
creepy with MOM inked on his jugular, but he was the wrong
guy.

Corey muttered "No, no, no," under his breath. He imagined correctly that the police had scoured the neighborhood for sex offenders on record and found this guy's rehabilitation less than stellar. The perp's building did look kind of like the serial killer's house but....

"He's over there, dummies," Corey mumbled to himself. He was referring to the serial killer's dilapidated home five houses down the block.

He didn't know what to do, but something. Something other than explaining himself had to happen here. In camera flash speed the solution lit him. He pedaled fast now so the cops wouldn't have a chance to notice him. He checked out the yards across the street from Nelson's layer and found one without a fence delineating properties. Lights were on in the home but no lookie-loos clustered on the stoop. Minivan and pickup truck slept in the drive. He was willing to chance these people being home because their lawn, situated diagonally across the street from the demon on the far side from the cops, was at a perfect angle for what he had in mind.

Corey stealthily leaned Old Faithful against the side of the house facing its open backyard. He purposefully did not extend the kickstand, planning a quick getaway. He hunted around for the largest rock he could chuck with accuracy and hurled it at the demon's closest window. He missed and bounced it off the wall. The impact was loud but not enough to perk a busy detective's ear or catch a nosy bystander by surprise. Undeterred, he found another stone and launched that fucker with extreme might fueled by adrenaline and bad intentions. He felt the strain on his arm and thought he might have pulled a bicep. No time to wince, this one soared through the old man's brittle pane shattering the glass. Shattering it loudly.

Several cops turned, startled. They signaled their party that they were going to check it out. Palms on holsters, they approached the nightmare that would make them talk-show famous, in long careful strides. By the time they stepped up to the door, Corey was gone.

But Nelson was home.

***

"Hello, sir. My name is Corey. I'm a friend of Lina's. I know it's late but if she's home may I see her?"

Mr. Igasho stared up at the tall young man befuddled. They made kids this polite in Taunton?

"Corey? I don't remember Lina mentioning you," he said more jogging his memory than trying to be rude. Mrs. Igasho appeared over her husband's left shoulder and froze when she beheld Corey. She was walking to the kitchen, not to the door, but when she saw him her head jerked and her eyes flew wide for a moment. Mr. Igasho was just doing the concerned fatherly act but something about Corey obviously stunned her in an embarrassing way. Embarrassing for Corey who felt locked out by these impenetrable guards eyeballing him for entirely separate reasons, their scrutiny keeping him out of the tower and away from his princess.

Mercifully, Mrs. Igasho broke free of her daze and fluttered up behind her husband. She slid a comforting hand onto his right shoulder and he reflexively, lovingly squeezed it. This was the type of affection Corey yearned for his parents to embrace.

"It is not too late," Mrs. Igasho cooed. Her voice was low and raspy, off-putting in its sensuality.

Corey hadn't met either parent in the other life but he'd seen close-ups of their faces in pictures. Mr. Igasho was as he remembered: a paunchy, squat man with a stern face but humorous eyes set in a light brown complexion. Mrs. Igasho was a different story. Far different. He expected a haggard and desperate stick figure with long stringy gray hair drizzling down her back who begrudgingly cleaned up good for family photos and special occasions—the prejudice that came to mind when he heard the word *psychic*. Standing before him was the opposite of that. Mrs. Igasho was voluptuous with shiny black hair and the sultriest voice he had ever heard in a woman. No hippy pubes under *those* arms. He thought, 'Damn, if Lina doesn't work out....' And then stifled a chuckle.

"Come in," the pot-bellied father relented with a sweep of the hand bidding him entrance.

Both parents were dark brunettes. Mother was taller than father by inches. When she walked her hips swished like a graceful belly dancer in that slinky negligee peaking underneath her blue bathrobe. Father shuffled along in a sweater vest and pleated dress pants. He looked like he needed to slip into something more comfortable: his wife.

How the fuck did he end up with her? Corey was dying to know their back-story and it better not begin and end with *arranged marriage* or he was going to hate America. He mentally slapped himself for the horny stir in his jeans but *Man, she's hot!* And the vampiric way she transfixed on him was accidentally seductive.

Mrs. Igasho called upstairs, "Lina? Lina, hon, you have a friend."

"I do? Be right down!" Lina sounded thrilled by the surprise, like an adolescent being given a wrapped box.

Mr. Igasho asked Corey for his last name then hollered up, "Corey Avon!"

There was a noticeable hesitation and then, "Oh. Be right down." Deflation. No gift inside *that* box.

Mr. Igasho gestured for Corey to take a seat on the couch in the living room. He did and nearly sank into it like the esophagus of a plush white Muppet. He forgot about that.

"Would you like some tea?" Mr. Igasho offered.

Corey smiled politely. "No thank you," he said while shifting his weight to maneuver his ass out of the cushion.

"Okay, I'll go put on some tea," Mrs. Igasho said smiling tightly. She retreated to the kitchen.

"Oh. Sure, yeah—tea would be nice," Corey stammered. What was it with this family and tea?

"So! How do you and Lina know each other?" Mr. Igasho asked. He bent and slowly lowered himself into an interrogation recliner opposite Corey. "My back's not so good," he confided. "I can really feel the weather here."

"Yeah, I know what you mean," Corey said. He nodded well past the words. He had no idea what the man meant.

"You... have a class together?" Mr. Igasho fished.

"Hmm? No. Ah, bus. We met on the bus."

And in another life where we were in love and she died unspeakably rescuing me from Freddy Krueger.

"Do you live around here?" Mr. Igasho asked.

"Not really, but kinda. It's bikeable."

Shit, should I have told him my street?

Mrs. Igasho bounded in and slunk down on the couch near the left arm furthest from Corey.

How come her ass doesn't sink into the couch? Because it's perfect. Duh.

"The water should be ready in a minute," she announced. "Do you want chamomile?"

"Sure, whatever is easiest for you. I'm fine either way." Corey thought he really hit his mark with that one.

"Alright, Corey." She spoke this with a slight yet perceptible condescending tinge of, *You're an idiot.* "Hon?" she asked.

"I'll have chamomile, yes," Mr. Igasho affirmed.

And now Corey got it: she wasn't asking him, she was asking her husband.

Please, God, save me.

"So, where did you two meet?" Mrs. Igasho asked.

"Me and your husband?" Corey joked.

Mr. Igasho chuckled heartily but she remained bemused in that tight grin and loose robe.

Oh, God, her cleavage. Glorious, boobalicious cleavage. No-no! Don't look!—Fucking SAVE ME!

He heard a door squeal open then feet bouncing down stairs. The obvious source of the ruckus was lost on him as he was lost in the perfectly defined mounds rolling underneath that sheer top daring him to stay trained on them.

"Hey," Lina called out.

Corey flitted his gaze past her mom to the window, to the wall—Is that a photo of baby Lina on the end table? That's what he was *really* looking at. Precious. To Mr. Igasho he mouthed the word *Hi*—and, Oh! There Lina is! Portrait of beauty draped over the railing like that.

He smiled broadly. "Hey," he replied with a nod. Somehow this was growing more uncomfortable not less. Did she catch him staring or did the eye flutter jujutsu work?

Mr. Igasho announced, "Corey is a funny boy. I like him!"

Corey cocked his head askance. "I like you, too, Mr. Igasho. You have a nice family." His inflection admitted that this was a revelation to himself.

"Can he come up?" Lina asked, still not thrilled with any of this.

"We were just going to have tea," Mr. Igasho informed her. He sounded like anything less would be a major disappointment.

Mrs. Igasho overruled him. "Tea can wait. Go." When she said it she waved her finger in an elegant looping swirl toward her daughter's room above the ceiling. Such poise in this MILF.

Corey thanked them and said, "Nice meeting you," as he shimmied off the couch.

"Likewise," Lina's parents replied, not quite in unison.

He trained his eyes on Lina's ass up the stairs to take his mind off her exquisite mother. It worked. He prayed she wouldn't look down and notice how well it worked.

***

Lina gently closed the door behind her. Corey belly flopped hard on her bed and delighted in the brief springy bounce. She glared at him sharply. "Make yourself at home," she said dryly and then rolled up the black swivel chair from her computer desk.

"Sorry," Corey chortled jovially. He flipped onto his back and regarded his love upside down. "Old habits die hard."

Lina plunked down in the chair and swung her right foot onto the edge of the bed just far enough from Corey's bobble head to not be rude. She rocked herself nervously and over-enunciated like a child reading a script when she said, "I received a call from Alex. It was really strange."

"I'll bet it was."

"And you know what the strangest thing was? It changed him."

"What did?"

"The story you told him."

Corey shrugged and dug his elbows into the mattress, arching his back. "He's still Alex," Corey offered nonchalantly.

"Yes but he's confident. It's in his voice. So I have to ask myself what kind of story has that power?"

Corey knew and responded hurriedly not letting this hang as a rhetorical. "The truth," he said.

"Not always," Lina countered.

"This time," he said.

She waved him off. "Oh, I don't know if I'm ready for that. That's a big bite to swallow. But I sure wish I had your gift, Corey. You spin one mean yarn, my friend."

Corey gyrated around on his ass and sat facing her. "It's not a yarn, Lina. It's what happened and we both know it."

"So you keep telling me. But my book, the one I'm writing...." She got up and rifled through the clutter on her bookcase.

"Top shelf by the photo album—How do you always forget where you put it, it's your favorite thing in the world."

He was right. She flushed slightly with embarrassment.

"So it is," she said. "But...." She tossed him the notebook, which he snatched from the air. ".... You're not in it."

He leafed through the handwritten chapters, skimmed a word here and there, but didn't really read.

"Okay," he said. "I'm prepared to accept that. Now how do I get in the book?"

"What do you—?"

"I mean I'm in love with you, Lina. And I've seen what our love means to you. It means everything. It meant your life."

He had to consciously will himself not to break eye contact and tear up. She saw his desperation and vulnerability and fucked-up crazy as it was she knew these were authentic emotions.

"That was another life," she reminded.

"Yeah, but they're both mine."

"Yes but this one's mine! I don't belong to that other world. I'm not the Lina you knew."

"No, you are! Of course you—Don't you see? You're exactly her, I just fucked it up by scaring you off."

She looked down. She couldn't face his pleading eyes anymore, couldn't give him what he needed. "Then why aren't you in my book?"

"I don't know why. But that psycho who killed you? Nelson? Did Alex tell you about—"

She raised her hand and acknowledged he had but let's not relive that and he said, "—Okay. That dude I called the cops on. He's going to jail. Watch the news for it. That'll be your proof. And it means we get to live happily ever after."

She didn't mean to but she exploded. "I *am* happy! Don't you get it? I'm not secretly searching for you!"

Her words punched him in the face. She saw it and immediately wished she'd self-censored. She lowered her tone to gentle and spoke, "I'm sorry, Corey. That girl isn't me. She's a different Lina. I'm just writing a sci fi story based on the Vedas because the spiritual history of my people fascinates me. Ever heard of vimanas?"

"Of course. I used to read all that ancient alien shit." He dropped her notebook on the bed and stared at his shoes when he uttered this. He didn't want to be here anymore. Not in this house. Not with her. Not alive.

"So I'm writing about that," she explained. "It's a fake back story to the ancient flying machines, like a fairytale. It's fun." She smiled weakly and felt ill. She didn't do confrontation.

"Alright. Sorry I barged in on you like this. I should get going."

Lina didn't protest or offer further apology. She wanted this to end as desperately as he, sloppy and uncomfortable a resolution as it was. She led him to the front door. On his way he waved goodbye to her folks in the living room and thanked them for their hospitality. They exchanged pleasantries but only Mrs. Igasho pried herself from the breaking news on TV. Mr. Igasho called out exasperatedly, "Lina, did you see this? They caught a serial killer and a pedophile living on the same street! And they have the same name! Nelson! Can you believe this? These men practically live in our neighborhood!"

"There's your proof," Corey said under breath.

Shocked, Lina froze. She jumped a little when her mother slinked up behind her and laid a soothing hand on her shoulder. "Would you like us to drive you home, Corey? I don't know how comfortable I am with you being out there alone," she offered in that sexy rasp.

He grinned and said, "No thank you, Mrs. Igasho. Very generous of you but I'll be fine."

"Are you sure, Dear?"

"Yeah. Besides, you look all cozy and stuff. I don't wanna make you get dressed."

She chuckled at the silly concerns of a sweet boy and adjusted her robe. Before she could press the issue he reassured her. After all, the cops nabbed the bad guys. Streets are that much safer. Plus, he needed the air.

He extended a hand to Lina who hesitated at what she considered an oddly formal gesture but then shook it. He bid them goodnight and once more hollered "Bye, sir!" to Mr. Igasho, then took off on his bike. Lina and her mom watched him ride away in the doorframe.

"That boy has a lot of power," Mrs. Igasho observed. The authority with which she stated it sent a chill up Lina's back.

"How so?"

"His aura is disarmingly bright. He is hard to look upon but it is impossible to take your eyes off him."

"Why don't you marry him," Lina quipped.

Mrs. Igasho played along. "I think your father might have a problem with that."

Lina looked thoughtful a moment. "Ma, do you believe in fate?"

"I do. Not all things but certain moments."

"How do you know when something is fated?"

Mom smiled warmly at her precious jewel and kissed her on the cheek. "You know it when you see it. The trick is to see it before the fact. Otherwise events unfold and you look back and say, 'Oh, I should have seen that coming.'"

Mrs. Igasho suspected they were talking about Corey but she did not ask. She respected her girl's distance.

Lina didn't feel distant. She felt disconnected. And she knew this wasn't anything Mother's wisdom or psychic abilities could fix. She was broken. This boy, this stranger on a bus, had broken her. Fixed Alex but broke her. And then she wondered if her resistance to him was what broke her.

Was Corey crazy? No. But was he fate?

God damn it, was he fate?

INTERLUDE
Earth

Abhavasimha Sharma was coated in a sheen of perpetual sweat and not much else. Loin cloth. No sandals. He was in love with Earth and refused to farm her unless he could dig his toes into her soft, giving belly.

He held deepest respect for sanyasis but he could never do what they did. Growing crops and bringing them to market was so much a part of who he was that he could not fathom renouncing all of that glorious process for a guru and begging bowl. Could not give up his attachment to the quaint township of Harappa where he was born and where he knew he would one day die.

Preferences aside he revered the great yoginis for their magic and their balance. If not for growing up hearing true tales of their mystical experiences he might have run for cover when the sky cut open and spat flying chariots out of its wound. Five, ten, twenty— They came at such blurring speed that he lost count.

Other villagers pointed up at the spectacle, jaws hanging. Some fled in terror. Some dropped to their knees and prayed thanks for the miracle in the sky. It was a sign. *Of what* would be deciphered much later and incorporated into the myths and parables that defined his Hindu people.

Abhavasimha kept his wits about him. He watched the mighty chariots zip around five hundred feet above his head as if they were searching for something. They were noiseless and stirred no wind along the treetops. By all other senses they were not there but his eyes did not deceive.

Abhavasimha's hypnotic stupor was broken by a shuddering boom. A new set of chariots came roaring into view from behind the mountains. These did sway the trees and their noise was such that Abhavasimha had to plug his ears with his fingers for the duration of the show. At first these chariots had the look of organisms. They were covered in soil and moss and roots the width of vines. But those organic veneers cracked off and fell apart like shells, giving birth to metallic objects, same to the last detail as their silent brothers.

Only they were not brothers. Clearly they were enemies and this was no show. This was a fight and one for which the silent chariots were grossly unprepared. The chariots from the mountain touched them with rays of the sun which sent them crashing all around.

Now all of the villagers ran for cover. All except Abhavasimha. He curled his toes in the dirt and mentally recorded the great battle in the sky. Someone needed to remember this precisely and recite it for the wise spiritual orators to till into useful metaphor.

Chapter 39

Monday morning the school bus pulled up on time for once. Normally Corey had a fifteen-minute buffer. He didn't want to leave his folks and the wonderful oatmeal Mom dished out, but he had to immerse himself in this antiquated life. In his previous incarnation school bored him. He expected the novelty of feeling like an objective outsider witnessing the mundane life that meant everything to him, like a ghost trapped amongst the living, to wear off eventually. Then he'd be back to caring about the typical dumb stuff. Even so, the thought of school bored him in a completely new context right now. Some things never changed and here he learned that clichés were repeated to death for good reason.

Corey hadn't heard peep from the boys on Sunday but he wouldn't make a stink about it when he saw them. They needed time. He was confident their silent treatment wouldn't last the day. He'd have to wait to test that theory, however, because none of them were on his bus route. But... 'That's right, Lina is.'

He barely acknowledged her with a nod and a quick grin as he passed her up to find a vacant seat. He found one toward the middle back section. He plunked down next to some tired loner kid he never bothered to meet the first go-round. Maybe in this life he would take the boy under his wing. What was he—a sophomore? Lesson One: Brush Your Fucking Teeth.

"Excuse me, you mind switching seats with me? I need to talk to him."

It was Lina. What were these shenanigans?

The exhausted loner muttered "Sure" with no fuss and scuttled up the aisle to where Lina had been sitting.

"Let's go, people, okay? Can't move the bus until every-one's seated," the driver scolded.

"Sorry! My fault," Lina copped to the angry eyes in the rearview mirror. She swooped down on Corey forcing him to push over faster. With a cough of engine the bus lazily sputtered into action.

"So, Mr. Destiny, tell me more about my fate."

"I don't know what you want from me, Lina."

"What do I want? Hmm…. Well, you could use your super powers to turn back time and not call me last Friday."

Corey rolled his eyes and faced out the window. He scraped at a fleck of dirt caked on the pane with a fingernail but retorted nothing.

"Can't do that? Okay, then make me believe," Lina continued.

"How can I do that." He stated this more than asked because there was nothing he *could* do to make her love him.

And yet she had an answer: "Tell me the story. I want to hear it from you, not Alex."

That broke his attention to window cake. "You serious?"

"Deadly."

He mentally ran through his itinerary then asked, "What do you have fourth period?"

"What's today, Monday? … Gym," she answered.

"Cool. I've got health. Let's skip and meet backstage at the auditorium. There's a loft back there—you know where I mean?"

"No."

"Well just meet me outside the band room and I'll take you there. Nobody goes there. It's perfect."

"Right on. Fourth period I'll see you. I didn't want to play bombardment anyway."

"Really? That's the only time I like gym class," he confessed.

"I like health better. I get to learn about penises."

Corey guffawed so loudly at the unforeseen punch line that the two junior girls in front of him swung around to stare.

"Sorry," he said. "Nothing to see here, ladies. Go back to hating your lives."

***

John Avon finished breakfast and kissed his wife goodbye. Kissed her on the mouth and she kissed back and there was a spark of lust surging through their bond again. He had forgotten what it was like to live up to the I Love You verbal contract they spoke to each other on occasion through force of habit.

He whistled some commercial jingle on his way out the door and only ceased twirling the key ring on his right index to press the orange plastic button that disarmed his car alarm with a double chirp. He didn't quite make it around the front to the driver's side when he saw a man in black business attire striding briskly toward him from across the street.

John smiled at the man while he backtracked to the passenger side to meet his visitor in the drive. "Hello," he announced cheerily.

The stranger smiled so widely and slowly underneath his fedora that it looked as if his lips tore apart at a seam to reveal perfect white dental work. He raised his left hand high. Odd. Was he waving or giving a Nazi salute?

"What can I do for you?" John asked, still chipper.

The stranger marched to him without a word but still showing those pearly whites. John thought, 'Salesman.' He didn't even know door-to-door salesmen existed. He thought they were a legend like the Puckwudgie.

Before John had a chance to take any of this seriously the visitor in black was on him, that outstretched left hand clamping down on his shoulder like a vice.

"Hey—!" was met with two bullets to the stomach from a silenced pistol. The man made sure John collapsed forward onto the gun as he opened the backseat door. He flung John in there and shot him once more to the head. Quickly he stuffed John's twitching legs in the car and shut the door. He straightened his neatly pressed suit and composed himself while scanning for neighbors, passersby, or the wife.

Or Corey. That little shit. Is he home?

Henry strode to the front door of the Avon house and knocked loudly. Meg answered. Her eyes fluttered between the stranger and John's car in the drive. No John. Her hackles immediately raised but she brushed it off as a baseless reaction. She tried not to look so concerned as she asked, "Can I help you?"

"Thanks, you sure can. Is Corey here?" Henry asked. He tried to insinuate his body into the house but Meg had enough sense not to fall for it. She raised a hand to his chest careful not to touch him.

"No, he's at school. What is this—"

"He's at school? The shit actually went to—Never mind. Meg, let me in."

"Who are you?"

"I'm the man with a gun telling you not to scream." He flashed his piece and she looked as if she were about to yell for help but he smothered her mouth with his free hand. "Don't scream! I just need to talk to you."

She shook his hand off and spit but to Henry's fantastic surprise it worked. He had rehearsed pretending to be FBI on the ride here but when it came time to perform he really wasn't in the mood.

"Whatever you want, just take it and go!" As Meg blurted the words her eyes darted for the nearest object with which she could club the burglar.

"I got what I wanted. You told me where your son is."

"What do you want with Corey?—Don't even think about touching him!"

"Or you'll kill me?—Please stop. His friend Darryl tried that one. It didn't take."

"Darryl? What are you even tal—"

Henry backed Meg into the kitchen and closed the door with the heel of his loafer. She stumbled into the rear of a chair at the table. He reached behind her and grabbed it, whirled it around, and sat her down. All of this so fast, so precise. Who was this guy? Not a common thief. She was in it deep and wished she'd screamed when the door was open. She almost did now but stopped herself. Who would save her beloved son if he killed her here and got away?

"My husband will be back any second. That's his car in the drive," she warned.

"Is that right?" Henry carefully took off his fedora and set it on the counter. Meg saw that the back of his head was a patchwork of stitches. He patted them delicately and winced. "I got a bit of a head injury, I'm not gonna lie. It, ah... REALLY FUCKING HURTS!" he exploded in her face. Then back to calm: "And I can't see." He giggled maniacally.

"If Darryl did this to you, I don't see what Corey—"

"Oh, sure! Pawn me off on Darryl! Scapegoat that kid to save your own. Mother of The Year, Mrs. Avon, Mother of The Year—No, the thing of it is, Darryl's not important. Corey is everything."

"What do you mean? I don't even know what you...." Meg's voice trailed off. She shook her head flabbergasted by the unreality of it all. She had just enough wits about her to try a tactic. She said, "Let's talk about this. Pull up a chair and we'll discuss it like adults."

His stare was ice and it shot through her eyes. "You can't control this, Meagan."

"I won't tell anyone," she whimpered. "Pull up a chair and let's talk." She didn't want to cry hysterically and transform into a human puddle of mucus and tears but her body reacted despite her will.

"How much did Corey tell you?" Henry asked.

"About what? He didn't—I know my son! He would never intentionally hurt anybody!" Meg sniffled and wiped at her tears.

Henry muttered, "He's at school, that's rich."

Meg came alive unaware how phony she sounded. "No! No, ah, he actually—Today is a day off! I forgot about that. He's probably at the tree house with Darryl!"

Henry snickered. The audacity of this woman! Now he knew which parent Corey got it from.

"Is that right?" he asked in mock-pleasant surprise. "They're both there, you say?"

Her pupils dilated. This was her first glimmer of survival if she could just keep the ruse up. "Yes! Yes," she assured. "It's where they hang out all the time!"

"Well I know that," he confided. "I hang out there all the time, too. Hell, I practically live there, Meagan."

She thought she spotted an opening to fake a real connection with this devil. She centered herself and calmly asked, "How do you know my name? Did Corey tell you my name?"

He was lost in a fog of what to do next. With the interest of an automaton he responded, "Hmm? No." He holstered the gun and went for his hat. He delicately fit it over his injured scalp.

Meg spotted a steak knife on the counter behind where his hat lay. It would be a leap in a dangerous direction if she went for it. He left her no time for that, swiveling around to make eye contact yet again. She smiled at him and kept up the connection.

"I didn't catch your name. You know my name. What's yours?" She was mounting with confidence but her face had a ways to go before it could formulate a proper friendly smile. Her lips contorted in jagged formations that amused Henry.

"My name is Henry. The government works for me. In another life I killed you. And I'm sorry to say—because you seem like a fine lady—that history repeats itself."

His draw was swift as a strong-jawed crook from the Old West. And after the click... and after the bang... blood and a thump. And then more blood. Lot's more.

That's how Henry left things. No time for cleanup. He was late for class.

INTERLUDE
Earth

On several occasions Earth Plane Council recon crews swooped down on the blue ball known by its inhabitants as "Earth." Each time the place was drastically transmogrified. For instance, the solitary gargantuan landmass this planet once housed had torn into continents split by ocean. Cold-blooded dinosaurs were replaced with warm-blooded cousins as well as giant mammals, all of which were replaced by smaller versions of everything.

One day they returned to find unevolved versions of squatch and the alien prisoner race roaming the lands together. Next time, it was just the prisoners. Humans. And the next these humans had stepped outside of their nature to tame the environment, enslave the animals, and erect stone megaliths and pyramids with nearly the calculation and exactitude of Earth Plane's masonry. The final time, they'd found that humans had invented weapons of mass extinction.

Humans were aggressive and they were evolving in quickening waves of transformation unaccounted for in Earth Plane science. What humans experienced as millions of years of evolution and thousands of years of cultural mutations, Earth Planers saw as days of abrupt random change. There was a natural lag between universes but nothing so drastic as this. Regardless, they should be able to witness any moment of humanity's unfolding by tapping into their unified field of conscious-ness. There wasn't one.

And what was happening to all of the recon crews? Where were they going? The closest the Earth Plane Council got to a reported act of war came when the ob-server team's ships were greeted by what they assumed were human ships—or maybe reptilian, it wasn't clear—over the Indus Valley. Unfortunately, as was always the case, communications mysteriously cut off before the team could relay anything definitive.

But then everything about the planet was bizarre. How had squatch, whom humans dubbed "Neanderthal," come to live there in the first place? They weren't the only Earth Planers accounted for, either. Later dis-patches of recon observed faerie rings, elf enclaves—pockets of various races from Earth Plane living clan-destine lives around the globe. Their stunned reports ended in permanent radio silence. Why?

How was this possible unless there were rogue clans of Earth Planers with their own portals and a means to keep them invisible from the council? Were they messing with time?

Whoever they were they wouldn't talk. Not the Earth Plane expatriates, not the excitable humans. Still no signs of reptilian life but they lived on in human myth and symbol. The elves, the faeries, the squatch—they, too, were consigned to mythological status by the latest incarnation of humans. Curious, because they actually lived alongside humans. Curiouser still because humans acknowledged the squatch as Neanderthal far back in history, yet denied their existence in modern times.

Nothing here made sense!

The deeper the council looked the more riveting they found this place. The fact that they kept losing people on rescue missions was a concern but not a prohibitive one. Not anything they couldn't resolve with a little ingenuity.

Faced with the impossible, Earth Planers' imaginations were on the mend. Earth had done that for them. Was it a gift or a bomb wrapped in a bow?

The council handed the project of building a sustainable bridge between worlds to the grays, who would soon unwrap that present and find out.

Chapter 40

"Lina, come on before the second bell. Don't wanna look suspicious."

"I've never done this before!"

"It's just one dumb class. The world won't end if you skip it."

Corey had her by the hand and was jogging her up the reverberant hallway of the backstage entrance to the Robert H. Park Auditorium. No one had witnessed them fleeing this way and the hall was barren. Drama Club didn't meet until after school. Still, everything from this side of the auditorium remained unlocked. Only the front doors were locked during school hours. For a school immersed in security panic this was a grave oversight and one that Corey took advantage of whenever the boys wanted to hang out or catch a nap.

He weaved them through the assorted props and lighting equipment strewn about the stage right dressing room like an obstacle course. It was pitch back there with no windows and no lights. He would never turn those on and risk catching some wandering janitor's eye or a goofy chorus kid who got his rocks off by rehearsing in solitude on the big stage.

They stopped at a metal ladder screwed into the wall of the loft. "Don't sweat the height. I've got you," Corey assured her.

Actually Lina didn't mind climbing. She wasn't afraid of heights, she was afraid of getting caught and ruining her GPA. At heart, she thought she had insecurities of the type someone like Corey would make fun of, not fall in love with. But then she didn't know what kind of boy Corey was, not really.

Had she known? Had she fallen in love with him? She craved the knowledge and thought that if he orated his wild tale it might spark something—if not love then an intuition that either he was deluded or telling the truth. In that other world

Alex described, their love sounded to her like machinations of a higher power writing about them through her. Might that be the truth? Not that she'd admit it to anyone but even now she felt like the story she was writing wasn't hers. Even so, not a drop of ink was committed to a love story between this strange boy and her.

What if their love died when she came alive again? What if love was used as a tool to save the world? If not for her would this timeline exist? Did she owe Corey anything for that? Would he be able to let her go if she denied him after all of this?

'Please, God, don't let me be trapped in the dark with a crazy man,' she faux prayed as she scaled the ladder.

"What's funny?" Corey whispered up to her.

She realized she'd been caught giggling under her breath. "Hmm? Nothing."

***

Breaking into Taunton High School was easier than killing John and Meagan Avon. The key was to dress affluently so that security assumed you belonged there and ushered you right in, no questions. Henry waltzed through the front door with a tip of the hat and a smile to the two rent-a-cops by the metal detectors. One smiled back sheepishly. The other didn't register any acknowledgment. That was enough detecting for one day.

Henry asked random teens if they knew who Corey was and if they'd seen him. No, but it was a big school and there weren't too many students meandering the halls without a bathroom pass. Most were in class. Henry checked his watch. "Or at lunch," he said to himself.

"I'm sorry?" a male freshman squeaked through his braces. He thought the old dude was talking to him.

"Cafeteria," Henry growled.

The startled boy snapped rigid and pointed a gangly arm to the hall leading to food.

"Thanks, kid." Henry patted the boy on the head and strolled by on a mission.

The boy sighed and collected himself before hitting the urinal. That must have been the new superintendent. What an asshole.

* * *

Lina's mouth hung slack through the second half of Corey's tale. She had been reduced to a saucer-eyed mouth breather whose feedback was all of, "Whoa! That was way better than Alex's version!"

So fucking cute! Corey felt caught in a slow drip torture being this close to his love, smelling her, lying next to her on the old foam mattress rotting in that dark loft, while unable to caress and hold her.

"What are you thinking right now?" Corey asked. Girls asked this all the time to the irritation of their boyfriends. Since they loved the question so much Corey thought he'd try it out here.

Lina regained her sense of environment. Darting her head around she said, "This place is moldy. Isn't it amazing how your eyes adjust to the dark? Where does that light come from to make out objects in blackness?"

Corey sank into the foam. "Whatever," he pouted.

"No, I'm just kidding." She placed her head and hand on his chest and cuddled up.

"Huh?" he peeped, taken aback by the gesture. She breathed with him for a bit, then he made a nervous move to gently stroke her hair. Not one stroke in and she absconded upright.

"Don't touch me." She didn't yell this but scolded him just the same.

"You were just on my chest," he defended.

"I was?"

"'I was?'" he mocked. "Are you high?—Yes!"

"I was. You're right. Sorry about that."

"Why sorry? I want you... on my chest."

They both burst into hysterics at the ridiculousness of it.

"Wait, that came out wrong!"

Lina hunted for his eyes in the dark and when she found them, twinkling like the Pleiades, she said, "Corey, I obviously feel something here. I can't say it's love, but…. Thank you." At that, she draped her hand across his chin and kissed his right cheek.

"For what?" Corey asked.

"For a lot of things. Too many things. Thanks for putting up with me and sharing this. And if it's true—"

"—It is all true."

"—I know it is. Thank you for loving me. I can't believe this is coming out of my mouth and not my pen…. Thank you for loving me through all time."

Her words socked him in the gut. His tear ducts were on the verge of pulling levees and he didn't want to stop them. He wanted to share a real emotion with this girl, this woman, his true love. He wanted her to know Corey Avon at his most vulnerable.

"I can't imagine what that must feel like from your perspective. I mean my God, Corey, what is it like to be you? And then to be rejected again is just…."

She trailed off. In Corey's head the proverbial record scratched and those tear ducts left their levees in place. His face scrunched queer. "Again?" he asked.

She looked at him shocked that he was shocked. "I told you I'm not in love with you."

"You put your head on my chest."

"I know." She sat up and clasped hands to knees looking like a ball.

"You put your head on my chest—What was that?!"

"I know! I don't know why!"

"This is...." Corey didn't have the words to finish that thought. He gripped his cheeks in his left hand and stroked his face down to the point of his chin as if he were erasing himself. The proper description flashed through him and he spoke it almost as quickly: "—Silly... comes to mind."

She nervously rocked in place. "I know! I'm sorry," she said honestly startled by her own affections.

"Useless? Fruitless?" The words were coming fast now. A whole other levee was about to break if he wasn't mindful.

"I said I know! God! Don't make me feel worse than I already do!"

He laughed reflexively at that one.

"Is it lunchtime yet? No, it's past lunchtime," he mumbled to himself.

Lina dug her atmosphone out of her purse and checked the time. "Oh, shit! It's way past lunchtime! We've got like fifteen minutes to get something and run," she said frantically.

She dropped the phone back in her purse and began to climb over the dead log that was Corey Avon, but he came alive and grabbed her. Before she could squeak out an obvious *What the hell do you think you're doing?* he pulled her to his lips. At first she tried to say something but each word was met with a passionate kiss. She sighed and melted into them and kissed back.

Corey sagged into the dank foam as she leaned him down. She stayed on top and lost herself to the ferociousness of her tongue. It acutely perceived what it wanted even if she didn't.

*   *   *

"God, these kids are a fucking mess."

Henry surveyed the cafeteria for Kiddo. Every table he spied a minimum of three teens blink-surfing the net and sexting on atmosphones. Woopty-shit if the cell batteries recharged on air pollution, they still caused brain cancer. The twitchy dopes blinking away their youth appeared leaps and bounds more retarded and bored than their friends, who were holding conversations and doing stupid impressions of class-mates and teachers they hated over pints of whole milk and grade D genetically modified horse meat.

No Corey, but he found next best and when he did he made a call of his own. The man on the other end knew who was ringing. "Go ahead," the voice said.

"I need a full lockdown with media blackout at Taunton High School. Mrs. Koma is coming. She's a wet job. Projecting a four-fold fatality response with fifth target option and whoever the fuck gets in my way," Henry murmured. He found speaking in code as juvenile as anything in this school.

"An overt with stagecraft? And what is this for, sir?" the gruff phone voice asked.

"This is for do what I tell you or lose your job, your wife, your children, and your balls for grandchildren." Henry cut the line and palmed his holster as he stalked over to Daryl, James, and Stephen. The trio looked genuinely innocent and well-behaved, slumped in chairs, hovering over picked-at lunches in funerary hush. Their table was a calm patch in this sea of ca-cophonous infants.

As an outsider looking in, Henry found the sights, the sounds, the smells of the hormonally challenged in their natural habitat as hypnotic as Vegas. He practically floated over to the boys' table. Darryl only first noticed him when he was upon them. He did a double take, then his eyes peeled wide in horror. "You!" he gnarled in a throaty voice beyond his years.

James looked up and yelled, "Gun!"

Henry shot James and Stephen in the chest. They had been sitting on either side of Darryl, Stephen to his right, James to his left. Now they were wriggling on the floor pawing their wounds and gurgling blood as Darryl stumbled over his chair, back to the wall.

Students, teachers, and lunch ladies ran screaming from the panther in black business suit. Not Alex. He dropped his orange plastic tray heaped with seconds. He froze there, thirty steps behind Henry to his diagonal left.

Was this happening? Was he really watching his brothers being mowed down by a psycho?

Corey. This had to have something to do with Corey. Good lord, what bloodthirsty wraith had he brought back with him from that other life?

"Where's Corey Avon?" Henry spat.

Darryl threw his hands up submissively. "I don't know what you're—"

Pop-pop. A bullet to Henry's left, a bullet to his right. Two kill shots through the brains of Darryl's best friends and the man hadn't so much as blinked in either direction.

"I am not going to ask you again."

He raised the gun to Darryl's head. Alex shrieked. Henry whipped around, turning his gun on the boy pissing his Dockers. Darryl instinctively pounced, hurling a chair at Henry who saw it coming and threw his guard up. The light plastic and metal seat bounced off of his right arm and then so did Darryl who had leaped across the table to tackle the sicko. Gravity didn't play along here as it did in the movies and he missed his mark. He clawed at Henry's arm on his way to crushing his sternum on the chair at the assassin's feet.

"You indolent shit!" Henry stomped Darryl's head with swift and furious force—a technique he sucked from the memory of Li Zicheng, emperor of the Shun Dynasty, over-thrower of the Ming. The boy's neck snapped cleanly over the lip of the chair.

"This is your fault, son. If I could still see I wouldn't be doing this," Henry justified to the convulsing mort. He then whipped around to extract Corey's whereabouts from the last of his prey but Alex was already in a full sprint down the hall and rounding a bend. Henry started after him. Mr. Gonzales, the new gym teacher, and Dr. Hanna, the beloved history professor, jumped out from behind a flipped lunch table. Henry shot them down before they could thwart him.

Two heroes. That was it. Everyone else had fled.

As Henry dropped the spent cartridge and reloaded his Sig Sauer he bellowed, "Don't run, Alex! I'm right behind ya! It doesn't have to end this way for you!"

Henry's words were as empty as the corridor. He chased the patter of running feet.

INTERLUDE
Earth

The grays, brilliant inventors through and through, suggested an experiment that was expeditiously approved and implemented.

First, they built a subspace hub that was like a secret room built into the wall between worlds. They modified the portal so that it was maneuverable and now they could place that window anywhere on Earth— and do so without ever closing it. This constant contact ended the time lag between dimensions. If Earth evolved by a hundred thousand years in an hour they'd see it happen.

Next, they crash-landed one of their vimanas along with three bodies of their own kind on the soil of what had just been declared the most powerful human nation in Earth's history. Then they watched. They waited to see what these "Americans" would do with it.

By every indication humans were a species terrified by the Earth Planer expatriates living clandestinely among them. They must have made brief random contact through the ages—and it must have gone poorly— for individuals spoke of these beings in hushed tones as if to name them is to invoke them and to invoke them is to invoke a calamitous exchange between species. Societies rarely addressed them as anything more than culture-dependent lore or ethereal spirit beings lining the rungs of "enlightened" hierarchical perception.

Human behavior confused the astute grays. How was it that these hominids did not know who the elves, faeries, and squatch living alongside them were? How was it that they had not figured out what they, themselves, were? Why were they psychically cut off from each other with rare and weak exception? Why did they tell juvenile, silly stories about Earth Planers involving worship, sex, food, love, and fear? Told these stories as if they were true and yet refused to acknowledge the beings as real! What a backwards people!

The grays were curious what would happen if they showed up in a way that humans could have control over: physically real but dead.

They crashed their props on a remote farm in New Mexico near a military base. In this way ordinary individuals would find the wreckage first and if they wanted to report it to their authorities, the debris would be close enough to the proper facilities for easy, quiet cleanup.

And if they didn't report it, how would they handle it? Would the farmer and his family speak of it? To whom? Would he make a religion of it?

If he reported it, would he go to the media first? The police? His government?

How would the government/military complex react? Would they sweep it all away? Would they bring it to humanity's full attention? Whatever the Americans wanted to do, this farm was the best location to afford them a plethora of free will options.

What ultimately came of it was more of the same: official denial, individual whispers keeping the story alive, and the denigration of this historic event into stories of worship, sex, food, love, and fear. One difference, the sole difference, was that the Americans kept the wreckage and bodies hidden for their own study. They wanted to know how to weaponize what they had found and how to commercialize it. These were their concerns in this time of monumental importance.

Even more confounding was that the story the humans most identified with was of this wreckage and these bodies being alien. The alien invaders declared Earth Planers aliens! What amnesia!

Many in the Earth Plane Council chortled at the irony as they scrutinized the unfolding of this latest mythology. It was the first hearty laugh they had shared since before the war. For that they were grateful. They were likewise thankful for the certainty. The certainty that these humans truly were divorced from reality and therefore each other. It wasn't an act, so what was it?

Thanks to the ingenuity of the grays the Earth Plane Council could crack Earth's code from the safety of subspace, without setting foot on land or ship in sky—without being swallowed by this foreign reality. They could search for their missing scout teams. They could keep trying to make contact with their own expats.

Most crucially, they could draw us in and study our souls. They could do the one thing we couldn't: figure us out.

Chapter 41

"Mmmm... hang on a sec."

Lina peeled her lips from Corey's to fish in her purse. She had set her atmosphone to vibrate and it was buzzing now, making her lipstick rattle annoyingly loud.

"It's a text from Alex. I told him I was coming here with you and to send help if he didn't hear back by—Shit!" She glanced at the time. "Do you know how long we've been here?"

"Not long enough," Corey chuckled. But he wasn't joking.

Her face suddenly read, *Oh no, this is weird.*

"What?" Corey sat up and peppered his sweet's shoulder with kisses.

"Alex said whatever we do, if we're not out of the building by now, stay here. And there are, like, twenty exclamation marks so it must be important."

As if a synchronistic nod, the school's fire alarm set off, bringing them both to panicked alertness.

"Fire drill?" Lina asked.

"Henry," Corey stated.

She knew that was right before she had asked.

***

"Psst! Hey! Dipshit!"

Alex didn't know where to hide from a trained killer so he crouched and plastered his body against the wall of the main stairwell on the third floor in B-House. Now a locker was speaking to him and he couldn't tell which.

"Over here, retard!"

A boy began clanking loudly on the inside of his locker. Alex saw the door jiggle and knew who it was. This wasn't the assassin. This was worse.

"Stop it! Stop!" Alex's voice cracked as he whisper-shrieked to that dumb-fuck bully, Brock Duwarte.

"Is the shooter gone?" Brock asked.

"I don't know! I don't think so. I think he's after me."

Brock's hideous disembodied voice cackled at the notion. "What the fuck would he want with you, your lunch money? That reminds me: you better give me your lunch money tomorrow or I'm gonna kick your ass."

"There isn't going to be a tomorrow if you don't shut the fuck up!" Alex hissed.

"Whoa, check out the balls on you! Unlock my locker so I can kick your ass."

"Are we really having this discussion?—Jesus Christ, where are the police?"

"I'm just kidding, dude, don't have a conniption. Hey, I saw you pull the alarm. Pretty badass. I did that once and got suspended for like a week or something. I don't fuckin' remember. I'm supposed to be suspended now but I fuckin' forgot. Can you believe that shit? I had a free day off and I fucked it up. But damn—Look what I would have missed!"

Alex thought if he ignored him he'd shut his mouth. Brock's mouth had other plans. "Yeah, so I was gonna call the cops and shit, but then I was like, 'Nah, they'll fuckin' figure it out.' So...."

Alex assumed someone had to have called 911 but then remembered Corey's story of the antennae, the Tesla Dream Machine. His eyes widened in terror. Was this whole school under the spell of computerized mind control or was Brock really this oblivious?

"Hey, Alex, can you let me out? I think it's safe now. The dude probably bolted when you pulled the fuckin' alarm."

"Okay, but you have to promise to be quiet."

"I won't be louder than this alarm, dude. Shit." Brock did an impression of the alarm, which made him giggle, then said, "It's bouncing off the metal walls in here, man. It's pretty fuckin' loud. Smells like sweat socks, too. Dude, I fuckin' stink! I didn't know that about myself."

"Yeah, well you're in a locker. That's what they smell like." Alex hustled like a ninja to Brock's door. "What's the combination?"

Brock gave him the digits and Alex released him. Brock slid his bulky frame out sideways. "Thanks, dude. You're all right," he said. He gave Alex a round of friendly if unwanted noogies and followed with, "So that's how the other half lives, huh? I ain't never been in a locker before."

Before Alex could respond they both heard Henry's voice loud and clear rising above the alarm and drawing closer. "Aaaaaleeeeex! Where are ya, kid? We need to talk!"

"Is that your friend?" Brock asked.

"He isn't my friend he's a fucking sniper—Hide!" Alex shoved the bully back into his locker and gently closed the door. Brock giggled uncontrollably.

Alex did his damndest not to flip out on the dunce and give away their location. In a slow trembling whisper he said, "Dude, you have to shut the fuck up. What's wrong with you? Are you high?"

He asked it rhetorically but Brock confessed anyway: "Yup." The peeping sound of his own answer made him laugh harder.

"All right, I'm out of here. Good luck, Brock."

"Thanks, dude. Fuckin' you too."

Alex patted the door mildly. As he turned to run away, Brock yelled, "Hey! He's over here!"

"You fucking asshole!" Alex teared up as he dented the locker with a furious punch.

"Dude, calm down, I'm fuckin' kidding," Brock slurred.

"You just got me killed, you fuck!"

Alex blindly picked a direction and ran. He had no clue where Henry was prowling. The blessing of the noisy alarm was also its curse.

Brock hollered after him, "Alex, I'm sorry, dude! I was just playin' around! Don't be a dick—Come let me out!"

Then he noted to himself, "It's so fuckin' ripe in here."

Then he giggled himself to hysterics.

***

Lina squeezed Corey's hand in their perch while they nervously listened for activity over the din of the fire alarm. They heard nothing. She spoke softly in his ear, "We can't stay here forever."

"Like hell we can't. I'm not losing you again, Lina. He'll never find us in this place. Never." His breath in her ear transitioned to a kiss on her cheek.

She fidgeted, unsure if she should say the obvious thing that hung there and distinguished predator from prey. She took the plunge and had out with it: "He will if he reads your mind."

Corey had actually forgotten about that. He said, "But he hasn't yet. I can feel it when he's in there."

She bowled over his weak answer: "Or me, or Alex—"

"—Shit! Alex! Yeah, you're right! He could have gotten it from Alex by now but... but you'd know if he read you, trust me. And so he'd have to know we're together to not read either of us, right? Because he wouldn't want us to see him coming, and... that's a lot of forethought."

Even while he tried to deny it he knew it was probably what happened. Forethought was Henry's specialty.

"Corey, stop being naïve. This is not protecting us. He's a mind reader for the ruling class. He knows where we are, face it."

"Yeah, okay. So then there *is* nowhere to run."

"Well running is better than waiting. We need to go. Now!"

She yanked his arm, snapping him out of a hopeless daze. He scaled the ladder and spotted her. She climbed halfway to his arms when someone flipped on the stage lights. They both turned heads at once. "Shit," Lina squealed.

"Go-go-go!"

She descended two more rungs then jumped the remainder. Corey hugged her tight for balance as her feet hit the floor. She kissed his right arm *thank you* and said, "Grab something."

He knew what she meant and they frantically scoured the cavernous dark room for anything they could use as weapons. She found a hammer and he was on the verge of testing the durability of a mannequin arm when Alex jogged into the doorframe. He stopped there and doubled over, a heaving backlit mess.

"Alex! What's going on?" Lina demanded. Corey and she ran to his side. She patted Alex's back not knowing how else to soothe hyperventilation while he relayed the death of their friends between gasps. They hugged him tight and all cried.

"I ran here... I ran here all the way... from B-House.... B-House, third floor," Alex managed to get out in chunks.

"Just breathe, buddy," Corey said.

"I don't think... I don't think he followed me, cuz... he didn't know where I am.... Doesn't know where I am.... Didn't know where I was...."

"It's okay, we got it. Focus on catching your breath," Corey instructed.

"Should we turn the lights back off?" Lina asked.

"No, he might see it under the doors out front if he's there or... up the hall," Corey said. He sure as fuck hoped this monster wasn't up the hall.

Alex huffed and sucked air and said, "Turn the lights... turns the lights *back* off?"

"They came on before you came in," Lina said. She was already ahead of where this was going and tapped her foot in a panic.

"I didn't... I didn't turn on the lights."

"Shit! We've got to move!" Lina yelled.

"No. It's too late. The trap's been set," Corey stated matter-of-factly, scanning the area for moving shadows. He understood Henry better than anyone here, maybe better than anyone at all. "Any move we make will be the wrong move."

Alex grabbed Corey's left shoulder for support and hefted his chunky frame. He felt woozy but was shivering from the power of another adrenaline rush surging through him. "Not... not if we run." He stammered this and then bolted onto the stage of the auditorium. He thought he had energy enough to get him to the front doors and then it would only be tens of feet in a straight dash to the nearest school exit. He also thought his friends would follow him on instinct but when he looked back they hadn't moved. He yelled, "Come on!" and waved them over but before Lina or Corey could react they heard a sound like the air being cut and watched Alex twist like a marionette in tangled strings before plunging backwards atop a dozen clanking music stands in the orchestra pit.

Lina screamed, "No!" Corey dropped the mannequin arm and held her from running out there to Alex and to her death. He hugged her tight, shielded her face in his chest—anything to rescue her from this appalling scene.

"Take a bow, Alex!"

Corey loathed that maniacal voice bouncing off the acoustics. He would rip the vocal chords from Henry's throat if given the slightest chance.

Henry stepped out from behind the scrim. He'd been hiding behind the curtain on the far side of a wooden prop throne for The King and I still under construction. He said, "I know we agreed not to throw one-liners at each other but really what's the point of killing a child if I can't FUCKING PUNCTUATE IT?!"

Wow, Henry was... insane. What happened to the refined man who had everything under control? Did Darryl whack the Zen out of him last Friday night?

In the midst of her own breakdown Lina slid the handle of the hammer she'd found in the dressing room down the back of

Corey's belt then collapsed in a heap on the floor. Corey didn't know how much of this was an act to hide the weapon on him but he left her to collect herself and, he prayed, give her an opening to run.

He also prayed the weighty hammer wouldn't bring his blue jeans to his ankles as he calmly marched to Henry center stage. He ignored the itchy tears caking on his hot blushing cheeks and fixed his gaze on Henry's proud, crazy eyes. He knew that if he turned and saw Alex mangled and dead—or worse, not dead but in so much pain he wished he were—he'd crumple like Lina.

Corey's skin didn't rise in bumps or tremble with fear and his voice didn't waiver when he unclenched his grinding teeth long enough to bark, "What!" so close to Henry's face that he blinked at the wind from the boy.

Henry feigned looking taken aback. "What *what*? ... Oh, you mean *why*," he toyed. "I'd show you the stapled gash on the back of my head but I'm afraid you'd take advantage of me with that hammer. How about you drop that thing on the floor?"

Corey sealed his eyes tight in that moment to stifle the urge to attack. "Fine," he acquiesced. He withdrew the tool from his belt and held it high when he dropped it. The clanking was loud enough that if police were sneaking around looking for the gunman outside the theater they should have heard it. Or his yell. Or Alex's dive. Where were they?

"Good boy, Kiddo. Your friend Darryl and I had a talk about what he did to me over lunch. He didn't apologize per se but I could tell he was sorry."

Henry's toothy grin was so wide, so obviously there to anger Corey that it no longer did. Henry just looked pathetic. Corey shrugged like he didn't get it and said, "So this is what you do now? Kill my friends and terrorize me with the details? What the fuck happened to you, Henry?"

Henry's smile was unrelenting. "Not just your friends."

That brought Corey back to anger and the death urge. He had the look of a tiger seconds from pouncing but Henry read him and stopped him. "Up-bup-bah," he warned. He retrained his pistol on Lina.

"Here's the thing, Corey, big reveal. I can't see. I don't know if your friend permanently damaged me or not but I haven't been able to see beyond my own two meatballs in three days. If I can't see I can't keep tabs on you. If I can't keep tabs on you and you do something stupid like disappear then the people who pretend *I* work for *them* will know I can't see. And I'd hate to embolden the ally. I don't particularly feel like being a deposed king if you know what I mean—So here's what's going to happen. You and Emily Dickinson over there are going to come with me to the alien bubble in Hockomock and I'm going to throw you in it. If your bodies rip apart at the seams in the transition between spaces then they'll just have to Frankenstein you back together—Not my concern. They want you so badly they'll figure it out and I'll have saved the world a few months ahead of schedule, capisce?"

"Don't you think they have a schedule for a reason?" Corey balked.

"Again, not my problem. I don't know what they want with you two and I don't care. They get you when they get you and nobody is the wiser about my little dysfunction." Henry tapped his left temple and continued. "I've got enough pertinent worldly knowledge up here to fake it for as long as it takes, but with aliens I can't read and kids I've got to babysit? Mmm... not so much."

Henry finished his speech but Corey had already tuned him out, lost in his own train of thought. When he responded with nothing Henry blurted, "Alright, kids, pack a lunch, we're going on a field trip!"

Corey's lids fluttered involuntarily as he came out of trance. "No, wai-wai-wait. You said 'you two.' The aliens want Lina and me—Is that what you said?"

"Am I on trial?—Yes. The prophesied Pair of Opposites."

"In the last incarnation it was just me."

"She was killed by accident. Don't let that happen again. Move!" Henry waggled his gun at Lina for emphasis.

"No, I'm sure of it. It was just me they wanted," Corey protested.

Henry smiled that shit-eating Cheshire. "*Now* who's the ego maniac? I am not going to tell you again: move."

Henry strayed fifteen paces behind Corey as he paraded his captive to Lina who lay sprawled on her stomach on the floor in a dark corner like a bored little girl in timeout. Her right hand, propped on elbow, held her head up while the index finger of her left etched the words I ACCEPT over and over on the grimy brick wall two inches from her face.

"What the fuck?" Corey gasped.

Henry ordered her to stand up but she was entranced, maybe even possessed, and unresponsive. It was so obviously not an act that Henry didn't question it. "That's interesting, Kiddo, but we've got to go. Pick her up."

Corey gently urged Lina to her feet. She stood and smiled and exhaled "Corey!" with the widened eyes of a long lost love. Then she passed out in his arms.

INTERLUDE
Earth

Flanked by two pairs of security guards he did not need, Trondant marched briskly down the winding metal corridor to the rarely utilized missing-in-action quarantine. His heavy purple cape fastened by three chains of gold symbolized his interim commandership. He was not Leader—never Leader—until or unless Leader was found dead. To be crowned Leader is to have survived a thousand deaths and caused thousands more. Millions more. Planets of them. Trondant had numerous genocides to his credit but nothing close to Leader's résumé.

Such a gifted and well-protected Leader could only be captured or killed if there was a flaw in the plan of attack that everyone missed. His demise indicated a broken system not a broken man. He would be found. He would be rescued. He would restructure the system and execute whomever an independent council named as the flaw.

Trondant knew he was innocent to the chain of mistakes that lead to this terrible moment in history because second in command was always shielded from grave error in the immediate moment. He also knew this was not a guarantee that he wouldn't be named as the flaw somewhere down the line. The longer Leader remained missing the more fall guys would be needed to appease Leader's lust for revenge upon his return. Shielding had its limits. Revenge did not.

***

There was only one reason a warrior would find his way home as the pilot awaiting Trondant had: to receive a hero's welcome and a proper funeral. Excluding Leader, of course, if one was so weak as to get shot down by enemy, one was as good as dead. Even so, bravery and service were the highest qualities of a warrior and if a fallen one somehow retreated back it was to die an honorable death among his own kind.

The Law of Self Sacrifice, as it was known, did not apply to the upper echelons of the command structure. Top tier fighters were so skilled that if they were struck down in battle the flaw was deemed one of planning. The ensuing investigation would run by the same rules as if Leader had been felled.

Trondant and his guards stepped through the evaporant wall into the quarantine room. Men and women in lab coats performed all of the proper scans and gave the pilot a clean bill of health. Trondant glanced at the name stitched into the left breast of the pilot's suit and exclaimed, "Krojah! Our brother hath returned home!"

He hugged Krojah in a fierce grasp that nearly took him off his feet. The pilot remained aloof, perhaps still in shock, as Trondant released him and patted his cheek. He smiled at his brave, failed warrior and asked, "Have you brought news of Leader?"

Krojah displayed thought-forms in Trondant's mind. This was against the law. How dare someone of warrior class invade the interior of his commander? Under the

circumstances Trondant assumed there was good reason and so did not slay his brother where he stood. Instead, he flung up a hand, waving off the pilot's psychic
communication, and boomed, "Why do you not speak
with your mouth, brother Krojah?"

Krojah choked out garbled nonsense while pointing
to his throat, indicating something wrong there.
Crushed vocal chords, perhaps. Trondant didn't bother
referring to the doctor's chart to confirm, he simply
gave this hero permission to thought-com.

Krojah regretfully informed the commander that
Leader was dead, truly dead, for his soul had not been
captured by the enemy. If Trondant was stunned by the
worst news he had ever received in his long, long life,
his body language didn't scream it. He was, after all, a
warrior's warrior and would take his rightful place as
Leader.

Krojah had one more thing to report—but not to
Trondant. He had a message for the Hive Queen and
only her. It was Leader's final utterance before he was
disintegrated in Krojah's arms by a long-range twert
blast.

Trondant comprehended the significance of this.
He alone would usher Krojah to the queen and stand in
frequency silence while the pilot delivered his telepathic message for her mind only.

***

"Enter." The Hive Queen had learned to speak the
invaders' linear, hierarchical language. However, permit-

ting the commander entrance was a mere formality. Beneath the surface pomp of being Leader's one true love, she was still a prisoner of war.

Trondant led Krojah through the evaporant wall of the queen's chamber and announced his intentions. "My queen: this fine pilot, brother Krojah, hath escaped the ruins of battle with a message for you from Leader."

The Queen's brilliant green eyes wafted from Trondant's to Krojah's. "Speak," she commanded.

Krojah did as told in her native frequency so that even if Trondant wanted to eavesdrop on their thought-com he could not. Nine seconds later, Trondant knew the conversation had ended when the Hive Queen's eyes bulged and she shot an accusatory finger like an arrow on outstretched arm at the glazed pilot. "Traitor!" she spat from mouth.

Reflexively, Trondant kicked out Krojah's left knee sending him crashing sideways to the red and orange fractal pattern carpet.

"This man is not Krojah! He is a faerie spy wearing your dead comrade's body," the queen alarmed.

Trondant snapped the intruder's neck, releasing the faerie soul inside. Without embarrassment, apology, or remorse, he called for the guards standing watch outside the evaporant wall to haul away the spy's twitching corpse as he stood and neatened his cape. The queen regarded him a moment and then spoke in his head: "Leader is alive."

The commander stopped primping and came to attention. Before he could ask anything, she cut him off:

"I know where he is and how to retrieve him. We must plan carefully but strike fast."

Trondant debated within himself a moment not if this was a trick—clearly not—but if it was proper under the circumstances to allow the queen of a conquered race, no matter how noble her intentions, to plan a retrieval mission of this ultimate caliber. Of *any* caliber.

No. He decided she should tell him everything she knew and stay put in the chamber. He was interim Leader. He could not bend to her, not even for the sake of her true love, his supreme officer. She would not see the inside of the war room or any other room on this mechanical planet until such time as Leader was extracted from the clutches of enemy and personally deemed her worthy of such an honor.

The Hive Queen was amenable to that.

Trondant smiled, white teeth glistening, when he told her that such an honor would likely come after Leader took her hand in marriage. The Hive Queen was fine with that, too. More than fine, thrilled. She contorted her facial muscles trying unsuccessfully to emulate Trondant's joy.

She still had not mastered smiling in this inferior human body.

Chapter 42

"You can't seriously be taking us out the front door." Corey uttered it and straight away beat himself internally. If ever there were a time to let a man make the most obvious mistake of his life he could set his watch by this moment.

Perhaps Henry felt the need to outdo himself after last Friday's most obvious mistake ever. Corey didn't know what motivated this man anymore. Was that from the conk on his former mentor's head or had he never known? Were any of those bonding moments in the last life real? Were they protocol?

"Trust me, Kiddo, this is all going to work out just fine." Henry wagged his gun at the kid. Corey knew what he wanted and he gave it to him, barreling the double doors to outside open with his right shoulder, while circumspectly hauling Lina's dead weight slunk over his left. He staggered out then froze a moment. His eyes adjusted to the brightness of day while his senses adjusted to the unexpected greeting.

Red fire engines with white trim stood by while black and white police cruisers littered the patio and lawn. There were young people being tended to by EMTs behind an ambulance cluster. Some reporters crowded them for sound bites while others waited patiently for the next breaking news moment in a sectioned off area to Corey's left. Police and news choppers hovered low, completing the noisy coordinated scene.

Corey focused on the spectacle by the ambulances. It was clear, even from this distance, that newscasters were asking dumb questions with insensitive timing to students and faculty who had just escaped the clutches of a killer. Blond cheerleaders in half shirts and minis pouted their full lips into the cameras while dimple-cheeked, square-jawed sharp young men rippling with muscle underneath sheer tops held their stoic composure. Two studious looking professor types cried through an explanation of what ill effects a tragedy like this will have on Taunton's precious youth.

The babble of people and of machines, the afternoon sun-rays... all of it dizzying to Corey who stumbled forward and almost dropped Lina. He did not drop her, he held on, but before he could get his bearings a buxom redhead outfitted in retro 80s sweatshirt falling off her right shoulder so that the purple cup of her lace bra drew the eye, shrieked and collapsed on the pavement before an EMT or anyone else could react and break her fall. As if her theatrics had pulled a trigger, the student body and teachers pointed almost in unison at Corey and Lina. A voice in the crowd yelled, "That's them!" And all of the cameras turned on the couple.

An arc of cops slowly moved in on them, guns drawn and menacing. A policeman shouted, "Freeze! Put the girl down and drop to the ground!"

Henry yelled back, "It's okay, I got them! They're unarmed!"

At that the police rushed them. Several thick-muscled brutes jammed knees on Corey's neck, arms and legs while an officer cuffed his hands behind his back. He heard Henry low-tone to another officer that Lina was fine, she just needed smelling salts. The officer hailed a medic who rushed over with her grab bag of supplies. She pulled out smelling salts and snapped the packet under Lina's nose. Lina coughed herself awake not knowing what the hell was going on but that her hands were shackled uncomfortably behind her.

"Get us to the car," Henry instructed the cop.

Ten police formed a barricade around Corey and Lina. They yanked the duo to their feet and escorted them to an awaiting squad car, where they unceremoniously stuffed them into the backseat. Corey didn't protest, didn't cry out, "You've got the wrong guys! Henry's the killer!" Didn't do this because he saw the faces of the students and teachers being interviewed and did not recognize any of them. It was as if they had been hired straight out of Hollywood's Central Casting.

Corey wondered what happened to the real Tauntonians— to his friends and teachers and the kids he'd passed in the halls. He wondered what would happen to Lina and him.

Henry jumped into the driver's seat and fiddled with the rearview. When he found Corey's wild eyes stalking him in the reflection he said, "Welcome to another layer of Oz, Kiddo."

Lina was coming out of her grog and asked Corey where they were. He was more worried about where they were going next.

Henry peeled away from the mob scene. He had a delivery to make.

INTERLUDE
Earth

For a faerie who had never lied once in his thousand-year existence, "Krojah" was a natural actor. He was top choice for the Earth Plane Council's plans to infiltrate the alien menace and when asked he did not blink. Of course he would live in a dead human pilot's body to reconnect with the Hive Queen—even if it meant his own permanent death.

Earth Plane Council put his body to sleep then transferred his soul to the body of a fallen alien pilot—the real Krojah—who lay in a deep coma. Five burley gnomes had retrieved him from his crashed vimana while it was burning to dross. Miraculously, the fires did not swallow him alive and his rescuers yanked him to safety just as the ship exploded. Yanked him, that is, to safety and now duty as an organic puppet who was being strung along and brought to life by this nameless faerie of great heart and valor.

The meat suit took some getting used to, as did the name. Earth Planers didn't go by names. So strong was their inner connection that they knew each other directly and instantly. They understood names to be a barrier to this type of connection. The faerie was all too eager to help stop this senseless war so that all of Earth Plane could reconnect in the purity and freedom they formerly took for granted.

The death toll was one affliction weighing mightily on Earth Plane, but the potentially longer-term danger

stemmed from this blocked flow of interspecies consciousness. Grays, elves, faeries, squatch, gnomes, mers
and on and on, had long forgotten the epoch when their
physical organisms meant everything to them. The very
notion of "my people and your people" had been assumed
extinct until this invasion. The faerie playing Krojah did
not consider himself a faerie until this war. He just
was. They all just *were*. They were beings being inside
of BEING. Diversity was not a virtue and neither was
conformity. Giving such notions meaning was a delusion
they had collectively sidestepped.

But now, back in their divided species, there was an
innate temptation to take it further, to walk that road
of illusion they had temporarily repaved as a precaution
against further treachery by any other Earth Plane
race who may have collaborated with the invaders. Because the Council forged this extreme agreement based
on the assumed betrayal by reptilians, they thought the
Hive Queen might have some insider knowledge that
would settle the issue. Earth Planers deeply longed to
move back into their normal, healthy state of connectivity. Krojah wasn't just the embodiment of a faerie
spy, he was the embodiment of all hope.

***

The alien invaders had such hubris that they never
planned on losing a war. Loss was not in them to believe,
such was their legacy as conquerors.

They implanted their warriors with nanotech hom-
ing beacons so that if anything ever went wrong a sol-

dier could always find his way back to his roaming mechanical planet. The faerie in Krojah smirked at this novelty and how there was no encryption code to keep out invading spirits such as him.

Were the aliens really this shortsighted or did they assume they could handle, say, a fleet of enemy who had confiscated warships to surprise attack their base? Did they also have a plan for just one? Just one wearing the body of their MIA pilot, Krojah? One who would swoop in on a ship cobbled together from crash-retrieved parts and stagger around the deck, presumably shell-shocked, but really because the spirit inside was not used to this tall, muscular body?

The Earth Plane Council had deduced one thing: not all of the invaders' blind spots were due to arrogance. The fact that they still used nanotechnology meant they were not as learned in the sciences of oneness as Earth Planers. They didn't have their technology encrypted because they didn't know an otherworldly spirit could thoroughly possess one of their own in a coma. More significantly, they knew little of the ether and its secret uses. Otherwise, they would have abandoned this rudimentary technology long ago.

If the faerie played the part of alien well enough he could permanently connect the Hive Queen with Earth Plane through the ether. And if the Hive Queen agreed to play her role to perfection, another faerie on the Earth Plane Council could sing him back to his own body by guiding his soul along an ethereal musical chord wherever his ship landed, provided it remained anchored in their universe.

   And provided someone killed the comatose pilot
named Krojah.

Chapter 43

It wouldn't be a long drive to Hockomock, yet Corey worried about Lina's finger all the same. She was fiercely scribbling nothing with her left index pressed hard against the window. The squad car was so clean that it still had that new car smell. There was no grime in which to hold the letters, if they were letters. It looked to Corey like she was spelling something but not repeating the same word. She was writing. Like in her journal.

Corey hoped she wasn't entranced in automatic pilot mode predicting their dark ending before it unfolded. On the other hand, if she was, maybe he could stop it. A tiny brilliant idea came to him: blow hot air on the glass as she writes and read the words before the mist dissolves.

He bent over the lap of his distressed sweet and exhaled over the back of her hand. "What are you doing?" Lina asked like he were nuts.

"Oh, you're awake," Corey said, puzzled.

"Yup, sure am," she replied. She didn't break her gaze out the window, though.

"What are you writing?" Corey asked.

"Just doodling."

"Doodling? Looks like you're writing a book."

She stopped manically fiddling the window and turned to the boy who had ruined her, the boy whom she loved through two lifetimes. Possibly three. "Corey," she said like a question.

"Yeah?"

"This is not going to end pretty."

"No."

Corey sounded genuinely thoughtful to her when he admitted that like it was a forgone conclusion. It didn't take a gift to see their future and yet the optimist followed up with hopeful questions: "You see something? In the future?"

"I see *now*," she stately flatly.

Henry stopped the car. Their conversation ended with the cutting of engine. Corey glanced out the window: Spooky Mansion. Castle In The Tank. Childhood shattered.

The polycarbonate partition that normally divided criminal from cop prevented Corey from lunging at Henry. No interior door handles meant no daring escape. This, even if he could summon the magic to Houdini his way out of steel cuffs and whisk Lina to safety. They were stuck.

Corey still had his wits but was tempted to abandon them for the silence that was deeply himself. Could he reach inwardly to beings who would help? There seemed to be a meeting ground in the clarity of internal stillness where eternity pressed against time—but had the beings there ever helped him? Were they not the reason for his fucked up life?

Finding out was not a chance worth taking because, as he recalled, the timelessness of that silence meant abandoning Lina indefinitely with a psychotic killer while his body fell lame. That could take seconds or minutes or hours. Time was too precious a variable to leave to chance when the answer from the other side might be, "Sorry, kid, you're on your own."

"Alright, last stop. Everybody out," Henry barked. He opened Lina's door and made Corey climb out her side. He knew the boy would try to fight this at some point but also knew all the tricks to minimizing Kiddo's opportunities.

Henry had to suppress a laugh when Corey tripped over his own feet and sent himself rolling to the ground while wiggling out the back in cuffs. He looked like a human inchworm. Henry helped him to his feet then Corey shrugged him off in a violent cloud of dirt.

"Temper, temper, Kiddo," Henry said. He flashed his gun and a smug face.

Corey huffed and rolled his eyes. He asked, "How you gonna get us past the guards?" then cleaned grit from his teeth with his tongue and spit out the dirt.

Henry looked bemused. "Guards, Corey?" he asked while circling around the boy, fishing for keys.

When Kiddo didn't answer Henry explained to his hostages that there were no guards, only an elite unit under his command. To question Henry's actions out there in the swamp with actors—even to surveil him—would be career suicide at best, actual suicide at worst. Drastic consequences for dissent are what you sign up for when you want in on secret keeping. Conventional morals and questioning orders die with your civilian identity. There is no American judicial system for these men and women. There is one golden rule: Do as you are told or be destroyed. It takes a very special breed of person to say yes to this life. Hence, elite unit.

"Yeah, special. A bunch of hyper-intelligent psychopaths circle jerking to keep that big secret from each other: they're insane. And you're their leader. Good for you," Corey mocked.

Without skipping a beat, Henry said, "Ah, Corey, I knew you'd understand." He uncuffed the boy and his girlfriend, then commanded, "Now walk."

Corey massaged the painful red grooves in his wrists where steel had constricted against the bone. He looked to Lina to do the same but she stood relatively motionless, almost like she was bored.

Henry waggled his Sig at the couple and dropped back fifteen paces, out of range of sudden attack. From behind he navigated them through the increasingly sticky muck of the swamp to the portal that would be their end. However that would pan out. Did this girl know? Did she receive insight from higher forces waiting to devour them whole?

Henry didn't ask. Henry didn't care.

INTERLUDE
Earth

"Enter." The Hive Queen had learned to speak the human invaders' linear, hierarchical language. These uncivilized beasts had a rudimentary understanding of psychic connection but not the natural bond of oneness enjoyed by Earth Planers. They had engineered a physical technological knockoff of the essential link that undulates in the core of all sentient life—the core to which they remained blind after... how many generations of learning and evolution?

Pitiful.

"My queen: this fine pilot, brother Krojah, hath escaped the ruins of battle with a message for you from Leader."

The Queen's brilliant green eyes wafted from Trondant's to Krojah's. "Speak," she commanded. She could tell by his eyes that Krojah was more than human, but not until he reached her on her native frequency did she realize, *faerie*. Before her lips quivered into a smile that reflected her emotion, he showed her everything. In a glance, everything.

He showed her that Leader and numerous other captives had been imprisoned in human/reptilian hybrid bodies on a reptilian world in a banished universe. That world had perished under mysterious circumstances, yet another near it lives. This second world contained all the signatures of the reptilian hand but no reptilians.

He showed her the millennial time slips that transformed everything from atmosphere to terrain to organisms in this wondrous place when the Earth Plane Council stopped paying attention; the data of the recon crews gone missing, including their ignored attempts at communicating with clans of exiled Earth Planers living invisibly alongside the new humans; how the grays had fixed the time slip dilemma by constructing a portable subspace hub where they could observe nonstop.

He showed her everything. All of it. All of it down to the minutiae. All of the pertinent events compacted into a striking series of virtual reality images that swirled around her interior domain and told the story like a dream. A dream that she absorbed; a dream that she became. It was, in the end, as if she had been making those discoveries with them all along.

She was there in 1947 when the grays crashed a ship in Roswell, New Mexico to study the effect on the population. She witnessed that effect and the surprising side effect—witnessed the original souls of human prisoners from Earth Zero popping up on radar as if reincarnating in response to the blatant crash, yet still blind to their true identity. Through trial and error the Council learned how to properly study them, and she was with them for those important discoveries, riding the winds of shared memory.

Earth Planers knew that body and soul inverted when leaving one's home dimension for another, unless one grasped the secret to controlling the flip of physicality. When the flip occurs, the organism naturally appears in the parallel universe as a luminous white egg.

Humans did not know the secret to controlling inversion—no surprise there—and when lured and abducted through the portal, they disintegrated! Hive Queen watched in awe and sadness as this happened trial after trial.

If nothing else Hive Queen was compassionate and relieved to find that the grays had worked a solution to obliterating their human subjects. They formed a protective bubble around the subspace hub so that they could herd human bodies on Earth's own soil while they examined the souls of these people in subspace. They called out to receptive humans on a subliminal level and normally it worked. Even so, on rare occasion one would slip back into his or her body and make a break for it in physical shock and immense terror.

Breaching the wall of the bubble while the shield was up had deleterious effects on the subatomic structures that comprised the human form. It caused random, chaotic mutations. Some of these people turned into monsters. Some turned into intelligent gasses. It sounded worse than it was, for the grays could very easily reverse the mutations if they could retrieve the runaways—but they refused to leave the safety of their bubble because they had not solved the riddle of why Earth Planers mysteriously disappeared here.

As if in answer to that dilemma, Earth's secret ruling elite did the grays' dirty work for them. Wherever the portal opened in the world, they would monitor it from a safe distance. If a runaway escaped, they caged them and left the mutated unfortunate back at the edge of the bubble. The grays lowered their shield in that spot, floated the subject through the window, repaired the humans, then left them unconscious for these people with secret occupations to return to their lives.

As it happened, the human ruling class was a good silent collaborator. They asked numerous questions through test subjects. Questions the Earth Plane Council refused to answer because it was clear to them that this warmongering race saw them as intruders and were feeling them out. Humans publicly promoted them as myth, legend, and sneer-worthy fiction while aiding them and studying the after effects of their "abductions."

The Hive Queen watched the evolution of these abductions, like a movie comprised of experiences, and was riveted. Initially the elves coaxed humans into isolated locations where the portal would open and the procedures begin. They reached out by "appearing" as nothing more than a sudden urge to drive or walk to the desolate spot. Sometimes they came in dreams. They were specifically tasked with this because they looked most like the modern colonial human ideal and so would cater to their racism. Humans felt safe with elves; they thought they were human, too. When the grays and others tried their hand later, the fear they instilled was so terrifying as to be comical. Nevertheless it worked well for decades of Earth time, days to the Earth Plane Council.

But something quite odd began occurring in the 1960s. Rogue clans of Earth Plane expatriates living invisibly on the new planet started approaching the portal wherever it relocated. Sometimes they interfered, scaring off the human subjects before they made their way to the clearing around which a protective bubble would manifest. In a handful of instances the interlopers outright killed the humans. Through it all they never dialogued with the watchers inside the portal. They were like feral monsters disguised as Earth Planers and they were their own mystery.

Finally, what the Queen saw was Leader. His soul signature was bright and strong and obvious, even though he was living obliviously as a boy surrounded by friends who were Royal Guard in another life. As they stumbled through life unconscious to their nature they acted out as if they knew. A piece of them must have.

The Earth Plane Council visited the special one in dreams and visions but they couldn't grab a hold of his mind like they could other abductees. They couldn't walk him to the portal for study. So, they finally gave the ruling elite what they wanted: a communiqué—*Give us the boy*. And they delivered it in a threatening language they knew humans understood, utilizing some date by the latest incarnation of the Western calendar that held mystical properties for these people.

The Hive Queen watched that date come to pass uneventfully, but saw that the boy must have found the portal on his own and brought his friends to play near there. This, despite the ruling elite's Dream Machine antennae influencing citizens away from the area. She wondered what manner of soul wields such power to taunt both the American establishment and the Earth Plane Council unconsciously?

The human divide between conscious and unconscious mind was another mystery Earth Planers had yet to fathom. They knew of creatures sleeping and wide awake. They knew how to modify sleeping creatures to wake them. Never had they encountered or created awake creatures controlled by a larger sleeping aspect of themselves for this long a duration. The induced amnesia of the original souls should have given way to full realization by now or else what was the point of reincarnation? Reincarnation was not an eternal situation yet these third-generation humans treated it as such in philosophy and practice. At the very least the original prisoner souls should have transcended into self-actualized people who took responsibility for their actions. That's what time itself was for.

These oddities got the Earth Plane Council to thinking: only recently did they learn of Hive Queen's secret that she was an overmind, a puppeteer to countless bodies. Was there a hive mind on Earth as well? Was there an amorphous queen buried somewhere, invisible to instrumentation? Or perhaps she swam the sea; perhaps she was the sea.

The Council would have treasured indulging the mysteries of Earth. They found themselves delighting in the newness here, craving physical exploration despite the evidence that past explorers didn't survive contact, and almost forgetting their mission. The Hive Queen felt their extreme wonderment as she absorbed the last of the vision, but knew that what the Council needed from her wasn't an opinion about human consciousness; rather, they needed to know if this ridiculous war was over and if reptilians were involved. As she stared into Krojah's dead-alive eyes, she showed the mind of the faerie inside the two answers he sought: *RESCUE*. And to the question of reptilian involvement, *NO*.

So. This war was not over. Not until Leader's soul has been recovered and revenge enacted. Revenge for proper self-defense. And they did this alone?

This human species was an abomination. How could they be so large, so mighty, and yet so tragically lost? And now, thanks to hasty judgments made in the paranoia of chaos, they occupied two universes in two breeds. Not good.

The whole of Hive Queen's visionary journey through the eyes of the faerie took exactly seven human seconds. Seven seconds to experience everything and accept an etheric implant that would untraceably connect her to the faerie through all distances. On the eighth she showed him what she knew of the human plot to retrieve Leader. And on the ninth second, she called Krojah a traitor, which was technically true, and had him killed. The faerie inside was vacuumed back into his sleeping body by the song of a dear friend on Earth Plane.

***

Hive Queen's implant worked flawlessly. And now she had an open line of communication to the council through the valiant faerie back home. If she was to aid them any further she had to experience Earth for herself. She had to figure out why they could not retrieve Leader, why they could not set foot there. She had to find out if their hunch was correct: was there another being like her born into existence on a random rock in this parallel universe?

If these parallel humans were marionettes to another queen—or king—she would know instantly, and she could talk to them, and she'd no longer be alone. Perhaps the mysterious being would have an organic body similar to her original and allow Earth Plane Council to grow her another from the DNA. This crazy twist in her destiny was begun in surprise and bloodshed, but the Hive Queen saw the ending and it was methodical. It was peaceful. It would be a type of resolution so new to the human invaders that it might just spark a lasting change in their conscious modality.

Assuming, that is, her counterpart lived on Earth.

***

Hive Queen required no mental preparation to scan Earth. She only needed her etherically bonded faerie channeler "Krojah" to sing her energy through the portal connecting Earth Plane with Earth. If there was anyone on the other side like her, or with an etheric technology like the faerie's to cling onto, she could just as easily link with them.

There was no psychological barrier to overcome for one such as she. Nonlocality came naturally to her. This human body was a nuisance but only in terms of walking, talking, eating, and touch. Internally, she was as capable as ever, for the heart and brain had achieved the capacity for full sentience even though her human captors disregarded the richness of their nature.

A tiny gray manning the portal opened the door to the new world for Krojah and he projected the Hive Queen's consciousness into the enigmatic place. The Hive Queen enveloped the globe like a vibrant mist. If humans felt her presence they didn't acknowledge it.

She saw the souls of the people dimly lit, a nightlight of a thing in each where star-quality radiance should be. Never before had she encountered this lack of clarity in sentient organisms, but the moment she realized what was missing the lights grew brighter. In particular, a small clan of boys and of them the one who should know himself as Leader shined like a beacon.

The growth in soul voltage was obviously a response to her concern and yet she did not pick up on a hive mind here. The signs of counterpart were here, but no being. As she marveled at this she felt herself dissolving as if being absorbed into this world. She did not want to leave until she solved Earth's riddle and yet she knew if she stayed she would not leave, not ever. The obvious choice was to withdraw and as she did, another light grew bright enough to attract her—a light tinged with her own unique brand of radiance. This human wasn't an original soul like Leader and the boys convalescing around him. She was a new soul. And she was, for Hive Queen, an open line of communication into this world.

How had that happened? How had all these lights brightened in response to Hive Queen's thoughts? How had an invitation to stay through this girl been sent? And by whom? What was this magical new sculpture zooming through the black canvass of space?

Hive Queen pulled back into her universe. She took the offering of connectivity to this young girl with her. She teetered on the brink of sharing her first sense of being overwhelmed by mystery ever felt during her long, ancient life with the faerie, the gray, and all the Earth Plane Council, but her awe was—*just like that!*—replaced with understanding. She understood the Earth mystery in the blink of a human eye, for even the most intricate quandaries resolved themselves in but a moment through one such as she. In seeing the answer to Earth she also found the resolution to the alien problem. These resolutions she shared with the council and together they hatched a plan to give the American leadership another ultimatum with precisely detailed hocus-pocus surrounding a completely meaningless upcoming planetary alignment in deep space.

They agreed that the council would relate through their chosen abductee mouthpiece precise instructions on where the boy Leader needed to be and when and the state of mind he needed to be in for them to peacefully transfer him to their dimension—or else they would utilize the energy of the alignment to manifest on Earth, unleash vengeance upon mankind, and take what was theirs anyway.

All of this discovery and plotting could be counted in human seconds.

***

Trondant did not allow the Hive Queen out of her palatial quarters but he rarely left her alone in there. Many were the evenings spent asking her for advice in secret. At least this is how he framed it in his head. What he was really doing—and she knew it if he didn't—was taking dictation on a plan of attack within a rescue mission. She was the architect and he was her mouthpiece. Trondant was far too proud a commander to admit the truth of the flowchart to himself and so his underlings had not a clue. Not in body language. Not in behavior. Not in any way.

Had they known they would have promptly removed Trondant from office. Then, after throwing a lavish ceremony in honor of his vast achievements, they would have promptly removed his head. This gruesome set of consequences despite the ingenious plan Hive Queen had worked out for them to retrieve her beloved fiancée and exact revenge on Earth Plane.

"My lady, what do you suggest we do?"

This was the most polite question Trondant had ever asked Hive Queen in all her time in captivity. He didn't even snarl when he asked it, though desperation broiled under the surface. She sensed it. He sensed she sensed it. They both kept up appearances—her with nervous, awkward smiles; he with that cold, hungry stare.

'He devours,' she thought in words—and he looked like his function. Actions etched the soul and then the body. Behold, a life in scars.

"We attack," she answered after a pregnant pause that emulated thoughtful concern.

Her two simple words uncaged a shark's grin up Trondant's weathered mug. Finally, they were conjoined in creepy facial gymnastics.

The words were simple but the execution would be so intricately designed as to look like a work of art.

She explained to him that Leader was one soul among many fallen heroes being held in new cloned bodies on a prison planet in a quarantined universe. Trondant balked, waving off the notion of rescuing subordinates, even if they were Royal Guard. Leader was the only mission.

Okay, then to confiscate him we must go in full force. That means everything we've got—not just the warships but also this roving artificial planet—because, she told him, in this prison universe the Earth was prison but surrounding planets housed guards. This is why the initial attack on Earth Plane was so easy: they concentrated their massive arms in a parallel where they hid the most evil of their kind. In fact, she confessed, this is why she never divulged her true nature: she feared being locked away in a forgotten realm. Anyway, Earth Plane Council figured the dragons would be enough to thwart any aggressor, but they had never met an opponent as strong and cunning as humanity.

The words dripping from her tongue... the scope and the dangers of the prison break... Trondant was so aroused that it took every ounce of military discipline not to rip into this woman and plunge her insides with a primal howl. If she wasn't already Leader's plaything,

Oh, what he would do to her with his engorging elite cock.

Chapter 44

The trudge through Hockomock felt longer and more tedious than Corey remembered. The discrepancy, he imagined, was like that between walking off the edge of a diving board into a pool full of friends and walking the plank with his true love. The brief cartoon of this playing in his mind's eye conjured a well-needed, if misplaced, chuckle. And then a deeper thought made him cackle loudly while they hiked.

"Something funny, Kiddo, or is this supposed to be the part where you throw me off balance and tackle me for the gun?" Henry mocked. He needed these two to know that he'd already worked through every escape plot they could hatch. He wasn't two steps ahead of them, he was miles beyond.

"You think you're balanced? That's funny enough," Corey shot back. "No, dude, what I'm laughing at is the ridiculousness of this. You know when something just hits you—like you wake up into yourself and you realize you're being held at gunpoint in skunkweed with the girl of your dreams? And the kicker is the asshole with the gun thinks he's in control as he marches you to the unknown. Like, you actually think you're gonna live through this and look how silly *this* is! None of it makes sense but you... You cling to this rational ending where the world goes back to normal and you, what? Steal back your power like a dictator? It's the... it's the depths of insanity that make me laugh."

Henry was too silent for too long. Corey egged him with, "What, no witty retort, Evil Guy With Gun? Did we just find the Tin Man's heart? Or is it the Scarecrow's brain?"

"That's enough, Corey. You're scaring him," Lina scolded.

Any words from her were shocking enough, but the fact that these were the first she'd spoken the entire walk led Corey to assume she was joking. "The Cowardly Lion," he responded. "Subtle. I hadn't thought of that."

"Christ, are you two finished or do I have to finish you?" Henry barked.

Corey launched into another giggle fit. "You should cock that trigger for emphasis. That way we remember who the cock is."

"I said enough!" Lina stomped her foot as she yelled, forcing the trio to stop in their tracks. It was the first break they had taken out here in the cold muck and sticks.

She exchanged glances with Corey: his askance; hers *shut up*. "I pity you both," she stated evenly.

A scowl took Henry's fed-up mug. "Does any part of me not falling for this elude you? Because here comes the cock, kids." He cocked the Sig. "I promise I will end this trip faster than you will."

Lina brushed past Corey and stepped to Henry. She put her chest to the barrel of the gun and met his wild glare with such lack of fear or even basic concern that Henry had to fight himself not to stumble back. "We don't have an escape plan. I don't want to escape," she said.

Corey gagged on a choppy laugh. This had to be part of her escape plan... right?

She continued unabated. "I've seen how this ends. I told you that."

Henry broke in with, "I don't care for your nonsense," but even as he did he could read in her eyes just how real she was being with him.

"It isn't nonsense. In fact, why don't we pick up the pace so we can get there already?" With that, she resumed the trek, walking briskly and with purpose. Corey caught up to her and Henry trailed his safe paces behind.

"How do you know where you're going?" Corey whispered.

"I know," was all she said.

"But... you said it doesn't end good."

"No. We all die."

"How?"

Lina kept moving but turned to her true love with compassionate eyes, honest and strong, and admitted, "I kill us."

The starkness of her words punched Corey. He felt his knees wobble a little at their bluntness. "Like a love pact suicide thing?" he asked weakly.

"No. I kill us all." Her face was strength when she said this and her voice unrepentant.

Corey groveled searching for an answer that wasn't this. "How do you kill Henry?—Maybe I can help you and we don't all have to die."

"No, Corey. I kill us. ALL."

INTERLUDE
Earth

In her final contemplative moments prior to the grandest double-cross in the history of her universe, Hive Queen lay on her bed made of air and reflected not upon all that could go wrong, making this the grandest bungle in her universe's history, but on how the human invaders had the exact same blind spot as Earth Planers in the polar opposite direction. These people were such fierce warriors that they didn't allow sheets and blankets on their beds like did their mysterious counterparts in the adjacent universe. Didn't allow them because would they were suddenly under attack during sleep, didn't want to risk their troops struggling with twisting, binding sheets for the few seconds it took to leap into action.

Leader had calculated this.

And yet in spite of—actually, because of—their ferocious mentality, they developed an arrogance, an assumption of invulnerability that would be their demise if the double-cross was meticulous.

What a black reflection of Hive Queen's beloved Earth Plane, where peace and harmony was so deeply lived that it rendered all the species complacent, defenseless. Writhing inside of their incalculable brilliance was a naivety that had danced them into evil's trap jaw. And if her plan did not unfurl perfectly—if her theory about this planet of new humans was incorrect—their purity would be their end. Dead immortals, all. Or enslaved. Forever. One of these would be the penalty for failure, as no third judgment existed on this mechanical planet.

Hive Queen's fantasy of a bloodless teachable moment for humanity was shattered the second she embraced Earth in her contemplative eye. Either the human race would be eradicated in one swift maneuver or they would become gods.

Gods who brought hell to everyone they touched.

Chapter 45

Corey observed two robins darting at a cluster of crane flies swarming between pines. The overcast sky made them easy to spot. The scene reminded him of what was missing: the paranormal hush that stopped nature and drew attention to itself when in close proximity to aliens.

"Where's the fucking portal!" Henry spat. "It should be here!" He marched Corey and Lina to the center of the clearing where aliens should be.

"Maybe the aliens don't want us now. You remember the timetable, Henry? The one I reminded you about before? The one they set? The one—"

"Alright, shut it, Kiddo. They'll be here."

"Yeah, on the timetable."

"On *my* timetable." Henry spun around and around searching out any surprises that might be lurking in the woods. "Evil Guy With Gun makes the rules, that's universal law, son. Our friends up there UNDERSTAND WHAT A COCKED TRIGGER INSINUATES, EH? IT INSINUATES *MY* FUCKING TIMETABLE!" He rattled his gun at the sky as he shrieked and his echoing words drew the unnatural silence Corey had expected to precede them.

Henry sighed and stared at his shoes contemplating his next move. What if the boy was right? What if they didn't come? How long should he wait out there? A night? A week? What would it take to get their attention if not their prized treasures held for ransom?

Lina broke her silence, and his, in a completely disinterested tone: "There is no timetable. Everything ran perfectly. Look up."

Henry jerked his head back but Corey lingered on her studying her face a moment before turning skyward. It was still Lina in there but she was something else now, something more.

Her lack of exaggerated body language—lack of any emotional interest in their predicament—told him this.

Slowly, Corey stopped training on his love and rolled his eyes then his head to the sky in time to witness a slit open in the atmosphere well below cloud cover but just above an ascending jetliner. From the wound triangular spaceships of conspiracy and nightmare bled into existence.

"Ho-ly mo-ther of—!" Henry's drawn out words of awe cut off when a mile-wide tanker of a vessel spilled into reality, shattering the 747 on its hull like a toy model airplane. The boom was impressive enough, but from the ground the black cloud of exploding machine and body parts looked like a cheap firework popping off. It left nary a scorch mark on the alien barge.

Debris crackled and whistled on its dive to its earthly grave. Corey buckled, dropping to his left knee. He concentrated on not losing his breath as the deaths of the sold-out flight socked him in the gut like a golden glove. Henry yanked him up screeching, "Take cover!" He dragged the boy all the way to the tree line and Lina jogged behind, zigzagging to avoid white hot metal raining down like bullets and bombs.

From the canvass of trees they watched human torsos buckled into numbered seats kicking their legs and spray-painting the sky with thick red blood. Hell had come to Hockomock. Corey wasn't sure he wanted to survive this but before he could acclimate himself to yet another abrupt transformation of everything he knew Lina bent into his ear and whispered, "Watch this, Corey." She cupped his chin in her soft hands and gently raised his head. From behind the false safety of oaks, pines, and birches, Corey locked eyes on the sky once again.

"Not good, Kiddo. *Really* not good." Henry muttered this while more calm behemoths poured in, devouring the sunset. Henry deduced from their trajectories that they were flying to key military installations and from the sonic booms rumbling like distant thunder that they were not here to negotiate. Was this assault local or global in scale?

"Fuck, fuck, fuck, fuck, fuck!" Henry knocked on his own forehead as he cursed himself for having the vision slammed out of him by some shit-ball high school punk. If he couldn't know the scope of this he couldn't plan an escape. If it turned out there was nowhere left to escape to, he needed to know that—needed to know how to survive. That survival was not an option never entered his thinking. He believed there was always a way to survive. And thrive. And eventually, even if as a shameful secret kept from themselves by themselves, rule the new rulers of this world.

Like an automaton, his right hand trained the gun steadily on the kids while his left fumbled for the atmosphone in his pocket. His mind was too preoccupied with survival to concentrate on what the body was doing. His hand found and retrieved the phone and this snapped him out of it in time to watch a pair of stealth bombers streak onto the scene. Long considered showstoppers of American military ingenuity, here they looked like the ancient toys of a retarded imagination. They were as ineffective as their flight was short-lived. Whatever ammunition these aliens used it was invisible to the eye. All Henry saw was the bombers arcing in a ninety-degree straight drop as if they had hit a wall and then been swatted to the ground by a giant hand before they had a chance to explode.

"Hello? Come on! Hello?" Every number Henry dialed ended in him barking at static or phony voicemail recordings, a hallmark of the legitimate elite. It wasn't just the elite, however; no one picked up. Not at Castle In The Tank. Not at Pease Air Force. Not at the Pentagon. Not at the White House. Not even at Glow Styxx. This attack was so meticulous and lightning quick that the phone system remained intact but there was no one left on the other end to pick up the line anywhere that mattered.

Henry dropped the phone on the ground and covered his mouth to breathe a warm squeal of delight into his hand. He ruled the world now and if nobody knew it that was only because they were dead or unaware of his two bargaining chips held at gunpoint. The irony that these advanced aliens hadn't located the only three ground targets that mattered—three puny humans witnessing the end of their world at the very gate of hell pried opened by these creatures—stirred an involuntary crazed chuckle for which Henry had no palliative.

Corey broke away from the sky. "This is funny?" he asked. He clenched his hands into tight fists as rage brewed in his solar plexus. Rage: his first burst of emotion since being struck catatonic by witnessing the inglorious results of his cursed destiny in that open field. Why was murder his fate? Not just murder, genocide. Not just genocide, everything. Everything dead because of the rash decisions of a small town boy, a nothing of a manchild.

And here he knelt at the end of time, soul mate forcing him to watch the dominoes he tipped collapsing into place while the enemy of all mankind coerced him to be still. Watch. Don't squirm. Don't resist. Watch.

"You cackling bastard—This is funny?!" Corey heaved words at the madman but Henry just waved them off as if to say, "Oh, shut up." Kiddo was ruining his moment.

"Corey, watch," Lina cooed. Her voice was sultry now, like her mother's. She again begged his gaze to the sky with her gentle touch and he retrained on the impossible movie above. What, he had to know, was coming that was so miraculous? What did she know that Henry didn't?

What could stop the torrential laughter of a maniac living his dream and reset the world?

Corey lightly nuzzled Lina's head resting on his shoulder. He felt guilty finding solace in her touch while humanity blew to extinction around them but it was the only thing keeping him from sinking into Henry's madness. He stroked her hair and pushed off his knee. Together, they stood as one. He could still smell the perfume of her after all of this.

"I know what you're trying to do, the... the... place you're trying to bring me. Emotionally. Playing off that asshole and... But I can't. I won't create another timeline to end this. I don't... I don't know if it's selfish or not but I can't go through this again, Lina. And... and it always ends like this, I think. I think I know that now. There's no escaping destiny. There's only making it worse."

Corey's eyes welled with tears as he confessed to his love the sins he refused to commit again in the name of hope. Lina hugged him tight and soothed him while he cried. She kissed him on the right temple and that kiss was strength. She was neither crying nor going through the motions. She was truly someplace else and yet more right here now than either Corey or Henry.

"Corey Avon, I love you—"

"—I love you, too." His reply chased hers too quickly for her to finish her sentence.

"I promise you I am not manipulating you into the silent place where time dies and blossoms to drop us off on the back of the bus," she said. Then she drew him close and whispered hurriedly, "Understand hither-thither and in that understanding be neither swept away nor carried on the seas of time. Come to me now, body and soul. Failsafe closing. Waste not another breath in prison, my love."

Corey's eyes bulged with recognition. He grabbed Lina by the shoulders and shook her harder than he meant to. "Who are you?" he demanded.

"I'm Lina Igasho, Corey. I am also Queen. And I am killing us all. But you will rescue us both. *That* is your true destiny, Love." With that she kissed him so passionately he thought he'd spill out of his body, then said, "Now please watch the sky, Love. Timing is all that we have."

INTERLUDE
Earth

These Earth humans were largely predictable and easily influenced, but not outright controllable. Hive Queen utilized her 17-year-old host to guide Leader's soul, but the boy's love for her became a hindrance. The American military response presented another setback. And, of course, the boy almost died in the dwelling of a madman. But those challenges were blessings in disguise because they lead to the boy revealing his power so immense that she could connect with him directly in his rare moments of clarity. So immense that he threw the prison universe into an altogether new timeline when clarity met rage. This was of no consequence to other dimensions such as Earth Plane's but it acted as a quick rewind where Hive Queen could course-correct for those variables, those mistakes she had made in the previous time.

If this boy were so in love that he would kill one time stream for another just to save the girl then in the new one she'd have to be important. She would have to live and be the dangling carrot he would follow to protect even if that meant following her into humanity's worst fear: eternal enslavement to aliens. Of course Hive Queen knew that was not what this was about—quite the opposite—but the boy didn't.

The boy, like the girl, was kept blind to the truth about himself and the truth of what lay ahead on the new predictable path he had forked into. Part of the reason she kept them ignorant was to make it easier to control them, to guide them where she needed them to be when she needed them to be there. Part of it... not.

***

The special boy's destruction of the original time-line of his universe set back Trondant's all-or-nothing attack by a few days. Ordinarily the commander's fury over this holdup would be such that Hive Queen would have been shoved out an airlock for it, but she didn't tell him the truth of what happened. She told him a much, much more enticing lie she had concocted with the Earth Plane Council—one that would turn the odds of this attack in his favor. First, however, she had to walk him through the original plan again. She discovered that this race found a peculiar joy in repetition. Trondant, especially, had a knack for reiterating what she had already stated as though they were his ideas—a most amusing flaw. And so, after apologizing to the point of prostration for insisting he hold off the blitz-krieg until he hear her new proposal, she requested he sit down across the table from her and allow her to lead him down the savior's warpath one final time....

Seizing control of the main portal undetected was a tricky proposition but not impossible. Trondant pre-ferred smash-mouth attacks to surreptitious ops but he was a master of both. Still, the control center for this thing was heavily guarded. Trondant didn't fear deadly conflict with those protecting the main gate. Casualties were a small matter. The bigger repercussion was what would happen at the other portal, the hidden one no civilian Earth Planer and very few leaders knew existed. This gateway was enormous and didn't open anywhere near that Earth planet. It was locked onto a point in the heart of the Milky Way Galaxy that connected Earth Plane with their stores of titanic weaponry. This, Hive Queen assured, was the vast military complex that existed to safeguard against extreme emergencies in the prison universe.

Because the mammoth portal was so well-hidden, it was assumed that no one who didn't know precisely where and how and when to look could ever find it. And if they did? Well that would be a suicide mission.

As the Hive Queen laid all of this out for Trondant, he predicted exactly where it was headed. He cut her off and finished the plot for her: "We must take the main portal by surprise and take the hidden one by storm! A two-front assault: one with a handful of my best men on the ground and one with everything I've got!"

Trondant's eyes bulged with delight as he came to the Hive Queen's epiphany on his own. He gazed past her enchanted by his world of private thoughts, which he continued to leak into the room. "We must bring the entire planet through that gate. We must completely overwhelm the enemy while they sleep." He paused to take it all in then exclaimed, "This will be the war to end all wars!"

Trondant sat back in his chair resting in his hubris, intoxicated with himself. But it wasn't over. "Commander, more good news. The faerie that possessed your man, Krojah... he wasn't the only one in the body," Hive Queen told him.

"What do you mean?"

"Respectfully, your people have much to learn of the ether. There was a stowaway, a royal pilot named 'Sheng-Ra.' He acquiesced to go with the Earth Plane Council to live as one of them and guard the main gate. He claimed he was reformed and this job would put him to the ultimate test. Of course they would be secretly monitoring his every move. Nevertheless, he must have learned etheric stealth from a sympathizer because he presented himself to me as a weak psychic pulse—a barely-perceptible signal in the noise barricade that prohibited the pilot Krojah from overtaking his faerie possessor."

"Sheng-Ra," Trondant repeated, jogging his memory for the name.

"Yes," Hive Queen assured.

"I shall look him up in our records."

"Do. And please hurry. He informed me that he is awaiting your instruction at the portal."

This really drew Trondant's attention. He sat forward, elbows on table, fingertips holding chin as he stared at her lovely face in search of the lie. "Continue," he said.

"I would have spoken of this earlier but truth be told, I thought I felt something weird at the time and assumed it was just the faerie. It kept nagging at me, though, and then last night the truth manifested in my dreams and when that happened I immediately reached out to Sheng-Ra and now we are linked. He and two other royals agreed to act as double agents on our be-half. It is clear to me that the Earth Plane leadership refuse to compromise their trusting nature even in these desperate times. This is not as foolish as it sounds. They hath an impeccable record of reforming and integrating off-world marauders into Earth Plane society."

Trondant flared his eyebrows skeptically. She read that and responded, "If you have a hard time believing that, you will encounter it for yourself. The prison planet is run by its inmates."

Trondant audibly scoffed at this and she chased it to regain his focus and keep his trust. "I know! I know it sounds impossible," she said, "but mark my words: you will be fighting humans there. Many have turned against you. They want another life. They have been repro-grammed—brainwashed. They are lost. But double agents can hand you the main portal and open the hid-den portal on my signal. Well... on your signal through me—this is why we had to call off the attack. It is not due to error on my part—it is due to fate handing you certain victory without the unnecessary risk of a ground attack.... And me, my one true love.

"Don't you see, Commander? You, my lord, in one swift act will have furious, bloody, unrelenting venge-ance. You will make history not just among your people but of all people everywhere. Your story will be legend the universe over. And I... I will have my dearest back at long last."

Hive Queen swooned at the last sentence but noth-ing so over the top as to be unbelievable. Then, in a switch of passions she yelled, "We all live as heroes!" and pounded the table with her fist for emphasis, shaking the fragile china.

Trondant seconded the brilliance of their destiny, yelling, "We all live as heroes!" He bolted to his feet and flipped the table over for emphasis. The rare delicates flew across the room and smashed when they landed. Hive Queen did not flinch. She smiled. In days she had mastered smiling.

The one thing she did not do... was dream. For hers was not a species that slept. Not even in this body, which looked exactly like someone Trondant could trust.

"All that we need, Commander, is three more days for our men on the inside to position themselves for the perfect attack. The perfect attack perfectly executed to conquer an artificial universe and rescue Leader. Then we shall dominate Earth Plane. And Leader will surely need someone to rule the new universe."

She watched his eyes bulge excitedly with the possibilities. He was in her grasp again and she knew it and she wrapped her fingers around him, squeezing tight. "Think of your future as ruler of not one world but all of them in a parallel reality. The power... such incredible power," she said, her words dripping with awe. And that was all she need say to him about the fake plan.

The real plan, however, required a new ally. And she would take a different type of convincing.

Chapter 46

A seemingly endless array of dark looming shapes zipped out of the slit above the clearing in Hockomock. Some of the smaller vessels looked aerodynamic but the larger tankers were defined by jagged edges and bulky contours. Nightmares, all.

These aliens had to have demolished whichever global power structures they found threatening by now, so what were all of these war craft for, Henry wondered? Did they expect a bigger fight from us? Or was this the search party looking for Corey and Lina?

"We're right here you idiots," Henry muttered. The rest of the world must have been devastated into unspeaking shock by this uprooting of every illusion they had planted to grow over their fears of the unknown and loss of control—but not Henry. He was bored.

'Find us and get on with the negotiations,' he thought. He thought this several times in deep concentration testing the theory that one of these advanced dopes would pick it up psychically and then pick them up physically before they accidentally squashed their human booty at forest's edge.

***

"It's coming. It has to be," Lina cooed in her love's ear. They were standing now, Corey in front, and she was holding him, arms draped around his waist. He hunched a little so she could rest her head on his right shoulder, allowing a comfortable view of the end of everything. He scritched her hair and kissed her cheek—God damn these perfect seconds in their final hour. But then if there was no savior coming to rescue the human race, these moments were all he had left. Thank God they were *these* moments.

Corey smooched Lina hard on the temple and slid to his left and back a step so that they were hugging tightly side by side. They settled in for the last act of the show when the heckler behind them broke their hypnosis. "It's almost enough to make you lose your faith, eh, Kiddo?" Henry grumbled.

Corey ignored him. Really, what did this assclown expect him to say? Who cares about any of the drama that led up to this? Their lives were over but Henry couldn't let go. He thought there was something here for him. He thought he was relevant in the storming end times. Pathetic.

Lina turned to Henry with her now trademark blasé confidence. "He doesn't need faith. He has me."

As if to punctuate her sentiment the ground began to tremble. And then quake. And then uproot itself and rise in gigantic clumps for miles around.

"Shit," was the first understated sentence Henry spoke in this timeline, as the trio was flung off balance in the marsh. Fortunately, the marsh and the meadow and the trees in their vicinity stayed anchored to Earth while all around them something in Earth was exploding alive.

***

The artificial planet that housed original humans and death loomed deep in the galactic core of the Milky Way. Alex, one of the three released prisoner double agents, made certain the planet would waft into existence like an unspeakably large heat mirage through a mighty tear in the fabric between realities, just as Hive Queen promised. Unlike her promise, though, the space around it was... space.

This foreign space was the same as any other space the humans had known and conquered, except this galaxy already looked conquered. Or barren. Where was the centralized military presence, Trondant asked himself? Where was the fight?

Trondant paced in front of his swivel throne on the deck of his command center. His brisk stride made his underlings squirm. The animal was out and felt caged and that never ended well for a random one of them. All of the soldiers on that deck understood Trondant's game of roulette was imminent if they didn't bump into a nest of enemy soon. Up and comers squirmed the most but they had less to fear. Likely the commander would send a pair of old, salty retiring generals to the gallows. Prone to mistakes and hardly missed, the retiring made wonderful patsies. They were on their way out anyway.

Trondant scratched the top of his ear manically. Nothing here, obviously, and no word from the fleet smothering Earth's atmosphere like a global superstorm. Bad news and helplessness made him itch. The commander realized he had been conned but since nobody knew his war plans had been drafted by the Hive Queen he could not, at this moment, dash into her chamber, rip her tits from her chest and feed them to her. To do thus would be to lose his own head, for his weakness would be undeniable. But, if he stayed put and rode her con out, maybe—just maybe—he could scapegoat some of these officers.

"How long 'til General Q'rvis' fight cams go live?" Trondant snapped at his first lieutenant. General Q'rvis was a bastard of a warrior—more of a sociopath, those who dared whispered—who delighted in visiting preschools during leave to orate his gruesome slaughters to children's circles at story time. As a teenager he had slain the heads of the six ruling clans in the Abacha Sector of his titanium planet, beginning with his father and ending with his brother's father-in-law. That he climbed the military ranks in record time surprised few. That he volunteered to oversee the war on second generation humanity from the frontline tanker on the first wave of assault surprised no one.

Trondant's first lieutenant smiled with relief as he informed, "Commander, General Q'rvis is hailing us at this time." He put the transmission through while he spoke so that Trondant wouldn't bark at him to do so, as if his expository words were a waste of precious time.

The general appeared life-size on a central wall that doubled as a monitor for all on deck to see and hear. "Commander, the war is almost over. The human resistance was disgraceful to our name. Like squashing bugs." General Q'rvis' droopy eyes twinkled and his sneer became joy with his next revelation: "But the Earth Plane forces hath arrived and they are putting up a fight!"

Q'rvis' exuberance was infectious. Trondant stopped tugging at his ear and patty-caked his fingertips with glee. "We shall join you posthaste, General. It is barren here. A traitor must have warned them we were coming. Save some for us!"

Trondant waited for a response from the general who had turned to consult with someone off camera. "Who is that there, General?" Trondant inquired.

From around the left side of the frame a new human face bulged onscreen. "Oh, hey…. Yeah, sorry about that. I was just sayin' that was me who alerted them. I thought if Earth Plane had all its forces in one spot you guys could, like, swoop in and fuck 'em up after the good general here softened 'em up."

It was James. Trondant's raised brow slowly compacted into a furl.

"I would have run it by you but I figured, *Eh. They'll figure it out.*"

"Who... is this *worm?*" Trondant demanded. His words breathed out of him like fire.

General Q'rvis yanked James into frame and stood him in the background like placing a mannequin. "Commander, this is one of the three Royal Guardsmen who helped make this possible."

James stood on his tiptoes to be seen over the general's massive left shoulder. "Yeah, I, ah... I helped make this possible. Less of a worm and more a bird of prey." There was a shocked silence, which James promptly filled with, "Go Team Humanity!" He fist-pumped his own cheer. Seeing he was alone in this, he added, "What, they don't have rally cries in the old world? I distinctly remember rally cries in another life!"

Trondant's face discolored to a drunk's shade of red and then choke-victim purple as this... this *thing* masquerading as human prattled word shit.

"General Q'rvis, do we need that creature anymore?"

"No, sir. He hath performed his function."

"Excellent. Kill it."

James lunged in front of the general and urgently thumped at the screen with his palms. "Kill it? But I'm it! And I helped make this possible! And actually, not to gloat, but I was *the* major factor in your success," he blurted.

"General?"

Q'rvis shoved James out of frame and answered, "Yes, Commander?"

"Kill it swiftly as a thank you for its service."

James drew in a long breath to register another protest but had his windpipe crushed by the general before his word-spew had opportunity to escape. The thrust of General Q'rvis' beefy hands was so fast and so strong that he tore James' brain stem from the spine rendering the boy a limp twitching rag doll. The general held the corpse by its bloated tongue and pushed on the mouth. James' body collapsed to the floor as his tongue wriggled in the general's hand like a giant bloody slug.

Trondant glared at General Q'rvis but said nothing. Q'rvis knew he had botched this one by allowing James to live as long as he had and Trondant knew that he knew.

"We anxiously await your arrival, Commander," the general said. He cut transmission before Trondant could consider cutting him. Then he ate James' tongue.

***

Corey pivoted in a dizzy waddle like he was bashfully slow dancing with a secret crush at prom. He surveyed the trees and houses, apartments and corner stores—Is that the court house?—schools and condos rising in the air at moped speed. In fact, he thought his squinting eyes made out a moped falling in the distance—as did all of the debris of civilization—from a shimmying, vibrating platform going straight up with the calm of a freight elevator. If these platforms made a sound it couldn't be heard over the crackle of snapping telephone wires and exploding pipes.

Asphalt blew to shrapnel in spots where gas lines twisted apart releasing giant orange fireballs that gave birth to inky black plumes. The trio was far enough away from the action not to be deafened by it but the acrid smells reached their nostrils and hit their tongues. Corey felt like retching at the oils of death but he held it. What the hell were these rising mounds living underneath Massachusetts, Corey asked himself? Were they everywhere? Was this happening around the world? Were they alien sleeper cells embedded here like death pods from *War of The Worlds*?

Flocks of birds ranging in the thousands rose higher and swifter than the remnants of their homes. For a time the sky was blotted out by a swarming feathery fog, but the squawking and flapping wasn't enough to dampen the noise of towns being shed from mobile clumps of… no, those aren't clumps of earth after all. Corey's eyes shot wide as the first of these things crashed through the wall of birds, zooming into action against the war machines that had flown through the portal. More and more of these vessels shook off the rubble of Western ingenuity that concealed them and swept into flight. Some shot pulsing laser knives at the invaders; others sliced through them physically in kamikaze games of chicken.

Unlike the invading ships these things looked slick, aerodynamic. They moved from zero to blinding in half a blink. They were incredible.

*Jesus, this **is** War of The Worlds, only the ships in the earth aren't killing us, they're protecting us!*

Lina broke Corey's daze with a breathy joyous laugh. Mouth agape, he turned to his love with a look that asked, *Are you seeing this shit?* Her wide, pleasant smile looked like relief... but not surprise. Corey's expression changed to one of concern, one that asked her, *Are you finally breaking?*

Lina planted her lips hard on his. He made a small sound of being taken aback but nimbly melted into her kiss. When she pulled away her eyes met his with great and, he thought, unnatural glee. "Corey," she said, "I was *so* right about this place."

"What place, Hockomock?"

She grabbed his shirt and pulled him tightly against her chest. Mouth to ear she whispered, "James is with me."

She released her grip and nodded at him confirming that what she had said was no joke. He stumbled back a step but before he could process her meaning Henry barged in between them and out to the meadow of smoldering humanity and jet parts. He was oblivious to whatever they were doing. Something up in that filthy sky entranced him—something beyond the dog fight. Something between here and the setting sun.

Henry's jaw slackened. The lines of his forehead twisted quizzical. There, far above a hole in the cloud cover, flew a sparkling dot. It was growing exponentially, which told him it was in a real fucking hurry to get here.

"A planet," Henry balked. The *Star Wars*-like air raid was unbelievable enough—but a traveling planet? A Death Star, perhaps? Craziness was about to be raped by a whole new insanity and all Henry could do was shake his head and mutter, "No, no, no."

Corey didn't give a shit what Henry was on about. He fixed his eyes on that gun dangling by the man's side. The devil finally let down his guard. Lina saw what he saw and what he was intending to do. She quickly grabbed for Corey's wrist to prevent him from tackling the bastard, but she was a hair late.

Corey pounced, spearing Henry in the center of his back while trying to strip him of his handgun. Henry took the full impact of the blow and lost his breath on his way to dirt. But he kept that gun. The surprise attack made him reflexively grip it fiercely, the opposite of how Corey expected this to go.

Henry rolled around on his belly like an Olympic wrestler searching for a way to buck this chimp off him and shoot if he had to. Break Kiddo's leg, definitely.

What Corey lacked in grappling skills he made up for in rage. And he was smart in the midst of rage, not blinded by it. Instead of trying to wrench the Sig Sauer from Henry's fingers he knocked fists on that cranial wound, opening it back up. Henry cried out but that cry morphed into one long snarling grunt.

Corey hefted his upper torso on his left arm as he threw haymakers with his right. Henry elbowed the boy's arm out from under him. Corey momentarily collapsed onto the back of the serpent, who immediately rolled out from under and then on top of this mouse of a boy.

"You fucking shit!" Henry growled. He slammed the butt of his gun into the sweet reverberant spot of Corey's skull, knocking him unconscious.

"Good try, Kiddo," he uttered more to himself than his beaten adversary while glaring at Lina who was standing behind them, watching. He wanted to make sure there were no more surprises yet the most surprising thing of all was her lack of re-action. She stood tall scratching a mosquito bite. He climbed off her boyfriend, cocked the gun trigger so she'd get the message anyway, and then patted his old head wound. It was a mess of blood and hair yet again. "Damn it!" It stung and he winced but there was no real damage done. Nothing he couldn't ignore.

Corey moaned and rolled onto his back after several groggy, failed attempts. He lay there sprawled in the grass, breathing heavily, and watching war toys disintegrate each other as his blurry vision worked itself back into focus. Was it his imagination or were the Earth ships transforming into alien ships? That must have been some blow to the head.

"Are we done here?" Henry barked the question sideways at Corey because he couldn't strip his eyes from Lina. Who was she? *What* was she? She was this insignificant little girl who also had the presence of a cunning apparition. "There's a planet coming," he informed her calmly.

"I know," she said. And there was that hint of grin Henry understood so well, like she were a cannibal assessing someone delicious, watching him simmer to perfection before ravenously devouring his flesh and his power.

"You *know*. Isn't that something." Henry dribbled his words like he was amused but he was far from amused. He was collected. Centered. For the first time since evolving into a living repository of all knowledge he fell between thoughts. There was silence in him, brief though it was, sweet, ticklish silence quenching a thirst he had long forgotten, a momentary reprieve from being himself. But the feeling was so fleeting that it immediately became like a childhood memory of the person he had been when the world was alive as a dream, the innocent creature he had slain and buried to make it as an adult.

Running from the stillness and back into the hell and now, he broke eye contact with Lina. "Get up, Kiddo! Back over there with Juliet!"

Corey couldn't hear him. He was again mesmerized by the machines dancing above them. The explosions and the dissonant rumbles echoed through him, their sounds recessed, his own blood pumping in the foreground. He heard his heart chugging in his ears and it was breaking. He had failed. Failed Lina. Failed himself. And as impossible as it sounded, failed the world.

Even the fleets from deep underground were morphing into the bad guys. He saw that clearly now; it was no concussive illusion. The two forces were merging into one of intricately designed death squads.

And there, alone at the end of the world, lay Corey Avon, the boy-god who couldn't stop this, broken and waiting to die.

***

Trondant fixated on the tiny blue dot out the windshield growing larger as his planet zoomed through the vacuum of space to destroy it.

"Commander, we hath a matter that requires your immediate concern," the first lieutenant spoke. He directed Trondant's attention to the main screen on which Earth's air war played in montage through cameras affixed to General Q'rvis' fleet.

The crew of the mobile planet were aching to brutalize enemy with their own cut scenes. There wasn't a fearful soul among them. No civilization in their ancient universe had provided them with real challenge; how could this unevolved speck housing prisoners be anything more than a training exercise? Obviously there was no Earth Plane force worth a damn or Q'rvis would have reported back by now.

"What is it, Lieutenant?" Trondant sighed. He was bored and frustrated and couldn't find any emergency onscreen.

The lieutenant hesitated. "Commander... sir...." No one wanted to bring dreadful news to Trondant—especially no one standing within throttling distance, as was the lieutenant.

"Stop playing sick and vomit your words, Lieutenant."

"Sir, we hath lost contact with General Q'rvis. Fatally... lost contact," the lieutenant informed him.

Trondant leaned forward in his swivel throne and squinted at the monitor. He pointed to the general's barge and said, "No, Lieutenant, his ship is right there. Hail him."

"We did, sir."

"Hail him again!"

"Sir, respectfully, that is not the general's barge."

Trondant shot eyes at the lieutenant like he was the foulest creature in six galaxies. What was a simpleton like him doing on Leader's deck?

The lieutenant did not wait for Trondant to decide his fate. He leaped in with an explanation—an explanation so impossible that he would have been decapitated where he stood if it did not play out on camera for Trondant to witness himself: the enemy vessels were shape-shifting into mirror images of the general's fleet and picking them off in the confusion.

The first lieutenant smiled nervously. Perhaps he would be promoted, not fired. "See, sir? That's not the general's ship. Over half the fleet is not the fleet. We are losing this war and losing it big."

The lieutenant was so relieved to have the proof that would save him he let the truth fly with abandon. As he began to drift into a daydream of promotion and hero's reception, Trondant leaped to his feet and snapped the lieutenant's neck. The fresh corpse's dead twitching nerves were not enough statement to the crew for Trondant's liking so he continued to twist the smug wonk's head until it clung to the body by flesh alone. Filling the deck with a primal scream, he yanked the lieutenant's head up off its torso and lobbed the bloody, smiling thing at the main wall monitor.

The crew fell silent to his rage. Entrails and sinew glopped onto the action scenes whizzing onscreen and trickled down like snail mucus.

Trondant ripped his shirt down the middle and smeared his chest and face with blood like war paint. Medals of honor flew off his jacket in the ruckus but he was too out of his mind to care.

At the top of his lungs he ordered, "Step on the fucking accelerator!"

Now they felt fear. And now Trondant had the perfect cue to make his exit and pay that filthy louse Hive Queen a visit that no one would question. Clearly this man was going to kill again and the crew would just feel relieved that it wasn't another one of them.

And the Hive Queen would be quite pleased that he chose her. Perhaps this is why her lips were smiling even though she lay in trance on her bed when he stormed into her quarters.

"Sow, wake up!"

He shook her but she did not stir. No matter. At this point he didn't care to enact a slow sadistic revenge, he wanted her gone. Plus, a quick death would look more like temporary insanity than premeditation.

Trondant whipped a silk pillow over her face and thrust down hard. Her body did not convulse but she had to be suffocating. Had to be!

"Fuck you! Fuck! Fuck!" he pouted. And then he beat her through the pillow with enormous tight fists.

Blood spread through the fabric like a red spider web but she didn't move. He ripped the pillow now clinging to her face by her own gore. She was dead. He snapped her neck anyway.

Now they both smiled. And he felt excitement in his pants. What he did with that excitement meant nothing to her for she was long gone from her horrid perfumed body cage. She was now on the blue jewel where he was heading and she was setting him up for the biggest fall in the history of two universes.

The Hive Queen had enough smiles for two bodies.

***

The gash in the sky finally sealed itself. Presumably all of the attack fleet were in yet something was terrible wrong and Henry felt it. He had missed the spectacle of buried tech reshaping into copies of alien fighters. He knew the alien exterminators were no longer wiping out humanity, they were fighting a technological presence buried here and he assumed they were also fighting amongst themselves. "Madness," he uttered to himself. But what he meant was *inconceivable*.

It was inconceivable to Henry that an alien air force had been buried in Earth's crust and not one secret keeper in all ages knew about it. He had broken into the minds of all the greats and never saw an inkling of this. A scenario much like this had been imagined, yes, and shared as fiction, sure—but not as a means to hide the truth in a lie. It simply did not exist as a real possibility and yet... here it was. Here *they* were.

Who the fuck are you?

How? *How?* Henry scratched his chin with the barrel of his Sig while gawking at two silver disks rushing off to battle somewhere in the world.

"Who kept this from me?!" The sky and ground were packed with noise. His yell barely made it to the treetops.

He glanced at Lina now. He wanted to chainsaw that all-knowing smirk off her face. Not moments ago she had grabbed at her temples and doubled over like someone was penetrating her brain the way Henry had done to countless victims.

Seeing her in pain was the only thing that got Corey off his ass and by her side but no sooner had he embraced his crying love than she dropped her hands and began giggling uncontrollably. She pinched Corey's cheeks and massaged the contours of his head as if she had never touched his flesh before. "I'm fine," she told him. "We both are." Humanity's final world war had been all smiles and joy for her since.

"That's it. That's fucking it," Henry scowled. He unfurled his long arm and aimed the pistol between Corey and Lina's heads. "On your knees, both of you."

Corey froze wondering if this really was it and should he attack again.

"Do it now!" Henry shrieked. He unloaded a round that whizzed between their heads nearly clipping the boy's ear. Corey reflexively ducked and then dropped to his knees—but his love. His possessed love standing her ground with the ecstatic joy of the clinically insane.

"So help me, little girl," Henry spat. Lina methodically raised her arms like a burglar caught and went to her knees in her own sweet time, eyes trained on Henry's through the slow ordeal.

"Henry, you can't kill us. We're all you have left." Corey spoke it so weakly even he didn't believe himself.

"Corey, you little shit, I am going to enjoy having nothing left. But you know what I'm going to enjoy more? Giving lover girl here a choice. What do you say, Lina? Should I kill your boyfriend or not? If not, I'll shoot you right in the all-knowing third eye." Henry snickered at his own word play. "If you say yes," he continued, "I will let you go. Go free, little bird! Fly to wherever it is you think you're safe from... this."

And he meant the world blowing up. Reassessing her pain-ful outbreak of Christ consciousness in the face of annihilation he deduced that she was not Lina but someone else. Perhaps there were not just sleeper cells embedded in the earth but also in people. Maybe she was one of these and maybe, just maybe, she had somewhere to be. If he let her go he could track her and capture her again before she embraced the safety of alien friends. Then he could bargain his way out of the asylum. It was his only play.

Lina didn't answer him but her face didn't register contem-plation. Did she even hear him? Maybe the being inside the body needed to get used to ears.

"Don't do it, Lina. You know it's a trick. He'll kill us both," Corey said. He anticipated the eye contact of his love but she kept them steady on the trained assassin.

"You're looking into my eyes, hon. Am I lying?" Henry asked gravely.

She looked into him; she looked through him. "No, Corey. Henry isn't lying. He will only shoot one of us."

Henry smiled almost as widely as she. "Good," he said, sat-isfied that she was about to choose life.

"Shoot yourself, Henry. It's the only way," she said.

"What?" Henry was incensed.

"Put the gun in your mouth and pull the trigger."

Corey cocked his head at his love. "Lina, what are you—?"

"—Do it, Henry."

To Henry and Corey's astonishment, the killer's right arm began to turn on him dilatorily. His hand shook and his wrist twitched as he fought for control of his own appendages. "What the fuck is—No," he protested, unable to even drop the gun.

"No! This is fucking ludicrous—Stop this!" He chastised his arm as much as Lina while the gun inched closer and closer to his lips. He tried in vain to will his left hand out of paralysis and grab the Sig but the struggle only caused his bicep to spasm.

"What the fuck is this?!"

Henry's screams, his protesting will—none of it made a difference. Some internal power overrode him. His jaws pried open wide enough for the Sig Sauer to rattle between his teeth.

"No! Don't do this! Don't do this, Lina!" Henry's saliva drooled out of him like a famished Rottweiler as he struggled to not choke on that acrid metal barrel.

"Lina's not doing this, Henry. You are. Now pull the trigger," she commanded.

Corey slumped back on his haunches dumbfounded. He didn't think he could be any more stunned than he had been today. Here it was.

Henry cried, "No! I don't want to die!"—But his words were deformed by the weapon penetrating him and pressing hard against his tongue.

At that moment the bubble in the meadow shimmered into the physical world. Henry couldn't see it behind him but he could tell something new was there by Corey's reaction. Lina didn't even look. She pushed herself to her feet and as she did she stayed even with Henry's eyes.

"See? There's our future, Corey. Now kill yourself, Henry. Pull. The. Trigger." Lina cooed the word *trigger* like it was an emasculating sexual request.

Henry shrieked his vocal cords raw but his trigger finger, slave to her voice, did her bidding. The pistol clicked once. Nothing. Clicked several shots in fast succession. Nothing. Was the gun jammed or out of bullets?

Henry winced through each yank of trigger but when he saw that she had failed to kill him he laughed. He laughed in relief and he laughed at the weakness of the stupid witch's power.

"You dumb bitch. I'm going to relish... *relish* killing you."

Corey revved up to lunge at the mad bastard but Lina draped a calming hand on his chest, which told him her spell wasn't broken after all.

"What's that, Henry? We couldn't hear you. You're choking on your gun. Choke on your gun, Henry."

Henry, the proud man of shadows who knew everything there was to know didn't know how to stop this. His eyes bulged as his hand forced the Sig down his throat. "What?—No," he barely said.

"That's it. I want you to eat the gun, Henry." Lina's voice was so soothing it struck Corey as grotesque.

Unable to bend at the waist Henry vomited on his shirt as his right hand lodged the pistol deep in his esophagus. He gasped hard, vacuuming chunky acid bile into his suffocating lungs. His eyes drained tears down his blue face while he choked on steel and breakfast. Finally the man who thought himself immortal crumpled into himself on the naked ground.

Henry wasn't afraid anymore, he was mesmerized. Mesmerized by an inner vision of his own truth. His eyes popped and his lips found a way to smile through their own messy death as he beheld himself as he really was in a flash—his final and greatest knowing.

"Oh, wow!" his mouth tried to exclaim around the gun. He now understood what the knowledge from the lives he absorbed really was. He knew what history was. He knew everything and it was nothing.

Henry's abdomen convulsed as if he were laughing at the greatest joke ever told, but a nasty gurgle released from him and then released him.

Corey thought he knew the worst of death. This stole it. Even after the torture circus Henry had led him through, at the end of it he had a sadness, a kernel of compassion for this man. "Lina," he said. "Are you Lina?" He was afraid to touch his love and that saddened him more.

"I will be. You need to take us home, Corey."

"Where, in that bubble? I'm not going in there."

"You have to, Corey. It's the only place that's safe."

He hesitated and she picked up on his reticence. "Do you trust me?" she asked.

He looked her in the eye a long moment as he processed the question. "I trust Lina," he said.

She touched his cheek with a graceful sweep of the hand. He almost flinched but caught himself. She smiled and said, "Then you *do* trust me." She collapsed into his arms and he hugged her tight. He knew then, even if he didn't understand why he knew, that she was his love and nothing other.

"Understand hither-thither...." she began reciting weakly.

".... And in that understanding be neither swept away nor carried on the seas of time," he finished. And when he finished she kissed him drowsily and that kiss was heaven, yet he did not feel it as a kiss from her to him because inwardly he had dissolved. Speaking the riddle in this moment, devoid of all the urgency that was him working to this emptiness, dropped the veil between worlds like a magical invocation. In that emptiness he didn't feel Lina's personal love wafting into his like the bonding ingredients of an intoxicating relationship, for he was that emptiness and she was love itself—love itself fulfilling him.

Love was the singular quality of emptiness. Together, Lina and Corey were everything, a bliss state Corey wished he could be forever. By wishing it he knew he was also still alive. This revelation born of desire brought him back to his senses and the couple back to form in the only place where their love could play out: on the inside of the bubble.

Corey looked around, discombobulated. His nervous system was humming and he felt loose in his skin like a sack of puzzle pieces. "Where are we?" he asked.

Lina looked up at the fine young man hugging her and softly kissed his lips. "We're almost home. We just have to walk through that door." She pointed to what he perceived as a glimmering wall of light. He recalled fearing this place but the feeling was insubstantial residue from another life.

Above them smoldering ash and fighter parts zapped to dust like moths on a bug light when vehicles hit the dome of the force field. Earth was hell now and that door led to a new home far away from here. Whatever unknowable challenges lurked there had to be better than this.

Corey squinted at a silhouette in the light door. "Is that…?"

"Come on, Coronimus! Time's a wastin'!" Darryl stood in the light waving his friends in.

"Move it or lose it!" Corey heard Stephen's voice, sharp and strong, before the shadow of his figure pierced the light.

Lina took Corey by the hand and urged him to walk with her to the light. He didn't hesitate. Wherever she wanted to go he was not losing her.

Together they stepped through and as soon as the last bit of fabric from his left pant leg crossed over, the light dimmed and the bubble expanded as if detonating, but then reversed in an instant and imploded like being sucked out of existence through an atomic straw.

The meadow returned to war-torn swampland once more. There were no signs that the bubble had ever been there. No singe marks. No crater in the soil. No radiation melting the trees.

The doors to this world had been erased forever.

Chapter 47

Corey's mind was a vortex of questions that swirled him dizzy. He fell against a blank gray wall and slid down it but instead of hitting the ground, his butt hit a bench that had self-created from the wall as if in response to his needs. Lina and Darryl spotted him as he bounced onto the sturdy new thing and sat next to him, Darryl to his right, Lina to his left.

He remembered this room or one just like it from his last Hockomock outing, the one where—

"I know, Corey. It's fantastic, isn't it? But it's a lot. Gather yourself and take your time. We're all safe now," Darryl said, responding to his unspoken concerns.

Corey sunk his head in his hands. They smelled earthy and it alerted him to the lack of any odor here. "Am I dead?"

"That's a complicated question," Darryl said.

"Is it?"

Stephen, who was standing in front of them, arms crossed, broke in thoughtfully: "Well look, the basic answer here is... This is physically you. But you can never go back there. Earth is dead to us."

"Obviously. I killed it."

"No, you killed the illusion of it."

Corey looked up at his friend hovering over him. "How are you alive?" he asked.

"And that's my cue," James said. He looked like a ghost to Corey the way he sauntered through the wall across the room. "We're not those cheap carbon knockoffs from the timeline you created. We're the real deal, baby.... No offense, Lina."

Lina looked pleasantly surprised to see James. She ran up and gave him a hug. "You made it out in one piece," she squealed.

"Yeah. Remind me never to live inside a girl's head. There's a lot going on in there."

Corey had no clue what that meant. He ignored it and asked, "Is Alex alive, too?"

"Yeah, he's kickin' it somewhere around this dump. He was in charge of the other portal. You saw that planet coming to Earth? His responsibility," James explained.

Corey leaned back, shaking his head and sighing. He glanced plaintively at Lina. "I don't get any of this. Why do you?"

Darryl asked, "Do you two need a minute?"

"Would you?" Lina said.

James put his arm around Stephen. "Don't have to tell us twice. We got stuff to do anyway. Like help rebuild a civilization, stuff like that. No biggie."

Stephen mimed a tip of the hat to Corey and Lina. As the trio were about to leave through the wall, James remembered what he really came to tell Corey and spun back around on his heels. "Hard Core, just don't be scared anymore, okay? There are some freaky-looking people here and I'm one of 'em. Remember how, like, we all got killed?"

Corey shot him a look like he was a fool for even asking— How could he forget that twice?

"Well, we all got souls, too," James continued. "And we all got put in new bodies. We're shape shifters now, which sounds—"

"—Stupid," Stephen completed.

"Yeah. But it's totally cool. I get to make faces in the mirror all day."

"Don't lie to the man—Corey, there are no mirrors here," Stephen noted. "Also, before I forget, sorry for putting on those dumb voices last time ya saw us—You remember?"

"No. What dumb voices?" Corey deadpanned.

"Yeah, it was stupid. We were fucking around with the shape shifting, thought it would be cool to come to you as light beings. Turns out you speak how you look but ya can't tell the difference until you shift back to normal. Light beings actually talk like douche bags!"

"But they're cool," James added.

"Yeah, everyone's cool," Stephen affirmed.

"So is this how you really look? As a shape shifter, I mean—Is this normal?" Corey asked.

"No, GOD no! But, dude: one freaky thing at a time," James said.

"Alright, good talk, idiots. Let's get outta their hair," Darryl said. He brushed at them to get moving through the wall.

"Laterz," James hollered over his shoulder with a clapping wave of the hand. Stephen and he took their exit.

Darryl straggled one moment longer to emphasize the importance of what James originally said. "Really, don't be scared anymore. This place isn't a nightmare. It's magical. We were just dumb kids."

"What are you now?" Corey asked.

Darryl grinned mischievously. "Dumb kids," he affirmed. And with that he abandoned Corey to the comforts of his love.

***

Lina draped an arm around Corey's neck and sat with him quietly for a while. She kissed his ear and whispered soothingly, "It's okay…. It's okay… I love you, Corey Avon."

"I love you," he whispered back. He wished he could cry away the knot in his feelings but he was still in shock and too lucid. He searched intensely Lina's eyes. Lina was definitely in there gazing back receptively.

"Am I ever going to understand this or is it too complex?" he finally asked her.

She waved the question off nonchalantly. "Oh, it's not complex. It's dreadful but it's not complex."

"Fantastic," he said. They chuckled a bit and he cherished sharing this with her no matter how bizarre the circumstances.

"Yeah, see, here's the thing: we're special, you and me and the boys. But especially you."

"Sounds good so far," he said drolly.

"No one from Earth has ever survived coming here and no one from here has survived going there," she told him.

"Why? Like a physics thing?" he asked.

"No. This is the shit part, Corey. Are you sitting?" They both giggled at her mock concern for the obvious. She continued, "There was a war here with these aliens. The aliens are human and they lost. Big surprise, right? But their leader and the souls of his fallen soldiers were banished to a parallel universe. Ours. To Mars, Corey."

"This sounds like that story you were writing. You were writing this?"

"Yes, and if you had read it like you were meant to...."

He smirked. "Sorry. I was never much of a reader."

"Right. An-y-way...." She over enunciated her words playfully scolding him. "There's a council of elders, the Earth Plane Council. They're, like, older than old. Oh, this is Earth Plane, by the way—Welcome. Nice to meet you." She extended her hand and they laughed as he shook it.

"They thought reptilians from here were covertly working with the aliens so they got banished to Mars, too, to oversee the development of this new species the souls of our forefathers were seeded in." Reading his confused face she added, "It's a reincarnation thing, just... go with it."

"Why would you have bad guys overseeing bad guys?" Corey laughed. "That's retarded!"

"Cuz they didn't know if they were bad guys. They had to prove themselves. That's how things work around here. People are connected in a way where trust isn't usually an issue. But here's the thing: when the council sent a team in to check up on them, they didn't find anyone. Mars was abandoned. They looked around the galaxy and saw life on Earth that looked pretty close to what Mars was so they went there, but they didn't find anyone on Earth either."

"Did they find dinosaurs? Was it that long ago?"

"Sort of. What they really found was an evolving ecosystem of complex life that drastically changed every time they took their eyes off the place. They found that and they found death," she said.

"Whoa, wait—Earth? *Our* Earth?" Corey asked.

"Yes. I can show you if you let me."

He scrunched his forehead and lips funny. "You have a movie of this?"

"No, I have better. I can immerse you in the experiences like virtual reality but without all the sticking needles into your brain or whatever."

"What do you stick into my brain?"

"Me."

He laughed. "Well get in there! I wanna see everything."

She put up a hand of caution. "It will be overpowering."

"After today I'm pretty sure I've got that base covered."

She hesitated a few moments then said, "Alright," and engaged his eyes with her own. Before he could make a staring contest joke his face went slack and he lost himself in a tornado of other peoples' memories—people from the fantasy movies he loved as a child and nightmarish abductions blocked from his own conscious recall; people who existed in legends and role-playing games; people he hunted with his friends in a swamp. People from here. These were the people from here.

No shit. Puckwudgies are real? No shit.

Lina's disembodied voice echoed in his mindscape like a chastising goddess: "Corey, you're paying attention to the wrong thing. Be amazed later. Learn now."

Her words galvanized him into proper focus. He watched and felt an onslaught of experiences flickering through him. There were cold-blooded dinosaurs then warm-blooded and small animals. Then large mammals and no dinosaurs. All just as he was taught, except these changes didn't unfold over millions of years, they happened in the turn of a back.

"This is how Earth Plane Council learned to never turn its back on Earth," Lina's voice confirmed.

Corey witnessed monkey-like humans engaging with the mythical beings from here. Lina explained those weren't really people from here, they were illusions, but he was too overwhelmed by all of this truth filling him, becoming him, that her words sounded fuzzy and garbled and distant.

This display wasn't just an answer to what happened with the war, this was the ultimate answer to the human struggle to comprehend self and purpose. This was everything. Did Henry know this? He never spoke of it.

Next time Earth Planers checked in the monkey humans were fully human. Outwardly they were perfect copies of the invaders. Inwardly they differed in that they had triune brains with a reptilian cortex reflecting their Martian origins. This evolution was not possibly random. Chance played no role here.

It appeared as though these new humans had forged large complex societies with architecture and mythical imagery straight out of Earth Plane. It was as if they were remaking Mars or worse: unconsciously building a replica of the first place they had fought and lost so they could go to war with it again and again in a never-ending bid for empowerment. Earth Planers didn't know. They only knew not to divert their attention again.

Corey watched and absorbed how the grays maneuvered a portal around Earth. He watched the Roswell crash and exclaimed, "That part Henry knew about."

He saw the Earth Plane Council's failed attempts at physically transporting humans through portal sites around the world for study and saw the same thing happen with soul extraction. "Henry knew about that, too," he said. Then he added, "But he didn't know why. They just wanted to know us. And we just wanted to know them. We had different ways of going about it. Ours was violent so we assumed theirs was, too."

"Corey, watch." Lina's voice was crisp and loud and galvanizing once more. He was immersed back in the remembrances of other people. He got the feeling from what he was seeing that it didn't matter how the governments of Earth or its citizens handled their visitors' presence—that was a smoke screen for something much deeper. He got that feeling because what he was now seeing through the eyes of a startled gray monitoring Earth was that the souls of the original Martian prisoners were being born into the world.

He saw Hockomock. He watched Earth Planers coaxing people oblivious to their nature through the force field to extract their souls from within the bubble.

Finally, he saw his mother in a hospital bed crying tears of elation as she held her newborn son. "Wow," was all he could say.

"And then you were born: Leader," Lina uttered solemnly. "And when you came of age, the Council didn't have to come for you, you went looking for them."

Corey broke eye contact, shook his head, and demanded, "Stop-stop-stop!" This was too much after all. The ramification of being Leader was that he was evil, a vicious brute, but he didn't feel evil. Then again his actions certainly did lead to—

"You're not evil, Corey." She read him but not psychically. His feelings were obvious. "You're not even Leader."

"But you just said—"

"I know, but... that's what the Council thought you were at first."

He waved her off to cut to the chase and said, "Lina... if you know what I am, just.... What the fuck am I?"

She took a deep breath, which reminded him of his breathing exercises in another life. He did the same to calm himself. She leaned back and stared at the clear gray wall across the room. Once she gathered herself she turned to her love and began down a path of explanation he only thought he wanted to follow and she knew it.

"You're… we're all—you, me, James, Stephen, Darryl, and Alex… illusions," she said.

She studied his face for reaction. At first he was a blank canvass but then exploded into mocking laughter. "Come oooo-oooon!" he drew out.

She stayed placid. "It's true."

"So what? What's devastating about that? I've seen that a million times in movies. Buddha said that."

"No, you don't get it: humanity is an illusion. All of life on Earth is an illusion. The terrain, the atmosphere…. The only thing that's real is Earth herself. Earth is alive, Corey, and she needs to feed. Do you understand?"

He thought he did. "She. Needs. To. Feed?" He over-enunciated the question like it was the stupidest thing he'd ever heard—worse than reptilian prisoners raising Martians. Could this be a silly nightmare after all? One from which he wakes up next to Lina on her bed having passed out, exhausted from reading her book all the way to the end?

He shook his head disapprovingly and scoffed, "Movie of the week. So… so she feeds on us?"

"No. She created us to attract others to feed on them. You want to know what we are? What all of Earthly existence is through all time? All of nature's rich complexity and beauty? All of humanity's art and war and boredom and ignorance and joy and bliss and sweeping global change—you want to know what all of that is? You don't, Corey, but here it comes anyway: it's bait."

Corey's throat knotted up tight like a Charlie horse. He slouched on the bench and rubbed at the pain in his Adam's apple. If he could melt away into the floor he would have.

"*Now* are you sitting?" she quipped. But he was beyond registering humor.

He paused a moment then spoke out loud to himself. "I'm not an alien leader. I'm the illusion of one. That's what *that* means. I'm not even human. I'm... an expectation. I'm fucking bait. I'm a fucking worm on a fucking hook."

Pleadingly and with brewing anger, Corey met Lina's eyes again. "I'm on a—a worm on a hook—Is that what you're telling me?"

She slapped a hand on his knee and said, "You're a perfect trap, Corey Avon. We all are. If you can own that you can move on because like I said, we're special. We're not just the last of our kind, we're transcendent versions of it. That's why we can live here. Our souls are real. All of this newness and change and confusion was a game Earth was playing to get Earth Planers to set foot on her soil again.

"Corey, my friend, are you ready for this one? ... Nothing even existed between ancient Egypt and the mid 1900s. You get it? Our entire sense of history is a perfect, brilliant lie. Life only exists on Earth when someone else is looking. All of that art, all of that knowledge... the wars, the advances, the setbacks, the... the human struggle.... None of it's real. It was just interesting. It was a mystery.

"The Earth Plane Council knew they hadn't been able to survive engaging the mystery in the past but also something was terribly wrong with the souls they examined. They were fake."

"So our planet whipped up some real souls, is that it?" Corey asked. Although none of this sat well with him, he recognized it was truth by the way his insides writhed and fought the knowledge.

Lina explained, "She drew the breath of life from the formless consciousness in which all life is embedded to make us more real than real. Earth's ability to not get caught resides in her ability to adapt to expectation."

"Then how did they catch her?"

"I caught her."

"You did. Of course you did," he sneered sarcastically.

She regarded him with a prideful smile. "I'm not just Lina anymore, Corey, I'm a synthesis."

"You're the alien woman from my flashbacks."

"Alien," she scoffed.

"Sorry. But you know what I meant."

Lina stroked his cheek softly with a lean finger and admitted, "Yes. I am her plus Lina in one and we both love you."

Corey stiffened his back. Lina thought she had said it melodramatically enough for him to pick up on the humor. Clearly not. He couldn't live with Lina and this other woman as a prism personality, never knowing who was regarding him, who was loving him, who was judging him, or, really, who and what this entity was.

Lina broke the tension with her sardonic giggle that was good-natured but also chastising him for being thick. "Kidding! There's only one of me in here! Think of me as two ingredients of a single recipe—or, okay—you know how, like, when you're forty you're still going to be a big dumb manchild? That's me now but the female remix version. Stop looking at me like that—I'm one person, promise. Earth whipped me up to rope in the woman you know as alien. She was trapped on that flying planet but got dialed into Earth by the Earth Plane Council. Earth liked her taste and wanted more but she was strong enough to break away. My whole psychic thing was basically a ploy to capture her interest and bring her back again but she figured this whole ruse out because... well... she had a lot in common with our home, let's just say that."

"She ate people?"

Lina laughed. "No! But she had many bodies until the war. I'll show you all that if you want. You can experience it for yourself. So I was used as an open line of communication and when the Hive Queen—sorry, the alien chick—figured out what Earth was and what we were, she hatched a plan with the Earth Plane Council. You kinda messed that up for them, though—no offense—so she approached Earth herself with a deal and here we are so it must have gone well."

"What was the plan?"

"Lure that nasty flying weapon planet into our universe and blow up the exits. But take you to Earth Plane. That was the trade: you for an entire planet of food. She made out like a bandit, I think. And actually, you know what? You almost blew the original plan a first time before you actually... well... did blow it the second—when you went camping with the boys that night. You should have died like people do walking through that force field when it's a shield. You're the only one who didn't."

Corey took this and a deep breath in and formulated a response. When he was ready he exhaled, "First of all, that's not an example of *no offense*. You're needling me."

"Point taken."

"—I'm no dummy. Second of all, I'm not the only one who lived. Darryl was there."

"Actually, he died. He just wasn't aware of it," she told him.

Corey tittered in frustration and she answered what she knew he was struggling with. "Yeah, I know. Totally jumping the shark here but that's life. Darryl was a ghost the second he zapped through that shield."

"Of course he was! And you were there! And you, and you, and you, Auntie Em!"

"—I know! Hey, listen—you wanted the truth! His consciousness struggled to maintain a solid form. That's what ghosts are. Denial is a powerful thing, Corey, but death always trumps it and if he didn't agree to come to Earth Plane.... Well, he did. So that's a good thing."

Corey balked. "Is that why they didn't just steal me then? I didn't agree to go with them? That's pretty lame."

"Well, no. I mean that's a problem for sure but in the end? Not really the bigger deal. The bigger deal was that Earth Planers didn't want you there yet. They still needed you on Earth as...." She giggled and let the answer hang in the air.

"Don't say *bait*," Corey warned. Lina smiled at him, debating how much truth he could handle at this moment. He caught this and dryly said, "Out with it."

"You really did screw it up when you hit the reset button on those timelines. You were just supposed to lie there in that box until the invaders came through and found you. The other woman of your dreams was going to guide you to Earth Plane at the last second, while Darryl and the boys slammed the doors shut on our world, sealing evil alien us's and her inside. The ol' disappearing from a magic box trick, except real. But your magic trick trumped her magic trick and the cool thing is it was a blessing in disguise because it showed her you had the power to willfully transcend time and space—not just physically survive the trip. Physically, you're the only human that could make it here to this dimension in one piece, and she could have made that happen for you. But mentally? Spiritually? You have yet to tap into what you are because you've never existed before. You are literally one of a kind."

Corey stretched. His fog was evaporating. "Okay, I get it. She used you to get off that planet and come back home."

"Yep. And bring James with us. He died, too, on a ship. It was planned. Jesus, how many times has that boy died?"

"Huh. So then the Hive Queen should be strolling through that wall in another body any second now, right?"

"Well... no. We're fused together forever. There were no bodies like hers. We made a pact back at Taunton High. Remember when I was freaking out?"

"Mmm."

"Yeah."

"So much stuff."

"I know. It was a lot for me to take then, hence the meltdown. But I agreed to let her see her plan through. Probably I didn't have a choice, now that I think about it. I mean Earth would have just made me do it anyway, like writing that book or Henry eating the gun. But the illusion of free will was pleasant enough."

They both chuckled at that and with a heavy sigh Corey sloughed off an enormous weight of muscular tension. He felt lightheaded and really didn't know what they were laughing about anymore. Lina hugged him. "We're gonna be okay, man," she said. "I am your true love, mister. And don't you forget it. I'll show you everything when you feel up to it. I've got every memory in this noggin the Queen ever had and—Hey, I can even teach you the psychic trick. They used to all be linked in a way in this place that is freaking marvelous. I can't wait to actually experience it. I just need you to get this now because the word 'illusion' isn't meaningful anymore. We're real. And we're not some evil reincarnation people or whatever. And the Hive Queen saved us and then really did give you a free will choice."

Lina began to tear up as she continued: "You've had two in your entire life. Both times you chose... me." She wiped the tears back with her forearm and tried to toughen up so she could get through this and get through to Corey. "You brought us here, buddy boy, and you fused us together when you did, which is why my body didn't explode when I stepped through the portal. The Hive Queen was cool with that. She wanted to experience something new. She's like a voice in the background—like my conscience, is the best way to describe it. No different than you and yours in feeling, really, because we are one in the same way, you know what I mean?"

He pondered a moment then came alive. "Yeah. Here's a scary thought: Who's to say we're not a clever ploy for Earth to branch out and lure more of these folks there? Or, like, what if I'm like Superman and I can will this planet onto Earth so she can go to town? Happy Thanksgiving, Earth!"

"No, see, you joke, but that's the beauty of what I'm telling you! Those are real possibilities! Who knows what you can do?

And Nelson, your favorite serial killer—Okay, here's another totally messed up thing. Ready?"

"Go."

"He was one of the mind control subjects used to transport abductees back to bed or their cars or wherever after abductions. The people at Spooky Mansion never did the dirty work because they couldn't risk getting caught, so they had these, like, pedophile zombie slaves do it."

"Jesus!"

"I mean not just that, but you know what I mean. Really messed up people—so that if they got caught they'd just be thrown in jail for robbery or kidnapping or whatever. They were perfect fall guys."

Corey dropped his shaking head in his hands. "This is fucking ludicrous," he said into his palms.

Lina was so giddy making all the big reveals that she forgot his life as he knew it was still real to him. She rattled, "You think so? Then you're gonna hate this! You wanna know why he did what he did to you and why he overshot the mansion and dragged you toward the portal?—Ohmigod, did you even know he did that?"

"Go ahead," Corey said wearily, head still in hands.

"You'd think, like, we did that. Well, not we *me* but we *the Earth Plane Council*—or maybe Henry or something, right? But no. He was just supposed to deliver you to the mansion, not torture you and kill me and all that. He did it to break you so you'd find a way to reassemble yourself."

"Well how the fuck did he know—"

"Ahp-bup-bup! ... Earth," she stated.

"Earth. Okay? So? What?"

"Earth did it. Earth controlled him."

"Of course she did," he said, deflated.

"Of course she did! Don't you see? She found a way to cook you different while the outside world was watching! She made you a new mystery in real time. Even though the Hive

Queen and the Earth Plane Council's instructions to have you on that roof in that chamber in a certain frame of mind were complete nonsense, Earth didn't know that. So she reshaped you to specification. But again, you're your own person, Corey—your own powerful person. You went back in time for love—which came as a shock to Earth—to everyone. We know this because when the second timeline happened, Hive Queen realized that she needed to bring Earth in on the double-cross. Earth agreed and became a conspirator. She shared a lot of info, you know?

"I mean you're right: this could all be a giant manipulation by her. She is cunning. Who really knows if she'll honor the deal or thinks she's going to double-cross Earth Plane after she eats that mechanical planet? But you're YOU, Corey. The grays can read your soul and it is a real soul. There are limits to what Earth can fake."

He broke out laughing and interrupted, "—Mother Earth fakes organisms to attract dinner dates. Ain't that just like a dame?"

"You're an asshole," she laughed.

"Well…" he said with pride.

"An-y-way…. You're you now, dude. Get over yourself. That's the whole point of being transcendent. You are not your programming. You are not your instinct. You are not her illusive creature on strings. You're not even your personal history or your cultural history or anything. You're you. You're Corey Avon. You are what freedom looks like when it breaks shackles for the first time. So are your pals. So am I."

"And as my first act of free will I chose you."

"You always choose me."

"Well, you make it so easy."

Lina beamed with the hope and joy of a comfortable soul. "And I will always choose you," she said.

She leaned in and kissed Corey so passionately then that he did know unquestionably who Lina was and it was as if he had known all along. This was a reminder. A reminder that she is love and love is indivisible. Love is either one's being or it isn't. The face of love matters not but that didn't stop him from lusting her.

Corey and Lina held each other for a timeless while in the room of light. When he was ready she took him by the hand and led him through the contracting gray wall to meet up with his friends and introduce him to his new family.

These few and precious humans were now an untouched species living endless lives. They lived in love. They lived in magic.

They lived for real.

Epilogue

A new planet blotted out the sun, one made of jagged edges, seamless metal, and fury. Warships burst out of Earth's mechanical twin like debris from colliding asteroids. Whoever demolished General Q'rvis's fleet would pay with extinction—even if they were brainwashed humans. This Trondant vowed as he barked orders from Leader's swivel throne on the deck of the mightiest vessel of them all.

Shark's grin swam upstream the corners of Trondant's face while he anxiously picked at his ear. That pathetic ball of oceans and minerals would be his to devour. If Leader was actually stranded there, all the better. He could still pull off the rescue that would secure his name in history. He didn't hold out for that any longer because the dead bitch lied but he was going to kill as many of Queeny's subjects as existed here and then he was going to return to her precious Earth Plane and finish the job there. He would crash his entire mechanical planet into Earth Plane if that's what it took— He didn't care.

Fuck.

All of them.

There Trondant sat projecting his rage into future plans, already overlooking Earth pulling up in front of him.

"Commander, sir... we hath a signal!" The new first lieutenant was so energized he forgot how he'd "earned" his promotion.

Trondant grunted. He didn't really hear the man, so caught in the spell of revenge fantasy was he.

"It is Leader, sir. We hath located Leader on the planet!"

Trondant's eyes popped wide and saliva dried up in his throat. He didn't know what he was feeling here but it was amazing. The most amazing news he had ever heard. "That's...." He could have cried then but instead punched the console in front of him so hard that it collapsed with a loud bang.

"Fucking right I did!" Trondant yelled this and the crew erupted into cheers, which gave way to them chanting, "Tron... dant! Tron... dant! Tron... dant!"

"Alright, people! You know what to do! Wipe these fuckers out of the sky and prepare my cruiser. I'm bringing Leader home myself!"

"HOORAAAAAAAY!"

Through the deck. Out the conquering globe. Across space. Into the exosphere of Earth this cheer flew. It was the tiniest muffled quark of sound by the time it reached, but she heard it. And as she drank in the blood and the ash and the metallic nutrients of her felled prey and their machines, she reorganized herself to lose the coming sky war.

She wanted them to conquer. She wanted them to land. She wanted them to wonder. She wanted them to claim her.

She wanted them all.

Earth overlooked no one.

Author's Note

Into The End is the definition of "A labor of love." I first wrote it when I was a junior in high school. It was a therapeutic means of working out what I thought were alien abductions happening to me at the time. (Now I try not to define them.) It was also something I simply could not put down. I compulsively wrote it during the school year and all through summer vacation.

In that incarnation there was no Lina, no Henry, and a completely different ending. Corey's name was "Johnny Mixx" and he was 15. The whole parallel universe plot didn't exist. It was a straight up alien abduction novel that ended with the serial killer delivering Johnny to the aliens, who convinced him that he was the Second Coming of Christ. He bought it and they plopped him back down on earth to "save" humanity in their name—but he was too late: the real Christ was back and had already saved the world. That's when Johnny realized he'd been played. He was the antichrist all along.

The demonic aliens flew away. Jesus stepped through his portal to Heaven with the remaining humans. And Johnny was the last person on earth—truly alone.

All of that is to say, a lot changes when you pick up a manuscript and dust it off twenty-plus years later. However, I kept much of the early dialogue between the boys intact, as well as the flavor of how my teen self felt about parents, authority, peers, relationships, and his place in the world. So all of that is authentically how one teen, at least, perceived the world.

It's as if I jumped in a time machine, traveled back to high school, and found myself as a writing partner! I just hope I did teen-me justice. I think he would be proud. He'd definitely take the credit.

About The Author

JEREMY VAENI is an award-winning writer. He is author of I Know Why The Aliens Don't Land! and Urgency. He is also a filmmaker whose work includes the feature documentary, *No One's Watching: An Alien Abductee's Story* and the Wholphin DVD short film, *David Huggins: Experienced*. He lives in Hawaii where he contemplates the value of a sequel, but you can visit him online at: http://www.jayvay.com

www.ingramcontent.com/pod-product-compliance
Lightning Source LLC
Chambersburg PA
CBHW051338250626
471 57 CB00001B/91